P9-BZT-830

AMERICAN BLOOD

AMERICAN BLOOD

BEN SANDERS

MINOTAUR BOOKS
THOMAS DUNNE BOOKS
NEW YORK

This is a work of fiction. All of the characters, organizations, and events portrayed in this novel are either products of the author's imagination or are used fictitiously.

A THOMAS DUNNE BOOK FOR MINOTAUR BOOKS.
An imprint of St. Martin's Publishing Group.

www.thomasdunnebooks.com
www.minotaurbooks.com

Designed by Omar Chapa

The Library of Congress Cataloging-in-Publication Data is available upon request.

ISBN 978-1-250-05879-9 (hardcover)
ISBN 978-1-4668-6317-0 (e-book)

First Edition: November 2015

10 9 8 7 6 5 4 3 2 1

For Thom Darlow and Tom Lucas.

Two of the very best.

AMERICAN BLOOD

PROLOGUE

Lauren Shore

She'd never picked this as her scene.

Bars by night. Some tableau of lost hope with these quiet men hunched glass-in-hand, the shared pursuit of emptiness.

She knew the feeling. That warm remedy, shot by shot the mind delaminating:

Present troubles gone.

Past troubles gone.

Names gone, and yours included.

All of it fading until that moment and that drink were the sum of your known world. Sometimes she'd wake lying clothed across the bed, recalling glimpses of city, a big neon montage blurred by liquor. Waiting at a corner. The backseat of a cab and beyond the window the night streaked and lurid.

And always that mantra: tonight won't be like last time.

Which is what she told herself now, in this low-ceilinged shit-hole. She had a corner table where she could see the door. Jack Daniel's with a beer back, almost gone. Let it be the last. To her right a guy in a suit sat staring at his drink like he wanted to fall through it. A second guy at a nearby table, same wardrobe and same fixation. Jacket over the back of his chair, a slack noose of a tie at his open collar.

Just the one bartender, late sixties or so, blue sleeves of tattoos in a faded mess up each arm. A lineup of three guys on stools in front of him: a tall blond man at the far end down the left, two others together on the right, gray and disheveled, a brief murmur swapped occasionally, like discussing grave matters.

The blond guy was side-on to the bar so he had a view of the room. She hadn't seen him before, and he didn't fit at this hour. Stella and a newspaper weren't the stuff of the ruined. He seemed to register the attention and glanced at her. She looked away toward the door, safe empty territory, so as the two guys in ski masks came in she was looking straight at them.

Young guys, jerky, probably loaded on something. Sneakers and torn jeans, gloves and jackets that hid skin color. One guy with the bag, one guy with the gun. Voices hoarse and strangled from adrenaline, words dropping out as they screamed:

"Get on the ground! Get on the fucking ground!"

Bag man yanked the two guys at the bar backward off their stools, a hand on each collar, arms flailing as they crashed. The guy beside her spilled his drink as he went down, fumbling a phone from his pocket. She could see 911 lit up. A few Jacks ago that could have been her.

Gunman with his pistol in the barkeep's face, screaming for him to empty the register. The second guy threw him the bag and began the rounds, patron to patron, wallets, cash, anything.

Seated at the edge of things the blond man hadn't moved, still just waiting there. An elbow on the bar, patient, unperturbed, like he'd seen such things before.

Barkeep with the drawer open now. This wasn't his first robbery: no shakes as he bagged the cash, "just be cool" intoned on repeat. Gunman finger-to-trigger, barkeep's head in his sights, urging him to hurry. The second guy moving clockwise through the room, a wallet each from the two guys he'd toppled, headed for the man whispering to his phone.

"Hey, the fuck you doing?"

He leaped and stomped the hand, a scream and a dry-wood crack of bone. Broken fingers raised weakly as the guy punched him in the head and then again and again and again, and then he was prone and crawling bloodied and she lost sight of him as the guy with the gun appeared huge and terrifying in her face.

So frantic that awful moment with the black wool mask like some raving nightmare vision and the smell of his sweat and so loud the screaming her ears rang with it.

"Money, little bitch, where's your fucking money?"

He dropped the bag and grabbed a fistful of her hair, and the gun was cool and hard and the terror so extreme she just couldn't respond.

And then somewhere back there, this calm, level tone: "Hey."

The guy released her and turned and rose. The blond man was standing easy behind him, arms at his sides, expression almost pleasant.

"Man, the fuck you doing? Get your fucking hands up."

Blond man obliged, unhurried, like he knew where things would end up.

"Man, shit, get on the ground."

Both guys approached, gunman with his weapon up, and as the muzzle touched his forehead the blond man moved his raised hands in a scissor motion across his face and rolled the pistol clean from the guy's grip and kicked him in the groin and wrapped a hand behind his head as he sagged and smashed his mouth against the edge of a table and lunged sideways and broke the bag man's leg at the knee with a kick through the side of the joint that crunched like a fall onto broken glass.

Three seconds.

Drinkers and barkeep alike stunned and motionless, united in shock. That spilled drink spread thinly on the table, a steady drip off one corner. The bloodied man was on his back, two fingers pinched to his nose. He stretched blindly a moment and found his phone, but didn't raise it. The backlight was dead, a spiderweb through the screen. The blond man glanced over at his Stella, like making a point to come back to it. At his feet the guy with the broken leg lay sprawled and hissing through locked teeth, injured limb kinked outward at the knee, toes on his good side arched backward in agony.

Blond man appraised him briefly with little interest and then stepped to the other guy and knelt. The man was on his side, mask pushed up, spitting teeth and blood.

"You going to stay where you are?"

No answer.

"Yeah. I thought so."

He stood and stepped to her table. He was in a T-shirt, arms roped with veins, a deep tan like he'd been soaked in resin.

He said, "Officer."

He'd guessed she was a cop. She cleared her throat to try and mask her surprise, Jack and adrenaline making the world swim. She said, "Detective, actually."

"Detective. Close."

He dropped the clip from the pistol and laid it on her table and drew back the slide to clear the live round. It was a Beretta M9. He placed the gun beside the clip and set the bullet upright on the flat of the slide.

"Probably best you look after these."

And then he went and picked up his paper and left.

ONE
Marshall

Sometimes at night he lay awake and thought of his dead.

Sins of others but they still robbed his sleep. That boy they'd left in South Brooklyn. That blown tail job in Koreatown. Midtown South Precinct said the transfusion almost saved him. What a prospect: the Big Exit, morphine and someone else's blood in your veins.

Sins of others, but he'd still borne witness.

Complicit. They were still his dead.

He thought of it as the night brigade. Misdeeds paraded for his musing. Maybe it was cathartic: daytime thoughts didn't stray there, so he reconciled by dark. Torture and opiate within the same dim reflection.

He pushed aside the sheet and sat on the edge of the bed. The clock readout floated disembodied: a bloodred four A.M. Beyond the window the night lay hushed and starless. He sat there a long time. Now and then the brief light from a car on the street below, the room in soft relief with each passing.

Four thirty A.M. On the bedside table his phone buzzed with an incoming call. It seemed to hover there on the glow of its screen.

He watched it a moment, some feeble thing crawling for the edge. Then he lay down again and answered the call. A blocked number.

"Is this Marshall?"

He lowered the phone and cleared his throat gently against the back of his wrist. "Yeah. This is Marshall."

"We spoke on the phone couple of days ago. You said you have some stuff we might like to look at."

So purposefully elliptic. He gave it a bit of time. He watched the shape of the fan above the bed through a few lazy cycles. He said, "I remember. You still want to talk?"

"Yeah. You know how these things work?"

"Tell me."

"We'll give you a general location to get to. Once you're there, we get a bit more specific."

Marshall said, "Okay."

"You in Albuquerque?"

"No. But I'm close."

"All right. We're talking a single-admission ticket. You know what I mean?"

"I can't bring any friends."

"Exactly. No friends."

Marshall didn't answer.

"You said you could sample us one key. That still okay?"

"Yes. That's fine."

"Good. That's exactly what we like to hear."

Marshall didn't answer.

"No need to bring any hardware either. In fact, we'll pat you down, so I'd say empty pockets are probably best. It just helps keep everything nice and relaxed, know what I mean?"

"Yeah. I know what you mean."

"Well, good. I think we're going to get along just fine."

Marshall didn't answer.

"Head up on I-25 toward Algodones. Keep your phone on."

The call ended. He laid the cell facedown where he'd found it and got up and dressed in the dark and walked through to the spare bedroom, a finger to the wall for his bearings. The cupboard light clicked on automatically as he opened the door. Waiting for him in the corner the old document safe he'd bought in El Paso. Standing half in shadow, like it knew it was wrought for nobler deeds. He knelt and spun the dial through its left-right routine, fluid and unthinking. Swing of the door almost unbidden. A chamber for his past life: guns, ammunition, the better part of two hundred grand cash. Everything so neat and orderly, like some court exhibit. Three shelves' testimony to his former self.

He straightened and removed the 870 from the shelf above and sat down cross-legged. He opened the breech and fed it seven 12-gauge rounds from the half-full box of Magnums in the safe. Same again for the Colt, .45 after .45. Each successive round a little more reluctant as the spring fought him.

He locked the safe and stood to leave. For an instant the light made art of the scene. This tall backlit figure, a gun in each hand.

He took the Corolla. The duffel with the samples was already in the trunk. Algodones was a forty-minute drive, south and west on I-25, right on the Rio Grande, maybe twenty miles from Albuquerque.

That stretch of I-25 is hard country. Out of La Cienega and it was arid for miles, barren hills and a few brave tufts of vegetation at the roadside. Like the last vestiges of a more verdant world, scoured to khaki by some vindictive god.

They rang again at five fifteen. He pulled to the shoulder to take the call. The same capitalized warning of blocked number.

"Where are you?"

He said, "I'm on 25."

"You anywhere near Bernalillo?"

"Not really."

"Oh. You coming in from the north?"

"Yeah. Santa Fe."

"How far are you from 22?"

"Close. Maybe ten minutes."

"Okay. Well, that works out pretty good then. Take a right when you get there. There's a diner a couple more miles up the road."

Marshall ended the call first. A minor victory, but it probably wasn't a bad thing to maintain an equal hang-up score. There was a psychological benefit there somewhere.

The diner itself was another fifteen minutes' drive. A roadside billboard on I-25 proclaimed its existence, together with a bold-print promise of twenty-four-hour service. The place was called Otto's. It was a plain rectangular structure like an oversize trailer home, lonely amidst a big gravel parking lot large enough to take eighteen-wheelers. There was a trailer-less truck cab parked nose-in by the entry and a Jeep Cherokee way over in a corner. A couple of dust-filmed sedans by a side exit. Above them the stub of an air-con unit slotted through the wall, drifts of steam rendered whitely on that dark vista.

Grit popping beneath the tires as he turned in. He parked beside the truck cab, headlight glare in tight focus on the cladding, each blemish in searing relief. Sudden darkness as he cut the motor. He sat a moment in the quiet with the engine ticking as his night vision recovered, and then he got out and locked the car with the key. He left the Colt in the glove compartment. Forewarned of a pat-down, it was probably best where it was.

He rounded the truck and headed for the entry. That cool taste of night. Northward the mountains all camouflaged by gloom. In the east the dawn just breaking. A thin blue seam in gentle flexure across the far edge of the world. A marvel this hard land could be coaxed to such a template.

A bell dinged as he entered. He let the door fall closed behind him. In front of him the counter lay behind a long glass display of food. A slice of apple pie caught his eye: cold, gelatinous, bulging against plastic wrap. To the left a long row of booths below the front-facing windows. Two guys side by side near the end, facing the door.

Marshall walked over. They didn't move, but their eyes followed him in. Both of them hunched slightly over folded arms, coffee cups standing half empty. He stood there in the aisle a moment, awaiting his pat-down, but the guy on the right signaled for him to take a seat. An issue of discretion, presumably. A gun-check in a diner is a fine way to draw attention.

"Don't worry about it. Sorry it ain't much of a respectable hour."

There was a wry smile on his face that detracted from the sincerity a bit, but Marshall reasoned even the pretense of civility was better than none at all. In any case, he'd met at less respectable hours with even less respectable people.

He said, "Sure," and sat down.

The vinyl creaked a little under his weight. He slid across and centered himself on the seat. He knew their backgrounds. On the left was Troy Rojas, Hispanic, six years' worth of Army followed by twelve years' worth of Walpole. In 1992, just back from the Gulf and high on something, he'd shot and paralyzed a Massachusetts State Police Trooper who'd pulled him over for speeding. Rojas's crucial error: discussing the events with a Boston PD informant two months later. His colleague on the right was Cyrus Bolt, twenty years of drug offenses on his résumé. Without doubt a consummate shit bag, but perhaps not quite in Rojas's orbit.

Bolt had some coffee. He wasn't an attractive guy: coke-fiend-thin, all lines and sinew. Like something chewed and spat out. He would have been pushing forty. He said, "And what is it that you do, Mr. Marshall?"

Marshall shrugged in a manner intended to convey versatility. "Bit of this, bit of that."

Bolt tipped his mug at him like a little toast and smiled knowingly. "Whatever's going. I like that."

A waitress came over, coffee flask in hand. Hispanic and heavyset, weary like she'd been doing the rounds since this time yesterday. Marshall hoped she was on the home stretch. He took the one remaining mug from the little stand in the center of the table and set it upright and requested coffee only, no food. She leaned and poured carefully, the four of them briefly captivated, and then she moved on.

Marshall looked around. Just one other customer. The truck driver, presumably, at a table over to the right. A coffee of his own, and what looked like eggs Benedict in a swamp of hollandaise. Overall not really an inspired choice of venue, given that a diner with one other customer is unlikely to afford much anonymity. Or maybe the waitress was in on it. He had some coffee.

Rojas ducked his head, smoothed a hand through his hair. There was a waxen gleam to it. "What we normally do, we take the sample off you, check it all out, and then maybe have another talk."

"All right."

Rojas turned his mug through a slow revolution on the tabletop, watched it carefully. He glanced up. "You got something for us to look at?"

"I do."

Which strictly speaking was the truth, because there was indeed something to look at. The fact that the sample's value as a stimulant was somewhat tenuous was information Marshall preferred to withhold.

Rojas said, "What's your supply like? We've got a real issue with keeping enough stock around. So the bigger the better, basically."

Marshall said, "We've got a hookup via Colombia."

An outright lie, but it seemed imprudent to undermine a happy discourse.

"So stock's no trouble."

"Yeah. Stock's no trouble."

Rojas nodded slowly and mulled on that. He was watching Marshall with something akin to cool indifference. Marshall didn't mind. He had some experience with the expression and was confident he could affect something of an equal if not greater standard. He did so for a few patient seconds. Then he had some coffee. Bolt had some coffee. Rojas had some coffee. The truck driver looked over idly and had some coffee.

Marshall said, "You guys out of Albuquerque?"

Rojas rocked his head, noncommittal. "Kinda."

Marshall nodded. He said, "Well."

He was quite partial to a good "well." He liked the quiet, reflective pause that it often inspired.

He said, "Why don't we go outside and have a look at my stuff."

Neither of them answered. Rojas reached up and took a napkin from the stainless-steel holder on the windowsill and balled it and dabbed his mouth.

He said, "We don't really check stuff out in this sort of environment. Public's not a good idea."

He gestured vaguely, like dispelling fumes. "And we're just talking in very general terms here. We haven't got down to discussing anything specific."

Bolt said, "Not that it's on record or anything. We just like to point out that at this stage we could be talking about anything here."

Marshall nodded and swept an upturned palm, conceding the merits of cautiousness. Beside him the windows were just a long bank of mirrors. A slight tilt the only flaw in that inverse world. He said, "So what do you want to do?"

Rojas said, "We can head somewhere a bit quiet. Or just . . . You know. Private."

Marshall said, "We could have gone straight there and avoided the preamble."

"Well. We like to get a sense of what our potential colleagues are like."

Marshall nodded slowly. "And your rivals?"

The tabletop was faded laminate, milky orbs where the neon was reflected. Rojas thrummed his nails a couple of times. "Coffee for the first meeting. Maybe something a little sharper for the next."

Bolt smiled.

Rojas smiled, almost lascivious.

Marshall smiled. He grasped the implicit warning, but he didn't think they were going to give him any trouble. It wasn't arrogance, just a calm certainty gained from experience. He'd met very few people who shared his faculties.

He said, "We don't have to dig around in the back of my car and make a scene. You can just take what I've got and do what you like with it. If you want to talk some more you've got my number. If you don't want to talk, that works, too."

Rojas thought about that. Marshall slid toward the aisle a fraction and laid an arm along the back of his seat. The waitress circled back around. Bolt waved off the offer of a refill.

Rojas said, "How much have you got?"

"A key. As requested."

Rojas didn't answer.

Marshall said, "Like I told you. You can do with it whatever you want. If you want to take things further, it's entirely up to you."

"This your standard practice?"

Marshall thought a bona-fide purveyor of illicit substances probably wouldn't make a habit of dispensing one-kilo product samples too regularly. But he wanted to leave the right impression, so he looked calmly down the barrel and said, "Yes."

"That's quite an expense."

He shrugged. "We don't do it every week. Like I said, we've got a lot of stock. Our issue is more to do with distribution as opposed to supply."

Rojas looked at him and nodded sagely, like this was a dilemma they were accustomed to resolving. He said, "Okay. Why don't we go outside."

Marshall patted the back of the chair slowly, like comforting a ghost. "All right. Let's do that."

He nodded at the trio of mugs. "It's on me."

He dug in his pocket. He had forty-seven dollars: two twenties, a five, and two singles. The five being the middle made it an easy find by touch. He laid it on the table and paired up the corners precisely and creased a sharp transverse fold, dead across the center, a perfect bisection.

Rojas and Bolt watched like it was street magic, some sleight of hand imminent. Marshall trapped the bill squarely under his mug and slid to the edge of the seat, stood up, and waited in the aisle.

Rojas nodded toward the door. "After you."

The waitress smiled as they went out and told them to have a nice day. Marshall reciprocated. He figured at the very least they were good for one out of three.

They'd been seated when he entered which meant it had been difficult to establish if they were armed. Walking ahead of them the situation was no better.

Out the door and the bell dinged merrily. Highway noise borne easily on the cool air. He could see headlights sliding across the gloomed distance. All motion rendered gradual by that huge landscape.

His choice of parking space was slightly problematic, because he wanted them behind him as he opened the trunk. The present configuration meant a straight path from the door to the car would put them on his left. A serviceable prospect, but not really ideal, because he wanted their view obstructed.

He dug the Corolla's keys from his pocket and spread them on his palm and pretended to search through them as he walked off to the right, toward the Cherokee parked in the corner. Six o'clock darkness, a plausible mistake for a preoccupied man.

Rojas and Bolt walking abreast behind him, trailing tight, maybe two feet. Halfway there and Bolt pulled him up.

"Wrong car."

Marshall glanced up and stopped. "Oh. Yeah."

He turned on his heel and threaded between them and headed back over to the Corolla. A slight arc so they would approach the trunk square. He heard them fall in behind, one or two feet, very close. Bolt on his right, Rojas left. This tight little procession. Breath rising palely like their own spirits departing.

He reached the Corolla. Morgue-cool to the touch. Rojas gave him no space. He stepped up tight against the taillight, close to his left shoulder. Trunk lid up and he'd have as good a view as any. Bolt was hanging a couple of steps back, off to his right. The low hum of the air-con and a softer, lonely note off the highway.

Marshall faux-searched his keys, the bunch on his palm again, that gentle chime of metal. Their positioning wasn't stupid. Rojas was near enough to be trouble. Bolt could shoot him in the back if things got difficult.

Rojas dug his hands in his pockets and tensed against the chill. He jiggled one knee. "Let's not make an event of it."

Marshall abandoned the ruse. He selected the correct key and inserted it in the lock. The metal grated gently. The sound of it so clear on that huge stage it seemed for a moment the focus of everything.

A quarter-turn.

The mechanism thunked cleanly. The lid popped up an inch proud. Marshall shifted his stance fractionally so his back was to Rojas. Crunch of gravel as he turned on the balls of his feet. And then he swung the lid up, just sudden finger pressure under the flat of the key, like flipping a switch.

The set dressing was good: the duffel's zip was open, clear baggies of white powder visible within. They drew Rojas's attention.

In a single easy motion Marshall leaned down and picked up the Remington 870 shotgun from where it lay against the bottom lip of the trunk and took a swift shuffle-step toward Bolt and smashed him in the face with the butt of the gun.

Bolt didn't even raise a hand.

The shotgun butt broke his nose. His head snapped back in a whiplash motion. He went down bleeding and Marshall, pulled by the momentum of the follow-through, stepped toward him to give himself space and brought the gun up and sighted on Rojas.

"Don't move."

Rojas was crouched in the gravel beside the car, one hand on the fender to steady himself, the other at the small of his back.

Marshall said, "What are you hiding back there?"

Rojas didn't answer. Quiet now in the aftermath. Just the three of them privy to the skirmish and in that hushed vastness it was as good as never happened. Rojas hunkered in the dust. Bolt fetal, hands to his face, blood seeping between his fingers. Marshall looming over him.

Rojas rose to full height, the hand still hidden. He stepped slowly away from the car, giving himself some room. Marshall tracked him with the gun barrel, nothing in his face.

"You're going to bring that arm round where I can see it and you better make sure there's only fresh air at the end of it."

"How old are you?"

"I'd say that's the very least of your worries."

"You're not old enough to be playing with guns."

Marshall prepped the trigger, took the slack out of it. "Playing or not. I've got pretty good at it."

Rojas didn't answer.

Marshall said, "Your friend here will attest to that."

"This is not the sort of thing you want to do."

Marshall said, "I wouldn't take your advice on things I would want to do. So I think we'll just carry on."

"You'll end up regretting this."

Marshall sighted down the barrel. Rojas's chest neatly centered. "Well. You just keep that hand hidden and we'll see where the balance of regret ends up."

Rojas nodded at the shotgun. "Haven't pumped a round yet."

"Take my word that I have."

Rojas didn't answer.

Marshall said, "It's your life you're betting. And I don't think I'm going to miss from this range."

No answer. They stood there a moment. Rojas locked on the bore and he could have been reflecting on things been or looking for a way out. Marshall moved a fraction closer. Six feet between them, a vaultlike silence, that gun their whole world.

Marshall said, "If you've got something back there, I'd drop it."

Nothing.

Marshall moved closer again, just a step. The 870 was a long weapon, and he couldn't afford to put it in grab range. He could sense Rojas willing the opposite. Marshall counted himself in, backward from three, and then he kicked him left-footed in the groin.

Rojas retched and doubled over, but kept his footing. Marshall moved in close and kicked him again in the gut, a big blow off the left instep. Rojas dumped his breath and fell prone. A nickel-plated .38 in his hand. Marshall stepped on his wrist and stooped and pried the gun from his fingers and slipped it in his belt.

"You carrying anything else you want to tell me about?"

Rojas gasping. Legs pulled double and an arm across his stomach, trying to pry his other wrist free. The skin all bunched and twisted where Marshall's sole had bit and turned. "No. Jesus, get off."

"What about Mr. Nose?"

"He's not carrying."

Which Marshall thought was probably untrue, but not problematic given Bolt's present condition. He said, "I see him hanging on to anything but his face I'm going to pop both of you."

Rojas still trying to jerk his wrist free.

Marshall said, "That's only going to make things more uncomfortable, doing that."

He checked the windows. No faces hovering there. His little reckoning still a private matter.

He dropped to his haunches and bridged the shotgun across his knees. "You should have done as you were told."

Rojas didn't reply. He seemed to have given up on the hand, like he'd accepted he wasn't getting it back. His breath was shallow, whistling.

Marshall said, "Sorry about the misdirection. But I'm not really in the business."

"What do you want?"

Marshall glanced back at Bolt to make sure he wasn't doing anything he shouldn't. The only nonconforming article was his nose, which was bleeding a lot.

Marshall said, "I'm looking for someone."

"Who?"

"A young lady."

"What's her name?"

"Alyce Ray. Alyce with a Y."

"Never heard of her."

"I thought you might say that."

"I haven't."

"Right. Well, either your boss or one of your colleagues or someone you sell to knows what's happened to her."

Rojas didn't answer.

Marshall said, "Point is someone's got answers, and I think you're in a good position to get them for me."

Rojas didn't answer.

Marshall scanned the distance. This light and this sparseness, he'd see red and blue a long way off. He said, "You can ask some questions. You've got my number."

"Get fucked."

"Yeah, well. Have a think about it."

"What are you, like a PI or something?"

"No. Just a concerned gentleman."

"You just made a pretty stupid mistake."

Marshall said, "Probably two of them. If you count him as well."

Rojas said, "How guys like you end up dead."

Marshall stood up. The windows still clear. "We'll see. If I don't hear from you, I'm going to have to come looking. And it's going to be the something sharper rather than the coffee. If you know what I mean."

Rojas smiled up at him. This awful grimace. "You don't have to come looking. I wouldn't fucking worry about that."

"Speed things up if I do. We'll meet somewhere in the middle."

Rojas didn't answer. Marshall could see him battling the urge to cradle the wrist. He laid the 870 in the back of the Corolla and took the .38 from his belt so he had a gun at hand. Then he closed the trunk lid and took the key from the lock and stepped over to where Bolt was lying. Still not a sound from him. Half-lidded and half-conscious. Marshall dragged him by his collar a few paces so he was clear of the car.

Marshall said, “I wouldn’t hang around.” He nodded at Bolt. “That’s not the kind of face you get from walking into a door.”

And then he got back into the Corolla and drove away.

It had started like this:

He had a job down in Albuquerque, a half-million-dollar build in North Valley. Two-way, two-story frames, three days' worth of welding.

He found a motel close by, his favorite sort of place, the desk guy content with fifty bucks as the price for no ID. There was a diner across the street. Seated one night at the counter where he could see the door, odor of cut steel still in his nose, fluorescent worms of arc flash in the darkness when he shut his eyes.

The guy beside him was a basketball fan, evidently a beer fan too, Marshall getting a detailed but drunken forecast of how this year the Mavericks would win that second championship. The TV was playing local news, good as mute due to his neighbor, but he watched anyway, indifferent to the content, hoping to convey disinterest as he waited for a meal.

"You see it last season?"

Marshall glanced at him. "Sorry?"

"I said, did you see it last season?"

"I don't think I saw it any season."

Back to the TV. It was the evening standard, crime scene tape and talking cop heads. He tried to lip-read as a distraction. A long shot of a house from the street, patrol cars in attendance. Tired clapboard and a dirt yard, chicken-wire fencing. His neighbor was still going, right in his ear. Marshall leaned away for some space—

Then:

An image of a young woman, maybe twenty years of age, dark hair and blue eyes. The beginnings of a smile that stirred memories, took him back a long time. He stared at the photograph through a slow zoom. No sound, but he guessed the gist of it.

You don't get news time unless you're dead or missing.

A cut to the next story and he blinked and lost the reverie. Returned to the diner, the talk beside him still in full flight and his plate now before him as if conjured, and the warm evening hubbub restored in full. A question in his ear:

"Don't you think it's gone downhill since they dropped him? It's fucking stupid, right?"

Marshall said, "Yes."

He replayed the image, tried to view it in detail. It felt like déjà vu, but it was false recall. He didn't know her. He'd just got the jolt, face and memory wrongly paired.

He dismissed it and started eating. The man beside him was gesturing widely as he spoke, warm beer breath on Marshall's cheek. Marshall offered a yes or a no when prompted. He'd ordered a burger and fries, but he didn't really taste them. The issue was their harmlessness: his attention was with those around him, and in a packed venue the known quantities didn't register. Years ago it had been a necessity, and he'd retained the habit. The result was inverted priorities: his focus the periphery, the minutiae of backgrounds. Everything others missed.

"But nobody beats Jordan, don't give a shit what they say, he's still the man. You know what I mean?"

Marshall said, "Yes."

It was ten P.M. In his pocket he had three twenties. He always used cash. It was a caution born with the move. He hadn't used a credit card since New York. He hated the notion of a trail. The driver's license and other ID the marshals had supplied were locked in the document safe. He never used them, complete anonymity preferable to a false identity.

He folded a bill crisply on the transverse and arranged it squarely beneath his mug and left, basketball man turning to address a new patron without missing a beat.

Outside it was cold and windless. A thin rain white as cut glass falling dead straight.

He stood at the curb a moment. His motel was across the street, lit windows a long and random sequence.

You don't get news time unless you're dead or missing.

He scrubbed his face with his hands. That slow zoom replayed.

Dead or missing.

"Shit."

He turned and walked up the gleamed street through the neon dark. A truck passed in a gust of road spray. At a gas station he bought a copy of the *Albuquerque Journal* and then he walked back across the street to the motel.

Hand shaking as he keyed the lock. He told himself it was the cold. He brushed rain from his hair and clicked on the light and locked the door behind him. That smell of inked newsprint. He laid the paper on the bed and scanned the front. Nothing. He turned the page, and there she was on A2. That same image that had grabbed him. Those eyes and her face on the brink of laughter. He'd never met her, but there was something in the photo. That false link to a former life and the better moments of a bad time.

He read the accompanying article. It was just a sidebar piece, probably a follow-up, light on hard content. Her name was Alyce Ray. She lived with her mother in a house on Comanche Road, just north of central Albuquerque. Mother had woken one morning and found the daughter gone. Any sightings please call this number.

She'd been missing five days.

He closed and folded the newspaper and smoothed it to its

original condition and lay on the bed, fingers knitted behind his head, legs crossed at the ankle, just quietly thinking. Outside, the traffic passed as a smooth hiss on the wet road. After a minute he got up and swept change from the table into a cupped palm and pocketed it and took his keys and went out. There was a pay phone at reception. The room a pale red from the vending machine light. Behind the desk a young guy sat nodding to headphone music, a camera up in a corner behind him. Marshall went to the phone and fed change in the slot and dialed a number.

"Hello?"

"Hey. It's Marshall."

"Marsh. What's happening?"

"I think something's come up. I'm not going to be able to finish this one."

He laughed. "You think something's come up, or something actually has come up?"

Marshall said, "Something actually has come up." He paused. "Just personal stuff."

"Oh. Okay." Quiet. "Didn't know you had personal stuff."

Marshall didn't answer. The door was open and he could hear the rain in its soft patter on the concrete outside. Smell of wet earth in the rain.

"Sorry. Didn't mean anything by it. Just, you know. Everything all right?"

"Yeah."

He could have explained, but it wouldn't have sounded rational. I want to find a missing girl, because she looks like someone I used to know. There was no way to pitch it as sensible.

"All right. Well. Why don't you just come by sometime when you're ready and get your pay? You did a couple of days, right?"

Marshall said, "Yeah, a couple of days. Thanks."

"Take care now."

The tone in his ear again. He fed some more change. It was a long time, but he still remembered the number for the apartment on Central Park West. For a few years he'd tried, and it would just ring and ring. Now just the tone. Every month another fruitless call and with them his faint hopes slowly dying.

Nothing.

The kid's foot was up on the desk, dipping back and forth to some tune. Marshall hung up the phone and stepped back out into the rain.

A storm that night. He lay listening to it. Still no wind and through the window he'd left ajar came the clean smell of rain. Periodically the curtains backlit by lightning and then the crump of thunder lagging the flash.

New York memories welling up, and he couldn't keep them down. In bed with her, the pair of them lying tangled. Her hand slightly curled, a light touch on his chest, her hair splayed out finely.

Marshall said, "We could leave."

Her smile just above him in the dark as she rolled toward him. The pause long enough he had time to hope. She said, "I told you I'd think about it."

"We could just do it."

She put her head on his shoulder. Warm breath as she laughed, a butterfly feeling, like it was too great a fantasy. "I promise I'll think about it."

He put his hand on hers. She made a fist, perfect in his palm. He said, "What if something happens?"

"Like what?"

"I don't know. What if something did."

Her face above him again. The quiet room even quieter with her hair touching him. She said, "Nothing's going to happen."

Rain on the motel roof. He sat on the edge of the bed, head in his hands, tried to focus on it. White noise to flood his recall. It took a long time. He thought about trying the New York number again. He didn't, but it made the memories re-loop.

Nothing's going to happen.

It was always the line he circled back to. He lay down again, hands over his eyes, as if blocking one sense might block the others.

Far from home and a woman on his mind whom he'd never see again. He felt very alone. He knew this life was never the ambition.

Gray the next morning but no rain. He had the Silverado pickup with his site gear in the tray. He drove south on I-25 and exited near the center of town onto Comanche Road and turned east through light industrial. A quirk of perception had the road ahead terminating on a low rise at the very foot of the mountains. Cresting it, he grasped the true geography: mile upon mile of suburb lay ahead on the plain.

Prosperity seemed to ebb as he worked east. Tired houses on dirt sections turned cracked and barren. Cars beset by rust parked in yards. He drove slow and scanned frontages as he went.

It took him forty minutes to find the house. He recognized it from TV footage. Mustard-colored clapboard with a carport to the left with an old maroon Impala parked inside. A yellow knot of crime scene tape at one of the columns. Another in a branch at the other end of the yard. Blinds drawn behind the windows. He parked a hundred yards up the street on the opposite side and crossed on the diagonal.

The front door was open behind an insect screen and beyond that a short corridor led into the house. Smell of cigarettes. He pushed the bell but it made no sound. He rapped on the siding near the doorframe.

A moment's wait, and then a short, heavy woman appeared at the end of the hall. The mesh screen obscured detail, but he could see her swaying as she approached, like her knees couldn't offer much bend.

"Maureen ain't here."

"Okay."

"Who are you?"

Marshall said, "I'm trying to find Alyce."

It sounded lame and naïve, even to his ears.

She stopped maybe six feet from the door. The bulk of her blotting the light from behind so she was just a dark shape, like some charcoal rubbing on the screen. “You a news man or police?”

“I used to be a police officer. I saw her on the television.”

“Well, it’s kind of you to come by, but used to be ain’t much good. There’s some proper ones on their way soon so I think you’d best be gone. We got warned about busybodies.”

“I’m sorry to hear she’s missing.”

“I think you’d best be on your way.”

He could see she wasn’t going to relent. He didn’t quite know what he’d expected. That he’d be invited in, all questions duly answered? He turned and walked back across the yard. When he reached the road he glanced back, but he couldn’t tell if she was still at the door. He crossed the street and got back into the car and waited.

Thirty minutes later an APD cruiser pulled up outside. Two officers got out and walked to the entry. He guessed they’d visited before because they didn’t bother with the bell, just knocked on the siding. A moment later the screen opened and they filed solemnly in, hats held at midriff, heads slightly bowed.

Marshall sat watching, a few options formulating.

Another ten minutes and a tan unmarked Crown Vic came along the street and slowed and U-turned and parked behind the cruiser. A plainclothes cop got out and walked across the yard. Pants riding low under a big gut, a wide swagger to keep them in place. The weight of his weapon and backup clips weren’t helping.

Light traffic, no one around. The two vehicles just sitting there.

Marshall waited for the cop to be admitted inside and then he got out of the Silverado and stepped to the rear and reached in and found his lockout tool. It was just a slender two-foot piece of flat steel with a hook-shaped cutout at one end. He slipped it from its plastic sheath and ran it up the inside of his sleeve, dropped his arm to his side with the tool standing on his curled fingers.

Back across the road, pacing it slow, heart really going for it.

He didn’t even bother with the cruiser. It was new and gleaming and decked out in loud livery and he thought there was a good chance it would have a loud alarm, too. He went to the Crown Vic. Ten or fifteen years old, smart but not state of the art. He cupped a hand and ducked and looked in the rear window, and then again through the front. Nothing in the back. In the front passenger footwell there was a black leather bag, unzipped. A file sitting there spine-down, a thick fan of paperwork just daring him. A take-out soft drink cup in an outrigger pocket and a balled wrapper on the seat.

He walked around to the passenger side. It put his back to the house, but he wouldn't be long. A car passed eastbound, and then another one westbound. No one slowed to look. He was just a guy standing by a car.

Head pounding, a chill down his spine, neck hairs on edge.

He let the lockout tool drop through his sleeve and caught the top of it midfall. Then he slipped the piece of metal hook-end first past the window, down into the door panel beside the handle. Ten seconds and he'd jimmied it. Door open, the tool returned to his sleeve. Another ten and he was back across the street, paperwork in hand.

He drove two blocks over and parked to read.

Pulse coming back in line, breathing steady.

You could get addicted to this.

He'd assumed the Crown Vic was an APD car, but it was a DEA case file. He'd just robbed a federal agent.

There were notes from Albuquerque Police first up, dated only a couple of days ago. He knew missing persons reports could only be filed seventy-two hours after the fact. Today was Friday. Alyce Ray had been missing since Saturday, the report officially filed Tuesday. Six days gone and three days' search time.

There was a statement from one Maureen Ray. She claimed that on the Friday evening prior to her disappearance her daughter had been out visiting friends. Maureen Ray had been home alone in bed at the Comanche Road address when she heard her daughter enter the house at approximately two A.M. Saturday. She assumed her daughter went to bed. When she woke in the morning she found the girl's bedroom empty. Purse and keys still in the room. Her car still out front. No other possessions unaccounted for. Just the girl herself gone.

Photographs of the bedroom. A bed with a corner of the sheet turned back and the pillow dented. Approach shots of the house and the entry he'd just stood at. No sign of blood, no evidence of forced entry. Maureen Ray claimed an abduction had occurred, but APD clearly hadn't been convinced. The prelims seemed cursory.

He thumbed the remaining papers. There was a thick sheaf of color photographs, time-stamped late-evening Friday.

2302. A blurred close-up of Alyce Ray, head turned, talking to someone out of shot. The next image provided context, Ray with three other women, all a similar age, strolling two by two on a sidewalk. A backdrop of cracked pink stucco and the four of them centered beneath a cone of light cast narrowly from above and the world beyond lost to the contrast.

2303. The four of them waiting at what appeared to be the entry to a club. CALOR in red lettering on the pink stucco lintel. A doorman checking IDs, a four-shot sequence, girl by girl. The doorman alone at the entry looking back along the street, and Alyce Ray stepping past him to darkness in the room beyond.

More images of people arriving. Singles and twos and threes. The sidewalk approach with the stucco behind. A Hispanic guy in his forties, dark hair swept back and a gray suit that caught the light in its creases. There was a computer printout a page over. Gray suit man was one Troy Rojas, a graduate of MCI-Walpole at Cedar Junction. He'd shot and paralyzed a state trooper up in Massachusetts in '92.

Marshall turned the page. Further printouts, internal DEA records listing all kinds of suspicions. Importation, manufacturing, supply. No apparent convictions. Current address unknown. Next of kin one Troy Rojas Jr. There was an Albuquerque address listed, together with a few credentials. Junior possessed similar proclivities to Senior, but he'd accrued some convictions: two separate counts of possession of methamphetamine, two ninety-day prison stints. One count of possession with intent to distribute that hadn't stuck.

Marshall flipped through. 2347. A photo of Rojas entering Calor. 2358. A trio of men entering single file. A blowup of the third man, followed by DEA records. Cyrus Llewellyn Bolt, thirty-nine years of age, the last twelve of them spent at the Federal Correctional Institution at Beaumont on a heroin trafficking charge. He was only five months out of prison. Current address unknown. He had an ex-wife over in Lubbock, Texas. The married/divorced dates implied they'd hitched and split while Bolt was still inside.

Marshall browsed on. There was a daytime shot inserted out of sequence: a blurry image of a guy in a black cowboy hat. Jackie Oswald Grace, Calor owner, fifty-one years old. He had some possession charges dating back twenty years, a few trafficking suspicions a little more recently. He sounded like Cyrus and Troy's kind of man.

Back to the night shots.

0031. Alyce Ray et al exiting, walking back the way they'd come. One of the girls unsteady on her feet, a friend at each elbow, Alyce Ray trailing, a handbag over each shoulder.

0032. Bolt's trio on the way out, headed in the same direction.

0034. Rojas and another man in his thirties, following.

Marshall closed the file. The images were all level shots, probably a standard DEA stakeout, a guy across the street snapping entry/exit photos. He'd done similar things before, a long time ago. He wondered how Albuquerque PD had got the DEA on board so soon. Maybe they knew the club was under surveillance and requested records when the name came up in questioning.

It didn't really matter.

All he cared was that at midnight Friday Alyce Ray had crossed paths with two men known to the DEA and by morning she was gone.

• • •

He drove back east, keeping south of Comanche, not wanting to come across that tan Crown Victoria. Tired street upon tired street. He quartered blocks, driving slow so he wouldn't miss the signs.

It didn't take him long. He passed a section host to two trailer homes, the structures joined in an L-shape, an awning off one side propped by tent poles. A Ford F-150 sitting on its rims in the yard. At the curb two kids in the front of an old Chevy Caprice, heads barely above sill level. Girl in the driver's seat, boy beside her. He drove slowly past. These pale wide-eyed faces turning smoothly to track him. He pulled over and parked and shut off the motor and looked in his side mirror. The car framed end-on, apparently empty. And then the kid in the passenger seat craned round to look, just his silhouette against the windshield.

Marshall said, "Please be wrong."

He got out. Dead quiet, not even a bird. The street just sitting there on a held breath while he did what he had to.

He walked to the car. The girl's window was down. She had perfect blond hair tied in a ponytail. She might have been nine years old. Marshall waited. The boy leaned across from the passenger seat to see his face and then he leaned back. Just the girl framed there, tiny on the seat, sitting on her hands. Blue veins webbed delicately at her temple.

She said, "Hey."

Marshall smiled. "Hey."

"How much you want?"

"Two grams, please."

"That's two hundred."

She held out a hand, waiting for it. He reached in his pocket and counted the bills by touch off his fold and passed them to her. She fanned them like cards to check the balance and then handed them across the console to the boy. He popped his door and clambered out and ran off across the yard to the trailer.

Marshall said, "How old are you?"

The girl didn't answer for a minute. A blank look on her face that could have been fear or surprise. She said, "Cain't say."

"What's your name?"

She shook her head. "Cain't say that either. Ain't allowed."

"All right. My name's Marshall."

She didn't answer. He knew that one day she would look back and realize she'd paid a toll without even knowing. He looked at the trailer. It would be nice to know without doubt if one person's end was another's good fortune. But he just couldn't call it. What's to say a good deed right now isn't just bad luck on a long fuse.

A moment later the boy came back with his purchase. The girl handed it to him, and then the pair of them sat watching until he walked away.

Rojas Junior lived in a place off Lomas Boulevard Northeast. Marshall drove south on the Pan American Expressway and then cut over on Central Ave.

The house was a newer design, clapboard with a tile roof, three grimed sedans in a lazy zigzag on the driveway. He parked at the curb and went and knocked on the front door. A guy in his mid-twenties answered. Torn jeans and the neck of his T-shirt stretched and sloping off one shoulder and his hair trying to go everywhere at once. Gloom in the house behind. A dog was barking somewhere.

Marshall said, "I'm looking for Troy."

The guy raked a hand through his hair. He cleared his throat. "Yeah. Me."

"Oh, right. I'm actually after your dad."

"He doesn't live here."

"You know where I can find him?"

The kid's eyes narrowed. "What for?"

Marshall said, "I got some stuff he might be interested in. If you've got a number or something."

"How do you know him?"

"Seen him at that club. Calor."

"How'd you find this place?"

Marshall ignored the question and just dug in his pocket, brought out the clear baggie with the two grams of meth he'd bought that morning. "I just got some stuff I could show him. You know. I could even leave this with you if you want. I mean, I got a lot of it."

The kid wiped his brow. "Yeah, man. Sure, okay." Quieter: "What have you got there, couple of grams?"

"Yeah. Couple of grams."

The guy staring at the bag. Ten hits, if he was good with it.

Marshall said, "You got a number or something. For your dad?"

It broke the trance. He looked at the ceiling, a hand rubbing at his neck. Track marks up his forearm, matted over by scarring. "Yeah. Hang on. Yeah, I do."

"Well, why don't you get it. And I'll just leave all this with you."

Marshall jiggled the baggie in his cupped palm. The kid turned and walked away into the house, this funny mincing gait, nudging the wall as he went. Marshall heard thumps, drawers banging, cursing. He waited. A minute later Junior reappeared, a torn scrap of paper in an outstretched hand.

"That's his cell. You can get him on that."

Marshall tossed him the meth and then he was gone.

He drove west on Lomas and pulled in at the university hospital and parked at a pay phone. He placed a call to Child Protective Services and explained the predicament of the little boy and girl he'd met that morning. He didn't give his name.

Then he dialed the number Junior had given him.

Rojas took a long time answering, but he did pick up. "Yeah?"

Marshall paused. Sun hot on his neck and the vicious glare of it off the concrete around him and he felt the sudden weight of all these things he could set in motion.

He said, "I've got some stuff you might want to look at."

THREE

Marshall

Twenty minutes northbound. Dawn now with the earth all coolly shadowed and domed above him this faultless blue hemisphere from horizon to horizon. He turned off the interstate and swung in beneath the overpass onto a crossroad. A thin lace of road dust strung crookedly in his wake. Just ahead on the right a few storefronts side by side: drugs, a diner, a hardware place. No vehicles in the lots out front. On the left and a little ways up a gas station. No customers and no movement that he could see. Waiting there clientless on that lonely stretch it seemed more a shrine to quietude than anything else. Like that was its purpose and no other.

He had a quarter tank but he parked up next to a pump and hit the lever to pop the flap. Through the office window the sales guy stood watching idly, arms folded, leaning on the counter. Marshall went in and exchanged pleasantries and paid for forty dollars' gas. Back outside he could hear sirens. Southbound, growing louder and peaking as they crossed the overpass and then fading again. Two cars. Maybe for him, but he doubted he'd been seen.

He unscrewed the cap and hooked the nozzle in the tank mouth and set the lever to keep it flowing. There was a pay phone over toward the road. He took some change from the console in the Corolla and walked over and fed the slot and dialed Felix's number at the house.

"Yeah?" Groggy, pushing away sleep.

"It's me."

"Hombre. That Cohen guy keeps calling me. I think you need to talk to him."

Marshall said, "What did he want?"

"I don't know. Shit, it's early."

Marshall said, "I think you need to get out of the house for a few days."

"Why? You moving in?"

"No. There're going to be some folks coming looking for me."

"That's all right."

"They're not really the friendly type."

Felix thought about it. It took a while. "So what. I just gotta scram?"

"I'd recommend it." A dull thunk behind him as the pump finished.

"Why? What have you done?"

"Not too much yet. But I think there'll be some more in store."

No answer.

Marshall said, "Bottom line is I've aggravated some people best not aggravated. So I reckon you might want to give everything a wide berth."

"But they'll know I'm me and not you."

"Yes. But I wouldn't really rely on that as a firm safety measure."

"What have you been up to?"

"That's for me to be worrying about."

"Illegal stuff?"

"No. But it's still worth keeping out of."

"I gotta move all my stuff out?"

Marshall said, "No. Just yourself."

"Ah, shit. How likely is it someone's going to come poking round?"

Marshall pondered that, likelihoods always tough to firmly quantify. He said, "I don't know. But even if it's a slim chance I'd say it's well worth avoiding."

Which he felt was good advice, given that in his experience it was the slim chances that made things all the worse.

"Man. Look. Thing is, I got some stuff round here that I probably shouldn't leave where people can see. Like, if people are coming by I mean."

Marshall let a quiet settle, like giving the admission a bit of gravity. In his right hand his last remaining quarter. He flipped it and caught it a couple of times, like heads or tails would dictate what he said. "What sort of things?"

"I'm just holding on to some stuff for a friend."

"A friend."

"Yeah. Well. You know. Some of it may or may not be stolen. I don't know."

Marshall felt his cell ringing in his pocket. That blocked number a fairly safe bet. He let it go to voice mail. He said, "These aren't the sorts of people who are going to worry if you've got a few extra DVD players lying round."

"Yeah. It's not really DVD players."

"Whatever. Look. You need to be operating on the basis you're going to have visitors fairly shortly."

"How shortly?"

"Like, pack a bag, but if it takes longer than thirty minutes I'd hightail without it."

"Shit. Sounds like you got some trouble."

Marshall said, "Trouble's selling it short. Thirty minutes."

He hung up the phone. The console on its short pole with its shadow laid neatly slantwise and beside it his own, hugely stretched. He went into the office and got change for his two remaining singles and walked outside to the Corolla and popped the trunk. What a sight: the duffel with his fake samples, the 870 laid next to it. He removed Rojas's .38 from his belt and dropped it on the bag. His hand came away grimed when he closed the lid. He dusted it on his thigh and walked back to the pay phone and dialed the U.S. Marshal's office at the district courthouse in Santa Fe. Cohen wasn't in yet, so Marshall asked to be put through to his cell.

When he picked up Marshall said, "It's me."

"Why are you so hard to get ahold of?"

Marshall said, "I'm out and about."

"Right. I guess that's your full-time occupation or something, don't think I've ever caught you at home."

Marshall didn't answer.

"Where you callin' from? It's a funny-lookin' number."

"I'm at a pay phone."

"Anyone listening?"

"I don't think so. But you're the government, you tell me."

Cohen paused and said, "Whenever I try the house it's that Felix feller who answers."

"He's my tenant."

"Right. I think the idea when the feds give you a house is that you actually live in it. Generally safest, as far as staying alive goes."

Marshall said, "I can look after myself."

"Someone's last words, I'm sure."

Marshall didn't answer.

Cohen said, "I think you and I need to sit down together. Sooner rather than later would be best. I've got time this morning."

Marshall leaned on the phone box, taking his time so he'd sound patient. He said, "Or you could just leave me alone."

Cohen laughed. "It doesn't work like that, I'm afraid. We need to sit down."

Some real firmness in that last bit. His cell phone started ringing. Blocked number. He could guess the gist of the message: You're a dead man.

Marshall said, "Let me call you back."

FOUR

Wayne Banister

Forty miles west of Albuquerque on I-40, just south of the Tohajiilee Reservation. No cloud cover and approaching summer, it wouldn't be hard to list places he'd rather be. Come midday and it would hit one hundred. Hell would be jealous.

They'd provided GPS coordinates for the rendezvous. The machine in the rental knew the way. He followed a dirt road north off the 40. If you could call it a road. Just wheel ruts wending through the undulations. A gentle arc this way and the other, one slope to the next. What a landscape, might as well be Mars.

He crested a shallow rise and below him he saw two vehicles parked nose-to-tail: a Bentley Continental coupe, and a Cadillac Escalade tight in behind. Black paintwork dulled by powdered grime. The Bentley's driver's door was open. A guy in the seat with a thumb hooked in the bottom of the wheel and one foot on the ground outside. Another guy in a T-shirt and wraparound shades leaning with arms folded against the rear door of the Caddy.

Wayne stopped thirty feet away. The GPS unit lost his position. They must have been running signal jammers. He cut the motor. The dials all collapsed in unison. A short, expectant quiet, and then the guy by the Cadillac unfolded his arms and walked over. His gait didn't fit him: a smallish man trying to fill a big swagger. Wayne wound down his window. A thin lip of dust accumulated at the sill. The guy leaned a hand on the roof and ducked his head to Wayne's level. A big loop of sweat beneath his arm. Below the black lenses his cheeks were honeycombed with old acne scars. Shape of a gun on his hip under the T-shirt.

"How you doing?" There was alcohol on his breath.

Wayne said, "Good."

"You carrying?"

Wayne nodded. "Shoulder and ankle."

"You'll need to lose them before you see Mr. Frazer."

The guy beckoned him out of the car. "Just step out slowly and I'll take them off you."

Wayne obliged. The guy patted him down and took the SIG from his shoulder rig and then crouched and removed the .22 from the ankle holster. He stood up and moved away a pace and sighted the SIG on the Cadillac, one-handed grip, frame tilted sideways.

"Nice piece. Good weight on these things."

"Yeah."

The guy opened the rear door of the rental and tossed the guns on the seat. "Revolver guy, myself. Don't have to worry about hunting for brass in the heat of the moment."

He smiled, as if all his heated moments got very hot indeed. A good spread of gold in his front teeth. Wayne didn't answer. The guy gestured at the Bentley. "Go on round to the passenger side."

Wayne walked around in front of the coupe. The guy in the driver's seat didn't seem to notice. His trouser leg had hiked above his sock, revealing a thin band of flesh.

Wayne opened the passenger door and slid in and closed it behind him. With the driver's door open a warning tone was chiming patiently, but the man beside him seemed unaware of it. *Ding, ding, ding, ding.* Wayne wondered why he didn't just seal himself in and run the air-con.

The guy said, "So you're the Dallas Man."

"That's what they call me."

The guy nodded, as if taking the measure of the name. The Bentley's interior was plush: all tan leather, sharply aromatic. "I like it. Got a certain something about it, you know?"

He clicked his fingers gently. "Dallas Man, Dallas Man." Not a local accent.

Wayne didn't reply. *Ding, ding, ding, ding—*

The guy said, "You can call me Mr. Frazer."

"All right."

The guy smiled, hiked a thumb at him. "Kinda funny. You cleanup guys are always so paranoid about being seen or whatever. So why the fuck you go around in a suit like that, coming into summer?"

"I could ask you the same question."

Frazer laughed. "Yeah. But I'm driving a Bentley. You've got that thing. People see the suit/car combo, they're gonna think out-of-towner, you know?"

"Out-of-towners are pretty ubiquitous."

The guy shrugged. "Yeah, well."

He smoothed a hand across the top of the wheel, gestured through the windshield. "I hope you like our little meeting spot. We got all sorts of jammer shit in the truck so you can't be listened in to. It's all real fucking fancy. Tell you what, thirty years ago it used to be easy to break the law in this country. Now they got surveillance that'll blow your mind. Satellites, tap your phones, whatever. Place's gone to the dogs, right, Chino? People's liberties, just, sayonara."

The guy by the Cadillac said, "Yeah, Mr. Frazer."

Frazer nodded to himself like he'd just imparted some deep wisdom. He looked close to sixty. Silver hair combed back off a receding hairline. A thick handlebar mustache that dripped down to a thick neck. Top button of his shirt open to accommodate it. Under his suit jacket he wore a leather shoulder rig, butt of a revolver visible. Maybe a .357.

Wayne said, "You got some work for me?"

Frazer looked at him. Sun still low, and on the cleared ground around them the shadows from the hills lay in wide curves. *Ding, ding, ding, ding.* "Thought with a name like that you'd be out of Texas. But you sound East Coast. New York or something."

Wayne said, "I'm not from around here."

"What's your background, Special Forces or something?"

"I can't really go into it. It's just an operational safety thing."

Frazer shrugged it off. "Just curious. I guess if you were shit I wouldn't have heard of you. Or maybe I would, but for different reasons." He laughed.

Wayne didn't answer. Big arcs across the windshield where the wipers had cleared dust.

Frazer brushed something off a lapel. His expression went solemn. Getting down to business. He said, "I want a takedown of a rival operation."

"Okay."

Quiet a moment, like letting the implications settle in. *Ding, ding, ding, ding—*

Wayne said, "Takedown, or takeover?"

"Takedown. As in, I want people dead."

"All right. How many targets are we talking?"

Frazer thought about it. "I don't know. It kinda depends."

Wayne waited.

Frazer said, "Look, situation is, I'm trying to broaden my operation a little, get some stuff into New York."

"And you're facing some resistance."

"Well, yeah. And it's not all that polite, either. I got stock gone missing, guys gone missing, ending up chopped. And when I say chopped I mean, you know."

He mimed starting a chain saw.

"I had two guys show up in pieces. Brought you the photos, holy shit. Everyone's doing the whole slice-and-dice thing these days. But it's ridiculous really, as if you can just scare me off, and I'll go try something else. I've been doing this for thirty years."

He stroked his mustache, checked his rearview mirror. Chino

was walking a big counterclockwise loop of the cars. "It's just fucking savage."

Wayne said, "So who am I looking for?"

"I only got rumors at this stage."

"Rumors will do."

Frazer looked out his open door. "Apparently the pushback is from some guy called Patriarch. Or the Patriarch or something. I don't know. It's some clever Web-based system where he can control everything anonymously and sort of keep back from it a bit. Guy I know reckons he's actually real young, like twenty, twenty-five maybe. Like, imagine that. Some fucking kid running an op where he's got guys running round doing shit with chain saws. Arrogance of some people. Just blows the mind."

"So you want him gone as well?"

"Well, yeah. I want fucking everyone gone. The people on the street actually stopping it coming in, and then whoever's calling the shots. Christ, this thing. It's put my blood pressure up about fifty points, I swear. Almost need a tire gauge to check it."

Wayne didn't answer.

Frazer said, "Look, I'm not after some showy vengeance murder or anything like that. This is all just business to me. I'm not looking to make anyone pay or regret or anything. I just want them out of the way, because it's costing me a lot of money."

Ding, ding, ding, ding. Chino was coming up alongside them, off to Wayne's right.

Wayne said, "We'd have to negotiate my fee scheme."

"Why's that?"

Chino rounded the front of the car. *Ding, ding, ding, ding.*

"Normally I charge on a per-hit basis. But if we're talking a long-winded thing where I have to do a bit of digging, it could drag on a long time. I'll need to have a think about it."

"All right."

"It really depends on what their security's like. If the guy really does have a safe, anonymous system going it could be hard to pin him down."

"Yeah, well. Sooner the better basically. It's all just lost profit."

Frazer paused and looked through the windshield. Lips slightly pursed like he was choosing words carefully. He said, "It just sounds like he's got a pretty cutthroat game plan up and running, and I think it would be good to get in and disestablish it before he starts thinking he's dealing with sissies. You know?"

Chino coming down the left-hand side. *Ding, ding, ding, ding—*

Wayne said, "Yeah. I understand."

"So is this something you're going to be able to look at for me?"

"Normally I would."

Frazer glanced at him. "But?"

Chino approaching that open door.

"It's kind of a conflict of interest."

"How so?"

Ding, ding, ding, ding—

Wayne leaned suddenly and trapped Frazer against the seat with his left arm, and with his right drew the revolver from inside Frazer's jacket and sighted on Chino one-handed and squeezed the trigger twice, a clean double-tap. Confines of the vehicle, the sound was colossal. Frazer tensed and shut his eyes, recoiled against the flash, cried out mutely beneath the blasts.

Chino caught both rounds. A tight group through the armpit. He was dead midstep. Lifeless form toppling and Wayne, still calmly in the moment, tracked the fall and fired a third time and shot him through the head.

Blood mist and a thump as he met the ground and a shallow wave of dust issued radially. Wayne eased himself upright and settled back in his seat. The leather creaked with the motion. He laid the gun on his thigh. Colt Python, chambered for the .357 Magnum. Smoke rose off the muzzle.

Ding, ding, ding, ding.

Frazer still crushed back against his seat, shock keeping him pinned there. Face averted from the horror and his cheek pressed to the headrest. Arms raised and hands clawed, some futile don't-hurt-me gesture.

Wayne waited.

Dignity returned gradually. Frazer lowered his hands, turned and faced forward. Breath heaving, face a shade paler than a moment ago. He passed a sleeve across his mouth and risked a glance outside the car. His backup man just dumped there, inanimate flesh and bone. Only movement his blood as it left him.

"Jesus. You killed him."

"I did."

Wayne just sitting there calmly, and Frazer must have wondered what other madness he'd witnessed for this to seem normal.

Wayne said, "Like I told you. Conflict of interest. If you'd contacted me six months ago things might have played differently. But I guess you've missed your chance."

"You're working for him?"

"On retainer, more or less."

Ding, ding, ding, ding—

"So now what happens?"

Resignation in his tone like he knew there was just the one outcome.

Wayne said, "It's binary. Either you die or I die." He smiled. "And then we go our separate ways."

"Jesus."

"He wasn't much help to Chino. So I doubt he'll be helping you."

"Please. There are other ways."

Lines he'd heard before. Wayne said, "You carry a gun, you keep an armed bodyguard. You must have envisioned a violent end."

Frazer didn't answer.

Wayne said, "Don't worry. This isn't some wild departure from likelihood. You were always going to end up here, more or less." He gestured with his free hand. "The specifics are irrelevant. This car. Chino. Me."

Frazer didn't answer. His lips parted, a rope of spit strung between them.

Wayne said, "Anyway. My point is that we have brought to fruition a scenario made inevitable a long time ago. You live this life, sooner or later you get clipped. It's not difficult."

Frazer didn't answer. Wayne could see his pulse leaping.

"Last words?"

No reply. His eyes were closed. Strange to waive the chance to shape the final moments. Although silence was, of course, a choice.

Wayne lifted the gun. Smell of cordite in the car. Dust and Chino's T-shirt lifting weakly as a breeze came through. He pulled the trigger.

Heading back east on the 40, he felt calm despite the blood flecks on his shirt from the blowback and the faint smell of cordite on his hands. He listened to an FM station as he drove. It helped mask the ringing in his ears.

Western limits of the city and I-40 became the Coronado Freeway. He stopped at the first gas station he saw and pulled in beside the car wash bay and used the hose to rinse off the rental. Safer than the drive-thru and being filmed paying. He stood there as if mesmerized as water off the roof fell in clean rivulets through the dusted windows. Evidence of his morning disintegrating, top down.

A mess of brown water at his feet. He used the hose and chased the murk to the drain until the eddies ran clear and then he turned off the water and coiled the hose neatly and set it on its cradle. Back into traffic and a twenty-minute run east to his motel just south of the freeway. A tan and low-rise neighborhood and in the east the indigo form of the Sandia Mountains, low and contoured beyond the city.

He parked in front of his room and got out, retrieved the gun bag from the trunk, and went inside. He locked the door behind him. Cool from the air-conditioning. A breeze from somewhere rolling fold-to-fold in the blind. He set the bag on the single bed below the window. He always found the transition strange. One moment fraught with bloodshed. The next tranquil, returned to normal life and its harmless trivia: sound of children in the pool outside. *TV Guide*. Nearby restaurant menus. Please check out by ten A.M. The ease with which he moved from one world to the other.

From the gun bag he removed a plastic trash liner and took it through to the bathroom. He undressed and balled his socks and bloodied garments and deposited them with his shoes in the liner and knotted the top. Then he showered and toweled dry and dressed in fresh clothes he'd left in the room and sat on the bed below the window. From the gun bag he took the SIG and slipped it in the belt holster and clipped it on his hip beneath his shirt, and then he found his blue phone and dialed a number.

Three rings and then the pickup. "How was Mr. Frazer?"

Wayne ran a hand through his hair, still damp with shower water. "Fine. Not quite so good now, but you're right, he was trying to get in on the New York market. He wanted help with reducing competition."

"I see."

"Obviously he named you as a rival."

"Code, or my actual name?"

"He used the term 'Patriarch.' "

"Right. And I take it he was proposing something fairly aggressive?"

"Yeah."

"How many hits?"

"Well. As many as it takes to stop what you're doing."

"And he wanted you to do it?"

"Yes."

"Has he approached anyone else?"

"I don't know."

"You didn't ask?"

"No."

"Okay. Where is he now?"

"Same place I met him, but dead. He had a bodyguard named Chino."

"You killed both of them?"

"Yes."

"Good, excellent. Obviously, I appreciate the loyalty."

"No, that's okay." Wayne laughed quietly. "Clearly there was a conflict of interest."

"Yeah. Did he give you any other information? What exactly did he have?"

"Most of it was vague. He said you were young and that you're operating things electronically."

"Okay. That's interesting. Were they carrying anything? Flash drives, that kind of thing?"

"Nothing like that."

"Computers?"

"No. Just some signal-jamming gear. It fucked with my GPS. No storage or hard disks or anything."

"Okay. Well, if people are operating this aggressively, then that's a concern."

Wayne didn't answer.

"What're your movements over the next few days? Are you able to stay local?"

Wayne said, "Sure."

"Okay, great. Yeah, I think if you could keep in the area for say the next week that would be helpful. If people are taking steps to try and push me out, I need to react pretty firmly."

"Frazer won't be having another go."

"No. Probably not. But I think it might be good just to see what plays out and respond accordingly."

"Sure."

"Where did you meet them?"

Wayne said, "Out west by that Navajo reservation."

"Okay."

"At a glance, it might look like Frazer drilled his bodyguard and then topped himself."

"Right. I imagine it won't take long to see past that. Sounds a bit incongruous."

Wayne said, "Possibly."

"And what about that other job? Have you checked the motel yet?"

"I went out last night. It sounds like it was Marshall. I showed the desk guy the photo and he was certain it was him."

"Did they let you see the register?"

"Yeah. He must've bribed someone. He checked in as John Adams, but there're literally no other details, no address or license plate or anything. Guy reckoned he stayed two, maybe three nights. But you know what he's like, probably said fuck-all, paid cash, so there's nothing to go on."

"Right. Well, they reckon the apartment's been getting calls maybe once a month, so hopefully when he tries again you'll be close enough to follow up."

"Sure. I'll need to be down here for the Frazer thing anyway."

"I appreciate it. There're other people I can put on Marshall, but I need to be sure it's done right. I just don't want him to stay in the wind like this, it's a real issue. I'll keep in touch, might have some more errands for you."

"Let me know."

Wayne ended the call. Sitting on the edge of the bed, elbows to knees. Sweat from his forehead dotting the carpet between his feet. What he hadn't said: Frazer had pictures of dead men. Men shot and men chainsawed, a whole garish ream of prints. He didn't want to go there. This whole catalogue of misery he'd be forced to describe. Too cold a prospect, even for Wayne. He found his red phone and dialed another number.

She always knew it was him. "Daddy."

"Hello, sweetheart."

"Where are you?"

"Just somewhere."

"That's not a place."

"I'm sitting on a bed."

She laughed. "No. That's not a place."

"Yes it is. You asked where I am and I said I'm sitting on a bed."

"Are you coming home soon?"

"Pretty soon."

"Tomorrow?"

"No. Not tomorrow. But not too long."

"Do you miss me?"

Wayne said, "Yes. I miss you so much."

She didn't answer.

He said, "What did you do today?"

"Painted a picture. What did you do today?"

"I had to go to a meeting."

"Have you had your lunch?"

"No. It's too early for lunch. It's only ten o'clock. I've had my breakfast, though."

"Is it a different time there?"

"Yes. It's a different time here."

She didn't answer. He said, "What did you paint a picture of?"

"Mommy."

It was too much for him. He clamped a hand across his mouth as his eyes welled. Quiet a long time.

"Daddy?"

He drew breath between fingers, eyes squeezed shut. He laid the phone on the bed beside him so she wouldn't hear. She was saying something, tinny and distant, another world. A ragged breath and he calmed himself. Composure could be fleeting, not long before he'd topple back. He picked up the phone.

"I'll be home soon, sweetheart. You be good."

She was saying something, but he ended the call and she was gone midsentence. He thought of Chino, departing midstep.

He lowered himself to the floor and sat with his back to the bed. Children in the pool outside. Please check out by ten A.M. The ease with which he stepped from one world to the other: his calm and his misery. The latter just a phone call away. He reached behind him to the bag and felt blindly and found the photographs. A4 sheets, glossed by laser print. Blood and the victims headless, armless, legless. He looked at the ceiling and tore the pages one by one.

FIVE

Marshall

He drove back north on I-25 to Santa Fe and went east on San Francisco Street through the center of town. Low-rise adobe, lots of Spanish detailing, the Saint Francis Cathedral framed neatly at road's end. He liked that sense of heritage. Oldest capital city in America and here he was, a chance player in a thousand-year lineage.

Marshall parked just beyond the plaza and checked his phone. Two missed calls from that blocked number, still awaiting action. Make them wait. Let them think his terms were the only ones that mattered.

He didn't want to use his cell to call the house, but he did.

"Hombre."

Marshall had hoped he'd be gone. He opened his door for some air and said, "I told you to pack a bag and go."

"You said thirty minutes."

"It's been thirty minutes. It's about fifty now."

"What sort of people you got coming round?"

"I don't know exactly. But I don't want you to be the one who finds out."

"Case they're unpleasant or something."

"I know they're unpleasant. It's all just a question of degrees."

"Like things could get pretty hot."

"Yes. Things could get hot."

"Well, I'm moving then."

Marshall said, "Hang on, wait. How much rent are you behind?"

"Don't know. You'd have to tell me."

"Right. I thought so. You got the car there?"

"You mean my car?"

Marshall said, "Yes. Your car."

"Uh-huh. Yeah. It's here."

"Are there many cars parked out on the street?"

"Hang on. Uh. Yeah. There's some. I don't know, five."

Passersby on the sidewalk, tourists mainly. Marshall closed the door again lest he be overheard. He said, "Anyone in them?"

"Don't think so. No."

Marshall said, "Okay. Pack a bag, get in the car, drive up the street where you can see the house, and just sit there and watch. If you can do that for me, we'll call everything square."

"My car?"

"Yes, your car. You're not taking mine."

"Okay. Yeah. All right. What am I watching for?"

"Anything."

"Like people coming?"

Marshall said, "Especially like people coming."

"All right. For how long?"

"Not long. I'll be back in about an hour."

"What if I see something?"

"If you see something you call me. But do not go back into the house. Is that clear? Do not go back into the house."

"Uh-huh. House off-limits."

"I'll be round in an hour or two. You need to get out of there in the next five minutes."

He ended the call and just sat there quietly, coming down off the tension of it. Then he got out and locked the car and walked back up the street. On his right the plaza was still green coming into summer, tourists with cameras out in force, buskers and the odd junkie looking for change. An old guy in a huge feathered hat was sitting on a bench, watching traffic slip by.

Marshall walked another block and made a left into the Starbucks on San Francisco Street. Lucas Cohen was seated at the table facing the window, reading *The New York Times*. Marshall ordered coffee and brought it over and sat down beside him, on the far side so he could put his back to the wall, keep the door in view.

Cohen said, "All the places in town we coulda met, you pick this." Running the words together in his Texas drawl, all part of being a smooth lawman. He closed the newspaper and held it at the centerfold so it fell together.

"What's wrong with Starbucks?"

Cohen raised his eyebrows, inoffensive. "Nothing. But there're parks, museums, got the cathedral just there. I don't know, some nice options."

Marshall tried some coffee. He said, "Did you want it like one of those spy movies, meet on a bench in the plaza, talk out the corner of your mouth?"

Cohen nodded. "Yeah, something like that. Both of us looking different ways. Maybe next time."

Marshall didn't answer. Cohen was wearing a yellow polo shirt tucked into tan trousers, razor-sharp down the creases. Folded sunglasses hanging in the neck of the shirt.

Marshall said, "I get you on your day off or something?"

Cohen set his coffee on the newspaper, looked down at his attire. "No. We got some Nazi wacko, skipped a court appearance for firearms in Dallas, had a tip-off he's working as a golf caddy down Sandia Heights."

Marshall said, "So you're going in undercover?"

Cohen nodded. "Yeah, swap my putter for a shotgun, that sort of thing. Trying to think of some good golf puns for the ride home." He smiled. "Actually picked him up once before, working at a course just up the 77. Coupla years back now. Funny how people have these instincts, you know? This guy, gets a bit of trouble, comes down here and does some caddying." He had a mouthful of coffee. "Anyway, should be good. Got along okay with him last time, he's a Texas man, I'm a Texas man, so we kinda bonded over that. But we'll see."

Marshall said, "Why do you keep calling me?"

Cohen glanced behind him, just regular coffee shop bustle. People lining up for caffeine, peering at cell phones while they waited. He said, "If you ever answered the phone I wouldn't have to." He unfolded the shades and slipped them on, the street getting pretty bright this time of morning. "But it's like asset management, good to check our witness protection folks aren't getting murdered."

"You don't have to worry about me."

Cohen tipped his cup high, getting the last mouthful. "If this tenant of yours was removed from the equation, I might be disinclined to doubt you." He liked a long-winded phrase every so often, take it slow, really play up the accent.

Marshall said, "It's extra security. Have him in the WITSEC house, keep myself somewhere else."

"Yeah. Thing is, when I drove past just now and ran his plates, they didn't actually match his car."

"How'd you know it was his?"

"It was parked in your driveway, so I put two and two together."

Marshall was quiet a second. He said, "So, what?"

"So, it tells me he's not exactly the most scrupulous individual. And the idea of being in federal protection is you try not to attract any attention." He leaned forward on folded arms and smiled out at the view. "Whereas people like whatshisname, Felix, can sometimes undermine that."

Marshall didn't answer.

They sat there a while, not talking. Cohen watched the window, oddly engrossed, like the street was careful theater. He said, "Looking forward to a bit of Albuquerque, actually. Might drop in at Tim's Place, grab a burger." He clucked his tongue. "Risky though. Mrs. Cohen gets sorta riled if I don't leave room for dinner."

Marshall said, "I think Felix is an acceptable risk."

Cohen looked at him. "Yeah? What exactly do you know about him?"

"Not much. But I'm a good judge of character."

Cohen kept watching him, Marshall just sitting there quietly, drinking his coffee. Traffic gliding by slowly on the narrow road, pedestrians chatting mutely beyond the glass.

Cohen said, "Problem is, if you're driving a car with swapped plates, chances are you've broken a law at some stage. Now if you want a tenant, I guess that's your prerogative, strange as it is. But bottom line is, you're going to have to find someone a little less. I don't know."

"Dubious?"

Cohen nodded. He tipped his cup back and forth, probably watching the last bead of fluid circle the base. He said, "Yeah. Dubious. Or even if it's just in the interests of irony. Like, bad PR if someone finds out we've got a wanted felon in a safe house, you know what I mean?"

"Right. So why'd we have to talk about this face-to-face?"

Cohen blew air through his teeth, a very faint whistle. "Because I wanted to make sure you'll do it."

Marshall said, "And if I get rid of him you'll leave me alone?"

"You don't sugarcoat it, do you?"

Marshall stood up. His coffee was only a quarter gone. He said, "Good seeing you, Cohen."

SIX

Rojas

More than an hour since the break, and Bolt was still bleeding. Face puffed like snakebite and the ooze spread all round. He'd been out a long time. Probably ten minutes before he could say his name.

Rojas drove, Bolt laid out on the rear bench of the Cherokee under a blanket like some cross-border run. The state of him. Jesus, they were going to get it.

The house was in east Santa Fe, brand-new place in a brand-new subdivision, big adobe structures on huge sections. Rojas called it Spanish pueblo revival. Vance called it pretentious fucking shit, but never in front of Leon.

Good roads and no traffic. He could get there fast, unseen. A nudge off the curb as he turned in and Bolt swore with the impact.

"Relax, we're here."

Ascending the drive and ahead of them the house laid out in a low sweep atop its artificial rise. Straight into the garage, a plunge into cool and gloom. He cut the motor and hit the button on the visor to drop the door behind them and got out and stepped to the rear.

Bolt shed the blanket and hauled himself upright and clambered out. Bone-white grip, clumsy from the knock. Blood streaked each side of his mouth, beading at his chin before the fall. He found his feet and pushed Rojas away, testing stability. Chin to chest, breath ragged. A good few seconds before the first lurching step. This solo horror show.

Slow progress as Rojas followed him through into the main house. Into what Leon called the great room, though he wasn't there. Just Vance and Dante laid out playing Xbox like a pair of kids. Vance shirtless on his side on the sofa, Dante on his stomach on the floor by the TV. Each of them fiddling with a controller, TV a split screen, a gun sight top and bottom.

And that perpetual mess, host to all manner of things:

Vance's Colt Anaconda on the floor by the sofa and beside it a gaping box of .44 shells. Two Berettas in Dante's grab range. The glass coffee table pushed aside, surface cloudy with powder. A razor blade in a field of scratch marks where they'd troweled and cut. Two tarred scraps of foil. A rubber tourniquet strap and a needle with syringe lying on a zippered pouch. A cloud of something dissipating near the ceiling and the rank smell of it still present. Windows curtained and between them the morning light slanting through in narrow rays and caught there the dust floating whitely.

Rojas said, "Could you at least do the dishes?"

Nothing from Dante.

Vance looked up. "Shit. Happened to you?"

No drugs in his voice. Vance and Dante being connoisseurs, it took a bit to shift them up or down. The gospel according to Vance: regular intake was beneficial. It bolstered mental resilience to foreign compounds and helped preclude the risk of an epic mindfuck. They had a coke/meth combo they favored. It was called Dante's Inferno.

Rojas said, "Got screwed on a deal."

Dante said, "Your nose broken?"

Bolt said, "Yeah."

Voice thick with fluid.

He stepped across Dante and lowered himself onto the other sofa and lay down. "Holy shit. Someone set it."

Vance said, "How long's it been?"

"Dunno."

"Not meant to do it if it's more than an hour or something. Can't see what you're doing with all the swelling and you just end up with a fucked face."

Dante said, "He looked half-fucked before so he may as well go all out."

Vance laughed so hard he had to pause the game. He was two years back from Afghanistan. Physique cut like some demigod, meth-and-bench-press his chosen regimen. He still had the tan, but he needed a UV bed for the upkeep. A maintenance zap every now and then.

Rojas said, "Where's Leon?"

Vance pulled himself together. "Where do you think?"

Which could have meant either the basement or the office. That basement an awful place: some dark-age gallows, natural light just weak through the vents, always damp, chains and anchor rings crusted with rust. Their own private Guantánamo. Vance's quip: the perfect place to be quartered. No noise out at the road but sound still made it through the floor. Chain saws and other things.

Rojas went to find ice. Doors in the house more often locked than not. Leon's doing. He had weapons, meth precursor, cash all stashed away. Rojas hadn't known Leon long, but Vance had served with him, Afghanistan and Iraq. Vance swore Leon had two million dollars cold in the house, stolen funds from a CIA drop in Baghdad he'd been in on. Rooms full of Marine ordnance freighted back from the Middle East that hadn't quite made it home.

Leon himself this strange, nocturnal man. By daylight locked in his sanctum with his books and his manuals scheming god knew what. By night hunched taut and shirtless with Vance at the coffee table in that great black-curtained room, the pair of them twisted feverish from toke after toke and then, delirious, descending to join the guests, and from then no one dared listen.

In bed one night with the noise of it filtering up from below, he realized there were scales for many things, that there was bad and there was evil, and in Leon lived proof that one was a long way from the other. The next day you could smell the aftermath, Leon reveling in it, standing there in the middle of the house with one hand lightly at his stomach and eyes closed as he slowly breathed.

He found a bag of ice in the freezer and gauze in one of the medic packs and took them through to the living room. Bolt got a start when he dropped them on his stomach.

"Jesus."

Rojas said, "You know how to fix a nose?"

"Not really."

Dante said, "Just shape it round with your fingers."

"How do you know the right shape when it's all puffed?"

"Have to guess."

"Shit. And then what?"

"You pack it out with the gauze and then you use tape or something over the top and it's fixed and hopefully only kinda fucked."

They all laughed.

With his yellow jeans and green hair, Dante seemed a strange source of advice, but Vance rated him. The verdict: crystal's fried his dress sense, but he's still a stand-up guy.

Vance dug around beneath him and found the TV remote between cushions. He flicked the set off. He and Dante sat watching the blank screen like some solemn remembrance, and then Vance said, "So how the fuck did that happen?"

Rojas said, "We went out this morning to do that pickup."

Vance lit a cigarette. "Which one was that?"

"We got a ring-in on the number. Some guy wanting to start up a new supply, had some sample stock for us."

"What'd he say?"

"I dunno. I got some stuff you might want to look at. Something like that."

"And what. You met him, and it went shit."

"Well, yeah. Pretty much."

Vance said, "Why you got this thing about always going early?"

"Because. You get someone when they're still asleep, it throws them. It's an actual proven thing."

Vance shrugged, kissed out a smoke ring. "Should have shot the fuck."

"Not that easy."

"Where'd you meet?"

"That diner down 25."

"Stupidest shit I ever heard, doing it there, when it's that quiet."

"Yeah, well."

"How big was the sample?"

"A kilo."

"And you didn't guess it's a setup. Holy shit."

Dante rolled on his back. "Where's the cigarettes?"

Vance tossed him the pack and then the lighter. Dante caught them, left hand then right. He said, "So, what. He think you'd have cash or something that he'd take off you?"

"No. We went to his car to do the pickup, and he nailed Cyrus in the face with a shotgun and then leveled it on me. Said he was looking for that girl."

Vance said, "What one?"

"That Alyce girl."

Dante rolled on his side to get a smoke going and then lay back down. Portrait of an overdose with his arms and legs spread starfish and the cigarette hanging out the edge of a smile. He laughed. "Shit. Not the one Leon did, is it?"

Vance said, "Maybe. I lost track." He laughed, midriff tensed in a perfect six-pack. "Old Leon's been a busy boy."

Rojas didn't answer.

Vance said, "What'd this prick want?"

"Well. Answers. Or he was gonna come looking."

"Answers. Classic, I love it."

Dante turned his head and tapped ash on the floor. Advantage of timber, you could just sweep it up every now and then. He said, "I like that 'come looking' part. Imagine that."

They all sat quietly, absorbed by fantasy. A quiet crunching noise as Bolt positioned the ice.

Vance said, "Guy give a name?"

Rojas said, "Marshall."

"Marshall, eh."

Rojas said, "I got his plate number."

"You called him since?"

"He's not picking up."

Vance grinned around the cigarette and spread his arms along the back of the sofa. He said, "Maybe Leon wants to try."

SEVEN

Lauren Shore

One of those mornings.

One of those mornings when she woke and it was nearly twelve. Still dressed and laid diagonally on tangled sheets, her feet at the pillow and a thin stripe of sunlight across the darkened room. Somewhere her phone was ringing.

She swept an arm and found where it had nested amidst the covers. It was Martinez.

She said, “Hey.”

“Hey. You sound like you just woke up.”

She laughed croakily, coughed. “If you hadn’t called I’d still be asleep.”

She rolled to the edge of the bed and sat up and found her feet. The room tipped one way and back the other. She crouched and steadied herself on the edge of the bed.

He said, “You doing okay?”

She went into the bathroom and looked at herself in the mirror, finger-combed her hair. She put an inch of water in the glass that stood at the basin and knocked it back like a shot. “Yeah, I’m okay.”

He said, "You sound like you just ate gravel for lunch or something."

She perused the medicine cabinet. No aspirin. "Ha. Yeah, I'm fine. Just, you know. I thought stress leave was meant to be relaxing. This is worse than being at work."

She walked down the hallway to the kitchen. The world steadying. Past the other bedroom door. Windows to the right, and on the left-hand wall these off-shade squares where the photographs had stopped the paint from fading.

He said, "Yeah, well. You gotta give it a bit of time. What's the doc been saying?"

"She says I'm not a nutcase."

"Really? You'd better go to someone else then."

"Hilarious."

In the kitchen she lifted the kettle, gauged it half full, and set it boiling. She leaned against the edge of the counter. "So what's happening? You got good stuff cooking, or did you just want to shoot the shit?"

He laughed. "I always want to shoot the shit. But I thought I better give you a ring. Even though I probably shouldn't."

She ran a hand through her hair. "Probably shouldn't. I'd better hear what it is then."

"Yeah. I thought you might say that."

She could picture him reclining side-on to his desk, kids' drawings all lined up in their frames.

He said, "Got a call from the staties this morning. Had a guy ring in a nine-one-one from this diner just off the 25, kind of up past Algodones."

She walked through to the living room to escape the kettle roar. "Okay. And?"

"Guy was a trucker, eating early breakfast or something, said the only other people in there were these three guys having a sit-down and a coffee. In there about fifteen minutes or whatever and then they just up and left. Anyway. He thought they were being kind of quiet, but didn't really make anything of it, so he pays and goes outside to the lot and two of the guys are laid out in the gravel, and the other one's gone."

Her files and news clippings and printouts spread on chairs, the coffee table, everywhere. She sat sidesaddle on the arm of the sofa. "What do you mean, laid out. Like dead?"

"No, not dead, just beat up. He reckoned one of the guys was on his back with a broken nose, blood everywhere, and the other guy was on his side and then sort of got up on all fours when the guy helped him. Wheezing away like he'd been kicked in the balls or kicked in the guts or something."

"Anybody say what happened?"

"No, but I mean, pretty clear the third guy nailed the other two and then hightailed it."

"Deal gone bad, maybe."

"That's what the truck driver thought. State police didn't think it was much of a trafficking area, but the descriptions this guy gave sounded like Troy Rojas and Cyrus Bolt. The beat-up guys, I mean. So they ended up calling the marshals because there's a BOLO on Bolt, and the feds put them through to our missing persons guys, because apparently there's some angle where they're connected to a missing girl. Anyway, then they called us just as a courtesy thing, too."

She said, "Quite the phone tree."

"Yeah."

The kettle clicked. She headed back to the kitchen. "So who was the third guy?"

"Umm, hang on. Yeah. Tall, well-built blond guy. Early to mid-thirties. Probably six-three, the guy reckoned, maybe two hundred."

She paused, midstride. "Huh. Shit."

"What?"

She kept walking. "Nothing."

"You know him or something?"

She laughed. "No. I doubt it."

He didn't answer. She rolled open a drawer and found a spoon and took a mug from a shelf and rinsed out the dust. "What did the staff think?"

"Couple of cooks out the back, didn't see a thing. Mexican waitress not too great with English. Cruiser went out but I mean, shit. Nothing to see, other than a bit of blood here and there."

"Truck driver still around?"

"Yeah. He's got a place here. Missing persons went out this morning, and I was going to have a word too, but I don't really have the time."

She tilted her head to hold the phone against her shoulder, spooned instant coffee into the mug. "So you thought . . . ?"

He laughed. "Yeah. So I thought if you felt up to it there's nothing says you can't just call round and see a truck driver for a chat. If you want to."

"Yeah. Okay."

"You want to?"

She watched water in the mug swirl as she poured. "Yeah. I'll go see him. What're his details?"

"Got a pen?"

She did. That marker for the whiteboard by the fridge they'd used to schedule out their week. She bit her lip a second. "Yeah. Go."

"Guy's name's Alvin Lemar."

He gave her a phone number and address. She scrawled in huge letters, trying to fill the space. Martinez thanked her and they traded some tail-off small talk, and then the good-byes, and then it was just her in the quiet house.

She set the phone on the cradle, resisted the urge to check the front door. It was locked when she went to bed, and she hadn't touched it since. No need to confirm. The windows were secure.

She sipped coffee, concentrated on staying still. The alarm had been useless during the break-in, so she'd left it unrepaired. To an extent, that felt empowering, as if the system was unneeded, but in practice she'd struggled. For weeks, unexplained sounds meant a check of all entries, and only in the past few days had she started to relax. She no longer carried the gun in the house, and daytime noises could sometimes be ignored. Nighttime was a different story, but she was getting there.

These were the hardest moments, though. Solitude felt most acute with no task at hand, no avoiding the fact that someone was gone. Work helped. Focused on a file, she was less prone to tearful lapses. She could disappear into others' misery, and it helped to keep her functional. It helped to hide her own tragedy.

She sipped coffee, tears making the kitchen blur.

Don't lose your grip.

She wiped her eyes hurriedly, trying to keep the Lemar guy front and center. She imagined what she'd say to him, running questions and answers in her head, keep her mind off other things. She tipped the coffee in the sink and dialed the number Martinez had given her.

He took a long time getting to the phone. She was thankful for the noise though, even just the ringtone.

When he answered she said, "Mr. Lemar, my name's Lauren Shore. I believe you spoke to my colleague Detective Martinez from the Albuquerque Police Department Narcotics Squad."

"I talked to a few people. I don't know about a Martinez. You a police lady, are you?"

She said, "I'm a colleague of Detective Martinez."

Voice shaking a little. Come on. You'll be all right.

He said, "Well, sure."

"Sir, I was hoping to come by and ask you a few questions about the incident you witnessed this morning, if that's okay."

"Well, sure. I mean, I didn't really witness anything. I just saw the start and the finish and made a good stab at what happened in the middle."

"I understand. That's fine." She read him back the address Martinez had given her.

Lemar said, “That’s the one. You just come on round any time. We’ll have a drink or something.”

The sooner the better. She didn’t want to face the quiet. She said, “I’ll be there in about forty minutes.”

EIGHT

Marshall

Early afternoon. The car so hot he could barely touch the wheel. At the bottom of Garcia Street his phone rang again. Blocked number. He turned right and put the car against the curb. Above him across the junction the power lines strung like the tatters of some great web, and higher still the birds cloak-black and jagged in their circling. Northward the land so flat the houses across the street obscured all but the distant hills. As if idling phone-in-hand he sat at some frontier.

He answered.

"Good you finally picked up." The tone digitized, androgynous. Deep and echoic on the line.

Marshall said, "I only missed two calls. There's not much finally about it."

"There's a finally for everything. You included."

Marshall didn't answer.

"I hear you're not an easy guy to deal with."

"I'm looking for someone."

"So I'm told. I think I got the message: give me some answers or I'll come and fuck you up. Am I in the ballpark?"

Marshall said, "More or less."

"Not a very safe thing to be telling people."

"Not a very safe thing to be refusing."

"Safe for me I think, my friend. I can give you some advice though: looking for disappeared people is a good way to end up disappeared yourself."

"So you know what happened."

"It doesn't matter. What I can say is that sometimes people go missing, and then they meet their end."

Marshall didn't answer. He shut off the motor.

"I think you've delivered a kind of ultimatum, so I hope you can accept one back. Well. Not an ultimatum, but a statement of the reality you've introduced."

Marshall said, "Which is?"

"Soon you'll be dead. Maybe you've been around long enough to live your dreams, I don't know. Any case, you'll get to live your nightmares. If not yours, then someone's. If briefly."

Marshall didn't answer.

"Are you a man of principle?"

Marshall said, "Everyone is. Some people just can't name it."

"Would you say you have something to lose?"

"Not really."

"Not really. Okay. But bear this in mind, because it's important: as soon as you hold someone dear, then you stand to lose something. Do you understand? Even if you don't value yourself, once everyone else is dead you realize how much has been taken. Wives, children, friends. Like that. Picture it, having no one. Earth with no sun, that kind of thing. Wheeling blind in the void."

Marshall didn't answer.

"Not to say that we won't come for you. But just to show there are alternatives. If you're elusive."

"I'm not elusive. I'd quite like to be found."

"I think you might renege on that at some point. We'll see. I think you're one of these people who think that because we inhabit the same territory, we also inhabit the same world. Not the case. I can live in yours, but you can't live in mine. You don't issue a threat from your realm into mine and expect to keep breathing."

Marshall didn't answer.

"Believe in God?"

Marshall said, "No."

"What about the devil?"

"Ditto."

"Maybe reassess that. You've got him on the phone right now."

The call ended.

The world and its features slowly forming: birds above and the traffic beside him and the phone warm on his cheek. A brief quiet in the hot confines of the vehicle as he replayed it all and wondered into what madness he'd entered for the sake of someone he'd never known. His phone buzzed again. He checked the screen. An image file: two arms and two legs coarsely severed, laid out side by side. Blackened concrete beneath.

He felt the blood draining from his head, edges of his vision softening as he leaned against his door. He stretched and opened the glove compartment, heft of the Colt instantly comforting. He leaned back in his seat. Gun in his lap, smooth curve of the trigger beneath his finger.

If it was her, there was no telling. But he'd got the message:

You're next.

NINE

Rojas

They listened to Leon make the call, sitting shirtless at his desk, a cigarette in two fingers held aloft.

Leon was IT proficient. The Marine Corps made him conversant. The phone was rigged to his computer, and there was a voice distortion applied. Everything he did was routed through some Internet substructure he called the dark web. It had been set up in the nineties by military intelligence for the purpose of safe communication, but somewhere along the line it had been hijacked for nonofficial activities:

Buying and selling porn.

Buying and selling kids.

Arranging fake IDs.

Contacting hit men.

The beauty of it was that by virtue of some complicated science, it was anonymous. Shit got bounced around through servers all over the place, and if you did things properly not even the geek kids at Fort Meade knew who you were. Leon hated the NSA. He believed eavesdropping was unconstitutional. He said the kicker about the dark web was that while one branch of the federal government was attempting to crack it, another was simultaneously bolstering its security. He called it a perfect dichotomy.

His office was full of books. Floor to ceiling on his shelves, great tomes lying open on the desk. Anatomy was his present interest. Vance said he liked to know exactly what he was cutting.

When he put down the phone Leon sat a moment with his back to them and then he swiveled smoothly in the chair.

He said, "Boy has to die."

He thought a moment.

"Probably best you all go. Take two cars, but not that Jeep he's already seen. I'll stay here with the guests. We might need to free up some living space."

Afternoon now as they readied the cars. First-aid kit for each, a ram for the door, a couple of M1s with spare thirty-round clips, backup Glocks, fake ATF badges and IDs Leon had procured online. Anyone stopped them, first glance they'd look like feds headed for a bust. Further checks and they'd just have to kill someone.

They donned Kevlar vests to wear under their jackets. Killing time before the roll-out, Dante and Vance did a few lines, standing there tensed, neck veins bulging, head-banging and screaming at a drum-bleed pitch, amping themselves up for the trip.

TEN
Marshall

He drove down onto East Alameda. This quiet residential street with the river reserve on the south side, just a shallow creek bed and in the curve of it the ash trees standing thin and gray. The river itself a weak dribble in this heat, like a drip line from a bygone passing.

Half a mile from the house the road split to either side of the reserve. He took the south route, rolling at walk speed, looking across through the trees. A few cars parked at the northern side. Light traffic. Nobody on the sidewalk, nothing really amiss. Felix's Saab station wagon parked straight out front of the house, the man himself in the driver's seat, hand on the wheel, nodding along to something. Marshall swore quietly and stopped abreast of him across the river and put the Corolla in reverse and with the engine in a high whine backed up fast all the way to the fork and came along the road on the north side and parked behind him. The Colt in his belt. He got out and stepped to Felix's window and tapped a knuckle one-two on the glass.

Felix got a start. He wound the window to half-mast. The rear of the car brimming with junk, boxes within an inch of the roof, his long board stuffed in there somehow. Felix in an orange Hawaiian shirt of all things, Fleetwood Mac on the stereo.

Marshall said, "I told you to go up the street."

"I am. Kind of."

"I'd describe this more as directly out front."

"Yeah, well. I watched for you. Why you all pale, dude?"

Marshall said, "Get out of here."

"Are we square?"

"Yeah. Get out of here."

He watched the car recede into the distance, and in the quiet he could hear the tone of the engine for a long time. He walked over to the garage and used his key to unlock the door and swung it up and open. Then he stepped back to the Corolla and started it up and reversed inside and shut off the engine. The Silverado was in the adjacent slot. He got out and looked left and right along the street and then lowered the door again, a dull boom as he shut himself in the shadows. Musty odor of concrete dust and cardboard. He popped the Corolla's trunk and removed the 870 shotgun and pushed the lid quietly closed and unlocked the Chevy and laid the gun on the rear bench and covered it with a drop sheet from the floor. Then he locked the truck and circled round to the internal door and entered the house.

He doubted he'd find the place clean, and he wasn't wrong. Empty beer cans through the kitchen, no flat plane spared. He resisted the urge to tidy. The cans irked him especially: he hated those ripped pull-tabs, all sitting up at different angles. It was a grating aesthetic. The clean, consistent geometry of a bottle was far preferable.

Open mail on the table, all bills addressed to him. Their arrangement was that Felix paid. The method could withstand a routine check of occupancy, and it meant Marshall didn't have to actually live there. He was inured to the idea of flawed systems. He believed that if his old life wanted to find him it would. No witness protection program would keep him hidden indefinitely. Hence this current initiative: sublet the dwelling the feds had provided, and rent a cheaper place elsewhere. All cash payments, the kind of anonymous economy folks like Felix appreciated. He was Californian, or so he said, and for crimes unspoken he was headed east in an effort to put as much distance as possible between himself and the Los Angeles Police Department. He'd been a tenant three months now, ever since Marshall had sat beside him on a stool in an Albuquerque bar and heard a tale of this great eastward trip that had been undertaken for unconvincing reasons. That the law was after him was the most detail he eventually gleaned, but Marshall figured that was perfect. When New York sent the cleaners, he didn't want mom and dad and the kids having to explain Marshall wasn't home.

The sweet, heady smell of marijuana in the living room, together with Felix's principal means of income: stacked cardboard boxes of stolen electrical equipment, DVD players, microwaves, hairdryers, all sorts. Marshall hoped this was just storage and not the showroom. He flicked on the light and then went upstairs and did the same in the bathroom. No effect now, but come sundown it would be perfect.

Back down the stairs. He stood at the front door for a minute and looked out the narrow strip window to the street. All clear. He went through to the garage and raised the door for the Silverado and got in and drove it out onto the driveway and set the brake. Then he closed the garage door again and slid into the truck and drove it up the street toward the fork in the road. Way up there in the blue a jet contrail like a stitch line across the crown of the earth. He took a left where the road split, and drove back along the south bank of the river. He stopped at a T-junction one hundred yards shy of the house and backed into the cross street and parked at the curb. Across the reserve and through the trees he had an oblique view of the front of the house.

From the glove compartment he took his Nikon Monarch binoculars and set them in his lap and took the Colt from his belt and laid it at his feet. He reached under his seat and found the little

Ziploc bag of emergency cash, two grand in twenties, and folded it and slipped it in his back pocket.

Northward the mountains. Seeing them he could never forget the scale of the world, and he knew that no trial was unique. Somewhere out there amongst the billions, someone else shared this same trouble in this same instant.

He waited.

2010

The back room of a restaurant down on Third Avenue, Gramercy Park, just a couple of blocks from the NYPD academy on East Twentieth. Marshall was at a table next to Mr. Asaro, seated opposite them a Russian guy in his late thirties, one Victor Bradlik, who Mr. Asaro called Vicki B. Kitchen had wound down for the night, but out here the air was still warm and close, fragrant with Italian cuisine.

Vicki B. saying, "And of course we appreciate the business opportunity, good to be back dealing with you. Lot of guys we've done this'n that with but, you know. Just not the same." All the right sentiments, a bit of ego preening for old Tony.

An interesting guy, this Vicki B. He'd been born in Russia, spent the first seventeen years of his life there, but his accent was all Brooklyn: A cawse we appreciate da business awpachoonity.

Vicki said, "What we're really after is to get our relationship back to where it was originally. You know. Before all this other shit went down."

Asaro smiled as he listened, the picture of serenity. He sat with his chair pushed back and at an angle to the table, hands linked behind his head, one foot laid across the other knee. The pose helped showcase his new footwear: leather boots by Gucci, laceless, a gleaming jet-black to match his hair.

He said, "That's good, Vicki. That's what we like to hear."

He spoke in a quiet voice that wasn't quite his norm: almost a whisper, let you know there was menace lurking behind the velvet.

Going on eleven P.M. now, nobody out front, traffic on Third

Ave. the only action. Just the one table in the back room they were in, not much else either: green paint, black-and-white checkerboard linoleum, curved up a couple inches where it met the walls. The place belonged to Tony's brother Danny. He'd been gone about thirty minutes, happy to serve coffee and then call it a night. A good decision given the nature of Tony's meetings. In the door to the kitchen Vicki B.'s backup man stood with his hands clasped in front of him. This huge, square guy in a dark suit and tie, hair buzzed so short it was like dust on his scalp. Over to Marshall's right one of Mr. Asaro's guys, Jimmy Wheels, rolling himself back and forth a few inches in his chair, not anxious, just idling away the time.

Mr. Asaro leaned forward and took a sip of his double espresso, set the cup back in the saucer, not a sound, even in the quiet room. Vicki B. and Marshall just had regular coffee, Vicki's almost gone, Marshall's untouched.

Asaro said, "Vicki, I'm pleased everything's getting under way with the right intentions this time."

Vicki B. spread his hands, face solemn. Least I can do, Mr. Asaro, sir. In appropriate mobster fashion, a black leather briefcase leaned against his chair, a second identical number on the floor between Asaro and Marshall, but the swap was yet to happen.

Asaro made a little gesture with one hand, like striking a cymbal, remembering something. He said, "You ever hear the story of how Jimmy ended up with fucked legs?"

Vicki B. raised his eyebrows a fraction, like come to think of it, no he hadn't. He glanced over at Jimmy in his wheelchair and said, "No." Stretching the word out a bit, like he'd be interested to know.

Asaro said, "Must've been a good fifteen or so years back now, would you say, Jim?"

Jimmy Wheels said, "It was that Jersey City shit, so yeah, fifteen."

"Right. So anyway, Jim was running a drop-off to a guy, Timmy Vegas, you know him?"

Vicki B. did not know Timmy V.

"Doesn't matter. So Jim shows up at Timmy's, and the load's what, ten thousand short, something like that?"

Jimmy Wheels said, "Nine six."

"Nine six short." Asaro laughed. "Which turns out to be a bit of a problem, because Timmy Vegas hasn't heard that Don't Shoot the Messenger saying. You know? Because Jim's just the fucking delivery guy, don't have a clue why it might be nine six down. Or even nine six up, if it came to it."

Vicki B. nodded, frowning slightly, a polite display of rapt attention.

Asaro leaned and picked up the teaspoon from his saucer and stirred his coffee gently, a delicate movement in the little espresso mug, laid the spoon down again. Vicki B. on tenterhooks, or so it seemed.

Asaro said, "So, a bit of a problem for old Jim. Or, I guess young Jim, at the time. Everyone's like, where's the rest, you musta took it, ra-de-ra. And anyway, long story short, they laid him out in the back of a pickup, facing upwards with his top half hanging out past the fender, and a coupla guys held his legs down, and Timmy and someone else jumped on his chest and—wham, broke his back. *Prrrck*."

Vicki B.'s eyebrows were up again, like he'd have to try it sometime, Asaro looking across at Jimmy Wheels, as if seeking corroboration. Jimmy Wheels nodding to himself with a far-off look, maybe reliving the magic.

Asaro said, "You're probably thinking, Yeah, yeah, Tony, good story. But what I'm getting at is, I've been pretty flexible and tolerant in business so far, and people have taken advantage of it. I've lost out to an extent. So you could say, with that in mind, I'm planning a more Timmy Vegas–type approach to doing things. If you follow."

Vicki B.'s backup man had been leaning gently on the doorframe, and he took a small step away from it, hands still clasped.

Vicki B said, "I'll bear it in mind, Tony."

Tony Asaro gave him the serene look again. "Terrific. That's great."

Vicki B. didn't answer.

Asaro had some coffee. He nodded at Marshall's mug. "Marsh, you haven't touched yours."

Marshall said, "I think I've had my fill for today."

"All right. Suit yourself."

He stirred his espresso again. He said, "So now really, we get down to it. Because the problem I've got is that you and I, Vicki, had some business go south a little while ago, and you've ended up owing me a bit of money."

Vicki, nodding as he listened, rolled with it pretty smooth. He said, "Sure, Tony, but that was six months back. And I'd sort of thought that what we're doing here today was like a good faith sign we're happy just to move on, kinda let it be."

Asaro said, "Vicki, time doesn't make debts go away. If anything, makes them bigger, appreciation 'cause of your interest and shit. So I'd say if there's any kind of good faith move being made, it would be me letting you know all's okay, not the other way round. That'd just be dumb."

Vicki B. looked set to say something, but drew a blank. He had some coffee to cover it.

Asaro said, "So by my estimate, you owe me about sixteen grand. We'll ignore the interest, because it's only six months, but we still need to square it. Because it's decent money, isn't it?"

Vicki B. didn't answer. His backup guy no longer had his hands clasped.

Asaro said, "Soooo." Stretching it out thin, something contentious on the way.

Vicki B waited.

Asaro said, "Way we're going to settle it all, I'm going to take your case"—he nodded at the floor—"but you're not having mine. Okay?"

Vicki B. dabbed a sleeve to his upper lip, swallowed like he was trying to keep something down. "Tony, that's ridiculous. I've got forty K here."

Asaro nodded. "I know you do. But remember, we were talking about the Timmy Vegas approach to life, and I think this is something Tim might approve of."

Had to hand it to him, Vicki B. knew how to roll with it. "Tone, come on. Shit was going so well, you want to end it like this? I mean, ain't even my money."

He dabbed his lip again. Asaro noticed and nodded at him. "Nixon had that same problem. Sweaty upper lip when he got nervous, happens to the best of 'em."

He and Jimmy Wheels shared a laugh.

Vicki B. gave it a moment, and then he came back, still keeping things calm. "Tone, seriously. If I call the deal off, we're going to walk out of here with our shit."

Asaro glanced around, mouth downturned, like he really couldn't see how that would come about. "Oh, is that right? Huh."

Vicki B. said, "I mean, no need to get vicious about it, but I'm packing, Mikhail's packing."

He nodded at Marshall. "Two on one. Easy." He laughed, bit shakier than normal.

Marshall's pulse ramped up, because if that was the plan, he'd have some work to do.

Asaro smiled. Leaning back in his chair with his suit jacket open, it was clear he didn't have a weapon. He said to Vicki B., "Have you heard the story about Marshall?"

"Tony, I think we've had enough stories."

He leaned down for his briefcase.

Asaro said, "Vicki. You leave that seat, shit is gonna go south very, very quickly. Understand?"

Vicki held the pose a brief moment, on a lean with one hand on the case. He looked at Asaro, looked at Marshall, and then he let it go and tipped upright again, very slow.

Asaro said, "Good decision. What was I saying? Marshall.

Yeah, Marshall's got some skills on him. Fastest draw-fire you've ever seen on a man, swear to god."

Vicki didn't answer. Marshall's heart tripping away at a steady gallop now, only thing he could picture, since Asaro had mentioned it, was the whole meeting going bad in a very bloody fashion. He glanced at Vicki's backup guy, the kid only twenty-three, twenty-four; last thing in the world he wanted to do was put a bullet through him.

Asaro said, "And you may think that's all very well, but." He held his jacket gently by the lapels, spread it slowly, just crisp blue shirt underneath, neatly tucked. "You know. I wouldn't walk unarmed into this sort of meet-and-greet unless I had someone with some pretty slick moves. Anyway."

He smoothed his jacket back in place. "End of the day, try any funny shit, Marshall's gonna tap the both of you."

He mimed it slowly with a finger gun, trying a couple of options. "Easy."

Vicki B. didn't answer. Marshall sat there riding the blood rush, hoping there was nothing in his face other than the sense he was in his element. Which, truth be told, he wasn't. Not because he feared his own well-being: way things were configured, Mikhail was just off Vicki's shoulder, Marshall could draw and nail them in less than a second if he had to. The issue was more that killing two guys he'd just met was fairly frosty on the scale of cold deeds, and it would be nice to know what good or bad they'd brought to the world before he showed them the door.

They all sat there quietly, Vicki B. sizing up a few exit strategies. Jimmy Wheels still rolling through his little two-inch amplitude. Tony Asaro with his foot up on his knee, arching his instep every now and then so his new leather caught the light.

Eventually Vicki B. raised his hands slowly, palms out, fingers very slightly curled. He said, "Tony, this the way you want to play it, fine. I don't want to end anything with guns."

He lowered his hands. "Just bear in mind, this is not going to be the last of it."

Asaro smiled. "I'll sleep with one eye open, Vicki, don't you worry about that."

"Sorry to rob you of a shootout."

Asaro laughed. "Oh, I don't know. You're not out the door yet."

And he picked up the teaspoon and leaned across the table and plunged the handle into Vicki B.'s right eye, deep, a solid two-inch thrust, and of course Mikhail flipped his jacket back and went for his piece, and Marshall pulled his Beretta from the shoulder rig and shot the guy through the gut.

End of show.

Vicki B. screaming and clutching his ruined eye, the spoon on the table in front of him, clots of jelly all up the handle. The backup guy fetal on the floor, retching and hugging himself, gun on the ground nearby. Jimmy wheeled over, leaned down, and picked it up.

Asaro spent a brief moment scoping the damage, and then he looked at Marshall and smiled. "Pretty fast there, kid. Maybe a record time."

Marshall didn't answer, shootings one of those things where the full awful gravity hit only in hindsight.

Tony Asaro leaned across and gripped his knee. "Best to tread easy now, I'd say. Bent cop isn't a good label to be wearing at the best of times, and I'd say you've as good as killed a man. So."

He stood up, put the same hand on Marshall's shoulder, warm breath in his ear as he bent close to whisper: "I'd say I pretty much own you now."

ELEVEN

Lauren Shore

Alvin Lemar lived in a trailer park down on Central Ave., which was the old Route 66 as it passed through town. At the gravel turn-in a low faded sign with slanted print read WELCOME TO GREEN HILLS. Opposite, a general store sat alone on a big lot and between them the road just straight and level through the tan landscape with the power lines strung endlessly pole to pole and no trees or wind to speak of.

She drove in slowly with the grit crackling under the tires and stopped at reception and the woman at the desk directed her to Mr. Lemar's unit. She cruised slowly round toward the back of the park. A Mexican boy grinned and shot a finger gun at her and his mother hanging clothes flicked him with a wet garment.

Lemar's trailer was olive green with some little planter boxes in the gravel out front and a Stars and Stripes on a short, sloped pole near the roofline. The flag just a lifeless sheaf in the heat. A timber deck was built off one side underneath a corrugated plastic veranda, and there was a plastic table and chairs and a few potted plants. A man, presumably Alvin Lemar, was seated dozing at the table with a magazine splayed on his paunch and a German shepherd lying beside him.

She parked behind a Kenworth tractor unit next to the trailer and the dog's ears pricked and its head came up off its front paws. Lemar woke with her door slam, blinking hugely as he adjusted his spectacles.

She stepped up onto the deck, feeling light without the gun. She proffered a hand for the dog, hot breath at her knuckles.

Lemar stood up and dropped the magazine on the table. "Don't worry about Maestro. He looks the part, but he's nothing really."

He shuffled around the table, hemmed in by his stomach, and shook her hand. "Why don't you just sit down out here. Think we've got some iced tea brewing away, if you'd fancy some."

She thanked him and took a seat, turned it so she faced the door. The car was only thirty feet away.

Relax, this is safe.

The dog took up post within petting distance, looking at her with round jewel eyes and its tail wagging gently.

Lemar called out from inside: "Popular man today. Couple of fellers were out this morning, but they weren't drugs people. Told them what I said to you on the phone, that I just saw the before and the after and had a guess at the middle. But anyway."

He appeared a moment later with two plastic highball tumblers iced and brimming, already working up a sweat.

He sat down, slid her a drink, ice tinkling. "See how hot it is. Jeepers." He traced a finger through the dew on his tumbler.

She said, "I appreciate your time. I understand you're a trucker, is that right?"

"Yeah. That's the one. Had a load I was running up from Phoenix, just to Santa Fe. Coming back and I was just dead at the wheel, you know how you get sometimes. Figured a bit of breakfast would set things straight. This was five A.M. or thereabouts I'd say."

"Okay. And were the three men you saw already there, or did they arrive after you?"

"They came in afterwards. I guess I sat down and had a bit of a ponder over the menu and said what I'd have. This place does twenty-four hours, but don't ask me how they turn a profit because hand to heart, I was the only one in there except the Mex lady. Waitress, I mean."

She sipped her drink. Just off to their right a timber fence and beyond it the road with cars back and forth every now and again. "How long before the others came in?"

"Not long. I'd say twenty minutes or close to it."

"They come in separately or together?"

He looked at the dog and sucked his lip as he remembered. "Separately. Well, I mean. The two guys who almost got their ticket clipped came in together. Mex feller and this ratty-looking guy. Nothing really funny about them I guess, other than that they seemed pretty grim sorts of characters you wouldn't want to argue with. You know how you get that sense. Anyhow, they just came in and sat at a booth. Mex feller made a call at one point, and then I guess the third guy came in maybe fifteen minutes later. Something like that."

"This is the blond guy?"

"Yeah, tall, good-looking kid. Very confident I guess, not hurrying along. Always liked folks like that. Used to say to people in a rush: What will you do with the time that you save?"

The dog nudged her wrist with a wet nose. She petted its head. "And he went and sat down with them?"

"Yeah. He sat down. That's right, the other two had some coffee and the new guy got some as well. Guess they talked for twenty minutes maybe. I mean, not causing a scene or anything, but you have to wonder when you get a kinda discreet-looking meeting like that at a funny hour of the day whether it's wholly honest business. I don't know."

"What did you think they were doing?"

Lemar squinted and tipped his chair back a fraction and then down. "At the time, nothing. But then when I went outside and saw the two of them in the state they were, all the bits clicked together pretty well. Only imagine they came inside for some negotiating and arranging prices or whatever, and then when they headed out to do the swap the blond character duped them and took off with the lot. Funny business. You look at a nice feller like that and you'd never know. But I mean, everyone on earth has got a private dimension, and the case with some people is you can't just look them in the eye and guess the nature of it."

He chuckled, patted his shirt pocket as if looking for cigarettes, came up empty. "Those other two looked like pretty capable characters, so to be done by some guy like that they must have thought they'd ventured into bad luck of a whole new kind. Slick-looking job, too. Like, they weren't all pummeled. It just seemed like bam, bam, and he was out of there. Not that they said anything. I told them, ought to get the law out here and press charges, but they wouldn't hear it. Had that sort of look where if you got police out there they'd just end up defending more claims than they could actually lay. Which I suppose might be pretty accurate because the drugs guys that came this morning said them two are good with their chemistry. If you follow."

She said, "What age would the blond man be?"

"Well. I wouldn't put my livelihood on it, but I figured he'd be nigh on the same as my boy Casper. Call it thirty-five."

"He use a credit card or anything? How'd they pay for the coffee?"

"Not sure, to be honest with you. Got the impression they just left money, but I couldn't swear by it."

"You see what sort of car he was driving?"

"Didn't see a car. Like I said, I just saw them come in the door and then walk out of it again. Them other two had a Cherokee that I saw when I came outside, but the boy I don't know. Not the sort of place to have a camera either, so unless he stopped for gas I don't know how you'd find him."

TWELVE

Rojas

They got his details through an online database Leon subscribed to. Just enter the license plate and it returned all kinds of personal information. Address, phone number, DUI history, nationwide felony arrest record. Not only was the government spying on people, but for an affordable monthly installment, people could spy on each other.

The guy's name was James Marshall Grade and he did in fact live in Santa Fe, in a place on West Alameda. They drove out there at a little after seven thirty, once Leon and Vance had been down to see the guests.

The sun had set. They were into the gloaming. Light traffic on Alameda as they cruised west, the trees along the river a twisted pale bonework in the headlights. Rojas and Bolt up ahead in the Chrysler 300C, Vance and Dante tailing in the Audi Quattro.

The cars had been a real slick move: Leon had found a guy online with direct access to New Mexico MVD. For a small fee you could nominate a plate number and associated details for inclusion in the state database. The practical benefit being you could boost any car you liked, swap out the tags, pay the guy to upload the information to MVD, and voilà, legit transport.

The Marshall guy's house up ahead on the right. There was a light on upstairs. They glided past. Looking back, a lit window at the rear of the house was visible, too. They continued a few hundred yards up the street and swung to the curb. They'd already scoped the place on Google Earth. The plan: leave the cars a little ways east and west, respectively, walk in, take the guy hostage at gunpoint, and then bring the Quattro into the garage and load him up.

Home for fun and games.

Vance called it Having One in the BAG.

Basement Abu Ghraib.

For coms they had earpieces rigged through digital radio. High-tech encrypted shit Leon had pilfered during the Iraq drawdown. It would help with the ATF cover story, if it came to it.

Vance radioed from the Quattro: "I think we're good to go. But we need to clear that street on the other side. He could have set it up so he's waiting out there with a long gun and then nail us when we hit the house."

Bolt said, "Nobody fucking long guns someone who comes to their house. That's fucked up. We could be anyone."

"You still need to do it."

"Why me?"

"Dante and I are hitting the house, you can clear the street."

"You guys are meant to be the fucking black-ops, you do it."

Vance said, "Listen, dipshit. I didn't spend six years wasting dudes in Sandstown on your behalf just to come back and be told what to do. You fucking owe us your liberty, and you can start repaying by walking along the street and checking it's clear. I don't give a shit who does it, all I know is it's not me, and it's not Dante."

Classic Vance, that hair-trigger temper. Crystal probably didn't help. Behind them the Audi's high beams came on and it U-turned and prowled back the opposite way.

Vance again: "Just call in when it's clear. It'll take two seconds."

Bolt said, "Jesus Christ."

But he wasn't going to argue it, not with Vance. He and Rojas had used him as backup when they were doing imports up from Coahuila. These dead-of-night cross-border runs in a Bronco, the two of them up front, Vance and a hundred-odd pounds of brown heroin in back. They'd been pulled over one night by two ICE guys and Vance had just stood up through the sunroof with a .357 and nailed the pair of them with a headshot each, and ten minutes later he was dozing in the backseat.

And with that in mind, one did not force the point, especially now the dynamic had shifted, and Leon was in charge.

Quiet as those realities settled. Gloom of the cabin and the smell of new leather and the dials all lit up like a flight deck.

Rojas said, "Just do it. Take that spare key."

"Yeah, yeah."

Like some petulant kid, packing heat and false ID. He opened his door and slid out of the car.

THIRTEEN

Marshall

Between the trees he could see the black Chrysler and tailing it the white Audi SUV. Almost predatory in their smooth and quiet glide, sharp headlight beams cast narrow and suspicious.

There was a bit of traffic so two cars in tight succession weren't that unusual. The only standout aspect was they were both late-model vehicles with tinted windows, and Marshall's grasp of likelihoods said that if the two most expensive cars he'd seen all afternoon came through as a pair, there was probably something to it.

He waited.

Very quiet on the street. He checked the river reserve. Darkness now between the trees. Nobody on his little side road. His own car plus a couple more. He dropped his window an inch. Cool evening air. A faint light throwing shadows in the woods and then the Audi slipped back along the street, no engine noise, the softest hush off the tires.

And he knew.

They'd cruised past for a once-over. The Chrysler had stayed west, now the Audi was moving back east.

They were setting up a perimeter.

If they were thorough they'd check the south side too, where he was, across the river reserve.

He listened. A gentle rustle as a breeze passed through the trees. In his mirror a lone streetlight framed there at the curb. His bathroom window growing brighter amidst the shadows.

He leaned and placed the binoculars in the glove compartment and picked up the .45 from the floor. There was a round already chambered. He reached up and set the dome light so it wouldn't come on, and then he slid out and pressed his door shut gently until he heard it click.

He stood a moment beside the car. The streetlight in its lonely vigil. The whispering of the trees. He crossed the road briskly to the junction where his side street met Alameda along the south of the reserve. There was a house on the corner site protected by a high adobe wall. He stood with his back against it and glanced out quickly along the reserve in the direction of the Chrysler. Nothing. The road narrow with no sidewalk, tall fences close against it on the left and the reserve on the right. Looking back the other direction, he couldn't see the Audi, either.

Blood roaring in his ears. High up the branches swaying gently.

He crossed to the reserve and dropped to a crouch and crept twenty yards up from the junction and put his back against a tree and risked another look along Alameda toward the black car.

Nothing coming. The bark flaking dryly where he touched it. Smell of dust and dead leaves. He couldn't hear the river. So weak, it was just standing water.

He stayed put. Five minutes. Ten. Every thirty seconds another glance out each way along the road. Waiting there amidst the trees, he knew he'd see before being seen.

Darkness drawing nearer. Cool air with some residual heat off the road. Across the reserve a ten-year-old Chevy sedan drove slowly along the street.

Footsteps.

Very quietly, out on the road. He risked a look between

branches. Cyrus Bolt. His face a swollen mess crisscrossed with flesh-tone tape. Maybe thirty yards away, hands buried in his jacket pockets, something concealed there.

Twenty-five yards.

The Chevy sedan pulled up a couple of doors down from his house. The lights died. Quiet a moment and then a woman got out and shut her door gently and glanced up at his lit window and headed for his driveway.

Marshall said, "Shit." Barely a whisper as he let his breath out.

He glanced back along the street. Bolt very close now, ten yards. Maybe his last short walk.

Marshall waited.

FOURTEEN

Lauren Shore

Finally better luck:

After her talk with Lemar she'd parked out front of that store across the road and checked the map to locate the diner he'd mentioned. North of Algodones, just off the 25. The next nearest turnoff was five miles north. Another one ten miles south. She called Martinez's desk line.

She said, "I just talked to Alvin."

"How did that go?"

She summarized the conversation. He thought about it a moment and said, "So it's nothing, really. Because all he saw was a meeting he didn't overhear."

She said, "I'm interested in this blond guy. Lemar thought he looked like he knew what he was doing. Troy's been around and Bolt's just come off ten years or something at Beaumont, but apparently this guy took them both down with no one noticing. Two on one can get pretty loud if you're not careful."

"So he's learned some stuff."

"Yeah. I'd say so."

He said, "Probably Special Forces. SEALs or Delta or something, probably good experience if you wanted to get into dealing meth. I mean, shit. It would seem like safe work."

"Yeah, maybe. Can you spare thirty minutes?"

"Well. Not really."

"I just saved you an hour and a half. You can at least give me thirty minutes back. Come on."

"What for?"

"I'm just having a look at where this place is."

"The diner?"

"Yeah, the diner. I was thinking if this guy's just taken down two dealers and made off with a pound of meth or coke or whatever, he probably wouldn't want to stay on the interstate too long. I mean, it's not even seven, there's not a lot of traffic. And if someone saw him and got the state cops out or even if Bolt and Rojas went after him it wouldn't be a hard chase."

"So what do you think?"

"I don't know. I just thought if he was shaken up or worried about being obvious he might have turned off and waited it out a bit. Let the traffic build some more."

"A Delta guy wouldn't be shaken up after breaking someone's nose."

"No. But you know what I mean? I don't think it's stupid that maybe either the blond guy or the other two turned off and stopped pretty quickly."

"Okay. So what am I meant to be doing?"

"Just have a look at the first couple of turnoffs north and south of the diner and see if there's anything worth stopping for. Store or gas station or something. I can't remember what's up there. Maybe he saw an Exxon sign on the 25 and thought it was a good idea to wait it out a bit. Time of day you'd get noticed, too. Nobody around."

"You mean he was worried about being noticed so left a quiet highway for an even quieter gas station."

"I still think it's worth checking. Wasn't necessarily gas."

He said, "Exactly the sort of job I could've got you to do."

She laughed. "You could have asked. You couldn't have actually got me to do it."

"Yeah. Probably. All right. Fifteen minutes."

"Thirty. You'll want to get your teeth into it."

"Twenty. I'll call you."

He rang her back in twenty-five. She was northbound on the Pan American, heading home.

He said, "Good guess."

"What, you found him?"

"Maybe. There's a gas station at an exit about twenty miles north. Guy reckons they had a blond man come in around seven or so. Filled up and used the pay phone."

Finally better luck.

She said, "Yeah, see? You shouldn't go brushing off my hunches."

He laughed. "Might be a coincidence."

"Might be. But I bet you still got his plate number and ran it."

"Possibly."

"Possibly. Give it up, you bastard."

"There's no need for that sort of language." Voice loud, making a real show of it. Someone in the office laughing.

"Come on. Where is he?"

"You're not going to go door-knocking, are you?"

She laughed, like it was ridiculous. "No. Don't be stupid."

So here she was, on West Alameda, up in Santa Fe. She'd managed a few tense hours at home, pacing, checking locks, back to her old habits. It was anticipation that did it. Wanting answers suppressed her logic. The need for truth trumped the fact it wasn't smart to go looking. She couldn't talk herself out of it.

She parked the car at the curb and got out and just walked up to the house.

What are you doing?

Which was a wasted thought, because the time to be toying with that was an hour ago, during the drive up. Once you're in the guy's front yard you're committed. If she backed out now she'd never sleep. That lingering "what if" would be a week's insomnia, even worse than it was now.

There was a light on upstairs. She walked along past the garage toward the entry. A window by the front door was backlit weakly, maybe a light in an adjoining room. She paused there.

Because what are you going to say? When he opens the door, what are you actually going to say?

Excuse me, sir. Given that this morning you took down two suspected narc traffickers, we believe you're currently in possession of a shitload of cash and hard drugs. Would you mind directing me to where you're keeping it all? No, I don't have ID. It's kind of a long story, but don't you worry.

Christ, you idiot.

It should have made her walk away. But there was a light on at the back of the house. She could just look in and see if it was him. If it wasn't, that would be the end of it. If it was, well. Bright ideas often hit you on the spot.

The darkness gaining ground. Lit windows up and down the street and all those within thought they knew their neighbor. She walked quietly down the side of the house. A coiled hose left on, misting weakly from a split. She felt it on the back of her hand.

Past a frosted-glass door. She put her back to the wall. Rough stucco, and it grabbed her jacket. The window was a ranch slider, no curtain. She edged closer.

Closer.

She could almost lean across and look.

And then he grabbed her. She jumped at the shock of it but a hand clamped her mouth, another wrapped her midriff, pinning her arms. Locked upright, immobile.

A whisper in her ear, breath warm on her lobe: "Where's your friend, bitch? Where's your friend?"

FIFTEEN

Marshall

He heard Bolt draw level. The footsteps pausing now and then as he looked into the trees. Marshall glanced up. This clawed black foreground of branches on a purple sky and he thought back to the birds in their circling as he'd talked on the phone.

Bolt continued, footsteps fading. Marshall rose from his crouch. The .45 a bright silver, finding light somewhere. He stepped out onto the road. This quiet specter. He crossed the lane to where Bolt had passed through and fell in behind. A long silent stride.

Bolt ahead, just a silhouette, slightly hunched. Shoulders dipping and rising as he moved. That dark picture of him growing as Marshall gained ground, and with his held breath and the tension of the moment the blood pounded in his ears. As they reached the corner of the adobe wall he hooked a hand in front of Bolt's face, clamped his mouth to pull his head back against his shoulder, jammed the .45 in his kidney. He felt Bolt tense with fright and then relax when he spoke in his ear:

"Walk with me."

He pulled him backward off balance and Bolt's feet scrabbled for purchase as Marshall dragged him into the trees. There was an earpiece corded down inside his collar. Marshall could feel a radio on his belt.

"Take the piece out of your pocket and drop it on the ground." He nudged him with the Colt. "I'm packing hollow points, so a gut shot will bust your whole engine."

A cushioned thump as Bolt tossed a pistol on the ground, maybe six feet away. Marshall shoved him against a tree with the gun between his shoulder blades, and then lifted his jacket and ripped the radio off his belt and held it at arm's length to tug out the earpiece. A little collar mike dragged his shirt neck and then plucked free. Marshall dropped the radio next to the gun and kicked the leads out of trip range.

"How many friends did you bring?"

Bolt didn't answer. A decade in federal lockup, he was probably accustomed to this sort of thing. Swap the trees for a shower block. His head was turned, cheek hard up against the trunk. From this range he didn't smell good.

Marshall said, "This is kind of nice. Rojas said you were going to come looking, and I told him we'd meet somewhere in the middle."

He put the muzzle on Bolt's spine. "Well. This is what the middle feels like."

"You're going to die, boy."

"I believe you're right. But you'll be first through the door, and damn soon if you don't answer my questions."

Bolt didn't answer.

Marshall glanced over toward the house. The light was still on, but he couldn't see anyone. He said, "I asked about a girl this morning. Maybe you didn't hear."

"I heard."

"Right. So tell me what happened."

"You ain't ever going to find her."

"So you know her."

"I know you ain't finding her. I know she's going to be all dead and chopped up before you get anywhere near. Hell. Maybe she already is."

So gleeful as he said it. Marshall had to wait a long time for calm to come back. His finger tightened up on the trigger and he knew if he gut-shot the man it would be a slow and awful death. Penance for every wicked action and utterance and then a bit to spare.

He kept his tone level: "I pulled you over here because I've got every intention of killing you. And you're not doing a good job of changing my mind."

"I ain't no snitch."

"Give it a try, you might get to keep living."

Bolt scoffed quietly. "Glad you picked me a pretty spot for it. I seen men die all sorts of twisted ways. Told their ghosts you'd rewind time and do them in trees by a river they'd be lining up for the shot. So don't think you're threatening me, boy. You ain't seen the world."

Marshall said, "Who was it who called me this morning?"

Bolt smiled, just the corner of his mouth, like it was snagged on something. "Probably the last person you'll see before you cross over."

That trigger urge again. Marshall kept it tethered. "What happened to the girl? Last chance."

Bolt laughed. "Don't kid yourself you're going to shoot me out here. They'll hear that thing all the way to fucking Kansas."

Marshall clamped his mouth with a hand and smashed him on the top of the head with the butt of the gun and felt the brief pressure on his palm as the man cried out. Bolt sagged at the knee and Marshall pocketed the Colt and shifted his left hand so it covered both mouth and chin, and then he laid his right forearm across the top of Bolt's head and jerked suddenly like cranking a vise handle and broke his neck. A flat crack, muted by flesh.

Marshall stepped away and let him fall. As he walked back toward the car, Bolt lay twitching.

Nearing full dark now. Hands in pockets and head bent as he crossed to the Silverado. He stepped to the rear and popped the handle for the tailgate and lowered it gently. Then he moved around to the driver's side and slid in and started up, kept the lights off as he cruised around the corner to where Bolt was.

He set the brake and left the motor idling and got out and walked back into the trees. He caught a fecal odor. Bolt must have loosed his bowels. He grabbed the body by the collar and dragged him over to the truck, leaves and dirt troweled up ahead of him. The rear suspension settled a fraction when he propped him on the tailgate. The corpse slack, walleyed. He'd hit him fairly flat with the gun and the blow hadn't drawn blood. Marshall got a hand through the rear of his belt and hefted him up into the tray, slid him forward, and closed him in, like shutting the morgue drawer. Flutter of the exhaust on his leg.

He walked back into the trees and kicked around blindly a moment until he found the radio and the gun. He picked them up and brought them back to the truck, slid in and laid them on the rear seat. Then he put the car in gear and rolled quietly up the road. When he reached the fork, he flicked on the lights and turned right and cruised back along Alameda on the north side of the reserve. After a moment he came up behind the black Chevrolet, just parked there at the curb. Dark tint, he couldn't tell if anyone was inside.

A Santa Fe PD radio car cruised past.

Marshall eased off the gas briefly, giving himself a second to think, and then he swung to the roadside and stopped with the rear of the Chrysler caught square in his headlights maybe twenty feet away.

He dropped his window and opened his door and slid half off his seat with one foot on the road and leveled the .45 across the sill.

SIXTEEN

Rojas

Vance opened the side door, one quick jiggle off his bump key, and went in first, gun up. Dante followed with the woman, and Rojas brought up the rear. He closed and locked the door behind them. Quiet in the house. No one home, no alarm sensors either.

Through a short hallway and left into the living room. Cardboard boxes stacked everywhere and the smell of reefer. Dante put the woman on the floor and cable-tied her wrists. Same again for her ankles. She seemed calm, no panic in her face. Compliant as Dante cuffed her. Vance cupped a whisper to Rojas: "I'm sure no one's home, but I'll just clear it. Stay away from that window."

He left the room. Not a word to Dante. They'd been paired so long they knew each other's game.

Dante kept a hand on the woman's mouth and leaned close. "Hush hush, sweetheart."

They waited. Five minutes. Ten. Even cranked on meth, Vance was smoke-quiet. Still no word from Bolt. Dante was crouched motionless, the woman lying in front of him. Brown hair fanned across the floor, so still she could have been dead.

Vance walked back into the room, gun at his leg, practically strolling. "Clear. There's that blue car in the garage, but it looks like there's another one missing. So where is he, sweetheart?"

He drew the curtain and sat down on the couch elbows-to-knees with the pistol hanging in one hand. Dante started to pat the woman down. Car keys and some cash, no weapons.

Dante said, "Man, you smell good."

Vance laughed. The woman tensed and lunged at him with a head butt. Dante leaned back and she missed, but not by much. He stood over her with the Glock aimed at her head. "Where's your friend? Don't make me start counting."

The woman looked up at the gun. No tension in the trigger finger and no tension in Dante's face either, and she must have realized they weren't out to do things by halves. She said, "He's not my friend. I don't know him."

"Who are you?"

She smiled. "You can call me Detective Shore."

Rojas thought: Shit. But Vance and Dante didn't even blink.

Dante said, "What you doing prowling round here?"

"Interviewing."

"Don't lie, bitch. You're the first cop I seen out at this hour with no badge and no gun."

The woman just looked straight up the barrel and smiled faintly and said, "Just keep that in mind when your cellmate's telling you to unzip him."

Vance cracked up. Dante didn't move. Rojas knew he must be close to putting a bullet in her.

Dante said, "What's your name?"

"Lauren Shore."

"What department?"

"APD. Narcotics."

"You're a long way off your beat, sweetheart. What're you after this guy for?"

The woman said, "He met a couple of traffickers this morning, down toward Albuquerque. Thought I'd ask him about it."

She turned her head and looked up at Rojas with these flat, calm eyes and said, "How you doing, Troy?"

Jesus. He ran a hand through his hair and walked into the dark kitchen. She knew who he was. He stood by the table with his arms folded tightly like they might slow his breathing, and when he turned there was Vance, right in his face.

"Christ, don't do that."

Vance didn't move, just watched him carefully. Eyes going left-right like following a far-off ball game. "Chill, Troy. You look like you just got spooked by a girl."

"I am. I didn't. But it's kinda hard when you've got a police detective hostage, and she knows your name."

Vance a foot away, voice a murmur. "We've got it handled. Me'n Dante know how to do this shit. She can say she goes to book club with Mrs. Obama, it don't mean jack, because she's not going anywhere. Why you looking all shook up, you're meant to be Mr. Badass."

"Yeah. I'm all up for making money, but when you've got a cop at gunpoint you sort of kick things into high gear."

Vance just stood there, and Rojas figured his blood must be cut with antifreeze. Vance said, "It's called civilian casualties. We do it in Sand Land all the time, don't worry about it."

"Someone might know where she is."

"Dude, look at me. This is what we do. We got trained how to do this. We are the fucking pride and joy of the United States military."

Rojas rubbed his face, ran his hands through his hair. "Cyrus still hasn't called in."

"He's probably changing his face tape or something, I don't know. It hasn't been that long. Just stop fucking twitching and hopping, and chill. We're under control." He ran a palm midair, flat line.

Rojas said, "So what's the plan?"

"The plan is self-evident: boyfriend isn't here, we can't drill the bitch in the house, we've gotta take her off site. Okay?"

"Back to the house?"

Vance nodded. "Back to the house."

"This all seems out of control."

"It's not. Remember, you rolled out here planning to kill a guy, but now it's a lady you've gone all cold feet. Man up."

Rojas didn't answer.

Vance said, "There's nobody for miles better at this than me'n Dante. So just go with it."

SEVENTEEN

Marshall

Nobody in the Chrysler.

He walked up the street on the reserve side, keeping to the trees. When he reached the house he could see the white Audi parked farther east. Hopefully it was empty, too. He imagined Bolt had been sent to clear the other side of the river and whoever had been in the cars was now in his home. With the woman either dead or hostage.

He stood in the trees, watching.

Light traffic on the road, maybe a car a minute. Gut feeling said there was no one in the Audi. The dilemma being if he was wrong, he'd be seen as he crossed the street.

Which was probably more than a slim chance, because leaving both cars unoccupied wasn't a bright move. Home invasion–cum-homicide, you want someone with eyes on the street. The very stupid or very arrogant might neglect it. Or maybe that had been Bolt's role, covering the approach.

Choices.

The Audi had tinted glass. There was no way to check it without breaking a window. He knew it would trigger the alarm, but he preferred that to being seen crossing the street and getting shot as a consequence.

He stood looking at the car. Plans formulating, tactics of varied bloodshed. He slipped the Colt in his belt and jumped down into the cut of the river and ran crouched back along the road. The weak trace of water just a silver thread in the dark. When he reached the Silverado he scrambled up the bank and unlocked the truck and took the 870 from beneath the blanket on the rear seat and slipped back down into the river.

Rocks and dead branches through the little gulley: it was hard to keep his footing. When he drew abreast of the Audi, he stretched and laid the shotgun up on dry ground and then clambered quietly up the sheer bank.

The car cold and silent.

Marshall in a crouch amidst the brush. He took the Colt from his belt and held it one-handed with the other steadying him, like a runner at the starting block.

Blood in his ears building to a roar again. No traffic.

Count it in:

Three.

Two.

One.

And he was off, up out of the trees, across the road. A silent dash to the Audi and he raised the .45 by the muzzle like a hammer in his left hand and smashed the butt against the rear window, shattering the glass, and as the alarm blared he swapped the gun to his right hand, and in his shooter's stance swung both ways to cover the whole cabin.

The car was empty.

The turn signals blinking orange in phase with the alarm. These huge shadows leaping away in all directions, and despite the commotion he felt calm standing there next to this empty vehicle. Better than death.

He backed up across the road and into the dark and slipped the pistol in his belt again and found the shotgun and dropped back down into the river. Doors opening and closing as a few people came to investigate the noise. The smashed window was out of sight on the river side, and with the Audi sitting there with no intruder, they must have brushed it off as some malfunction. The car playing cry wolf. He watched them go back inside, one by one.

When he reached the house he climbed back up the side of the cut and waited at the tree line in a crouch with the shotgun across his knees. The alarm clear in the cold night and with each flash the woods looming orange above him.

Two minutes. Three. The crouch burning him, but he didn't move.

He saw a man in black emerge from the darkness beside his house, like he'd slipped out the side door. Marshall's size and bearing and in the streetlight he could see the guy's dyed green hair.

The man looked to his left along the street and saw the Audi sitting there blinking and blaring. He looked back right toward the black Chrysler, and then briefly into the trees, and then he jogged up the road toward the car. From thirty feet away he blipped a remote fob and the alarm quit and he opened the driver's door and slid in.

Quiet a moment. What's with that broken window?

The engine started.

The car's lights came on, twin blue-white flares.

Marshall stood up, the shotgun in one hand, down along his leg. Across the street someone in his darkened garage raised the door.

The Audi pulled out into the lane and cruised toward him, heading for the house.

Marshall raised the shotgun. He jacked a round. Eerie and full of promise, and in the quiet it might have been heard across the street.

The car a hundred feet away.

Fifty.

Marshall moved out of the trees and onto the road. To the right the glare of the car, and to the left his shadow reaching long and thin for the dark, like he'd been stretched from the void.

One step. Two, three, four.

Gun to shoulder.

The driver anonymous behind the black tint and the white paint gleaming and Marshall sighted quickly and squeezed the trigger just as the driver saw him and jerked the wheel. The massive boom of the shot and the radial kiss of gun smoke as the stock kicked him and the pellets blitzed the door pillar and shattered the front window. The roar of it still dispersing through the quiet evening as Marshall corrected and jacked his next shell and with the car still in motion he fired again through the driver's door.

The Audi lost control and bounced up onto the sidewalk and ripped to a halt, straddling the curb. Marshall was gone. Moving backward at a jog to the safety of the reserve. The guy from the garage was caught in the headlights, and he could see it was Troy Rojas. Gun in hand, shuffle-stepping left and right, unsure of the next play.

Witnesses now, just glances between blinds. Gunfire bringing them out. The green-haired guy from the Audi popped his door and practically fell on the road. His left side was bloodied, arm hanging limp. Twin swathes of rubber in the car's wake, broken glass winking sharply.

Marshall lay prone, sighting the .45 two-handed, the shotgun beside him. He knew they'd seen him drop back into the trees. He waited, the gun on the green-haired guy. Every instinct said drop them right there, cold blood or not, but with an audience he didn't want to see his escapades on a sworn statement.

So he just lay there.

Five seconds. The 911s would be going out. The green-haired guy circled to the other side of the car. Rojas, as they say, between a rock and a hard place:

Come across the street, or bail out.

He chose the latter.

He ran out into the road, heading for the Chrysler, calling behind him as he went: "I'll get Cyrus, you get the girl."

Someone at a window, phone to ear. Another guy came out the open garage door onto the driveway. Marshall tracked him with the gun. The guy saw the green-haired man hunkered down all bloodied beside the Audi, the car itself wearing a nice spread of buckshot. Rojas's form receding into the distance.

The guy glanced into the trees, and his mouth opened a fraction, like in that instant he could see the whole debacle.

He said, "Shit. Get in, get in."

The green-haired man opened the passenger door and clambered into the car, and the new guy circled round and got in the driver's side and they roared away.

Marshall gave it another few seconds, gun on the open garage, and then he got to his feet and picked up the shotgun and sprinted across the street. Colt in his belt, 870 raised as he went through the front door.

That shortness of breath.

Every sense hyper-tuned.

The roaring adrenaline.

Shit, it had been a while. And never in his own house.

Clear in the entry.

Clear in the kitchen.

Into the living room and there she was, bound on the floor. Cable ties at wrist and ankle. She raised her head to look at him and let it tip back gently to the floor.

She let her breath out. "God. Get me out of here."

He went to the kitchen and took a knife from the block on the counter and walked through to the living room and cut her cable ties.

The cuffs had bit deep. She rubbed each wrist in turn and sat up and got slowly to her feet. Her hands were shaking and she'd lost some color, but she was keeping it together. He wouldn't have blamed her for being less composed.

Two minutes. Don't hang around.

He bent and picked up the curved scraps of plastic. "What are you doing in my house?"

She kissed blood off a wrist. "I thought you might say, 'Are you all right?' "

"I can see you're all right. Anything else will need some explaining."

She followed him into the kitchen. He returned the knife to its slot and opened the cupboard under the sink and stood on the bin pedal and dropped the cuffs in the trash. He said, "This is the second time I've saved your life. If you were banking on me showing up, you must be damn good at wishing."

He looked at the 870. "Or maybe you've got the patron saint of the NRA as your guardian angel. Wouldn't that be good."

She didn't answer.

Marshall said, "Well. We'll call it luck, then."

She said, "I wanted to ask you about your meeting this morning."

He glanced at her. "Which meeting was that?"

She laughed quietly but didn't answer.

He leaned across the counter and looked out the window. He said, "I don't know what your plans are, but I need to get out of here in about ninety seconds."

"This is a crime scene. You can't leave."

"I think it's more that I'm not supposed to. But permitted or not I can definitely pull it off."

She didn't answer.

He said, "Maybe you didn't hear, but there was a bit of a ruckus out there a moment ago, and I don't want any trigger-happy lawmen showing up and finding me with this." He raised the shotgun briefly. "Also, I plan on finding those other three. You can join if you want."

He went and cracked the side door and listened. No sirens yet.

He waited, seeing if she would follow. Getting up around the four-minute mark.

No time to wait around—

Footsteps behind him. He glanced back. She said, “I’ll drive.”

EIGHTEEN

Rojas

They went east.

Breakneck on the straights, almost skidding through the corners.

"Cyrus, where the fuck are you? We had to bail."

Digital radio, not even static on the line. Like putting your ear to the void. He keyed it again:

"Vance, how's Dante doing?"

"He's shot all down one side. He's bleeding pretty good."

"Shit. Is the woman tied down?"

Vance braked hard for a corner. His taillights filled the Chrysler's windshield. Rojas stomped the brake and the car shuddered with the ABS as he fought the wheel through the turn.

"We don't have her, man. There wasn't time."

"What? What the fuck? You don't have her?"

"There wasn't time, Troy."

He felt this cold seep outward from his gut and fill him that special way bad truths do. He took his foot off the gas and the Audi shrank away ahead of him. The Chrysler drifted to the curb.

Free fall. He couldn't catch his breath. He felt the blood dropping from his head, heartbeat thundering on nothing. His head tipped against the wheel and he felt himself losing it, Vance in his ear, words that breezed straight through because:

She knows your name.

The cop knows your name.

You held a cop at gunpoint, and she knows your name.

A cruiser flew past in the opposite direction and the blue-and-red light was starry in the mist on his windows, almost beautiful but for the fact he knew what was coming and he turned and looked behind him and saw Bolt lying dead on the backseat with his eyes aimed somewhere distant and the spare keys hanging from his mouth.

Somehow he made it home. Autopilot. The Audi was in the garage, both front doors open and a trail of blood leading into the house.

She knows your name.

Cyrus dead, Dante a pint short, and the cop was all he could think of. He walked into the living room, saw Dante on his back with his shirt cut open. Black pockmarks on his chest and down his arm where the shot embedded. The whole side of him scarlet and the floor slick with blood. Vance rigging up an IV stand, prepping a line for his arm.

"Troy, help me with this. Shit, he might need the hospital."

He patted Dante's cheek. "Stay with me, dude. We got you covered. I'm gonna shoot you up. Troy, help me with this."

But his phone was ringing.

"Hang on." Anything to get away from the blood. The color so vivid, and the sweet copper smell filling his head.

He put a finger in his free ear and answered.

"Troy. Why you not ring?" His mother. Only she had such timing.

He walked toward the garage, but saw the mess and turned and headed for the kitchen. "I've been working."

"When we gonna see you? You been gone so long, ages. Your sister's worse again, Troy, she not good. She's gotta get the marrow thing to try fix it."

"I know she's sick."

"So why you not here?"

He didn't answer.

"When I not hear I worry what you're doing, and I think maybe you're doing something's gonna make you go back inside. I can't live with that again. I can't have my girl dead and you inside."

He wiped his mouth and swallowed and waited a moment for it to pass. "She's not going to die. I'm making money and I can pay for her to get better. It just takes a little while. But I promise."

"What you promise?"

He sat down with his back against the counter, covered his eyes with a hand. "I want to be there, but I can't. I want to more than anything, but I need to be here. Did you get the money I sent?"

"What? No. We didn't get no money. How much you send?"

So much he couldn't bring himself to say it. "Shit. Are you sure you didn't get it?"

"No. We had friends of Marco stay and maybe it went with them, I dunno. How much you send?"

He just couldn't say it.

You took a cop at gunpoint and she knows your name—

"Look, don't worry about me."

"How you can say that when I don't see you. Troy? How you can say that."

"Soon. I'll be with you soon. But I just need time to get everything together."

She didn't answer.

"And when I do I can fix it. Okay?"

"You been saying your prayers, Troy? You pray you go to heaven?"

"Yes." Not strictly true: he'd given up years ago. In the hallway, he saw Leon headed for the living room.

"Troy." God, she was crying. "I love you so much."

He closed his eyes and eked it out: "I love you, too."

"And your sister."

"Yes. So much."

Shuddering breaths as she composed herself. "People ask where you at, and I say you away living the dream. I say Troy living the American Dream, but I never know if I'm true."

A gunshot and he jumped. He saw Leon walking back down the hallway.

Shit. He got that panicked lightness again. She was talking, but he left the phone on the floor, scrambled to his feet, ran to the living room even though he could bet his life what he'd find.

Dante on his back in his own blood and a bullet hole in his forehead. Vance kneeling by the drip stand, rocking and cradling him.

NINETEEN

Marshall

He didn't want to leave the Silverado, so they took separate cars. Marshall told her he'd talk anywhere, provided there was food. She drove lead, which was a good arrangement: tailing close he could see if she was on the phone.

She led him down onto Cerrillos Road heading south and west, and stopped at a diner about fifteen minutes out of town. It was a low brick building with cars nosed in on three sides below the windows, as if peering into the light. The sign on the pole by the turn-in read BIG CHIP AND SMALL FRY's. In the dark with the mountains obscured the six-lane appeared to stretch forever through the cold and barren world, and the bright diner looked like the last friendly waypoint you'd ever see.

Sitting opposite her in a booth at a window, he wondered what trauma you'd have to live through to come out the other end of the last two hours and not be rattled. Maybe she was having the same thoughts about him.

A waitress came by and poured them each a cup of coffee. Marshall ordered a short stack of pancakes, and she asked for a grilled cheese sandwich. Even speaking to the waitress, she never took her eyes off him. Marshall sat there relaxed, his arm along the top of the seat like he had with Rojas and Bolt that morning. He quite liked that unexpected symmetry, bookending the day with diners and the same little pose.

The waitress moved away and she said, "You talk first."

Marshall said, "You going to ask questions, or do you want a soliloquy?"

She had some coffee. He noticed the liquid quivering when she lowered the mug. She was scanning the room every minute or so, and it made him feel better about having his back to the door. She said, "Can't be a soliloquy if I'm here. Monologue."

Marshall rocked his head a little: same difference.

She said, "What were you doing down in Albuquerque?"

"When?"

"That night in the bar with the robbery."

"Attempted robbery. I think I cut it short."

"Why were you in there?"

He looked at her a while, one of those instances where he couldn't find a simple lie for a complicated truth. The complicated truth being he preferred to avoid lying awake in the dark regretting things. After a while he said, "I like to drink."

She said, "Huh," like she knew there was more to it.

He said, "I was down there on a job for a couple of days."

"Do I want to know what sort of job?"

"I have no idea."

She didn't answer.

Marshall said, "I'm a welder. I stick bits of steel together."

"Don't normally see welders that good with guns."

Marshall said, "I watch a lot of YouTube."

She didn't smile. She said, "What were you doing in that diner this morning talking to Troy Rojas and Cyrus Bolt?"

"Nothing you need to worry about."

"What makes you say that?"

"The DEA's acquainted with them, but you're not federal, so I'm guessing you're a narc detective."

She didn't answer.

Marshall said, "But my meeting wasn't about illicit substances, so I'd say strictly speaking what was discussed is beyond your purview."

She smiled thinly. "Maybe just tell me anyway."

Marshall took his time, thinking how he'd lay it all out for her. He said, "You keep up with stuff about missing folks?"

"I try to."

"There was a girl named Alyce Ray, disappeared down in Albuquerque."

"How do you know about that?"

"I saw it on TV. Night after I rescued you in that bar, I was in a diner and saw it on the ten o'clock news."

"And what?"

"And I thought I'd better find out what happened to her."

"Why?"

He took a sip, buying time, not wanting to talk about it. He said, "Because it seemed like a decent thing to do."

"Thought you might have a better reason."

He thumbed the stack of napkins slowly, like looking for something between the papers. He said, "What better reason do you need than it's a good thing? If people observed that rule, I think the world would be in a far better state."

She said, "I mean I thought you might have a more personal reason." Getting closer to it than he liked.

Marshall said, "It was personal. I thought I wouldn't feel too swell about myself if I did nothing, knowing I could have been proactive."

"You call this proactive?"

Marshall looked out the window expecting to see the world, but just saw himself sitting there. He thrummed his fingers on the top of the seat, crossed his legs at the knee under the table. "Well. Whatever it is, it's certainly caused a bit of a stir."

They fell quiet as the waitress set their meals on the table. Marshall pulled his plate toward him and turned it to get it just so, and cut a segment of pancake with a single stroke near the edge, and ate it. The trick was to go no deeper than the top layer. He chased it with some coffee.

She watched this little procedure and said, "What makes you think Rojas and Bolt had anything to do with it?"

"She came into contact with them the night before she disappeared."

"But they didn't necessarily do the disappearing."

"No. But they'll know something about it. You run into shitbags one day and then go missing the next, chances are said shitbags had something to do with it."

"What's that, the law of shitbags?"

"No. It's common sense."

Quiet a moment as they ate. That faint squeal of cutlery on plates. She said, "How'd you get this information? That she'd been in contact with them."

"It's just something I know."

He sensed she wanted to push it, but she let it slide.

She said, "Right. How did you contact them?"

"I called Rojas."

"How did you get his number?"

Marshall shrugged, worked carefully on his meal, not looking at her.

She said, "What did you say to him?"

"I said, I have some stuff you might want to look at."

She looked around the room, taking everyone's measure, and then settled back on him. "So he thought you'd lined him up for a deal."

"Yeah. He thought he was getting a free product sample. But I broke Bolt's nose and kicked Troy in the balls and asked them about the girl."

"How did that go?"

Marshall chewed. He said, "They didn't seem that pleased about it at the time. Which I guess explains their behavior this evening."

"If you wanted to ask them what happened to the girl, you

missed your opportunity. In fact, I'd say you made a bit of a meal of it."

Marshall shook his head. He was down to his last pancake. He halved it carefully and damnit if that wasn't a perfect fifty-fifty. He made a neat incision and cut the bottom point from the left segment and ate it. He said, "I don't think so. They would have got home and taken stock of everything, and realized they're dealing with someone who takes life mighty seriously."

She didn't answer. Marshall sat there chewing slowly with his forearms on the table either side of his plate. He looked at her and she looked back as she drank her coffee.

He said, "Besides. I figured they had you tied up so I didn't want to rush in and risk you getting bulleted."

"Bulleted?"

He nodded, faint amusement in his face. "It's like billeted, but faster." He looked at the window. "And they don't send you anyplace nice."

She didn't answer.

He said, "How'd you find me?"

"Someone in the diner saw your little meeting. And then the same someone saw the state of Bolt and Rojas."

"Was it the truck driver?"

She just looked at him and said nothing, but he figured he was right.

He said, "But then how did you find me?"

"You stopped for gas. I got your plate off the video and got your address."

He nodded slowly, seeing her side of things. The Corolla had been a gamble. It was in his name, so it led back to the house on West Alameda. He needed Rojas and Bolt to find him, but it meant Shore had, too. He said, "And then you came looking at the same time as the rest of them."

"Yeah."

They sat quietly eating again. He finished his coffee, tipped the mug vertical to catch the dregs. He set it back in the little moisture ring it had made for itself. Down to his last half pancake now. "Can I ask you a question?"

She spread her hands, be my guest.

He said, "Why are you sitting here chewing the fat with me, rather than sending out the cavalry for Troy and Co.?"

She said, "Your neighbors would have called nine-one-one. Plus it was a case of issuing another lookout notice for a guy we're already after, or trying to figure out what your deal might be."

"And have you?"

She shrugged. "I don't know. But it was worthwhile."

Marshall nodded. "I think so, too. I certainly like a good pancake."

She said, "Never seen someone eat them like that."

"Like what?"

"One at a time. Normally have them as a stack."

Marshall nodded slowly, thinking it through. "More than one way to eat a pancake. My way's best though. Take each one on its own merits."

She didn't answer. She'd only managed half the sandwich and didn't seem to pose a threat to the rest of it. Marshall chased some crumbs and mashed them.

She said, "How did you get them out of the house?"

Marshall said, "I triggered the alarm on one of their cars and when the guy with the hair came out for a look, I caused a bit of a commotion."

"I heard gunfire."

"I imagine you would have."

"Did you kill anyone?"

He took a moment to respond, the contents of his plate apparently demanding some focus. He said, "I didn't shoot anyone to death."

"Did you kill anyone?"

Marshall didn't seem to register the question. Last quarter now.

She folded her arms on the edge of the table and leaned

forward slightly, like now they were getting down to it. She said, "So what's your story?"

"What do you mean?"

But he knew what she meant. She waited.

He said, "Well. The parts worth listening to are the same parts I don't like discussing. So it leaves us in a bit of a pickle, narrative wise."

He thought for a moment, looking out the window. "I'd say it's Bible black and best forgotten."

The thin smile again. "Dylan Thomas."

Done. He paired up his cutlery in the center of the plate and pushed it aside. "Bible black? I thought it was Wilco."

She shook her head. They sat there a moment, no pressure to fill the quiet. One the other's mirrored stillness.

At length he said, "You're a little light in the badge and gun department compared to most detectives I've seen."

"How many have you seen?"

He shrugged, and then pitched the question that was really nagging him: "How come you just got held at gunpoint and don't seem fazed?"

She shrugged. "Training."

Which Marshall supposed could claim a little credit but certainly not all of it. To reach the point where a hostage situation is nothing drastic, you've either seen a few minor dramas or perhaps one major crisis, and he guessed it was an even bet either way.

She sat watching him with her head on a slight tilt, and he got the funny sense she could see his thoughts as they surfaced.

She slid to the edge of the seat. "Been a pleasure. Wait here."

She stood up and headed for the restroom. He watched her walk away. Poor choice of words, that parting line: too final and imperative, and he knew straightaway her little departure was more to do with making a private call than anything else. He just got that gut feeling.

Wait here.

Lucky he drove. This sort of place, the alternatives were limited should you be without wheels.

He rolled slightly on his seat and slipped his cash from his back pocket. All hundreds. It would be the evening's biggest tip by a fat margin. He took a bill from the stack and arranged it in his usual fashion and quietly left.

A cool and starry night, and on the highway the traffic spent a long time as distant light before and after passing. Smell of dust and dry grass. He got in the Silverado, started up, and headed north, back toward town.

One after the other he dialed Felix's three throwaways, but he didn't get an answer. He tossed the phone on the seat. Beneath him the road unspooling in a blur. The shotgun was on the rear bench, the Colt in his belt. He liked traveling at night. Cabin warmth felt like safety from the world.

He drove.

TWENTY

Lauren Shore

She locked herself in a toilet stall for privacy. First up was 911:

"This is APD Detective Lauren Shore. I need a cruiser at Big Chip and Small Fry's Diner down on Cerrillos Road. I've got a witness in a shooting on West Alameda from earlier this evening."

She gave the operator Marshall's details.

"Yes, Detective. ETA twelve minutes."

She dialed Martinez.

He said, "This some sort of retribution for earlier? Waking me up?"

She told him what had happened.

"Holy shit. Are you there now?"

"No. There's been a nine-one-one, but I left with Marshall."

"Who's Marshall, the blond guy?"

"Yeah."

Quiet a moment. Puddles on the white tiled floor. A long tail off the toilet roll dangling just out of reach.

He said, "Where are you now?"

"At a diner up on Cerrillos Road. I'm in the restroom. Sheriffs've got a cruiser on the way for him."

At his end she heard a door closing. "Holy shit, Lauren. Jesus. I can't believe you went up there. What did you think you were going to say to him when he answered the door?"

"I don't know. I never got that far. They grabbed me outside."

"Was Bolt there, or just Rojas?"

"Just Troy, plus two other guys I didn't know. I think Bolt might actually be dead."

"Really?"

"Yeah, well, I heard Troy say Cyrus hasn't called in yet, or something like that. I think maybe they sent him to clear the street, and Marshall killed him."

"Has he said anything?"

"No."

"How's he acting?"

"Normal, I guess. He doesn't look like he's got a lot of worries."

"Oh, man. I can't believe you left the scene."

"Well, he wasn't going to hang around. And I figured it was worth going with him to figure out his deal."

"Which is what exactly?"

"I'll run you through it later. Look, I need to get off the phone. He's going to wonder what I'm doing."

"Hang on, hang on. I'm just thinking."

She waited.

He said, "I'm going to come up. Once you get him in the cruiser you need to get back to the house. I'll give SFPD a call and make sure they know what's happening."

"Okay."

"Is he armed?"

"Probably. But he's not hostile. He probably saved my life. I just had coffee and pancakes with him."

"Fantastic. Look, call me again when they pick him up. I'll see you later."

He clicked off.

She stepped out of the stall and pocketed the phone. Her first time in a diner in months, but she'd coped well enough. No quiet times to let in memories. She stood a moment at the door, and then she pushed back out into the restaurant.

He was gone.

Shit.

She walked over to the table. There was a folded hundred-dollar bill trapped under his mug. She went outside. His truck was gone. She walked out to the highway and looked left and right, as if she might discern which light was his, but of course she couldn't. She called the sheriffs back and told them to cancel the cruiser.

Couldn't call the man stupid.

She went back inside and spoke to their waitress.

"That blond man who was sitting with me over there, did you see where he went?"

"Sorry, miss. No'zing. He just go, I think. He pay though, I can see."

She went back outside and stood a moment at the highway shoulder in the cool midnight. With the stars arrayed brightly and the flat plain unbounded in the dark she'd seen no truer glimpse of vastness. She walked back to her car and got in and drove up toward Santa Fe.

TWENTY-ONE

Lucas Cohen

He got the call just before midnight. Cohen eased out of bed and took the phone out to the hall, pulled the door gently behind him. Important not to wake the beloved, else sure as sunrise there'd be some pointed words come morning. He checked the ID. It was Bill Masters, the Santa Fe sheriff's CIB lieutenant.

He stood at the upstairs landing with his phone elbow propped on the balustrade and said, "Good evening, Deputy United States Marshal Lucas Cohen speaking."

Which was a bit more elaborate than his standard greeting, but dealing with the local fellers he liked to err on the side of fancy.

Masters said, "They haven't fired you, yet."

Cohen laughed. "Probably just because I look the part. See my reflection with the badge and gun and I say to myself, Lucas Cohen, if you don't look like a million dollars I don't know a man who does."

Masters didn't laugh. Folks called him Bull Mastiff, due to his canine droopiness, but no one ever said it to his face. Cohen sometimes toyed with the notion of being the first. He reckoned you'd get a prize, probably a mug or something with it written on the side.

He said, "You get the short straw or something? What are you doing on the graveyard shift?"

Masters laughed. "No, I'm at home. Just got off the phone with APD."

"Who've they shot this week?"

Masters let his breath out, white noise on the line, like even the telling of it could get ugly. "Well, I'm not sure, but sounds like there's been something. One of theirs had a shots-fired incident up here this evening, fair bit of lead exchanged. Wouldn't be bothering you, but the name Cyrus Bolt came up. Believe we were talking about him just the other day."

Cohen swapped his weight one leg to the other, stop the pins and needles setting in. "I believe we were. Hope you're not gearing to tell me he's put a bullet in someone."

"Well, I don't know. But like I said, there's been some lead exchanged, whether someone's ended up wearing any I don't have the specifics."

Cohen said, "Any bodies on the premises?"

"Not that I've been told. You'd think with what's gone on there'd be a whole bunch of 'em. APD guy said it was real chaos, people out on the road firing guns, if you can imagine that."

Cohen said, "I can. In fact, I'm imagining it right now."

Masters didn't answer.

Cohen put his head in the kids' bedroom, check they were still under, and yes, all was right with the world. He said, "Is Bolt still there?"

"No, just someone from APD. Alive and breathing, thank god. I's hoping they were going to tell me good news, like old Cyrus'd taken a .45 on the bridge of the nose or something, you know? Like, taunted bad luck enough, this time it's finally got him."

Cohen felt that little worldly nugget merited some reflection, so he gave it a moment before replying.

He said, "You got an address or anything?"

"Yeah, somewhere, let me see. Incident on West Alameda, just up by the river there."

And Cohen said, "Shit," because sure as anything it would be the Marshall boy's house.

Masters said, "Everything all right?"

"I certainly hope so, but I think it warrants some investigating. You planning on coming out? I can meet you."

Forty minutes later he was out there. Two sheriff's cruisers in a chevron blocking the road, a long queue of Santa Fe PD cars along each curb. Light bars throwing wild shapes through the woods along the river.

He parked short of the cordon and got out and took his jacket from the trunk. Dapper in charcoal gray, the Glock slim on his hip. Thirty-five years old, the novelty wasn't gone: he'd done three years with APD before he joined the feds, and for whatever reason the little dress-up buzz of being in uniform just couldn't touch the magic of having a marshal's star on your belt.

He walked to the driver's door of one of the roadblock cruisers and opened his jacket, letting the guy see the gun-and-star combo.

"Masters around?"

The guy hiked a thumb. "Lieutenant's up the street. Just head along. Need to sign the log if you want to go in the house."

Cohen thanked him and walked on up the street. The door of an unmarked opened and Masters swiveled on the seat and hauled himself out. Fifty or thereabouts, a wide and paunchy guy with a droopy mustache and jowls that took things even further. They shook hands.

"Lucas, how you doing?"

"I'm just merry, thank you."

Not even a smile. Masters never seemed to get his humor. He said, "Thing's looking like a circus. Got us and Santa Fe PD, and now you, and APD's sending some people up as well. Felt like telling them to stay put, give them a call if we need anyone else shot. Jeez."

Cohen said, "I did some time with APD, I'll make them play nice. And you and I always get along, don't we, Bill?"

That got a chuckle out of him. Masters said, "Fuck off." Then: "Heard you had some trouble up in Farmington recently."

Cohen said, "Yeah. Couple months back. Not a pretty thing."

"So I heard. But glad it all wrapped up for the best."

Cohen didn't answer, hoping to put it to bed. They walked over toward the house, but Masters had some flow now, shootings a subject he could run with: "Heard people discussing it every now and then. Folks like to make the point nineteen's young to be getting drilled and all, but shit."

Masters ran a hand round his jaw, collecting his thoughts. "Evil's evil, don't matter what age it is. Makes me want to swap to open-top holster. Looking at a thing like that and you're clipped in, you don't have a show. But anyway. I'm sure they'll make a case study of it over at Glynco." He laughed. "Call it the LC drawdown, something like that."

Cohen said, "Maybe," because now didn't seem the occasion to offer his views. Shooting that boy didn't turn out to be for the best at all. He always found it interesting, these guys like Masters, the way they spoke about things. He got the impression that come the time their own finger was on the trigger they'd be clipping out the news stories and popping them in a scrapbook.

They walked up the driveway to the garage. A deputy proffered an attendance log and Cohen signed, Masters asking the guy when CSU was due on-scene, the pair of them swapping grumbles about the PD stepping on their toes. Cohen, biting back a smile, almost suggested they get the state police out to cover forensics, make it a full-blown carnival, but there's only so far you can push a man.

He said to Masters, "You had a walk-through?"

"Just a quickie. I didn't actually hear that Mr. Bolt was part of this, but there was another feller he goes around with that got mentioned."

He flattened his tie on his chest and fussed with the knot. "Think it was speculated that where there's the one, there could be the other. Which makes sense."

Cohen nodded and didn't answer. He stood in the open garage

door with his hands on his hips and his jacket pushed back, taking it all in. He said, "Heard anything more from APD?"

"Yeah, spoke to Martinez, don't know if you know him. Sounds like a funny one: off-duty detective of theirs was up here wanting to question the owner about something or other. Guy's not home, so she has a bit of a look around, three guys grab her, take her inside, hold her at gunpoint."

"One of them being Bolt's friend?"

"Yeah, the Rojas feller, plus two other guys. Anyway. They hold her awhile. Then one of them goes off outside and apparently she hears this gunfire out on the street, couple of rounds I think, and the guys holding her just skedaddle." He snapped his fingers to underline the effect. "Another minute and the owner, the guy she'd come to talk to in the first place, runs in packing a fucking pump-action shotgun, and sets her loose."

Cohen looked at the floor as he pondered all that and then he said, "Sounds like quite the evening."

Masters said, "I'd say it's that plus a little more." He shook his head. "Shit."

An internal door into the house stood open. Cohen brushed past sheriff's deputies and stepped through to the entry hall. Faint smell of weed somewhere, but it all seemed neat and tidy, no real sign someone had been held captive.

Masters followed, saying, "Guy obviously leads a busy life, got APD chasing him on one thing, these other guys coming in on the other front."

They stopped in the kitchen.

Masters said, "I'd say if you've got guys after you prepared to hold a police detective at gunpoint, you're into something fairly hair-raising."

Cohen nodded slowly. He eased open a cupboard with his boot toe and saw the bin hiding there. He stood on the pedal and noticed bloodied cable ties. He said, "I was just mullin' on a very similar thought."

Masters didn't answer.

Cohen said, "Where's the APD cop they were holding?"

"She's here. One of my guys is talking to her."

Cohen nodded. "How come SFPD's been pushed out of it?"

"They haven't, I'm just taking lead." He winked. "Looked like a scary one, so they wanted the pros on it."

Cohen said, "How'd you get in the house?"

"Garage door was open. First response just came straight in. Some rubber and broken glass out on the street, but the PD guys've parked all over it. But come have a look at the living room. All these boxes here. Looks like stolen goods or something."

Cohen drifted through after him and did a circuit, nothing seeming to pique his interest. He moved back to the kitchen. He said, "Believe he actually rents this out. I'd say it's the tenant's."

Finally showing his hand.

Masters glanced at him. "How'd you know that?"

Cohen said, "I've met him. Owner, I mean."

"What, through the marshals?"

Cohen nodded. "Yeah. Through the marshals."

Masters said, "Well thanks for sharing. Better late than never, I suppose."

"Maybe I'm only just rememberin'."

Masters said, "Yeah, like hell." He chewed on it a moment and said, "Not some ten-most-wanted fugitive or something, is he?"

"Not to my knowledge."

"So how do you know him?"

"Just through a thing."

"A thing."

"That's correct."

Trying to sound final, avoid the WITSEC subject, but Masters kept at it. "Must've been quite the situation, needing input from the likes of yourself." Tongue only slightly in his cheek.

Cohen nodded, mouth downturned a little at the edges. He said, "Bill, I do believe I'll concur wholly with that."

He looked around a final time before walking back toward the entry.

Masters said, "So what's his background?" Not about to give up easily.

Cohen didn't answer.

"This some witness protection thing?"

"No comment."

"Well that's as good as a yes, isn't it?"

Cohen shrugged. "Ain't at liberty to say." He stood in the front door and looked out, quietly pleased he'd had a question that warranted the phrase. "Other than that I reckon he's come from the sort of life that'd make him tough to mess with. Evidenced by what you've just told me."

Masters didn't answer.

Cohen said, "So. Where are we now?"

"Well." Letting his breath out as he said it, trying to sound miffed. "Where we are now is we've got a lot of stuff we've been told about, but not a lot to actually look at, given no one's here."

A deputy came through from the garage, said to Masters, "Sir, we opened up the Corolla, looks like cocaine or something in the back."

Masters looked at Cohen. "Gonna write that off as the tenant's, too?"

Cohen said, "I don't know. I think we can say that at present there's a bit more to this than meets the eye."

A little twitch of a smile lighting up under that mustache and Masters said, "Lucas, I do believe I'll concur wholly with that."

"You spoken to the neighbors?"

Masters shook his head. "I haven't. But be my guest."

He did just that.

The woman next door was one Ada Lawton, midsixties or so. They spoke outside on her porch, the woman bespectacled and slightly stooped, a rolled issue of *Time* in her hand for ease of gesturing.

She said, "Heard the first one maybe nine thirty or something. Gunshot I mean."

"Sound like a pistol or something bigger?"

"Can't say I know a helluva lot about these things, but to be honest I'd pegged it as something a bit bigger. But I was sitting right there by the window so when I heard the first I thought, Lord, what was that? And I looked out and blam, saw the second shot clear as day."

"And what did you see?"

"Well, there was a great big white car, a really great big thing, in the middle of the road there, and a man with a rifle or something up at his shoulder standing kinda next to it, and I saw him shoot into the side of it. Just the one time mind, but I'd heard the first one. And then."

She put a hand on her hip and gazed past him, looking back through the evening. "And then the car just stopped sort of crossways on the walk, and the gun feller was trotting backwards in reverse and fore you knew it he's gone." She clicked her fingers.

Cohen said, "Brave of you to stay at the window like you did."

The lady clucked her tongue, bit of a smile showing. "Yeah, well. Better'n cable, and you don't have to pay."

Cohen said, "You recognize the man with the gun?"

"No, not sure that I did. Dark, mind you."

"So what happened after the car stopped? Were you still at the window?"

"Yeah, still there. Had the cordless with me for the nine-one-one. Guy got out of the car and by the looks of it he was all bloodied down one side. Kinda limping."

She gripped her thigh with one hand and took a lock-legged step to demonstrate. She said, "Coupla guys came out the garage. One of them ran off thataways, and the other got in the white car with the injured feller, and then they were off. I stayed on the phone just commentating it all, and I s'pose it was about a minute or so, and then the guy'd done the shooting comes tearing out of the trees, vroom, straight across like that, into the house. And I'm thinking, What the heck? Anyway. Minute later out come two of them, gun feller and this lady, too. And I mean, phwoar. Of all the things you could guess you'd end up watching, this would not be one of them."

She chuckled. "But hell. It happened."

Cohen was half-turned, looking across at one of the unmarked cars, where a woman was climbing out of the backseat. A plain-clothes guy exiting the other side. He said, "It certainly did."

He reached in his shirt pocket for a card and passed it to her, just two fingers right on the corner, a smooth little move people sometimes took a liking to.

He said, "Appreciate it. Anything else, you just give me a call."

He winked and doffed a pretend hat, and she seemed to like that just fine. He walked across the street. The woman was talking to the plainclothes, a Santa Fe PD detective he recognized but couldn't name. He walked over slowly, and by the time he reached her, the cop had moved on.

Cohen offered a handshake, and backed it up with a smile. "I'm Deputy U.S. Marshal Lucas Cohen. Are you the off-duty APD detective I keep hearing about?"

She took his hand. "I'd say so. Lauren Shore."

"You mind if I have a word?"

She smiled tiredly. "Why not? I'm getting good at it."

Cohen laughed. "My car's just up here. You can even sit in the front this time."

A minute later and she was seated next to him, elbow on the sill and her head on her knuckles. The windshield view was all blues and reds, seemed to have her in a trance.

Cohen broke the spell: "Sounds like quite the evening you had."

"Yeah. I prefer them a bit quieter, have to admit." She rubbed a wrist, and he thought of those bloody cable ties. She said, "What's the marshal's interest in all this?"

Cohen said, "Cyrus Bolt's known to us."

"How so?"

"Kind of a long story." Which it wasn't, but in general he preferred listening to sharing.

She said, "I've got time."

Cohen dropped the visor and looked at his shadowed self in the little mirror, and then raised it again. He said, "Cyrus did time over in Beaumont for trafficking. He's out on supervised release but he ain't been filing his reports, so there's a warrant out on him."

She folded her arms, leaned against her door. "That's not a very long story."

Cohen smiled. "There's some subplots I omitted."

"Such as?"

Cohen rocked his head. "There's a bit of stuff no one's managed to hang on him. Coupla ICE guys got drilled near the border shortly before he went inside, got some hearsay it was him and Troy Rojas. Don't know how much you know about old Cyrus, but he's got an ex living up in Lubbock. Sent a coupla deputies out to visit with her, see if she'd got word recently, pair of them ended up shot, stone dead. Neighbor found them in the yard. This was two, three months back." He hitched his gun round so he could settle in the seat. "Texas man myself actually, so it pains me especially."

"Wasn't the wife that shot them?"

Cohen shook his head. "No, I don't believe it was. Takes a special breed to be killing people where they stand, and I'd say Mrs. Bolt isn't one of them, though I'm sure she's a fierce lady. Plus she was actually out of town."

She didn't answer.

Cohen said, "Anyway. You could say that knowin' what I do about Cyrus, there's a special place in my heart for the man, in that I'd like to see him with a bullet between his eyes." He touched his forehead to mark the spot. "But anyhow. I understand you didn't actually see him?"

She raked her hair back, and he could see her hands were shaking.

Cohen said, "I'd offer you some coffee, if I had any. Sometimes on the long days my Mrs. Cohen sends me out with a little thermos, take a hit if I need it."

Shore turned her head on the rest and smiled at him. "I didn't see Bolt, just Troy Rojas."

"They normally come as a pair, or so I'm told."

She nodded, still looking at him. "I think Bolt might be dead."

Cohen hadn't seen that one coming. He said, "How'd you conclude that?"

She nodded toward the house. "You hear what went on tonight?"

"I'd say I got the gist of it."

"You know about the occupant?"

Cohen nodded. "I do know about Marshall. Quite the boy."

She glanced at him suddenly, like this was some fresh angle. "What have the marshals got to do with him?"

"Oh. This'n that."

"Is he WITSEC?"

"I can't comment."

She watched him a while. He wasn't used to getting such scrutiny to one side of the face. He counted off the seconds in his head, studying the light show. At five she said, "That sounds like a yes to me."

Cohen didn't answer.

She said, "Are the feds after him?"

"I don't know about feds in general, but I'm certainly not."

Shore said, "I think he might have killed Bolt."

Thinking back on what he knew of the man, it didn't strike Cohen as an unlikely prospect. At length he said, "Well, until I've got a warrant from a U.S. federal court saying I need to go after him, then I don't care what he does. Just prefer he get some less dangerous pursuits."

Shore took all that onboard with a slow nod. She said, "So who are you out here for? Marshall or Bolt?"

The car was fogging up. Cohen turned the key and dropped his window an inch. He said, "They're both official business. I want Bolt in handcuffs and Marshall out of trouble."

"Might've left it late. Far as the trouble part goes."

Cohen rubbed his jaw. He had a trim little beard he was cultivating, coupled to his hair by a pair of neat sideburns. He said, "I suspect you're right. Where'd you last see him?"

"In a diner down on Cerrillos Road, couple of hours ago. No idea where he is now."

She put her elbow back up on the sill. "Get the sense he's got a knack for keeping out of sight."

Cohen nodded. He hooked a thumb in his belt and he could feel his star clipped there and hell if that wasn't a fine sensation. He said, "Had a knack for keeping out of trouble, it might serve him a little better. You talked with him a bit, did you?"

She nodded. "He's on a missing persons hunt. Girl named Alyce Ray, disappeared down in Albuquerque. He was out this morning questioning Bolt and Rojas about where she is. Somehow he knew they'd been in contact with her."

She gestured out the windshield. "Obviously they didn't appreciate the interest."

"Clearly not." He watched the street a while, theories circulating, drawing a little clearer now. He said, "What exactly did he tell you?"

TWENTY-TWO

Wayne Banister

He'd returned the rental earlier that day and used different ID at a different place to check out a second car. The new motel was down on Gibson Boulevard, just east of the airport. Two-story with a concrete balcony that ran the length of the upper level, and in the late evening he stood out there leaning on the rail, below him the gridwise city lights reaching flatly to the black horizon. Ash trees swaying in a slow waltz, and high above, the measured blinking of airplanes on south approach. Engine noise a thin and far-off rumble.

Strange life, this. Motel to motel, no real friends, business contacts anonymous or dead. He sometimes wondered if his real self had meaning, whether it actually could, when every move was hidden by a false name. How many people actually knew him as Wayne? To whom was he more than just the Dallas Man?

In the room the blue phone rang.

He stepped inside and found it on the table, brought it outside to answer.

The Patriarch said, "Having a nice time?"

Wayne put his hip against the rail. Out on Gibson Boulevard traffic stopped at the light, and in the motel office he saw a lone guest with a carry bag waiting at the empty desk. Perhaps a different version of himself: another room in a string of many and the guy would check in with a fake ID and proceed to his unit and take instructions on an encrypted phone from a nameless employer. He said, "Can't complain. I got a quiet place. There's a Starbucks just down the road."

"Just keeping you in the loop. I haven't heard anything about Frazer."

Wayne said, "Lonely spot out there. Could be a while before someone spots them."

"Yeah, that's what I thought. I've done some background on him. He's got a business down in South Albuquerque. Razor Rentals."

"Car hire or something?"

"I guess so. It's him and another Frazer running it, probably his son. I'll just find the name, hang on."

Wayne waited.

"Yeah, Sean Frazer. I bet it's his son."

"Okay."

"I'm sure it's a front. Tweak the records a little, easy laundering setup. Probably tell the IRS they've got a fleet of fifty Ferraris hired out. Get some nice meth money coming through."

"You want me to go for a visit?"

"Yeah. Emile's been aggressive enough, I think you'd better go see Sean. Really make a firm statement, if you follow."

Firm statement, read as: put some lead in him. Wayne was long past the point where he missed the euphemisms. He said, "Sure."

"Thanks, it's down on Fourth Street Southwest. I found it on Google Maps, just look for the sign."

A hollow echo of feet on the metal stairs at the end of the building, and then the girl he'd called for earlier emerged on the balcony. She made her way over like it was the catwalk: upright and courtly, casting about with this prim, cool look on her face, lips slightly parted like she was blowing smoke. Handbag slung over one shoulder and slim long legs beneath her miniskirt, each step dead ahead of the last, like staying on the tightrope. Words in his ear, but he was briefly in another world.

She tipped her head toward his room, eyebrow raised. "This twelve?"

"Yeah. You can go on in."

She went inside, a slight shimmer in her hair with each step.

The phone finally coming back to him: "You there?"

Wayne said, "Yeah. Sorry. Still here."

"Company for tonight or something?"

Wayne laughed. "No. Just room service."

"Okay. What I was saying, I may send you some more guys to help with this Marshall thing. He's either got federal protection, or he's completely off the grid, so he's going to be very difficult to find. But hopefully he's going to call again."

"Yeah."

"Can you give me another week down there, just to coordinate things if I send in some more people?"

"Of course."

"Great. Well, call me once the Frazer issue's resolved, and we can go from there. I want to try and set up a rapid-response type thing so you can actually move in as soon as he tries the number. But enjoy your room service."

Something knowing in that parting sentiment, and Wayne clicked off without a good-bye.

He stood a minute just looking out across the city, and then he stepped inside and closed the door gently and locked it. She emerged from the bathroom, already in her underwear, head tilted as she fixed an earring, and any excitement that had been brewing out there collapsed. The bright light showed her for what she was: pale, bruised, needle-marked, overly made up, unenthused. Overused.

It felt a long way from the real thing.

She said, "Room service, huh? Wouldn't that be something."

Wayne didn't answer.

She said, "What should I call you?"

"You can call me Wayne."

He sat down at the table. He said, "Where are you from?"

She paused there in the middle of the room, still fussing with the jewelry. She looked at him a moment, maybe sensing his second thoughts, catching some sort of cold vibe. "If we're just going to talk, do you mind if I put my clothes back on? If that's cool."

He nodded. "Yeah. You can put your clothes back on."

She turned and went back into the bathroom and left the door ajar as she dressed. She called out, "Mind if I smoke in here?

He said, "Only if I can have one."

He got up and took the alarm off the wall from above the bathroom door and set it outside on the balcony by the doorstep, wondering why undressing was a private matter. Maybe it was all about the startling entry.

When she reappeared fully clothed the catwalk gait was back on display and her bag was over her shoulder. She sat down on the bed and found a pack of cigarettes in the bag and placed one in her mouth, passed a lighter flame back and forth on the tip until it was going. She leaked smoke out her nose, cigarette hanging off her lip as she spoke: "You want one, come and get it."

She waved the pack, and it rattled gently.

He got a mug from the kitchen and came and sat next to her on the bed. He put a cigarette in his mouth and she lit it for him, leaning across to cup the flame with her other hand. This close, the air was just perfume.

She said, "So." She tapped her cigarette against the makeshift ashtray. With the mug in his lap it seemed an easy, familiar gesture, like they'd known each other a long time. "What are we going to talk about?"

Good question.

He wanted to talk about himself and about her, like people did.

The quiet dragged out while he thought about it and she said, "Where you from?"

He said, "New York. Before that, New Orleans. I was born there."

"New Orleans, huh. How do you end up being born there?"

Reflex and insincere. He wondered what you'd have to do to make her give a shit.

He shrugged and said, "Same as any place. My father was there." He laughed. "And I guess by default my mother must have been, too."

"What did they do?" Breezy and automatic, just the normal pillow talk.

Wayne said, "My father was an FBI agent. After that he was a private investigator. Actually pretty well known. Very anti-communist, used to send cash and weapons down to Cuba for the anti-Castro movement. Never knew my mother."

Her eyebrows arched slowly, stayed there a second. She hiked one leg, rocked the knee side to side as she worked on the cigarette. She said, "Who's Castro?"

He smiled faintly. "Never mind."

He held her hand. She didn't seem to mind. He crossed his legs at the ankle and realized that the gun bag by the bed was open and that his SIG was visible. Not that she seemed fazed. He guessed on the scale of oddities a pistol in a bag was fairly pedestrian compared to what else she would have seen.

He said, "How old are you?"

"Twenty-nine. Thirty next month."

He nodded to himself, like it married with prediction. It felt good being here, in this warm room in the light with another hand in his.

He blew some smoke.

It felt good being like everybody else.

TWENTY-THREE

Marshall

A dead-end residential street, just south of Rodeo Road in Santa Fe. Quiet but for the low hum of breeze in the window he'd slightly lowered, and he could smell mesquite in the night air. Here and there a lit window, but mostly it was dark. He hadn't seen another car in nearly thirty minutes. He sat low in the driver's seat, eyeline on the crest of the wheel, the .45 gripped two-handed between his knees.

After midnight now. A cat crept along the far fence line, and he alone saw it. A car approached. Still hidden beyond the corner, but its lights played weakly on the road ahead. He slipped lower in his seat. The view sharpened as the vehicle turned, Marshall's cabin bright as it drew nearer. He waited motionless as the car pulled into a driveway, darkness panning back across him.

He opened his door, held it ajar.

The car's lights died. The engine quit. Marshall got out and pushed his door closed and crossed the street quietly, the gun under his shirt.

The driver was out of the car now, crunch of footsteps on the shell path leading to the door, Marshall silent across the lawn, and even as they reached the step he was still unseen.

He said, "Sarah."

She gasped and dropped her keys, a loud ring on the concrete. She laughed weakly and closed her eyes when she recognized him. "Jesus, Marshall. You scared the shit out of me."

"Sorry. Not one of my best approaches."

"Good if you plan to kidnap me. God."

She was still in hospital scrubs, a jacket over the top. He bent and picked up the dropped keys and found the one for the door and passed it to her.

She opened up and hesitated briefly and said, "Come on in, I guess."

He followed her inside and locked the door behind him. She hung the jacket in the entry and stood heel-toe to kick off her shoes. A light was on in the living room, and she led the way through. A woman was seated on the sofa reading a newspaper. She lowered it as they entered and smiled and looked at them across the top of her spectacles.

"You have good day, Sarah?"

"Yeah, it was okay. How about you?"

"Yes. Good, good. How you, Mr. Marshall?" Like this was nothing unusual.

"I'm fine, thanks, Juanita. How are you?"

"Very well, I think."

"Pleased to hear it."

"You like some coffee before I go? I put some on, you want."

Sarah said, "No, you get on your way. Sorry I was a bit later than I thought."

He sat in the living room and waited as she showed Juanita out. Quiet voices in the entry he couldn't quite overhear. It felt strange sitting here with a gun in his belt, a fresh angle on an old scene, but the room itself was a close match to memory. A few subtle changes that drew him: the armchairs had switched positions, and the television was closer to the corner, and there was a new side table, an antique piece that clashed with the otherwise clean and modern look. After a minute or so he heard the door close gently and the bolt scrape across, and then she came and sat down opposite him, leaning forward with her hands clasped.

She said, "Funny time for a visit."

"I remembered you have the late shift, thought I should drop by."

She didn't answer.

Marshall said, "I like the new table."

"What's going on?"

He smiled. "What do you mean?"

"You're looking kind of stressed. Last time I saw you, I don't think you had frown lines."

"Oh. Yeah. I guess."

"So what's going on?"

"Oh. Nothing. How've you been? I haven't seen you in a while."

Quiet. In the kitchen he could hear the clock ticking, and that was the only sound in the house. She said, "Marshall. Do you really want to do this now?"

He said, "Depends what you have in mind. I thought you might just want to have a talk. And maybe a coffee."

She glanced at her watch, and he knew it was only to underline a point. "I would, but it's after midnight. And it's been a long day."

"So some other time, then."

She leaned back and laid an arm on the rest. The way she was biting her lip, he knew she was trying to tread lightly. She said, "I don't know if we should."

"Why not?"

"Well, because it didn't turn out well once, and I just . . . I think it will maybe end up much the same way. So."

"Maybe. It doesn't have to."

They sat a while without talking. He'd always been comfortable with lulls, but he could sense her trying to pick the best way forward. She said, "Marshall. The parts of you I know, I like a lot."

He smiled and said, "Back atcha."

She made a bracket with her thumb and first finger. "But I feel like there's about a five-year gap somewhere back there that's kind of a blank area, and it scares me."

"There's nothing to be scared about."

"I feel like we're having the same conversation."

"Maybe I can do better the second time round."

She sighed through her nose and looked at him and smiled sadly, her eyes not in it. "I feel like I don't really know you. Does that make sense?"

"What do you want to know?"

"I think we've been here before."

"What do you want to know?"

She shrugged. "I don't know. The normal things. Your parents. Your friends from back then. What you did. It just . . . It scares me that you've put a block on so many parts of your life. Or that you just don't want to tell me about them. It's scary. I don't know if you understand that."

"No. I get it."

"So maybe you can tell me some stuff."

He leaned forward in his seat and in his mind he could see the whole story scripted neatly for the telling, but as always there was that block and he said, "I was a cop in New York."

Other phrases coming to him, but he stalled, because he knew they were the well-worn explanations she'd heard before and they weren't the truth. So he just sat there quietly, and he couldn't help but ponder that strange reality of never being short of a word other than when it came to talking about himself.

She said, "Marsh. I have a little girl. I can't have you with . . . you know."

Quiet. He said, "What?"

"This sort of secret element. I don't really know anything about your past and sometimes what you even do day to day. Like . . . I ask you what's got you on edge and you say nothing, but it's more than nothing if you show up here at this hour and you've got a gun under your shirt. You know. It doesn't exactly make me relaxed about things."

He knew his face didn't change, but she said, "Don't be all surprised. They don't make cell phones that big these days."

Marshall didn't answer.

She said, "Are you in trouble?"

He shook his head. "No."

"So for god's sake. Why are you carrying a gun?"

"I had some trouble before. But it's pretty much gone."

"Sounds like there's a bit left."

"Yeah. But it's probably not like you think it is."

"Why? How do I think it is?"

"Well. There's trouble. But I'm the one dispensing it."

She passed the back of her hand across her brow and let her breath out through her teeth. "Shit, Marshall. That doesn't mean anything to me. It's just dumb talk."

"Whatever. You don't need to worry."

"Well I don't think I could. I don't think I'd have the energy."

Just the clock, carrying on patiently.

He said, "Can I see Abby?"

"Marshall."

"Just a look in."

He counted off the seconds, holding his breath. She said, "Yes. But you leave the gun here. Or you can go."

He lifted his shirt and took the .45 from his belt and laid it on the coffee table between them. Out of place in that peaceful context, like some prelude to tragedy, lying there with its hammer cocked.

She got up, and he followed her very quietly down the hallway. The little girl's bedroom door was open and she was awake, looking at him as he glanced in, fistfuls of sheet bunched up under her grin.

"Marshy Marsh!"

He feigned shock and went and sat on the edge of the bed. "You shouldn't be awake at this hour. Little girls should be tucked in and off to sleep by this time."

"I am tucked in. See?"

She scooted down under the covers, the sheet pale blue with yellow ducks.

He said, "Yeah. But you're not asleep though."

"Your talking woke me up. And I'm big. Not little."

"You're littler than me."

"But everyone is. So that doesn't count." A little moth-wing flutter in the sheet as she talked.

"All right. How's school been going?"

"Good."

"Have you learned any new words?"

"Some."

"Some. That's not a new word. You've known 'some' for ages."

"No, like . . . I learned some new words."

"Oh, right. I thought 'some' was the new word."

"No. It's an old word."

She came out from under the sheet. "How come you're here?"

"I just came for a little visit."

"Did you see Juanita?"

"Yes. I saw Juanita."

"She has a new cat."

"Huh. She didn't tell me that. Have you had any more wiggly teeth?"

"Yep. Wiggly and gone." She grinned to flaunt the evidence: a gap front and center down the bottom.

Marshall said, "Wow. Look at that. Tooth fairy wouldn't have been pleased he had to pay up."

"Tooth fairy's a girl."

"Yours might be. Mine was definitely a boy, though. Probably retired by now, I'd say."

She giggled. She said, "Do you miss me?"

"Yes. Lots."

"Are you coming back for more visits?"

"Well, I don't know. I hope so."

From the doorway he heard, "Marshall has to go now, sweetie."

"Where do you have to go, Marshy?"

"Oh. Just home."

"Why don't you just stay here?"

Right then, there were very few things he'd rather do.

He said, "Because my bed will be sad."

She giggled again and raised her arms. "Good-bye hug?"

He leaned down and hugged her, couldn't help but think of Cyrus Bolt's last embrace. Handling that slack-jawed corpse, shoving it in the car. God. And here he was with this kid.

"See ya, Marshy."

"See you, sweetheart. Be good."

Sarah was leaning on the doorframe with her arms folded and he stepped past her into the hall and she trailed him back to the living room. He picked up the gun and slipped it in his belt. She stood watching and the blank expression was disapproval enough. She led him back to the entry, opened the door and held it for him, like coming out of county lockup.

He paused on the step, trying to think of parting sentiments.

She said, "Well. See you later." She was fanning the door very gently.

He felt he needed something more than just a bye. The phone call from that morning kept looping away, the guy laying out his threats. As soon as you hold someone dear then you stand to lose something.

What would you do if someone hurt them?

Standing there at the threshold he said, "Spoke to someone today. Just made me remember how much I miss you both."

He'd hoped she'd offer something back that he could cling to, but she didn't answer. The way her mouth was set he could tell what she was thinking: too bad.

He stepped outside. He said, "I'll give you a call."

"See you, Marshall."

She closed the door.

2010

Lloyd came by. He had a key and let himself in the front, the Third Avenue entry. Marshall figured him for about thirty. He was like Tony minus twenty years and twenty pounds, the same sleek tailoring, more Wall Street than gangster.

He came out back and saw Mikhail curled on the floor, blood leaking through his fingers, lips shining with it. He ran a hand through his hair, looked at Tony Asaro still seated at the table. The espresso was gone now.

"Jesus, Dad, what happened?"

Asaro said, "Vicki's backup guy tried to pull, Marshall put him down."

"Shit. That must have been something." Unfazed, trying to impress the old man.

He took a step back from the table, looked over at Mikhail, trying to figure the blow-by-blow. Marshall was leaning on the doorframe, gun in hand, watching the front room. Defied belief they had a man here on the verge of dying, Tony Asaro sitting there like this was his living room. A calm and distant look in his eye, like reflecting on a pretty normal day.

Lloyd said, "Where's Vicki B.?"

Asaro said, "He had somewhere else to be."

"Is he hurt?"

"Yeah. Don't touch that spoon."

"Oh, god." He leaned in for a look, a hand on his midriff to stop his tie dangling. "Is that an eye?"

Jimmy Wheels dropped his voice an octave, like the fight-night announcer: "Gets it on the first try."

The three of them laughed. Lloyd looked around, checking everyone was enjoying the moment, though he'd actually lost some color. "Marsh, you're looking worried there. Chill."

Marshall glanced at him and then away, didn't move. Pulling the trigger was bad enough, but humor while the vitals waned was verging on depravity.

Lloyd came closer, the smile hanging in there, keeping it friendly. "Not a good look for a cop, is it? Shooting a guy like that."

Marshall didn't answer.

"Are you carrying your badge? Must be some sort of bad-luck omen or whatever. Killing someone while you got your silver on you."

The smile had gone. He had a light-switch personality, the smooth corporate side only there while he needed it. He said, "Should make you assume the position, pat you down for it."

Jimmy Wheels said, "Lloyd, come on."

Lloyd grinned and punched Marshall lightly. He stepped away, back in character. "No, you're right. Things to do."

He went and stood over Mikhail and said, "What's the plan?"

Marshall said, "He needs a doctor."

Asaro ignored him. He said, "I'm going home. You three are going to take this guy home."

"Which is where?"

"Brooklyn. Return-to-sender type thing." He laughed. "Shit, imagine we had a stamp."

Jimmy Wheels had a custom Escalade, blacked-out windows and a nice tan leather interior, modified controls with no foot pedals. They put Mikhail in back and headed out down Third Ave., Jimmy and Lloyd up front, Marshall and Jimmy's chair in the seats behind.

Jim wasn't happy. "Wish he'd fucking tell me when he's planning things to turn out like this. Like, I woulda at least brought some plastic or something. Gonna be shit all through the trunk now, fucking nightmare."

Lloyd had his color back now Mikhail was out of sight. He said, "Just use some bleach, give it a good clean."

"Yeah, you gotta be so careful though. Some of the CSI shit they can do these days, blow your mind. Eh, Marsh? Get blood out of anywhere, can't they?"

Marshall said, "They can."

"See. Nothing for it, you'll just have to get me a new car."

Lloyd checked his cuff links. He said, "What, you angling for a new Ferrari or something?"

"Yeah, Ferrari would actually be kinda good. SUV's hard with the chair 'cause I gotta reach down so far to pick it up, you know."

"Just go to the gym more. Do some weights."

Jimmy took a right on Ninth, left on Broadway, southbound again. The old buildings through Noho tight on the curb, leaning in for a view. Marshall took a look over the back of the seat. The guy's breathing quick and shallow, scalp white beneath his hair. The Beretta was silenced, so the bullet had lost its kick. It had gone in and hadn't made it out.

Lloyd saw him looking and said, "What do you reckon, Jim. What's a good drop-off point?"

"I don't know. Somewhere. They're Bensonhurst, aren't they?"

"Yeah, I don't know. Could drop him off down on Eighty-sixth under the bridge or something." He put his elbow up on the door, thrummed his lip slowly, like pondering something complicated. He said, "Reminds me there's this big park somewhere, acres and acres, some kind of farm, but it's just full of dead bodies. Put them all sorts of places, so you can see how they rot and decompose or whatever."

Jimmy cracked a small smile. "Is it a legit science thing, or is it some sorta wacko place?"

"How'd you mean?"

"I don't know. Like a necrophilia resort or something."

Lloyd laughed. He played with his window button, shot the glass up and down a couple inches. "Yeah, maybe it is. Have to check them out on Google, get a day pass for you, Jim."

"Or a family pass. Take your dad."

"Fuck you."

They cut west on Houston.

Marshall said, "Let's drop him at a hospital. We can just kick him out and run."

Lloyd said, "That's the second time you've said that."

"Because he needs a doctor."

Lloyd turned in his seat, expression bored. "Look, man. Being on the take means you work for us. And when you're working for us, and you're riding in our car, you drop the protect-and-serve bullshit, okay? Just me and Jim you need to look after. Only thing you got to worry about is if some NYPD asshole pulls us over with this guy in back, how fast can you kill them."

Marshall didn't answer.

"Don't just sit there doing the hard man thing, I never know if you've heard me."

Marshall looked back at him nice and steady. He had one arm laid along the sill, and he tapped a finger gently while he thought. The patient clockwork of it. Like each added second was an added tactic to some private scheme. He said, "Pretty fast."

"Pretty fast." Lloyd shrugged one shoulder. "Means nothing."

"It might if you're the one getting shot."

Lloyd didn't answer.

Marshall said, "We can try it, if you like."

Lloyd held the stare, propped an arm up on the back of his seat. He said, "I wouldn't threaten me. That'd be pretty fucking stupid." Still nice and smooth, taking a leaf from Tony's book.

"Why, you going to tell Dad?"

Lloyd laughed. "Wouldn't be Dad. Might be his cleaner, though. You heard of the Dallas Man?"

Marshall said, "Can't say I have."

"Yeah, well. My father uses him for the tough jobs. People just end up dead without knowing it. Pays to just behave yourself. Otherwise." He clicked his fingers. "Sometimes shit just happens."

Marshall nodded slowly, looked out his window like he was slowly grasping the concept. He said, "Lloyd, if I killed you, I'd want you to know all about it."

Lloyd didn't answer. No change in expression, he reached in his jacket and drew a snub-nose .38 and put it against Marshall's forehead.

Jimmy Wheels said, "Ooooo, shit, Lloyd. That's not a good idea on the road."

Lloyd cocked the hammer. A faint metallic creaking as the cylinder stepped round, lining up a shell. "You got all the right lines, but you don't know your place. That's the difference between you and me." He smiled. "I put a bullet in you, no one cares. Other way round, you probably can't say the same."

With the gun right in his face it was hard not to look at it, but he forced himself to keep his eyes with Lloyd.

Marshall said, "You kill me and you're going to get pretty well acquainted with NYPD. Probably lockup, too."

Lloyd said, "Maybe. I didn't think they'd be all that bothered by bent cops dying. Maybe they'd just think I'd done them a favor. Who knows."

Marshall didn't answer.

Lloyd said, "Not for you to have to worry about anyway. This sort of distance, you wouldn't have much brain left."

They held the pose a few more seconds. The muzzle cool on his skin and the car gliding swiftly through the bright electric night in a trail of yellow cabs, and he and Lloyd swaying gently with the motion.

Lloyd lowered the hammer and withdrew the gun. He looked at Marshall a moment longer and then he turned in his seat. "Let's put it on record, Jim. Marsh doesn't know his place."

Jimmy Wheels said, "It's on the record, Lloyd."

Lloyd reached up and turned the mirror so he could see Marshall's reflection. He touched his forehead. "Should get a tattoo of where the muzzle was, like one of those religious dots. Remind you who's in charge."

They followed West Street down into the Battery Tunnel and took 278 through the western edge of Brooklyn. Jimmy exited at Eighty-sixth and headed east toward Bensonhurst. They passed the Dyker Beach Golf Course on their right.

Jimmy Wheels hiked a thumb. "Could drop him in here. Some bunkers pretty close, could even bury him. Imagine that: someone plays a shot out of the sand, take a bit too much, boom, the fuck is this?"

Lloyd said, "I like the idea of the bridge."

"What, the West End line?"

"Yeah, one that goes over Eighty-sixth."

"Whatever. Don't say I don't give good options though."

They could see it when they reached the light at Eighteenth Avenue. The huge steel bridgework of the train line where it curved out of the leftward distance to lurk on huge frames above the Eighty-sixth Street traffic. Driving now beneath the soot-grimed underbelly with its vaulted gussets and massive girder matrix all rust-streaked, and the rivets in studded rows without end. He remembered the shattering iron clatter of the D train rushing through in its great howl of wind, trash dancing in the eddies.

Coming up to Twentieth Avenue, the light went red. Jimmy hit the gas and snuck through. No traffic coming toward them. Lloyd turned in his seat and checked the road behind, but it was all cars headed north/south on Twentieth.

"Okay stop, stop, this'll do."

Jimmy braked and the front of the car dipped hard as they slowed. Lloyd's belt was already off. He got out and ran to the rear and opened the door and dragged Mikhail out onto the road. The thump as he landed, nothing else. Lloyd slammed the back door and then ran up front, jumped in, and they were off, the Escalade roaring through the gears, and in the rear window the guy was just a suited jumble with the huge bridge truss like some giant portal framed above him.

Lloyd breathing hard with the rush, the car swerving slightly as Jimmy turned to check behind.

Marshall glanced over the back of the seat again. All that blood, the guy can't have been conscious. How long you could last with a nine-mil bullet in your gut, he didn't know.

They stopped at Twenty-first Street, traffic backed up at a red light.

Lloyd, still short of wind, said, "Even better than that time you took out that guy over in Queens, Jim."

Jimmy Wheels said, "Oh, yeah. Forgot about that. In that old Lincoln, weren't we?"

Marshall ran a hand through his hair. They'd be talking shit all the way back to Manhattan. He wasn't sure he could take it. He opened his door.

Lloyd turned and looked at him. "Hey, what're you doing?"

"That's enough for me for one night."

He slid out and threw his door closed, caught Lloyd calling out: "You just remember all that. Step out of line, I'll turn you into roadkill on Eighty-sixth." He wagged a finger, like he still had the .38. "You tell your uncle that, too. He owes us money, don't want him ending up like this guy."

The light went green. Marshall stepped back as the Escalade took off. He could picture Lloyd watching him across his shoulder, Marshall's figure receding as the black car bore him away.

He headed back west along Eighty-sixth to where they'd made the drop-off, called Ashcroft on his cell phone while he walked.

He said, "I've got a problem. Asaro had a meeting tonight with Victor Bradlik, things got rough, I ended up shooting his backup guy."

"What? Bradlik's backup guy?"

"Yeah. I don't think he's dead, but he's heading there."

"Where are you?"

"Eighty-sixth Street in Bensonhurst."

"Shit, you got an ambulance there or something?"

Up ahead: a stopped car and three people standing in the street, just silhouettes against the headlights.

Please don't be dead.

Marshall said, "There's one on the way."

"What happened?"

Marshall leaned on the roller door of a Radio Shack and ran it down for him. He said, "Lee, I want to come in tomorrow. Get those Bureau guys, too. This is crazy."

"Marshall—"

"No, I think I probably just killed a guy. I need to come in or I swear, next call I make is to Tony Asaro, tell him what the situation is. Jesus Christ, Lloyd almost patted me down for my wire."

"Marshall—"

"Tomorrow."

"Shut the fuck up and listen a minute. Give it two days. You need to just chill out, give it some time, act normal. Otherwise stuff comes apart."

Marshall said, "Tell them I want a meeting or I'm gone."

He hung up and kept walking.

He caught a D train at Twentieth and got off at Atlantic Avenue and waited for a Q train.

Standing at the platform with his shoulder against a column and the tracks fading into the dark of the tunnel he looked down and saw a rat: coal-black fur in wet spikes sleek on its bloated form, the finger-thick tail dragging ropelike as it crawled across the rail. All that trash down there, begging for plunder.

One A.M. now.

When the train arrived he stood in the aisle of an empty car, no handhold, swaying on his feet with the motion. The clatter and rush of the crazy free-fall speed through tunnels, car rocking with the pace, the sudden quiet as they breezed through bright and empty stations.

He got off at Parkside and walked up Flatbush Avenue. His uncle's place was the corner unit of an old block of brownstones, the barber downstairs, accommodation on the floor above.

Marshall stood at the front window and called him on the cell, looking at his reflection as he stood there, EDDIE's in an arch of white letters on the glass, bordered by red, white, and blue.

"Marsh, what's up?"

"I'm downstairs. Come let me in."

He clicked off. A minute's wait and then Eddie was at the door, a ding of the bell as it opened. Marshall walked over and stepped inside.

"I just saw Lloyd Asaro."

"Yeah. And?" He closed the door. No lights on, the pair of them just shadows.

"And he says you owe them money."

"Why'd he tell you that?"

"I don't know. Maybe he doesn't like having debtors."

"Look, Marsh. You don't need to worry about it. It's mine to figure out."

"How much do you owe?"

"Don't worry about it."

"How much do you owe?"

"Marsh, it's not your business, seriously."

"Are we going to do this all night? Because I'm patient."

"Jesus. All right." He made a motion with one hand, stirring up the words. "Sixteen grand."

"Sixteen. Ah, shit. How'd you manage that?"

"I don't know, it's easy. They keep bringing me all this money to try and put through my books, clean it up, thought I should just take a bit more here and there. Not all at once, but it just adds up, you know. 'Fore you know it, yeah. Sixteen grand."

Marshall didn't answer. He stood at the window and looked out at the street. Sixteen grand, just like Vicki B. He couldn't hold back Lloyd's last jab:

Roadkill on Eighty-sixth.

Marshall said, "How long have you got?"

TWENTY-FOUR

Rojas

Carnage.

Dante spread-eagled, the toppled IV stand lying beside him, a bag of clear fluid tethered to the crook of his arm. Eyes round and vacant like the fatal wound. An oval pool of blood creeping radially, a brass shell caught in the mess, the Colt Anaconda only just on dry land. Vance sat with his back to the wall, Rojas arranged similarly, propped against the TV.

Vance lit a cigarette as Leon walked in.

Vance said, "Can't believe you fucking killed him."

The cigarette fell off his lip, rolled through a short arc on the floor. He didn't pick it up, didn't close his mouth either.

Leon stood by the coffee table. No shirt, faded jeans with the .22 Ruger in the waistband at the small of his back. Rojas didn't get this no-shirt policy. Maybe it reminded them of the 'Stan. Leon crouched and used Dante's Visa to push some of the coke around, build up a short line. Delicate click of plastic on glass, leaning this way and that to check the symmetry. He dipped his head and snorted and rocked back on his heels with the hit, rose to his feet.

He said, "What, you think you were going to patch him up, get the pellets out? Not a chance. Would've bled to death before you were done. I mean, look at the floor. The leg one probably got his femoral."

"So he needed a hospital."

Leon still had the credit card. He flicked it backhand out of two fingers, sent it spinning dead flat on a beeline across the room. It hit the wall above Vance's head and skittered across the floor. Vance didn't flinch.

Leon said, "Sending him to the ER would have worked out well for everyone, I'm sure."

"And your answer was to shoot him in the head? Holy shit. You're a wacko."

Leon didn't answer, just stood there square, hands in pockets. A real *I dare you* stance. He smiled and pointed at the IV bag, draped across the center pole of the stand. "Looks like a fat guy climbing through a window."

He glanced at Rojas, looking for a laugh. No joy: he was lost in his own head, picturing the wanted posters.

Leon said, "Gone a bit white under the tan there, Troy."

Rojas surfaced, put the words together. He said, "You would too, if you took a cop at gunpoint and someone let her get away."

Leon said, "Now, now. Let's not have a blame culture. You could have taken responsibility."

Rojas didn't answer.

Vance kept his eyes on Leon, felt around for the cigarette, stuck it back in his mouth. He leaned over and picked up the Anaconda.

Leon said, "What, you're going to shoot me? Good plan."

"Yeah. I thought so, too."

Leon said, "You'll need a round in there."

"Cut your shit, Leon. You killed my friend."

Leon knuckled his nostril, sniffed. "Yeah. Because he fucked up."

Vance turned out his pockets, looking for a shell. Some cable ties and his set of bump keys fell in a jumble. He saw the box of .44s sitting by the couch and leaned and tipped it over, bullets rolling in a wide spread with a sound like marbles. He picked one up and swung the cylinder out of the gun.

Rojas could see him shaking, eyes wet. Cool Vance had checked out for the day.

Leon stood watching from beside the coffee table and said, "What are you doing, dipshit?"

"Take a guess."

"Right. And what are you going to do when I'm dead? I run this thing, Vance. If I'm gone, you're done."

Vance didn't answer, busy thumbing the shell home. He flicked his wrist and flipped the cylinder back into the frame. Leon could see where the bullet was seated, just left of the muzzle. Looking from the danger end, Colt cylinders step round counterclockwise: he was safe for five pulls. He didn't blink when Vance aimed one-handed and squeezed.

Click.

Vance kept the gun up, one eye shut. He said, "Pow."

Even with coke, Leon never seemed wired. Rojas thought he must pop downers to stay mellow.

Leon said, "After that mess tonight you're going to have state, federal, everyone looking for you. And you're going to find yourself in shit without me watching your back."

Vance squeezed the trigger again. Click. "I've got pretty good at looking after myself, gonna need some better reasons than that. Come on. Three more squeezes and then you're dog food."

Click.

"Oops. Two."

Leon seemed pretty confident about where everything would end up. He said, "You think you're hot shit, Vance, but you don't know how to live in the world. You know how to kill people, and that's it. I'm the only reason you get by without the other half of the equation."

Vance held the gun steady, looking down it through one eye. "Those going to be your last words? You don't want to grab some Shakespeare or something?"

Leon drew the Ruger and leveled it. Not a bad little feat: complete in a blink, somehow unrushed.

Leon said, "Didn't think we'd get this far."

Vance didn't answer.

Leon said, "You've gotta squeeze twice to beat me. Pretty hard to do it fast, gun like that. This thing's got a nice light trigger. Shit, I'm almost there. We'd better be careful."

Vance didn't answer.

Leon said, "Don't kid yourself you want me dead. When you dream of all the murdered kids in 'Stan Land, no one else is going to say there, there, because no one else knows what it's actually like. Other than you and me. And if you get rid of me it's just going to be you left. Not much fun."

Vance kept it up for another few seconds, and then he put the gun down and slid it aside, scrape of steel on timber. Nothing in his face, the cigarette seesawing as he worked his jaw slowly back and forth. Leon kept the Ruger on him a bit longer, make sure they'd drawn a line under it, and then he reached behind him and stuck it in his waistband.

He said, "Bring him downstairs. Cyrus, too. We'll have to use the Skilsaw."

He bent and wiped a finger through the coke dust, rubbed it round his gums as he left the room.

They went and fetched Bolt from the Chrysler. The corpse facedown as they lugged it, sparing them that awful stare.

Down to the cells, the body awkward, locked with rigor.

It was more garage than basement: the artificial rise the house was built on abutted it on three sides. From outdoors it looked innocuous, but the main door was backed by an eight-inch layer of concrete block. They'd drilled and epoxied rebar into the floor slab as a footprint for the new internal walls and formed them from masonry. Guest accommodation, plus Leon's cutting suite, plumbed to a cesspit outside.

No noise from the guests. Leon was in an apron, wiping down

the band saw. Tools of the trade on a pegboard on the wall behind, stenciled outlines denoting absent items.

They laid Bolt out on the floor beside Dante, just inside the door.

Leon threw the rag on the table and clapped his hands once. "All right. Who's going to help?"

Quiet for a moment, and then Vance said, "I'll do it."

"Great."

Rojas stepped out of the room. He'd known Cyrus Bolt a long time, and this was the parting moment. He knew that if life's purpose was to witness the twisted, then right now he could die.

Leon closed the door.

He sat in the living room. The coke on the coffee table suddenly very tempting. He waited there in the clutter. The Xbox, one of Dante's guns, the coffee table, Vance's Anaconda, just two pulls from more bloodshed.

Very faintly, the sound of the Skilsaw. A high-pitched rotary whistle, muted intermittently as it cut. He ran his hands through his hair, blocked his ears, listened to the ringing. Who was first: Cyrus or Dante?

He rested his face in his hands. Emerging from the dark the memory of the cop tied up on the floor, arching to look at him.

How you doing, Troy?

He needed to get out of here.

So just take a gun and a car and go.

But you need money.

The daunting road ahead: help his mother, help Troy Junior, keep himself out of prison. All three would need some funding.

He glanced around. Dante's Visa on the floor. It wouldn't be good for much, maybe a few hundred. Bad taste using it when the true owner was dead. He shook his head to lose the image, noticed Vance's set of bump keys, lying in the tangle of cable ties.

Bump keys.

A plan cohered in flashes. Tempting glimpses of a brazen departure.

Imagine what you could do.

He got slowly to his feet and walked over and picked them up by the ring. Like regular keys, except the teeth were even and equidistant, with a single larger tooth at the end.

He held the crouch and jiggled them on a flat palm and they fanned in a gentle curve, perfect size order.

The dizzy screech of the saw, dropping out as it cut.

Through limbs.

Through bone and cold, dead flesh.

He pocketed the set and picked up the Colt and flipped out the cylinder and fed in another five .44 shells. Then he stuck it in his belt at the small of his back and walked quietly along the hall to Leon's office.

The whistle of the saw. He pictured big arcs of blood. Spray patterns on the heavy aprons.

He tried the handle. Locked.

He took the keys from his pocket and spread them on his hand again and crouched so he could match one to the lock. It was a nine-key set. He tried eight, the second largest. It slotted cleanly home, the gentlest grating as the pins met the notches.

Easy.

He let his breath out. It clouded on the handle, fingerprint whorls in the mist. He waited with empty lungs trying to bring his heartbeat to one a second. Sound of the saw again.

He moved the key in and out a couple of times, feeling for the last pin. That subtle, subtle nudge.

He'd only bumped a lock a few times. Simple in theory: insert the key so it sat just before the final pin, twist gently, and then shunt it all the way home. In principle the sudden impact made the lock pins leap upward, and the applied rotation to the barrel let them settle on the shear line in the freed position.

He tried it. Twist and bump.

Nothing.

He listened for the saw. There it is.

Fingers slick on the metal. It's hard when you're shaking. He tried a second time. No luck. Vance had the knack: he'd picked that side door, one pop.

Three's the charm. Twist and bump.

Nothing. He withdrew the key, inspected it. Precision steel, defect-free. His sweat standing up on the finish. He tried key nine.

All the way to the last pin, twist, and bump.

The lock turned.

A little leap in his chest and he pocketed the keys and pushed the handle and stepped into the office, the long wedge of light from the door revealing the setup:

Leon's chair pulled back at an angle, almost welcoming him in, do sit down. Books open on the desk. Computers and modem humming. The smell of warm plastic. He stepped to the desk. On the keyboard lay a color print of a naked torso, limbless and headless. He turned it over, rolled open a drawer, found a fat bunch of keys and a white swipe card.

He picked them up and shut the drawer. The saw up and running again, in the midst of something big. He set the lock again before he closed the door.

Down the corridor to one of Leon's off-limits rooms. He guessed it was a bedroom turned storage locker. He picked through the bunch of keys until he found the one that fit the lock, and then he opened the door.

Light from the corridor filtered in, and he saw metal wall racks loaded with M16s, submachine guns he couldn't name, shotguns, pistols, helmets and body armor in different shades of camouflage. Boxes of stacked ammunition, any caliber you like. Scent of oil and cardboard. Nothing that looked like money.

He closed the door quietly. He was about to lock it, and then he realized he couldn't hear the saw.

He slipped the keys in his pocket, kept his hand there to stop them ringing. He moved closer to the stairs, back against the wall, like walking a narrow ledge.

Quiet.

He reached the stairwell door and glanced down, and shit, there was Vance right in his face, standing at the top tread.

Rojas said, "Holy shit, you walk quiet."

Vance glanced at him. "What are you doing?"

"Heard the saw stop. Thought you must have finished already."

"I can see the pulse in your neck." Chilled Vance back in action, the brush with Leon behind him.

Rojas put two fingers below his jaw, suddenly conscious of Vance's Anaconda jammed in the back of his belt. He said, "Yeah, shit. I keep thinking about that cop."

Vance studied him a while, just eyes moving in a blank face. He said, "You know if there's any of that nitric acid left?"

"No. I'm pretty sure it's gone."

Vance stepped into the hall. "What about the sulfuric stuff?"

Rojas turned a little, not wanting to put his back to him and reveal the gun. He leaned on the wall. "I think we're almost out of everything. Might be enough to do one of them, but not both. Just use a gallon and water it down."

"Tried that before, Leon said it makes the pH go too high or something."

"So just hose off all the sections and wrap them in the plastic and I'll bury them."

Vance looked at the ground, rubbed the back of his neck. "Oh, yeah. Could do that, I guess." He gripped the doorframe and leaned down the stairs to yell. "Leon. Troy says just hose off all the sections and put them in the plastic and we can dump them."

They waited as he thought about it. Vance still hanging from one arm, Rojas could just shoot him in the back. Colt .44 at this range, wouldn't be any maybe about it.

But then you'd have to face Leon, in the dark, by yourself.

Name a greater danger and you'd be wrong.

God.

He felt his heart thud dully, a wave of cool dispersing.

Only way to do it was get them both in the same room, give them no time. But Leon was so fast. He just seemed to know what you were lining up, some sixth sense forewarning.

Quiet still. A long, thin gurgle of a drain in the quiet. Blood or water. Leon called, “Yeah. Okay.”

Vance turned on the stair. “Come give us some help.”

Rojas shook his head. “You wrap, I’ll bury.”

“You got a thing about blood or something?”

He backed away, careful not to turn. “No. I got a thing about chopping up guys I’ve known. Just yell when it’s done.”

“Whatever.” Not thrilled about it, but he was heading back down the stairs.

Rojas let his breath out and took his pulse again. Still going like it was trying to top some kind of record. He walked quietly back along the hallway, relocked that door he’d just opened.

Trembling like his first holdup, must be twenty-five years back now: sticking the barrel in the guy’s face, screaming for him to get out of the car, gun wobbling like Parkinson’s. Should be used to it by now.

He moved to the next door and tried some keys and got lucky at number four. He turned the handle gently, and then stepped into the room. The same wall-rack setup, guns galore, body armor, foil packs of ready-to-eat meals.

In the corner the timber flooring had been cut back to expose the foundation slab, and a safe maybe five feet by three square was bolted into the concrete. It had a keypad combination lock and a swipe card slot with a glowing red light. He threaded his way over between the boxes. The light like some demon’s eye, watching the whole way. He paused a moment, card hovering, and he knew that behind this door lay a one-way trip, no turning back now.

He ran the card through the slot.

The light went green. He heard a soft click.

He pulled the door open, dug in his pocket for his cell phone and used the screen glow as a flashlight.

Shelves of bundled bills, dozens of them. He thumbed a stack, all hundreds, snug inside a paper ribbon stamped *$10,000.*

Leon's CIA cash.

A few seconds lost to quiet awe. His phone light timed out. He woke it up and scanned the shelves again. Had to be two or three million dollars here. Enough money to get him anywhere he wanted, keep him out of sight a long time.

He left the safe open and walked back to the top of the stairs and leaned on the frame and listened. A noise like water jetting against plastic sheeting, followed by murmurs he couldn't catch. It sounded one-sided, probably Vance getting a firm word, reassured of the nature of things.

The water again. He padded down the hallway to the bunk-room he'd shared with Bolt and knelt beside his camp stretcher and pulled out his canvas duffel and took it with him back down the corridor.

As he reached the room he could hear an alarm trilling sharply. Shit—he slipped quickly inside and the light on the safe was flashing orange, text he couldn't read scrolling on a narrow display above the keypad.

How loud is that hose—

He rushed over, fumbled the keys, ran the card through the slot again. The alarm quit, the light held a steady green. He left the bag on the floor and took the gun from his belt and darted back to the door and waited a second and then stepped to the stairs. Nothing. Sound of plastic being folded, water falling on concrete. That eerie cleanup noise.

Back to the room, back to work. He laid the Anaconda on the floor and opened the bag very gently, stop-start on the stiff zipper, drew the flaps wide. Then he reached inside the safe with both arms like hugging someone large and drew the contents of the top shelf slowly toward him and off the edge. Bundles tumbling, filling the duffel. That rich smell of currency, oil and grime, scent of all those beckoning dreams.

He cleared the next shelf. Fast, keep the alarm quiet.

Bottom shelf. He could smell it on his hands. Maybe bona fide Baghdad dust in those creases. He closed the safe door. The light switched from green to red. The lock clicked. He glanced around and gathered the errant bills that had fallen shy of the mark and tugged the zipper closed.

He slung the bag on his shoulder and with the gun in his other hand walked out and through the kitchen into the living room, followed the bloodstains to the garage. He still had Leon's keys, but it was too late to bump the office door again and return them to the drawer. It didn't matter. He felt better now, lugging three million. It instilled a devil-may-care mind-set: get out of my way, or I'll fucking shoot you.

He hit the switch and the lights draped the cars in sequence, front to back: the Chrysler, the shot Audi, the Jeep down the end. They kept the keys in the ignitions. He walked down to the Jeep and opened the passenger door and dumped the bag and Leon's keys in the footwell. Then he stuck the Colt in his belt and tugged his shirt out to cover it and walked back to the living room.

Vance was just coming through, a big black-wrapped parcel in his arms. He said, "We did Dante in the acid."

He hefted the package. "This is Bolt."

Rojas didn't say anything. He turned and walked back to the garage and after a moment Vance followed.

Rojas went to the back of the Jeep and swung out the rack for the spare tire and opened the door. Vance set the package in the rear and the suspension dropped with the weight. He crouched slightly to shunt the plastic shape forward and stepped back and slammed the door.

"Where you gonna take him?"

"I don't know. Somewhere." He swung the tire rack home.

Vance didn't answer.

Rojas opened the driver's door and pushed the button on the visor to raise the garage door. They waited without talking as it rumbled open. When the motor cut he said, "I'm taking your gun."

"What, the Anaconda? You can't."

Rojas drew it from his belt and held it at his side, cocked it with a noise like breaking a wishbone. "Don't worry. I'll look after it."

"You don't have a shovel."

Rojas didn't answer. He got into the truck and let down the hammer on the pistol and set it on the seat beside him. The cabin smelled like money. He started the motor and flicked on the lights and backed out toward the road.

TWENTY-FIVE

Marshall

Heading back north, he turned off Highway 84 at St. Michael's Drive, three miles south of town, and pulled in at a motel on the left. It was a newish-looking place, two-story, tan plaster with a steep gable roof in orange tile. The sort of color scheme that reminded you this was Santa Fe.

There were a handful of cars in the lot, and he parked up beside another Silverado. The phone was in three pieces on the seat beside him: handset, battery, and SIM. An antitracking precaution, necessary now both sides of the law were after him, but he reassembled the device and turned it on. It was slow to wake up, almost a minute before it let him access the settings and disable the GPS. They could still triangulate him off cell tower pings, but it was far less accurate than going by the phone's onboard chip, which he knew would broadcast his position every few seconds, good to within about ten feet.

Not that he had a penchant for mischief, but part of him almost hoped he was being tracked. Maybe they'd see a dot sitting there on the map and peg him as a motel guest. Or perhaps they'd see it all in context with the highway right beside him and figure he was a southbound runner. There'd be some arguing about what was planned, guys speculating about misdirection.

He left the phone balanced on his knee while it decided if he had messages. He counted off a minute. Nothing. He picked up the phone and dialed his voice mail service for the WITSEC address, the number Cohen normally got him on.

Three messages, standard where-are-you inquiries:

Bill Masters from sheriff's CIB. Delete.

Someone Martinez from Albuquerque PD. Delete.

Lucas Cohen from the marshal's service.

Marshall clicked off and started shutting down the phone, had second thoughts and took his finger off the button.

He clucked his tongue and sat a while, just weighing up what was sensible. Then he called the message service again and the machine recited Cohen's number, halting and stilted. Marshall dialed. Cohen made him wait a while, but he got there.

Marshall said, "Did you find your Nazi golf caddy?"

"Yeah, we got our boy. Didn't come as quietly this time. Found out I'm a Cohen, so he kicked up quite a fuss. Some kind of fascist thing."

Marshall waited.

Cohen said, "I see you got yourself in some alarmin'-looking events tonight."

"You could call it that, I guess."

"I'm glad I didn't find that tenant of yours all chock-full of bullets."

"Felix is long gone."

Cohen said, "I reckon it might be best if you come in. Have a talk about things."

"You're not tracking my phone, are you?"

"No, I most certainly am not. I don't have those sorts of facilities in my kitchen."

"Well that's good."

Cohen said, "You have any idea where Troy Rojas might be?"

"No."

"What about Cyrus Bolt?"

"Same again."

"You know if he's still breathin'?"

"That's a slightly different kettle of fish."

Cohen said, "Right." Drawing it out a bit, like he heard the unspoken bits, too. He said, "I think we at least need to sit down with one another. If you're not going to come in."

"You've got a trustworthy-looking face, you're not going to set me up, are you?"

"No. I wouldn't do that."

Quiet for a spell. Marshall pictured him pacing slowly, watching his feet, figuring how to put things in the best light.

Cohen said, "I just think there's elements to this that only you yourself are privy to, and I think it would be prudent to have someone of more official standing know what all the pieces are."

Marshall didn't answer.

Cohen said, "Put it like this: I met you enough times I reckon your heart's probably in the right place, so I got no issue with you. Even if your grasp of the law might be kinda tenuous."

Marshall didn't answer.

Cohen gave it one more go: "Look. I've been hearing about all manner of craziness and I'd like to find the truth in it, if there is any. Needless to say I look kindly on the prospect of you not getting hurt, too. Other than that I don't know what else to say."

Marshall said, "Can I get you on this number?"

"You can. You going to meet me?"

"You going to tell anyone?"

"No, I won't. Bring me a stack of Bibles, and I'll swear to it."

Marshall said, "Good to talk to you, Lucas. Keep your phone on."

He clicked off.

He drove up Pacheco Street to his apartment. Peaceful in these early hours, lonely cars at crawl speed on distant cross streets.

He'd been using the Pacheco place eight months now. He

always sublet for cash, rented out the WITSEC house at a steeper rate. It was good to turn a profit. He had a few addresses on rotation, dotted round Santa Fe. So far eight months was his longest tenure.

The building was a two-story, the requisite tan adobe, parking around back. He flicked his lights off as he turned in, and drove the Silverado behind the building. He eased into the narrow garage and set the brake and shut off the engine. In the dark with the exhaust ticking, out of sight from the world, it almost felt like safety.

He left the shotgun on the rear bench and got out with the Colt in his belt under his shirt and the phone in three pieces in his pocket. A hollow boom as he lowered the door, but there was no one in sight. He kept odd hours and never saw his neighbors. It made it feel like New York, feel more like home.

The apartment was warm with stale air. He set the locks on the front door and opened a street-facing window to the catch. The curtains stayed drawn, lights off. He took the gun from his belt and laid it on the table and sat down. A slight tremor in his fingertips, featherlight on the cool laminate, so weak maybe it was just the table. Like a far-off train approaching. Shivers in the earth as it neared, that shake along the rails.

He had very few possessions. The bed and the document safe and the items it protected. The square Formica table and two chairs. A couch and armchair in the living room. The shelves with his books: Franzen and Richard Ford, stories of a way of life he'd witnessed, but never lived. Above them his music collection: Wilco, Ryan Adams, Cat Power, Tracy Chapman, among others. Come evening he'd listen through headphones with one ear to the melody and the other to the dark. Sometimes things came back to him, but not always. On good nights there was nothing else on his mind.

So what are you going to do?

Cohen had asked about Rojas and Bolt.

Maybe Cohen could help him find Rojas. Or maybe he should have just killed him this evening.

The curve of the trigger on his finger. No slack. Rojas a half-squeeze from dead. Maybe in another universe he'd followed through.

He took the pieces of phone from his pocket and set them on the table, neatly spaced and square to one another. Ascending size order left to right.

Who else had the number?

He guessed just Cohen, and probably no one else.

Probably.

He could just put it all together quickly, check his messages, break it down again. Too fast to be tracked, surely.

He clicked the SIM home, working mainly by touch, some weak streetlight between the curtains. He attached the battery, a dull gleam on the terminal revealing the alignment. He powered the thing on and set it carefully faceup in front of him. He and the room tinged palely by the glow. Sitting slightly hunched with his arms resting either side of the phone, it looked like grace before a meal. A different kind of prayer, maybe.

Find me some bad, bad people.

The phone buzzed. One missed call, one message. He dialed voice mail. It had come in only thirty minutes ago. He listened to the menu options, and then Troy Rojas's voice came on, two words only: "Call me."

Marshall sat a moment, phone in hand, running through the risks. He looked at the screen. Rojas must have swapped phones: no more blocked number warning. Marshall dialed.

Four rings, and then Rojas said, "Bit rude, sent me straight to voice mail."

Marshall said, "My phone was off. Got to leave a message, otherwise I'll never know. Be a waste of everyone's time."

"I'll keep it in mind."

Marshall said, "I saw you this evening."

He took his time answering. Heavy static in the lull, like maybe he was driving. Rojas said, "Yeah. I thought maybe you had."

"How's Mr. Bolt?"

"He's with me right now, actually."

Marshall didn't answer.

"In a better place, I think."

Marshall said, "I certainly hope not."

"I'd be respectful of death, I were you."

"It's not respectful of living."

Rojas didn't answer.

Marshall said, "I've found you twice, now. I'd say I can go three without too much bother."

Rojas laughed. "I was calling because I wanted to save you the trouble of looking. I'm headed out of town for a while. But I'll see you again one day. I promise."

Marshall said, "Will it be the something sharper, or are we back to coffee?"

"Oh. I think you'll get the picture."

"Sure. So what's brought this on?"

"Better luck. Things have just suddenly turned my way, and I've taken them. Which, you know, is nice when it happens."

Marshall said, "I'll save you some luck as well, but I won't tell you what it is till I see you. Maybe try and guess beforehand."

"I think maybe I can. Look, I shouldn't string you along, I'm planning on killing you, there's no two ways about it. That lady cop, too."

Marshall didn't answer.

Rojas said, "Might take some time, but that's how good things work. Just don't forget me while I'm gone. You and the lady are at the top of my to-do list."

Marshall didn't answer. Sitting there quietly with the phone, and the only motion in the darkened room a tiny swaying of the curtain lit white along its edges.

Rojas said, "I'll tell you about that girl though, just as you're crossing over. Our little secret as you're on the way out. Some comfort to line your grave."

That girl.

Marshall heard the blood in his ears, counted to five to let it ease off, ensure things played out cool and measured. He said, "I was planning something along those lines, too. But I had you doing the dying."

"You killed Bolt."

"I'll kill you as well. Just give it some time."

Rojas said, "I'll see you again, Marshall. One day. Don't bother sleeping. Plenty coming your way."

2010

Only a day since the Vicki B. fiasco and Asaro threw a party, celebration for a real estate deal closed earlier in the week. Marshall attended, ostensibly as security. He didn't think he was needed. They were in the cocktail lounge of the Standard Hotel on Washington Street in the Meatpacking District. Eighteenth floor, full-height windows looking west across the Hudson and downtown to the Financial District. Marshall guessed it was a five-figure tab.

Asaro sleek in charcoal with a faint pinstripe, and the same shoes he'd worn when he stabbed Vicki B. Shirt cuff sitting just above a TAG Heuer watch Marshall hadn't seen before. Had to hand it to the man, he had style: moving guest-to-guest with a measured clockwork, smiles and quiet laughter for his anecdotes.

Lloyd was there, dressed like the old man, and Asaro's daughter, Chloe, whom Marshall had only met a couple times. The rest were earnest corporate types grouped in threes and fours, nodding and studying the floor as they listened.

Cool décor in Marshall's opinion: gold carpet, honey-colored bar, tan leather and timber for the furniture. He ordered another drink, took a stool while he waited. Someone touched his elbow. He turned.

"Hey."

Chloe said, "Hey. What are you having?"

"Dark and stormy."

She signaled the barkeep, tilted her head at Marshall. "Same for me. Extra ginger."

She took a stool next to him, side-on to the bar so she could look at him in profile. He thought she was twenty, twenty-one. Petite figure in a blue cocktail dress, long dark hair with just a hint of a wave. She was drawing some glances, more than a couple of stares.

She said, "Should've come earlier. Great sunset from up here."

The barkeep slid a napkin in front of him, centered his drink on it. Marshall set the glass to one side and removed the straw and folded it loosely in the napkin. He said, "The night lights aren't bad, either."

Her own drink arrived. She mimicked his routine with the straw and took a sip. She said, "Is this what they call moonlighting?"

He laughed. "I'm just having a drink."

"Yeah, but my father's paying."

He took a sip, held it, swallowed. It was his third cocktail: repartee took some thinking. "Nothing to say I can't accept free drinks on my own time."

She smiled. Red lipstick, a slim curve of white teeth. "I think it's all the rest that goes with it that's the issue."

Marshall didn't answer.

She said, "You're NYPD, right?"

Marshall nodded.

"Good to have around, then."

He took a sip. "I like to think so."

She nudged him lightly with a toe. "Nice to value yourself."

He didn't answer.

She said, "What do you do for the police?"

He took a drink and looked her in the eye, see how she'd play it. He said, "I work for the Organized Crime Control Bureau."

All poise: when she raised her eyebrows it was just faint curiosity. "Sounds like a gun-in-your-briefcase type job."

He smiled. "Not quite. I'm with Brooklyn South Narcotics. I go around looking for drugs."

She appraised the shelves of liquor above them, just mild interest. She leaned toward him. "I do that sometimes, too. Though I'm not with Brooklyn South Narcotics."

Marshall held her look a few seconds.

She said, "My father's not a criminal."

"I didn't say he was."

"Mmm."

"What does that mean?"

She looked over toward Asaro. She said, "My father's a pretty good judge of character, but I'm sure he doesn't always get it right."

"Like?"

She laughed quietly, keeping things polite. "He's probably got you made as a cop just wanting some extra coin. I don't know. Maybe you're here on cop business, see if my father's making some extra coin, too."

He didn't look away. "You've got a good imagination."

She toed his leg again. "You've got no idea."

Marshall didn't answer.

She said, "Whatever you're thinking, my father isn't breaking the law. I can promise you that."

Marshall could have offered evidence to the contrary, but now was one of those times when now was not the time. He thought a change of subject wasn't a bad idea.

He said, "What do you do?"

"Computer science. NYU."

She said it prim enough he didn't ask for more details.

She said, "So you live down South Brooklyn, or do you just venture in for work?"

"I'm up by Prospect Park."

"Oh. With your uncle?"

He nodded. He wondered how she knew about Eddie. Hopefully that sixteen-grand debt wasn't common knowledge.

Across the bar, Asaro was beckoning for her to come meet someone. She smiled and lifted a finger. One minute.

She turned to Marshall, smile still in place, and when she spoke her mouth hardly moved. "Well, this has been nice. You should come visit sometime."

He laughed. "I'll bear it in mind."

She seemed not to hear. "How old are you, Marshall?"

"Twenty-nine."

"Twenty-nine. I think we'd get on fine, personally. I've got an apartment, same building as my father's, one floor below. You know where I mean?"

He said, "Fourth floor."

She pushed her hair behind her shoulder, glanced at Asaro to check his back was turned. "Good boy."

She leaned in, and when she spoke her lips touched his ear: "Central Park West."

It wrapped up around midnight. He ended up in an elevator with Lloyd.

"Always love the toilet in this place. They got that floor-to-ceiling glass, must be the best place in the world to take a piss."

Marshall didn't answer. Lloyd was behind him. Marshall watched him via the mirror on the door.

Lloyd said, "What were you saying to my sister? Saw you talking."

"Oh. This and that."

They reached the ground floor. Lloyd followed him through the lobby, heel clicks ten or so feet back. Marshall ignored him and walked outside. He waved down a cab. Lloyd grabbed his arm.

"What is it?"

"Relax."

Lloyd pushed an envelope into his hand.

"What's this?"

He smiled. "Just a little something. Remind you how much we appreciate loyalty."

Marshall watched him through the back window as the cab pulled away, Lloyd with an arm raised, waving Hitler-style.

He checked the envelope. There was a photograph inside: Vicki B., two bullet holes in his forehead. Marshall turned it over. Penciled handwriting, block capitals: GREETINGS FROM DALLAS.

• • •

The cab went east on Twelfth and then turned south on Seventh Avenue. He leaned against the door with a leg along the seat, looking out the far window as he tapped the photograph edgewise on his thigh. The West Village night with the traffic and the old brick apartment buildings a different shade of red one to the next and the bars hosting drinkers in the warm light beneath the sidewalk awnings. When they stopped at Charles Street, he took his phone from his pocket and dialed one of the support numbers Ashcroft had given him.

A man answered on the third ring. "West Insurance."

"It's me. Do you have Chloe Asaro's number?"

"That's the daughter, right?"

"Yeah. Cell phone, if you can get it."

"Give me a minute." He clicked off.

Two blocks. He got a text message at Grove Street. One line only: a ten-digit cell number. He looked at it until the screen timed out and went dark. Dialing wasn't a good idea. Now he was on the verge of calling, the just-do-it impulse that had got him this far was fading. He could see the reasons it was a bad idea, probably a whole litany if he put his mind to it, but the main issue being: she's Tony Asaro's daughter.

He ran his thumb over the Dallas Man's photograph.

Just a little something. Remind you how much we appreciate loyalty.

Remind him fairly graphically that life was short.

Marshall dialed.

Three rings, but she sent it straight to voice mail. She wouldn't recognize the number. He tried again, and when this time she answered he said, "I thought we could continue that drink."

She laughed. "I thought I gave you my address, not my phone number."

Marshall said, "You would have given it to me if I asked."

Quiet a moment and then she said, "You're not still on guard duty?"

"No. I'm off the clock."

"Where are you?"

He glanced out the window to check progress. He said, "Seventh and Houston."

"What do you feel like?"

Marshall said, "Anything, so long as you're paying."

"What a gentleman. How about the Soho Grand. You know where it is?"

"Broadway and Grand."

She said, "See you soon," and he liked the way she drew out that last word.

He got out at Canal and walked around the corner onto West Broadway. She was in the Grand Bar on one of the high leather stools, a cocktail on a napkin in front of her. He leaned on the bar but didn't sit down.

She raised her glass to the barkeep. "One more. Cast iron."

She looked at Marshall. "Rum and honey. You'll like it."

Matter-of-fact, like there was no chance he'd disapprove.

She set her glass down and he shifted it slightly on the napkin so it stood in the same moisture ring. Humor in her eye as she watched, but she didn't comment.

She said, "You could have raced me home, had the drinks waiting."

He pretended to think it through, shook his head. "The concierge would have seen me. And I don't have a key. And even if I got in I'd have to hunt around for where you keep everything, so I'd be all flustered when you showed up."

"Flustered."

He nodded.

She nudged him with a knee. "Could have been interesting. Come home and find you trying to pick the lock."

Marshall thought about it and said, "I'd probably hear the elevator and duck out of sight while you went in. Then knock gentlemanly."

She smiled and watched her drink as she swirled it. "Well, we can work on that. But I wouldn't worry about the concierge."

The barkeep set his drink in front of him. Marshall said, "I'm more concerned about who the concierge might talk to."

"Scared of Daddy?" Playful smile widening. That nice curve of teeth.

He had a sip and looked around. Soho suave: the bar itself looked like polished oak, blond with dark trim, and the shaded lamps between the tall windows facing West Broadway gave a honey-colored light. He said, "No. But I think when something involves the boss's daughter it's good to be discreet."

"We're just having drinks."

The way she said it, like a stage whisper, made him think this was just the appetizer. She took a sip as she looked at him. Not a bad feeling: an evening's worth of alcohol mixed with the happy prospect of a good night getting better.

He took another drink and said, "How did you get here so fast?"

"I was out with friends. But I decided you were a better option."

"That's nice to know."

"Not for them."

Quiet between them a little while, background bar noise disguising the lull.

Marshall said, "What are you going to do when you graduate?"

"I don't know. Something that makes money." She raised her glass. "I don't want to give this up."

"Liquor, or the high life?"

She smiled. "Both. The high life especially."

He watched her as she drank. That dress hadn't got any less appealing. He said, "Maybe you'd better do whatever it is your father does."

"What do you mean, whatever it is my father does?"

He shrugged. "I don't know. Whatever people do when they say they're in real estate."

"Like buy and sell property. I don't think there's much more to it than that."

He smiled, trying to draw her out, but the look he got back was cool enough he knew he wouldn't be getting anything worth sharing.

She said, "What?"

Marshall said, "You're actually quite hard to talk to."

"Why's that?"

Really going for it now, half a cocktail helping him along. He said, "Well, you're very attractive. It's sort of distracting."

Amused, playing the game, she had a little sip and nudged him with a knee again. "Well, I'm glad we've both got the same issues."

He nodded solemnly, like they were facing a real challenge. Then he finished his drink and raised the glass for a refill.

She said, "I think the idea is that you sip it."

"Maybe. You did tell me I'd like it."

She didn't answer. He felt in his pocket for cash and remembered the Dallas Man's photo. A dead Vicki B. trying to spoil the moment. He found twenty dollars and sharpened the fold before sliding it across the bar.

She said, "I'll pay. I've got a tab."

Marshall said, "This is a hotel."

"So?"

"So you can pay for the room."

They had an elevator to themselves, which was quite a lot of fun.

The room was on the fourteenth floor, so the ride up permitted a brief but energetic first act, and enough time to regain composure before the doors opened. In the room she paused long enough to push his jacket off, a brief distraction as he felt her hand on the photo, but it didn't last because then she was working on his belt and in the excitement he pushed the dress up but she stopped him and turned so he could reach the zipper, and tight as the dress seemed it fell off her pretty easily, and she put a hand in his underwear to lead him to the bed and any reservations he'd had about calling her were gone and never coming back.

He liked the view from the bed, the trail of clothes leading to the door. Lying on his back with Chloe pressed against his side, he decided this wasn't a bad way to spend a very long time. He wondered if he should call the precinct now, tell them he wouldn't be coming in. Then he could get back to forgetting about the world.

He said, "How long do we have the room for?"

"Just tonight."

"What time's checkout?"

"I don't know."

"Should've asked."

"I had other things on my mind."

"Like what?"

"Haha."

He said, "If I could reach the phone, I could book another night. But there's just no way of getting to it."

"Then I guess we're screwed."

"I'll think of something."

She said, "There's always round two."

Marshall rolled toward her and said, "Two's just getting started."

TWENTY-SIX

Marshall

When he slept he didn't dream. He woke just after seven A.M. and lay in the gloom and remembered New York.

He feared he'd lived on autopilot, too consumed by role playing to see the moral side of things. For a long time he'd been Cold Marshall, concern for good and bad absent from the ruse. Things happened and he reacted, and maybe if the stoic front had been less effort he might have viewed things in a different light.

He might have got out sooner.

He rose and used the bathroom, and then returned to the bedroom and dressed in jeans and a denim work shirt. He liked his sleeves with a good square fold at the elbow, and he spent a moment getting things nice and balanced. Then he donned a pair of steel-capped boots and laced them firmly and pulled his cuffs down to hide the knot. He stuck the Colt in the back of his belt with the shirt hem covering it.

Pacheco to the middle of town was only a forty-minute walk. He took his cash and the pieces of cell phone and his keys and was out the door by 7:30.

• • •

The marshal's office was on South Federal Place in the U.S. District Courthouse. He stopped just round the corner on Washington Avenue and reassembled the phone and switched it on. He dialed Cohen's number.

"You at your desk yet?"

Cohen said, "No, I'm puttin' together a sandwich for my little girl."

Marshall said, "If we're going to have this meeting we should do it sooner rather than later."

"Where are you?"

"Washington Avenue."

"Okay. Why don't you head along to that Anasazi place and get us one of them outdoor tables on the patio."

"All right."

"I'll be along directly. Order me some French toast, I reckon it'll beat me there."

Marshall said, "See you soon."

He found an outdoor table for two and moved the chairs so they could sit side by side with their backs to the wall, the table between them.

A waiter poured coffee and Marshall ordered Spanish eggs Benedict for himself and French toast for Cohen, as requested. The food took ten minutes. Another two, and a Lincoln Town Car pulled up at the opposite curb. Lucas Cohen got out and blipped the locks and crossed the street, one hand on his tie to keep it flat in the breeze. Neat as a razor in gleaming aviators, silver star on his belt bright against his all-black getup.

He sat down and put a dash of cream in his coffee, looked out across the street as he stirred. A tired smile under the lenses, like the world was a tough place and coffee in the sunshine was a welcome refuge.

Marshall said, "You ever tempted to go all out, dye your hair black as well?"

Cohen leaned forward a fraction, laid one thigh across the

other. He said, "Can't say I haven't toyed with the prospect, but truth be told it's a dangerous thing to pursue." He tapped the spoon on the lip of the mug, sound like a wind chime. "Issue is, where does a man stop? Eyebrows, mustache, nose hair. It's no small thing to undertake a re-color."

Marshall didn't answer.

Cohen said, "Anyway. My Mrs. Cohen approves of the status quo, so I won't be modifyin' anything, 'less there's some change of heart. But let's not go tempting bad luck."

Marshall didn't answer.

Cohen said, "How's the eggs?"

"Fine."

Cohen nodded. "That's been my experience of them, too."

Marshall said, "I still don't know if I'm trusting you or not."

Cohen pushed his plate to the edge of the table so he wouldn't have to twist too far to reach it. "Gave you that stack of Bibles line, didn't I? Wouldn't have said it if I was planning on screwin' you."

Marshall prodded some food round, like checking for signs of life. He said, "Wasn't sure you're a believer. Couldn't tell if you meant it or not."

"I meant it." He tried some coffee, added a splash more cream. "But you're right. I'm about as spiritual as that lump of eggs."

Marshall didn't answer.

Cohen said, "I seen a lot more bad than good, so if they happen to decide he's keener on misery than compassion, sign me up. But until then."

Marshall said, "I need to find Troy Rojas, and I thought you might help me."

Cohen smiled a little as he cut himself some toast. "I can find you some friendlier opponents to play hide-and-seek with. And that's just on our ten most wanted."

"Are you interested or not?"

Cohen nodded. "I am. It's actually his friend Mr. Bolt I've been looking for, but from what I'm told it's a find-one-get-one-free type situation."

"I'd say that's more or less what we're looking at."

Cohen removed his glasses, wiped a lens with his tie. "You made a good mess of your house last night."

"Personal best."

"I spoke to the police lady from APD you saved."

Marshall had some coffee, watched the street. "And what did she have to say? Other than that I saved her?"

"She said you were looking for a missing girl, disappeared down in Albuquerque."

"That's right."

Cohen gave it a bit of time, in case he had more. When there was just silence he said, "So what she didn't know was how you'd reached the conclusion Bolt and Rojas or one of them knows something about it."

"What's it to you?"

Cohen dipped his head, slipped the aviators back on. "Well, like I said on the phone. Just think it'd be prudent for someone of official standing to know what all the pieces are."

"I'm not sure I can be entirely frank with you."

Cohen ate some toast. He used his cutlery like Marshall did, one clean knife stroke at a time. He said, "Get into those eggs or they'll cool down on you."

Marshall ate a few mouthfuls.

Cohen turned toward him and in the lenses Marshall saw his twin reflections in convex miniature. Cohen said, "If I was entirely frank with you, would it put you more at ease?"

"It'd help."

Cohen had some coffee, grinned thinly on the swallow, like downing hard liquor. He said, "Killed a cartel guy up in Farmington couple of months back."

"Good for you."

Cohen didn't answer.

Marshall said, "How'd you manage that?"

Cohen propped his arm along the table, hand hanging easy off the end. He said, "Had a couple of them we were after, two brothers, actually. Got a tip-off one night the younger one was at a motel up there, so we rounded up the staties, moved in early mornin', got him while he was still sleeping. Never saw us coming obviously, pretty clean wrap-up. So that was fine. Problem was the older guy was coming back from something across the street, food or diner or whatever, sees us paradin' his brother out of the room in cuffs. And, you know. Of course he's got a gun with him, so he holds up a car that's coming through, shoots the driver, boom, two head shots, blood everywhere, takes her eight-year-old son hostage, drags him over at gunpoint."

Marshall said, "And you shot him."

Cohen nodded. "I did. Was holstered at the time, so it was a draw-fire thing." He slid his mug in a small circle on the table. "Not to be heroic about it or anythin', but that's how it happened. All sort of frantic and instinct."

Marshall didn't answer.

Cohen said, "Bullet went in his mouth while he was talking too, didn't even clip his teeth."

Marshall said, "Could have done open casket, rigged up a big smile."

Cohen adjusted the glasses, a tiny nudge to get them level. "Indeed they could have."

Marshall said, "Good story."

"Yeah. Point I was working round to is: I've got a wife, not so different to the lady was shot, and two little girls before long'll be eight years old themselves. So given all that, my little Farmington adventure resonated a bit, and I guess I've lost any meager tolerance I mighta had for gun thugs." He chewed and looked out across the street. "Funny, you have a family, kids, you realize you'd do anything to keep'm safe." He looked at Marshall. "But then, what is it about anyone else on this earth that makes them undeserving of the same devotion, other'n that you don't share blood."

Marshall ate his eggs. They spent a moment not talking. At length, Marshall said, "So what's Bolt done that you're after him?"

The wind kicked up, laid Cohen's tie across his shoulder. He restored order without looking down. He said, "He's out of federal lockup on supervised release, wasn't filing his reports, which I believe is a Class D felony all by itself. Anyway. He's got a former missus out in Lubbock, marshal's sent two deputies along to reconnoiter, pair of them met a pretty insalubrious end." He drained his mug. "And I'd say the good money is on Mr. Bolt having a hand in their departure. Needless to say, death of anyone's a tragedy, but to my mind Texas men are among the very finest, so I'm extra saddened by that sort of news."

Marshall said, "So you want him dead."

Cohen made a claw of one hand, inspected his nails. "I think that's a dangerous thing for a federal officer to be putting honest comment to. But I think society would be radically improved should Mr. Bolt stop living. Never met him of course, but Cyrus strikes me as the sort of man doesn't like to go quietly when given the option; check out in a hail of gunfire, if he got the chance. So yeah. I think I'm lookin' forward to seeing him in the flesh."

Marshall didn't answer.

Cohen said, "That nice police detective lady. Shore. She speculated maybe you'd showed Mr. Bolt his grave."

Watching him carefully now. Marshall said, "Speculating's her prerogative."

"Mmm. I guess what I'm fishing for is whether there's any merit to her wonderings, or if it's just a bunch of fanciful what-ifs."

Marshall said, "If I killed someone I wouldn't tell you about it."

Cohen looked at him over the top of the aviators, add some weight to things. "What if I told you that whatever's shared between us during a nice session of eggs and toast remains our private business?"

Marshall sat a while, toying with words, didn't get the feeling he was being taken for a ride. He said, "I don't think you need to worry about him."

"And what about Mr. Rojas?"

"He's still worth investing some serious time in."

Cohen nodded slowly to himself. "Right. I had a suspicion that might be the case."

"Is there a federal warrant out on him?"

Cohen clasped his hands on his knee, tilted his head while he thought about it. "I'm not entirely sure that there is. But I do know APD missing persons would dearly like to talk with him, and he held a police officer at gunpoint last night, so I'd say the feds'll be after him sooner or later." He paired up his cutlery. "Troy's had a busy time, so there's bound to be something in Title 18 he's violated. Section 1201, maybe."

"That the part about kidnapping?"

Cohen nodded. "I do believe that is the part about kidnapping."

Marshall set his fork down, finished his coffee. He sat up in his chair a bit and folded his legs the way Cohen had, and the two of them sat looking out at the street. The wall behind them shadowing the little courtyard, and at the opposite curb the square adobe frontage of the old public library was warm and blemish-free in the sun. The sky a clear and pale blue.

Cohen said, "You going to help me find Mr. Rojas?"

"I asked you first."

"What I meant more broadly is, are you going to cooperate with me?"

"Well. What are the alternatives? Hypothetically."

Cohen smiled, Cheshire cat, like a dentist's brochure. "Hypothetically. I could take you in, put some questions to you about those drugs in the back of your car, or all them boxes of shit stacked in your living room. Asset forfeiture type concern."

"The drugs are fake. And the boxes are my tenant's."

Cohen said, "Unofficially, I believe you. Officially though, we've heard it all before, son."

"Can you make me a special deputy?"

"You be on your best behavior, maybe we'll work something out."

Marshall didn't answer. He stood up, walked around the table toward the door. He said, "I'll pay. Meet you in the car."

TWENTY-SEVEN

Wayne Banister

Eight A.M. he went looking for Sean Frazer. He had visions of killing him in a car, give him the same fate as the old man.

Fourth Street was in a narrow band of development between I-25 and the Rio Grande, not a prosperous-looking area, and Razor Rentals fit in fine. It was in a low off-white building that might have been a grocery store at one stage: big plywood-backed windows facing the street, timber signage along the eave, whited out to leave just a red hue. RAZOR RENTALS had been stenciled over in chrome blue.

The building adjoined a large concrete lot, chain-link fence along the other three sides, a wide swing gate to permit vehicle access. There were maybe twenty cars parked in there: sedans, SUVs, a few pickups. Nothing less than ten years old. Down the back he could see an old Dodge Charger with its hood up, two Hispanic guys leaning in over the engine bay.

Wayne parked a block away and sat watching. No traffic. The storefronts tired, untenanted. A bars-over-windows type of neighborhood. He took the red phone from his pocket and looked at it and thought of calling home, but he didn't. Too great a distraction. Talk to the child and all those moral questions start weighing in.

It's just a job, you're good at it, it's a single-variable problem: How are you going to do it this time?

He sat there working it through, watched the two guys jack up the front of the Charger. A moment later the quick squeal of a pneumatic wrench. He leaned and put the phone in the glove compartment and checked his mirrors. Then he got out and blipped the locks and crossed the street without looking, buttoning his jacket as he walked.

There was a steel security screen over the front door, but it wasn't locked. He stepped in and mariachi greeted him, radio cranked way up to catch a weak signal, the noise equal parts static and music. He was in a small office, a new partition in the front half of the original building, bright new gypsum board on the rear wall. No cameras. There was a fat guy of about fifty wearing a ball cap seated behind a desk, a Jewish man in full black attire bent over to sign documents. Sidelocks gently pendulous as he wrote. A door to the left accessed the lot, and the shrill tone of the wrench was clear over the radio.

Wayne stood at the entry until the customer had left with a key, and then he sat down in a torn office chair on casters in front of the desk. He rolled himself back slightly so he could see through the door to where the two guys were working on the Charger.

The man behind the desk gathered the documents and tamped the edges square. He said, "Been doing this a while, but that's my first whaddya call it. Orthodox Jew. All dressed up like that."

He looked out at the lot, like the sight of the guy had been some kind of rare spectacle he wanted to savor. "Asked for one of them people mover things, but we didn't have one, had to give him an SUV. Funny, knew a guy in Brooklyn did this, said Jews always want big cars. Especially on weekends, you know, move their big families around."

Wayne sat quietly, and when he felt they were done with Jews he said, "I'm looking for Frazer."

"What?"

Hard to hear over the radio. Wayne turned his fingers in a little dial motion and the guy leaned and turned down the volume. The noise faded back to static only.

Wayne said, "I'm looking for Frazer."

The guy dropped the papers in a drawer, scraped it shut. "Which one, Senior or Junior?"

Wayne thought about it and said, "Either."

"They're not here. You can leave a message I guess."

"I'd rather just talk to them."

The guy shrugged.

Wayne said, "It's Junior I'm really after."

The guy leaned forward, put his elbows on the desk. He smiled and touched his hat brim, pushed it back a fraction. He said, "If it's a rental you're after I can probably help you."

"I'm not after a car."

The guy didn't answer.

Wayne heard an engine start and watched the man in black ease a Subaru Forester out the gate onto the road. He said, "You know where Junior is?"

The guy spread his hands. "Look, he's on an errand."

"Where?"

"I don't think he'll be too much longer."

Wayne smiled, patient. He put a foot up on the edge of the desk. "Is there anyone else here who might be a little more forthcoming?"

"Forthcoming. Well, what's your Spanish like? You could try those two out there." He laughed.

Wayne leaned back and looked at them. The old wheel was off and a new one was being rolled into place. Give it a minute and that wrench would be up and running again. He drew the silenced SIG from the shoulder holster and propped it on his raised knee.

The guy's face went slack and his mouth fell open very slowly. He cleared his throat but kept his voice low. "You don't, we can." He closed his eyes, showed Wayne his palms. "Just, relax."

Wayne said, "I am relaxed. What do you think relaxed is?"

"Just. You don't need that."

"Where's Frazer?"

"I don't know where Emile is."

"I told you. I'm after Junior."

"What for?"

He was watching the gun. Wayne said, "You just need to tell me where he is."

"Okay, okay." Head lowered as he spoke. "He's at Andrea's. You probably drove past it. That Mexican place. He likes breakfast there."

"Back a couple blocks?"

"Yeah. Two, three blocks, not far. Look, man, I just do the car stuff, I promise. I have absolutely zero involvement in, you know." Eyes still downcast, like if he didn't look it wouldn't happen. "The other stuff they're running. I mean, I know nothing about it."

Wayne said, "But you do know there's other stuff they're running."

The guy didn't answer.

Quiet a long time and then finally the squeal of the wrench. The guy looked up slowly. "We good?"

Wayne nodded. "Yeah, we're good."

The wrench again, perfect sound cover, and Wayne squeezed the trigger. The round caught the guy on the bridge of the nose and sprayed his brains on that clean white gypsum. The limp corpse tipping slowly back, squeak of springs as it went almost horizontal, like a dentist's chair.

Wayne let his breath out.

Blood and pink matter dripping on the floor. A final blast off the wrench. He took his foot off the desk and stood up and holstered his piece. Sharp smell of gun smoke. Standing in the doorway watching, one hand on the frame, was a little boy about four or five years old.

Wayne still had his hand on the SIG. He said, "Ah, shit."

• • •

He drove slow to Andrea's. It gave him time to call home. Bad form being diverted midjob, but he needed to hear her voice. He dialed on the red phone, and she was always so happy it was him.

He could see the sign up ahead, but he still got to talk to her for two blocks, and it made the rest of it disappear.

Andrea's Restaurante Mexicana was in a low concrete-block building opposite a supermarket turned Mormon headquarters. A security gate covered the door and there were mesh screens over the windows, the steelwork all bright yellow, like it was purely adornment.

There was a line of cars parked nose-in at an angle along one side of the building beneath a metal verandah. Wayne turned in and parked next to a gleaming red Humvee and got out and locked the car and walked around to the front. A sandwich board at the curb announced today's special: sopapilla with green or red chili. He went in, and more mariachi music greeted him, probably the same station as the dead man's. To the left was a counter and register surrounded by potted plants, and behind it a door through to the kitchen. Two families of four seated separately, and down the back facing the entry a man of about thirty eating alone.

Wayne went over and pulled out a metal chair and sat down opposite. He leaned forward and rested his clasped hands on the edge of the table.

The guy looked up. He had Emile's features but with less droop and less neck. He wiped his mouth with the back of a wrist. "Help you?"

Wayne said, "I'm the Dallas Man."

Frazer laughed quietly and looked around. "Well shit, I wondered when I'd see you." He let his fork drift idly through his meal, like doodling on a blotter. He had rice and enchiladas in a big plate of green chili. He said, "Haven't heard from Dad since he met you yesterday."

Wayne said, "Not answering his phone?"

Frazer shook his head. "Nah, nothing."

Wayne nodded slowly. He clucked his tongue. He said, "Doesn't that make you wonder a little?"

"What do you mean?"

"Well. Doesn't it make you wonder? About where he might be?"

The guy didn't answer.

Wayne said, "Why didn't you have the special?"

"What?"

"Why didn't you have the special? Sopapilla."

The guy chewed some enchilada. "I dunno, I don't like it as much."

Wayne sat watching him over his clasped hands, the other man clearly unsettled.

Frazer said, "Do you know where he is?"

Wayne nodded. "Yeah, I know where he is."

Frazer loading another forkful, waiting for it.

Wayne said, "He's in the desert out west with a bullet in his head."

The fork was en route to Frazer's mouth when he dropped it on the table. He gave Wayne the same slack expression as the guy at the desk.

"Jesus, you killed him?"

His hand went to his mouth and his voice broke on the last word.

Wayne said, "It was a conflict-of-interest issue. He wanted me to take out someone I'm already working for. It was just a professionalism thing."

He unwrapped the napkin from his cutlery and wiped up the spilled mouthful and balled it carefully.

Frazer's lip wavered, eyes filling as he looked at him. "God, you really killed him?"

"I really killed him. Keep it together, we don't want a scene."

Frazer started panting, glancing around, touched a hand to his brow. "God. Shit."

Wayne said, "Just keep it together. You've got an important decision to make."

Frazer leaned back, gripped the edge of the table. This little moment of desperation and the mariachi music just pushing on cheerily. Wayne liked the juxtaposition. He said, "We can either do it in here, or we can do it outside in the car." Hoping for the car. Like father, like son.

Frazer panting through his teeth. "Do what?"

"Guess."

The guy didn't answer.

Wayne said, "What, you think this was a courtesy call? Let you know what happened?"

Frazer wiped his brow, looked at his knife. Not worth the risk: no point on it.

Wayne said, "That your Humvee out there?"

"You piece of shit. Go to hell."

Wayne gave that a few seconds' grace and then he repeated the question.

Frazer nodded.

Wayne said, "I always like guys like you. You know. Most days you got plenty of attitude, drive the sort of car that lets people know it, but then you hit a situation like this and we're not getting much of a fight. Could of stabbed me with the fork or something."

Frazer didn't answer.

Wayne said, "You can choose where we do it, and you're probably best to go for the car. I've got a gun in a shoulder rig so I can draw pretty fast, and I don't think you'd have much hope. In the car I'm more hemmed in, so you'll have more of a show."

Disbelief in the guy's face and Wayne felt duty bound to answer the unspoken question. He said, "If I give you some options it eliminates the certainty of the outcome. It's a gamble, which is sort of the essence of life. That element of unknowing. Suddenly we're within a spectrum of likelihoods, which is more fun for me, because there's that suspense factor, which is what we live for, and what you might die for."

Clench-jawed silence and then Frazer said, "Where is he?"

"I told you. Out in the desert."

Frazer didn't answer.

Wayne said, "He was telling me he wanted to get to someone called the Patriarch. You know anything about that?"

Frazer shook his head, eyes full of tears.

Wayne said, "I thought that might be the case. You want to finish your meal, or shall we head outside?"

Frazer chose the latter. Wayne left money on the table, a careful pincer motion so he wouldn't leave a print, and then followed him out and round to where the Humvee was parked. He could see Frazer was unarmed.

Wayne said, "You want driver or passenger seat?"

Frazer said, "Passenger."

Wayne didn't answer, just slid into the driver's seat when Frazer unlocked the car. Frazer climbed slowly in and closed his door and then there was just the two of them and the quiet and Frazer looking at the glove compartment.

Wayne said, "What have you got in there?"

Frazer didn't answer. He closed his eyes.

Wayne said, "You're not going to be much good for it if you're not looking."

"How did you find me?"

"I went and talked to the guy at the shop."

"Oh, god. You didn't hurt my boy?"

Wayne shook his head. "No, I didn't hurt your boy. I've got a little girl not much older."

He cupped both hands round his mouth and nose. "So he's okay?"

"Yes, he's okay. Promise."

"Thank Christ."

He lost some posture as he let his breath out, visibly shaking. Truth be told, "okay" was a slight embellishment: Wayne had locked the kid in the office with the body.

Frazer back to staring at the glove compartment.

Wayne said, "You have to make a move at some point. Otherwise I'll have to, and you'll just be a bystander to something you could have intervened with. Maybe."

Frazer didn't answer.

Wayne said, "Situation like this, it's better to take an active role. You're changing a certainty into a small chance in your favor. So why wouldn't you?"

Frazer choked as he said, "Why are you here?"

Wayne said, "Bad luck really. Your father tried to hire the wrong man. Sometimes that's just how it goes."

Frazer wiped his eyes with his wrist. "Maybe we could make a deal."

"I don't think so."

"No, wait, just listen. I've got information. We know the other players down here. We've got workups on all of them."

Wayne said, "Show me."

"You've got to let me walk away from this."

Wayne shook his head. "I haven't even seen what you're offering yet. We're still dealing in hypotheticals."

"Okay, just . . . Let's take it easy."

He wiped his eyes again, turned very carefully on his seat and eased his wallet out of his pocket with two fingers. Wayne sat there calmly, looking out the windshield. Frazer opened a zippered pocket and removed an SD card.

"I'm not shitting you, we've got everything. Names, addresses, phone numbers, access codes, stock levels, all of it. We had these ex-Mossad guys do it. Like, total pros, we don't even know what they look like."

Wayne held out a hand. Frazer gave him the card. Wayne said, "You have photos, too?"

Frazer raised his hands. "Man, it's thirty-two gigs. We have everything. Honestly, that's a hundred grand worth of intel, right there."

Wayne didn't answer.

"What do you say?"

A few seconds of tense quiet, just Frazer's breathing. Wayne kept his eyes straight ahead, slipped the card in his jacket pocket, and then he went for it, swung the fork he'd taken off the table in the restaurant and stabbed Frazer in the left carotid.

Gouts of blood hitting the windshield and Frazer sat thrashing and clutching his neck. Wayne got out of the car and used his sleeve to clean blood off his face, wiped the door handle with his tie. He took the fork with him.

TWENTY-EIGHT

Rojas

He was wrecked.

He'd had visions of a nonstop drive, reaching his mother's place that day. The look on her face when she saw the money. He could picture it: hands to mouth, eyes bright with tears.

Three million cold.

And a Colt .44, dead cold.

But an hour on the road and he felt himself drifting, the road yielding to dreams. He kept seeing that cop. The fear of being wanted fought the trauma of Bolt dead. The money kept him grounded. He was almost high on the smell of it. The warm, giddy hit of perfect, endless promise.

Three A.M.

He was southbound on 25, turned off at Bernalillo onto U.S. 550. He found a motel less than a quarter mile off the freeway. The night guy was in a worse state than he was: slouched on the counter, eyes hidden under the peak of his cap.

He could smell his own sweat, but all he could do was lie down. He fell on the bed and dropped the bag on the floor, reached for the gun and slid it under the covers beside him.

He smiled before he drifted off. When was the last time he'd done this? Safe behind a locked door with no one he couldn't trust.

He woke a little after eight. Nothing gentle about that morning: azure sky promising awful heat, four lanes of heavy traffic out on 550. There was another motel across the street, handful of cars in the lot, a Ford Bronco just pulling in. A pizza place on the right and a gas station to the left, sign on its pole probably the tallest thing for miles, just a flat, tan plain all the way to the northern tip of the Sandias, blue-green coming into summer.

He showered, and he reckoned he'd pissed at higher pressure, but it still felt good. Cleansing in more ways than one.

He left his shirt off, water beaded on his torso, just like Leon would do it.

I'm the new king.

He stuck the .44 in the back of his jeans, like Leon had with the Ruger, and picked up the bag and tipped it on the center of the table. The bills piling and spilling, that lovely smell. He drew back a chair and sat down, hair in his eyes, drips running down his back.

I'm the new king.

He started stacking.

Ten bundles, a three-four-three lineup, a hundred grand. He pulled it toward him and sat cradling it.

It took him more than five minutes just to count it all.

Not a bad first guess. Total value: $3.1 million. He slipped a bundle in his pocket, got up and walked the room, giving it some swagger.

This is what it feels like. So loaded, 10K is just petty cash, don't matter if you drop it.

Get used to the feeling.

He paced in front of the bed, fists clenched, riding the rush. He drew the Colt and held it sideways at eye level.

Guess what's in my pocket, asshole. Ten grand. You know how it got there? 'Cause when some dipshit gives me attitude, I drill them and take them for what they're worth.

And I've been doing it a long time.

Think you're smooth, Leon? I just rolled you.

He stood in the bathroom and gave the mirror some poses. Hair raked back, leaning on the basin, bringing the gun right in close.

Colt .44, asshole. Pray I don't pull.

A cold laugh for a fake antagonist: I've got three million cash, man. I don't care who's chasing me.

He cruised the room again, gun out, giving it heaps of cool, used the cell phone and called his mother.

Marco answered.

Rojas said, "Put her on." He jabbed the pistol for emphasis.

"Don't give me that attitude, man."

Rojas cocked the gun, wondered if he could hear it. "You tell that to me when I'm standing in your face, see if you can take the consequences."

No reply. He heard the phone being passed round, murmurs like they were still in bed. His mother came on.

"Why you gotta talk to him like that all the time? Troy?"

He was still on the move, chest thudding with the hype.

"I got it all, Ma. I'm coming to see you."

"What? Troy—"

"I'm coming to see you. You're not going to believe how much I got till you see. But I'm coming. I might even be there today."

"Troy, where you get it from? I don't want no crime money. Where you get it?"

He laughed.

"Troy—"

"No, don't worry. Ma, it's been coming to me a long time and finally it's here. It's been coming to you a long time as well, you just maybe didn't know it. But now all you got to do is wait, sit tight."

She didn't answer, but he had momentum, didn't let things ebb. He said, "How many times in life does good stuff just come to you? People always saying, you gotta go out and make your own luck, all that shit, but not today. You just got to sit there, and it's fucking coming for you."

He nodded the beat for the last line, water flicking from his hair.

She said, "Troy, your language, please."

"Ma, don't sound so scared. It's all okay. I'm coming to see you. You don't gotta worry about a thing ever again."

"Troy, where you get it all?"

"Forget it, you don't have to think about it. It all works exactly the same."

He ended the call, cutting her off in the middle of something.

Exactly the same.

He dialed Troy Junior, wouldn't the kid be proud, but he didn't answer. Probably juiced on something. He tossed the phone on the bed and started bagging the money, a soft buzzing as another call came through.

He collapsed across the bed, answered without checking the screen.

Leon said, "Why'd you do it?"

Rojas didn't answer, caught off guard.

Leon said, "You left that photo on my desk upside down. So that was the first clue. And then of course the money's gone, so I put it all together pretty quickly."

Rojas found his voice. "It'll work out. You can make some more."

"I'd like what you've got, too. Seeing as how it's mine."

A minute ago he'd been humming, but it was hard to keep it up, talking to Leon. Man put a frost on anything. He said, "That's not going to happen."

He heard the crack in his own voice.

Leon didn't answer.

Rojas said, "I only ever wanted to make money. But it just got too heavy. It isn't what I wanted. I mean, Jesus. You cut up Cyrus."

"Doesn't matter if it's what you want." Quiet a while, like there was a tough lesson coming: "When there's dollars at stake you have to accept some amount of moral abandon. I mean, you give a man enough, he'll cut all ties with decency, just the way it is. World we live in, Troy, there's no act can't be bought. Maybe you know that already."

Rojas didn't answer.

Leon said, "Have you looked out the window this morning?"

"Don't think you can screw with me."

"I'm not. It's a nice morning down there in Bernalillo."

Rojas almost threw up in his mouth. He sat up on the bed, everything suddenly very hushed. Don't be stupid—

Leon said, "Didn't you know I have trackers on the cars?"

He got up and checked the window, just a peep at the edge of the blind. "Prove it."

"I just did. You're in Bernalillo."

"Sorry."

Leon laughed. "Bear with me. You see that motel across the street? There're guys in a room on the upper level. Just be careful when you step out the door."

Shit, that Bronco that showed up.

Rojas didn't answer. Leon probably heard him let his breath out, sensed the panic gaining ground.

"If there's a window out back, you'll see a parking lot across that vacant lot, couple of guys in there, too."

Come on, get back level with him.

"Maybe I'll just call the cops on them."

But his tone said he'd never follow through.

Leon laughed. "Not a good game to play. You've got a dead man in your truck, remember? All chopped up, Dahmer-style."

"I dropped him off miles back."

"No you didn't. I've got the GPS record right here."

"Jesus." He was pacing again, not in a good way. "What do you want?"

"I want my three million back. Or three point one, whatever it is."

"So let me the fuck out of here, or I'll burn it."

"That wouldn't be a good idea at all. Have a good day, Troy. Vance'll be along soon. Don't leave the room."

End of call. He pictured a heart-rate monitor, every time. That flat tone sounded like doom.

He dropped the phone on the bed, pulled his shirt on, so frantic he almost ripped it. There's got to be an angle. He crouch-walked to the window, risked another glance. Just a normal-looking morning out there. They could be anywhere.

Jesus Christ.

He checked the lock on the door, and then pocketed the phone and knelt beside the bed. He heaved and turned it up on its long edge. Pillows tumbling to the floor. He steadied it and moved to the end and gripped the base, hands and knees both, and dragged and shuffled and leaned the thing against the window. A few good kicks along the bottom edge, get it sloping even, a solid backstop for the glass.

Relax, you're safe in here.

The shirt clinging to his back, probably more sweat now than shower water.

The room suddenly dark, he almost needed the light. Things were going to get warm, trapped in here with closed windows.

There's got to be an angle.

He thought for a moment. Then he took the phone from his pocket and dialed a number. Straight to voice mail.

"Shit."

He jammed it in his pocket again and drew the Colt and checked the bathroom window. Frosted glass, hanging open an inch. He tugged it closed, a sudden furtive flick, like testing an electric fence.

He left the bathroom door open so he could hear a break-in and sat with his back against the partition wall, facing the entry. Legs in a V-shape like some mannequin dumped there. He leaned and pulled a chair over from the table, used it to prop the Anaconda, keep the door handle in his sights.

The phone rang again.

He fumbled it without looking, scared to take his eyes from the entry, hit the button.

Marshall said, "Troy, just returning your call from a moment ago."

Like they were fucking pals.

Rojas said, "Hey, look, things have changed, I've got a deal for you."

Relief in his voice, faint and breathless, sounding like a little bitch.

The guy said, "Uh-huh."

Relaxed and smooth, like this wasn't a new dance. It made him want to spill it all the faster:

"Shit's been shaken up, forget about what I said yesterday. Look. I'm at a motel down in Bernalillo, I've got three million cash right here, if you get me out I'll split it with you."

"What's the situation, Troy? You're sounding kind of wired."

"Shit. It's kinda complicated. The guy me'n Cyrus were working for's gone kinda funny. I'm stuck here in a room, he's got cartel guys staking it."

"Because you stole three million dollars from him?"

"Yeah, you're a fast learner. Jesus, look, it's easy. He says he's got two guys in the upstairs of a motel across the street, probably with a long gun on me or something, someone else in a parking lot out back covering the rear."

"How does he know where you are?"

"He tracked my fucking car, okay?"

Marshall said, "That was silly."

"Yeah, fuck you. Listen. If you come and get me the fuck out of here, I'll tell you everything you want to know. About the girl, where she is, everything. And I'll cut you in on the three mil. But you need to get here literally now, otherwise I'll be dead and you'll be too late."

"I don't care about the money. I just want to find the girl."

"Okay. All right. I promise, you get me out of this, I'll give you all of it. Anything you want to know, I'll talk till I fucking bleed. But you gotta get me out of this. They're going to kill me."

"Is she alive?"

"Yes, she's alive. I promise you. I promise you she's alive. But please, you gotta hurry, he's sending Vance to kill me."

"Who's Vance?"

"He was at the house yesterday, you musta seen him."

A long, awful quiet on the line, and then the guy said, "Where exactly are you?"

TWENTY-NINE

Marshall

When he went inside to pay, he'd reassembled the phone and discovered Rojas's one-word message: Shit. He stepped outside and stood by the table and called him back, Cohen in the car with his window down, watching the little exchange. After he clicked off, Marshall walked across the street and stood with a hand against the edge of the roof, one leg crossed and tiptoe.

Cohen nodded at him. "You still got the moves."

"Like what?"

"Like how you're standin'. Probably straight out of the NYPD manual of how you talk to a feller sitting in a motor vehicle."

Marshall didn't answer.

Cohen said, "Who was that on the telephone?"

"Guess."

"Huh." He put a hand on the top of the wheel. "Speak of the devil. He say where he was?"

Marshall said, "Can you and I arrange a little deal?"

Cohen smiled at him pleasantly. "I thought we just did. You arranged to help me."

"He's holed up in a motel, says if I come see him he'll answer some questions."

"Questions about what?"

"Alyce Ray."

Cohen worked his jaw, savoring the breakfast, pondering this and that. "So he does know."

Marshall didn't answer.

Cohen said, "And what's the catch?"

"If I bring anyone, he won't cooperate."

"Well now. That's an absolute classic, isn't it?"

Marshall nodded. "It is something I've heard before."

Cohen started the engine. "Where is he?"

"Are you and I just going to have a quiet look?"

"We'll reassess when we get there. I ain't making no promises about a thing I never even seen. But you can ride shotgun, I'll grant you that."

"If you call people in and he makes them, he'll take off. Or get ugly, might be his more likely reaction."

"So we'll check it out first. I got no problem with that."

It sounded honest. Marshall looked at him a while, trying to see the hidden angle, but didn't feel he was being taken for a ride. He hoped Cohen wouldn't hold a grudge. He said, "He's in Bernalillo."

"Get in."

"I've got a .45-caliber pistol in my jeans, that going to be an issue?"

"You got a concealed carry permit?"

Marshall said, "I'm a skilled and responsible owner."

Cohen whistled through his teeth. He said, "Get in the car."

THIRTY

Marshall

Santa Fe to Bernalillo was only a forty-five-minute drive south and west. Cohen took the 84 out of town, called the New Mexico State Police when they turned onto I-25. He said they had a possible Rojas-related situation developing down in Bernalillo, please have people on standby, further details coming.

When he hung up he said, "What exactly did he tell you?"

"He told me where he was and said come and have a talk."

"Seemed you were talkin' a while."

"He didn't have time to be more concise."

Cohen thought about that. "Right."

Marshall looked out his window. He had a few dilemmas going, namely how he was going to handle these motel watchers, how best to put some questions to this Vance character, lastly and most crucially, how to keep Rojas in one place while events were unraveling, run some queries by him once things were tidier.

Cohen being nothing if not astute, Marshall worried he could sense the issues percolating. That knowing look in his eye, like he couldn't tell you the details, but all the same he guessed it was something noteworthy.

He thought it was best to avoid silence, cut down on Cohen's thinking time, so he said, "I didn't know you had kids."

Cohen nodded. He liked things laid back, drove with his elbow on the sill, a thumb hooked in the wheel. He said, "Well, I do. Think my oldest was still cookin' when we first met. Would've only had my Mrs. Cohen a small while, too."

There were some business cards in the center console. Marshall took one and read it like he was interested and put it in his shirt pocket. He said, "Does Mrs. Cohen have a first name?"

"She does. In fact it's Loretta. And she's not actually a Mrs. Cohen. Kept her maiden name, but I just like to call her that to wind her up a little."

Marshall didn't answer, hoping Cohen would get some momentum, let him just sit there and muse.

Cohen said, "Funny the way I met her, actually. Was at the sheriff's Trivial Pursuit night, Duke Garrett useta run it on a Thursday before his kidneys got bad. And I think it was down to the last question, sudden death. Forget what they asked, but anyway it got read out and straightaway she goes: 'Robert Louis Stevenson!' Which they noted down as correct, and I have to say I took my time, but after a while I shook my head and said, 'No, it's Robert Lewis Stevenson.' Because that's how you say it: Lewis. Even though it's written down 'Louis' you say it 'Lewis,' because that was his name originally until he changed the spellin', but of course he kept the pronunciation. Lot of folks don't actually know that. And I guess she was one of them."

Marshall said, "So who got the point?"

"Well I don't actually recall which way the score fell. The critical thing of course being that I was correct, so in all strictness I should've won."

"Should've."

"Well, like I say. I don't recall."

A mile or two of not talking. Marshall said, "You ever think about that Farmington guy you killed?"

Cohen studied his side mirror. "I think about what might've

happened if I'd missed. But I don't go losing any sleep over him if that's what you mean."

He sucked a tooth gently, very still as he stared off down the coming road, and Marshall knew he was gearing to philosophize. Cohen said, "Way I see it, you go into something with a gun, you're pretty much agreein' that things can be resolved in a bloody manner. So you get what's coming to you. And anyway. I figure if there's a God and he's welcomed him to heaven, I've done him a favor."

"What if he's gone to hell?"

He took a moment with that. "Then it was obviously a righteous shootin', wasn't it?"

Marshall said, "What if he's gone to neither and he's just completely dead?"

"Then he's certainly not worrying about me, is he, so I may's well reciprocate."

Marshall didn't answer. Cohen looked at him, a smile just showing at one edge. "What's with the questions, anyway? You don't give a shit about personal stuff."

"I'm trying to improve."

"I thought you were more fond of quiet reflection."

"I am. We can give it a try if you like."

Cohen said, "All right. We can at least see how we get on. Feel free to cut in with something if it gets unbearable."

2010

There was a gun range in Brooklyn that he used. It was a converted sugar refinery on the East River, probably eighty years old. Brick walls darkened by city grime, a high truss roof underslung with girders, all rust streaks and rivets. Marshall thought it was a good aesthetic. Old steelwork seemed well suited to gunfire.

The morning after his night with Chloe, he got there at five minutes after seven. He'd dreamed of Russian thugs, voices in his sleep telling him Mikhail was dead and now they were coming for him. He didn't know if the guy was alive, but practice seemed like a good idea anyway.

Seven was his normal time. At that hour the only other patrons were diehard enthusiasts, tattooed guys with camo and close-cropped hair, dressed to show they were serious. Just two of them today, adjacent booths, four revolvers each. Marshall only ever brought one weapon, either his service Glock or the Beretta Asaro had given him. He didn't care for modified pistols. He used standard weapons and factory ammunition, and he shot at close distances, ten to fifteen yards. He saw skilled shooting as a pragmatic imperative, not a hobby. When someone tried to kill him it would be close range, no warning, no second chance.

Today he ran draw-fire exercises: tight double-tap shots on side-by-side targets. At his quickest he could clear the holster and hit both in less than a second. Today he was slightly out, 1.10, but he knew why.

Too much on his mind.

A gut-shot Russian gangster he prayed he hadn't murdered, and his night with Chloe Asaro: a bad idea he didn't actually regret.

He shot another twelve rounds, three sets of two double-taps. The timer was hands-free and worked on acoustics. You drew as the buzzer sounded, and the clock stopped on the fourth shot, the second double-tap.

His fastest down to 1.08 now.

Chloe.

He knew even one-time-only was not a great decision, but that was why he came here. Preparation for when a wrong move meant a bullet. Him or someone else. He was resigned to the notion of bad endings.

He shot another twelve. Back up to 1.10. He wouldn't leave until he'd cracked one second. That was Marshall's rule. It had got him this far, and he had a feeling he might need it again, too.

THIRTY-ONE

Marshall

Going on 10:00 by the time they got down there. Rolling slow on 550, the far right lane, getting a good feel for the place.

Cohen said, "Where is it?"

"Said it was about a quarter mile. Just pull in here. There's a Subway."

Cohen indicated and turned in. Marshall unclicked his belt and leaned forward in his seat and took the Colt from his jeans. He checked the load and cocked it and set the safety.

Cohen parked. "That's a fairly serious talk you're gearing up for."

Marshall sat back. Lonely spot out here. The shop's small bright frontage, and beyond it the dry and yellow countryside, windswept grass standing almost plumb on the flat terrain. Gray trees stark and brittle in the clear morning.

Marshall said, "There's another element to this I haven't mentioned."

Cohen was looking at the gun. "Right. Better late than never and all that."

"He reckons there's guys across the street in a motel, probably got a scope on his front door, and then another couple of guys out the back of the place."

Cohen slipped the shades off, inspected them, put them back on. "If you'd mentioned this at the get-go, would've been terrific."

"Then you would've been hesitant about taxiing me down here right away. And that might've been a problem."

Cohen didn't answer.

Marshall said, "Rojas said he's had a falling-out with his employer. There's a guy called Vance coming down to kill him."

Cohen looked out his window along the road, like maybe he could see all this precipitating. He said, "When?"

"Right this very minute, I'd imagine."

"Terrific. A falling-out, that's what he called it?"

"Well. He said the guy'd gone kinda funny."

"Right. And by virtue of them folks across the street he can't go anywhere in the meantime."

"Exactly."

Marshall opened the glove compartment in case there was something good, saw a cheap pair of Wayfarers hiding near the back. Black plastic frame with bright pink legs. He slipped them on.

"Jesus. That's your disguise?"

Marshall nodded. "No one'll think I'm official with these on. What they're doing in your car, I hate to think."

"It's a pool vehicle, gets shared around."

"Right."

Cohen said, "So you intend to do what, exactly?"

"Well. While you no doubt make some phone calls, I'll go check this motel, see where these guys are."

"You gonna come on all gentlemanly, say excuse me ma'am at the front desk?"

Marshall said, "Something like that. Get your backup people some decent info, lock things down nice and discreet before this Vance guy shows up, or Rojas hears a siren and decides he doesn't want to talk to me anymore."

Cohen took the keys from the ignition, twirled them on his

finger. "Why's it you nominated yourself for the checking, and not me?"

Marshall nodded at him. "You're dressed up as Gatsby, so they'll see you coming."

Cohen looked away into the distance, pushed his lower jaw out a bit. "And what makes you think you're adequate?"

Marshall opened his door and put his feet on the ground, looked back across his shoulder. He said, "I've had some practice."

He put the gun in his belt and walked up the highway along the shoulder. Four lanes of intermittent traffic. Low-rise commercial along both sides. Storefronts behind deep parking lots and the parched country beyond.

After a hundred yards, he noticed the motel diagonally opposite. Parked nose-in at a room midway down was the red Cherokee he'd seen yesterday morning. He slowed but kept walking, a dead stop too eye-catching. Nothing really happening over there: a couple of doors open, handful of cars in the lot. Rojas had his blinds drawn.

Coming up on the near side of the street was a pizza place and next to it another motel, two-level, maybe ten rooms top and bottom. A Chevron station on the next lot.

Gas was doing a good trade, but the motel had just seven cars, only two getting pizza. Marshall walked along the drive-thru lane. The girl at the window with the headset watched his progress, didn't say anything. Marshall put his hands in his pockets and kept an eye across the street. Rojas's place still quiet. A door down the end opened and a bald guy in his sixties came out hands-to-hip, appraised the day, went back inside.

Marshall crossed the little strip of lawn at the edge of the parking lot and walked fast for the nearside motel. It wasn't an attractive building: precast concrete panels in lime green. A walkway cantilevered off the upper floor. Reception was in a little annex at the near end. An old Toyota Camry was parked out front, three kids between five and ten on the backseat. The driver's door was open and a woman in her thirties was in the office, leaning on the counter with her arms folded. She glanced back over her shoulder as Marshall entered.

"Nice shades."

"Thanks." He pushed the Wayfarers up on his head.

Through a door behind the counter he could see an office space with desks and a chair and a metal filing cabinet.

No sign of management.

The woman kept an eye on him as he sized everything up and said, "I thought you might work here or something."

Marshall shook his head. "How long you been waiting?"

She checked her watch. She was a short woman, everything about her a tight fit. Feet wedged into tiny stiletto heels, and a skirt that was just a high, taut band on her thighs. A sleeveless top with a deep V-neck struggling to keep everything where it should be. "Dunno. Fifteen minutes maybe."

The room had filled up with her perfume. Marshall pushed through the little swing gate to get behind the counter. There was a computer running, but when he nudged the mouse a window prompted him for a password.

"I don't think you're meant to be back there."

"I don't think you're wrong."

He glanced in the back office. No one home. Instinct told him draw the gun, but he didn't. Keep it quiet, get her out of here.

He said, "I think you'd best find another motel."

"What? We had a reservation, though."

There was a coffee cup beside the keyboard, half full, cold to the touch. Marshall lowered the sunglasses, make things look more official. He reached in his shirt pocket and showed her Cohen's card.

"We've got a bit of a situation developing here, I think it's best you be on your way."

She leaned over to read. "Dammit. You know where a good motel is?"

Marshall said, "Long as it's not this one, or the one across the street there, I'd say they're all pretty terrific."

He stood in the doorway to reception and watched the lot as the Camry drove away, rear suspension nearly bottomed out.

Six cars remaining.

Two Chevy sedans, a GMC pickup, a Ford Focus hatch, a Toyota Prius, a Ford Bronco pickup.

He drew the gun and leaned on the frame and looked along the length of the building. All quiet. From the upper level the view across the street to the other motel would be above the traffic. An unobstructed sight line. Up there right now, someone with a rifle waited at a window.

All he had to do was find them.

THIRTY-TWO

Lucas Cohen

He called the state police back and explained the situation.

They put him through to SWAT. The call went on hold. Cohen drove out of the Subway lot onto 550 and rolled slowly westward on the shoulder. When the motel came into view diagonally opposite he set the brake and sat there with the engine idling.

He waited. A minute. Two.

Over at the motel he saw a tan Chevy Tahoe turn in off the highway by reception and cruise quietly down the length of the building and cut a sharp U-turn and park facing the Cherokee. Two guys about thirty up front, dark close-cropped hair, tank tops, tattoos on their arms.

The call came off hold. A guy called Henry Lee picked up. Cohen had met him a few times. Looking across the street with his chin ducked to see over the aviators he said, "Henry Lee, I'd bet the New Mexico State Police is the last institution in America that doesn't have hold music. Just defies belief."

"Make it quick, Cohen, this is the crisis line."

He could have come back with something biting about how

three minutes was a long time to be left waiting in a crisis, but he let it go. He said, "How fast can you get a team up to Bernalillo?"

"Thirty minutes. But depends what for."

Cohen gave him the gist of it.

Henry Lee said, "You got confirmation on the sniper or is this just a maybe?"

"I'm waitin' on more details. Can you put a team on standby just off I-25?"

What he didn't want to tell him: he had a civilian making inquiries, trying to find the guy.

Henry Lee said, "I think we need more details."

"Here I was thinking I could just say the name Rojas and you'd be straight out the door."

"Some positions would be nice."

Cohen didn't answer. He could see the two boys in the Tahoe looking over at the Cherokee, heads turning as they talked, the driver leaning back in his seat to see past the windshield pillar, passenger checking his watch.

Cohen said, "Just put them on standby. I'll call you back."

He clicked off.

He sat there tense a moment, thrumming the wheel, wondering if he was about to broach a whole new realm of brave, or just plain stupid.

Shit. He shut off the engine and removed the key. If the Tahoe boys moved he'd just have to sit and watch, lest he end up getting sniped. Only way to get them was to move first, preemptive action, don't let them know what's happening.

It was one of his long days, so Mrs. Cohen had packed a thermos. He reached in back for it and had a little pick-me-up hit, started undoing his tie. He took his time with it too, figuring his coming actions probably warranted some serious thought, so he did his best to grasp the full bell-curve spread of likely outcomes while he worked on the knot. Then he pulled the tie through his collar with that whisper noise and looped it round his fingers and laid it carefully on the passenger seat and popped the trunk and got out.

Light traffic. A truck roaring as it down-shifted. He waited a moment, buffeted by the wake. The road straight and endless both ways and confronted by the enormity of the plain with the distant mountains the one feature of note, he got that cold fear of being a worthless element of a much larger thing.

He removed his suit jacket and folded it and laid it in the load space and tugged his shirt from his belt to hide his star. Then he arched sideways and slipped the Glock .40 off his hip and took his backup SIG from the small of his back and put the pistols in the gun bag with the 12-gauge. The Tahoe guys still watching the Cherokee. Nothing happening at the other motel. A beat-up old Camry just pulling out, exhaust mist scurrying behind. Someone at reception, maybe Marshall, half-hidden in the doorway. He slung the gun bag on his shoulder and slammed the lid, locked the car with the remote and walked up the highway toward the pizza place.

As he came along the drive-thru lane the girl at the window in the headphones watched him but said nothing. He went straight in the front door, showed his badge to a kid at the counter, no line this time of day.

"Manager in?"

They were happy to fit him out: when he came outside he was wearing a cap and a T-shirt emblazoned with the company logo and he had a zippered pizza box concealing both pistols. They didn't have anything that could accommodate the 12-gauge, but in all fairness he imagined that was typical of every fast-food establishment on earth.

He stood at the shoulder waiting to cross. Looking back along the road he realized he'd parked the Town Car closer than he initially thought.

The traffic cleared but he hesitated.

What if there's surveillance he hadn't seen? They could have witnessed his little reinvention. Could be cross hairs on him right now.

He didn't move. The road's edge a yes-or-no junction:

Go back to the car and continue living. Cross the street and maybe don't.

Only death cut things so binary. It was hard to overcome: the prospect that what he saw right now could well be his end point. Thirty-five years, love and fear and all the rest of it, and this could be the dreary terminus.

Lord.

It was too much to properly consider, standing at the edge of a highway dressed as a delivery man. When the road cleared again he let his breath out through his teeth.

He started walking.

THIRTY-THREE

Marshall

Across the highway Rojas's Jeep hadn't moved, the blind still drawn. Marshall tensed as he heard a siren and then with little warning a state police car flashed past, headed for the interstate. Marshall held the gun behind him along his leg and stepped out from beneath the balcony, scanned the length of the upper level.

Heart thudding as he broke cover. You could lose your head doing this.

Nothing.

No faces at the glass, no twitches in the curtains.

He kept the pistol at hand and went back inside the office and moved behind the counter and started taking files from shelves.

Insurance, expenses, employment contracts, finally the guest register.

He flipped through, glancing door to page as he read. The check-in form had a box for vehicle make and license number:

There's that GMC pickup.

Chevy sedan, times one—

And times two.

The Focus.

The Prius.

Where's that Bronco?

He licked a finger and walked through the pages. Yesterday. Two days back. A week.

Nothing.

No Ford Bronco.

He kept his eyes on the entry and took a backward step to the office door and glanced in. Keys on a pegboard on the far wall, plastic tags denoting room number. Seven, eight, ten, thirteen, and twenty were missing.

Five legitimate guests, five keys gone. Which implied the Bronco men had taken a master, and probably the manager, too. He'd known it when he saw the empty office. Now the adrenaline caught up.

A near-dead silence, just the computer hum breaking it.

He could see it all converging: Rojas and the answers Marshall needed, locked across the street. A killer inbound.

How much time did he have?

Gut feeling again: none. Maybe these were the final seconds, break-in imminent, a sniper upstairs supplying cover.

He stepped to the desk and picked up the phone and jammed it with his shoulder so he could keep hold of the gun and dialed Cohen. No answer. He dabbed the cradle and broke the line. On the console was a list of numbers, one marked "Day Manager." He punched it in. A short pause, and then on the desk beside him a cell phone started ringing, a cheerful little tune that was dreadful at the same time.

He put down the handset and gave himself a few seconds just to run it in his head, and then he entered the office and took key five from its peg, which he figured was ground floor, center unit. Then he stepped outside and walked along the front of the building beneath the walkway, the Colt .45 still held against his leg. Outwardly calm but as he moved he checked windows and checked the street and checked parked cars and amongst that mental threat register a catalogue of fallback tactics grew, a Plan B if he'd missed something, contingencies if things came apart.

The Bronco was parked midway along, nose-in between units five and six, almost dead-level with the Cherokee across the highway.

His footsteps on the concrete, like a countdown to something.

When he reached room five he keyed the lock and let himself in and left the door open behind him. The same tired setup that always greeted him. He was glad he wasn't staying. He glanced around for what he needed and then checked the bathroom. Across the window a white lace blind was suspended on a plastic-coated wire maybe four feet long tensioned between two screws.

That'll do.

He unhooked the little eyelet at each end and bunched the material in a tight concertina to keep it on the wire, and then brought it back outside.

Standing by the Bronco at its rear wheel, he was out of cover from the balcony, visible from the second floor. Chest thundering as he scanned each way. This range with a rifle, he'd make an easy target. Steady breaths. He counted to ten, just watching.

No sign of movement.

Head still turned to watch the upper windows, he trapped the blind under his arm and dropped the clip from the Colt. He found the latch edge of the fuel door by touch and jammed the steel lip at the base of the magazine into the quarter-inch gap and cranked it violently and popped the flap.

Still nothing upstairs.

Marshall unscrewed the cap. A faint sigh, a haze as the fumes wafted. Odor deep in his nose. He raised the curtain wire one-handed like a spear and pushed it halfway down the tank and withdrew it carefully, a six-inch length of curtain soaked with fuel. He inverted the wire and fed the dry end down the tank again and bent the free section out at right angles, the material wadded tightly at the opening, what he hoped was a good vapor plug.

In the room he took the fire evacuation notice from where it hung from a nail on the fake timber veneer of the bathroom wall and slipped it from its laminated cover.

Irony not lost on him as he used the gas element to light one corner of the paper. A long tongue of flame starting eagerly, dying back to smoky embers as he angled the page carefully, keep it to a slow burn.

The smoke alarm trilled.

Marshall walked outside, smoldered paper held aloft. He touched the blackened edge to the soaked blind and the flames leapt brightly for an instant and then subsided, working patiently on the white lace.

Marshall dropped the paper and walked away, gun in hand, headed for the stairs at the end of the building. A ground-floor door opened, room seven, and a young guy in a tank top stood framed there, aghast, pants gaping at an open zipper.

He spread his arms. "Dude, the hell you doing?"

Maybe he couldn't see the gun.

Marshall glanced behind him, improvised fuse making steady progress. He said, "Might be best you went back indoors."

THIRTY-FOUR

Lucas Cohen

Walking across the highway, over the shoulder, he could feel the point on his spine where the gun sights surely settled. Eyelash to the lens. Aim quivering on each heartbeat. The smooth and gradual tightening of a trigger.

Don't think about it.

Into the motel parking lot. The guy in the passenger seat of the Tahoe glanced at him and then away. He was just a pizza guy. But he saw the front windows were down. It would make things easier.

He looped around the nose of the Tahoe, careful not to look at them, and headed for one of the end rooms. There was a Ford Taurus sedan parked out front. Cohen balanced the box on one hand and knocked on the door. A man in his sixties answered. A lean, tan guy, bespectacled and combed over, neck and waistline just starting to slacken.

Cohen said, "Sir, did you order a double, extra-large pepperoni pizza with mustard crust?"

The guy said, "No, I didn't."

Lucky he'd found someone honest or it might have got interesting. The lid was already unzipped, and he lifted it and peered in, perplexed, like he might be checking an order or something.

"Funny. Told me it's a motel pretty close, but guess they had a mix-up."

All the while wondering how the man would react if he tried for a glimpse of the good stuff and saw only guns. It would take some smooth talking to placate.

The guy nodded across the street, closed the door a little. "Could be that place over there."

Cohen glanced behind him, like noticing the other motel for the first time. "Oh, thanks. I'll check it out."

The guy gave him a nod and a sort of thin parting smile and Cohen turned and the door was closed before he'd even stepped away.

Now it got tense. Just keep everything steady.

He kept the lid up, head slightly bent like he was grappling with something tricky. He walked back across the lot toward the highway, coming up on the driver's side of the Tahoe. The pair of them were still fixed on the Cherokee. As he drew closer the car blocked the view of the motel across the street, and he reached beneath the lid and put one hand on the Glock .40, and then two paces from the truck he let go of the box completely and in a deft move caught the SIG as everything fell. He raised both guns and aimed through the driver's window.

"Gentlemen."

They weren't looking his way, but they didn't get a fright. They both had pistols held low between their knees: the passenger a .357, the driver a Colt M1911 like Marshall's.

The driver had a thin scar down his neck, looked like pink melted plastic. He smiled a little, and Cohen saw he had some gold caps up front. "What you want, pizza boy?"

Cohen said, "Deputy U.S. marshal, actually."

"Not what your hat says."

"I'm what's called undercover. Drop the guns and get out of the car and you can have a look at my ID."

The driver put the Colt up on his knee, very slowly. Then he thumbed the hammer back, just as gentle. No expression, like the hand was doing its own thing. He said, "How dudes get hurt, doing silly shit like this."

Cohen said, "You'll learn."

No answer.

Cohen said, "That thing comes off your knee I'm going to put one through your nose."

"Then maybe take a step back. Less you want my brains on your face."

Cohen said, "Don't push me. I killed a guy a few weeks back, I'm happy to make it three for the year."

Which was a long, long way from the truth, but acting soulless and trigger-happy struck him as tactful, given this was something of a life-or-death matter.

They didn't move. The passenger hadn't spoken. He was tattooed from jaw to wrist, white tank top stark on the ink, prison art by the looks of it.

Movement across the highway: Cohen glanced and saw a black Chrysler 300C with black-tint windows ease out of a parking space and turn onto the road. It slowed as it drew level with his Town Car and then accelerated again and came smoothly along the street and switched lanes and pulled in at reception. Then it rolled quietly through the lot and stopped just short of the red Jeep.

The Tahoe driver saw him looking and smiled, and Cohen hadn't met many people who could do that to a .40-caliber Glock.

He could almost read the guy's mind: Didn't you know we had backup?

The driver said, "Deputy, this isn't something you want to be a part of."

The Chrysler still idling and Cohen saw the driver's door open and as the guy put a foot on the ground something across the street exploded.

A colossal, shaking boom.

He glanced across to the other motel in time to see a blue Ford Bronco leaping off its back axle, a cushion of yellow flame beneath it. A mushroom of black smoke already rising, and as the truck crashed to earth he heard the tinkle of shattered glass, and the guy in the passenger seat of the Tahoe lost some color, ink on his neck gaining definition.

Cohen said, "Drop them, or I'll start counting."

The driver said, "Counting for what?"

Cohen didn't answer, and he could see in his periphery the window of the open door of the Chrysler slowly lowering and when he next looked a man was crouched there with a gun leveled at him two-handed.

The driver drew the Colt slowly up his thigh. "Back off, pizza man."

"And then what? You murder Rojas?"

The guy smiled. "You're first on the list. I wouldn't worry about who's next."

Cohen didn't answer.

The driver said, "Five."

Enunciating clearly, big lip movements the Chrysler guy could read.

"Four."

Jesus.

"Three."

"Two."

Crack.

They all looked.

Across the street on the balcony of the motel he saw a figure with a rifle, smoke from the gutted Bronco a roiling black pillar adjacent, and when he looked back the guy at the Chrysler was slumped dead across his door and blood was running down the paintwork.

That awful sight drew him, and he stayed with it a fraction too long, so when he turned back to the Tahoe the driver's gun was coming up and Cohen fired, hit something nonvital, the Colt still rising and the passenger's .357 coming for him too, and he fell backward and fired and fired and fired, pockmarks in the polished sheet metal, and finally just lay there with both weapons raised and the gun smoke drifting white and acrid. He heard a door slam, but by the time he looked the red Jeep was already speeding backward out of the lot, and shit that's Troy Rojas at the wheel.

THIRTY-FIVE

Marshall

The rifle was a Springfield M25, box-fed with .308 Winchesters. Marshall stayed on the balcony and watched through the scope as Rojas made his getaway, tearing for the interstate. He couldn't risk another shot. He swung back to the Chrysler. Vance was slumped dead on the door. Marshall recognized him from last night. In the short time it had taken him to sight and fire, Rojas had made it to the Jeep.

He scanned left and found Cohen getting to his feet. People were screaming, here and across the highway. The two guys in the Tahoe were motionless and the windshield was cracked and bloodied. This picture of godlike ruin and he'd played a hand in it.

He stood watching for a few seconds, and then he lowered the gun and went back into the motel room where the two men from the Bronco lay dead and the duty manager was bound and gagged in the bathroom.

Marshall checked the bodies. No phones. They were probably in the truck. The first guy had some cash and a set of keys and a canvas pouch of lock picks. He found a knife on the second guy and used it to cut the masking tape securing the manager's wrists. The man spat his gag and lay gasping with weak relief and Marshall knew his frame of reference for terror had been skewed a long way.

"Thank you. Thank you so much. They were going to kill me. Oh, man."

Marshall wondered why they hadn't. He said, "It's okay. Can you stand?"

He helped the guy to his feet.

"Just close your eyes. I can lead you out. Are you okay?"

"Yes. Just get me out. Please." Shaking and pale.

"It's okay. You're safe. Shut your eyes now."

Marshall took him by the elbow and with the man shuffling like an invalid they left the room. The sliding window above the bed had been opened to permit a clear shot, and the table had been moved to the center of the room to support the rifle on its bipod.

Outside, the smoke from the burning truck was blowing in a loose and noxious skein across the front of the building and a few cars had stopped at the edge of the highway. Guests in the other units were at their windows and a woman came out to take the man's other elbow, and Marshall walked with them a few steps and then turned back to the room.

He could hear sirens, several cars inbound. He stood by the table and made a last brief scan. Their final seconds chronicled in blood. Marshall knelt and pocketed the canvas lock pick bag and crossed the unit to the bathroom. He lowered the seat on the toilet and stepped up and pushed the window wide and put one leg outside so he was straddling the sill. The ground-floor units were stepped beyond the line of the upper-level wall, forming a lower roof. He gripped the sash and pulled the other leg through, and then lowered himself carefully. He crouched at the gutter a moment, gauging the impact, and then he jumped down and walked away.

There was a Denny's farther up the highway, a few places past the Chevron station. The motel action had it low on patrons. Marshall went in and checked faces and saw that everyone's attention was with the blue and red lights down the road. He leaned on the counter.

A waitress saw him and smiled. "Hon, you go round wearing pink glasses, people'll wonder."

"Wonder what?"

She shrugged. The gum she was chewing smacked wetly. "I dunno. Something."

"Do you have a phone I can borrow?"

"Yeah. But you got to buy something."

He ordered coffee and paid with his breakfast change. Once she'd poured him a cup she brought him a cordless handset, smiling as she chewed, like there'd been something flirty in the request.

"Thanks."

"You know what's going on down there?"

He looked out the window. Three state police cars and a sheriff's unit over by the Tahoe. Smoke from the Bronco was blowing across the highway. He said, "Car on fire, I think."

"Quite a turnout, whatever it is."

Marshall didn't answer. He sipped the coffee, standing side-on to the counter so he could see the door, and when she moved away he called Cohen.

"Gather it was you who incinerated that truck I'm lookin' at."

Marshall said, "Had to get them out of the room before they shot someone."

"And I imagine that would've done the trick."

"Yeah."

Cohen said, "Where are you?"

"I'm at that Denny's you can probably see."

"You going to come back and give a statement?"

"No."

"Why's that?"

"I'm going after Rojas."

"You know where he's headin'?"

"No. But I'm good at making guesses."

Cohen didn't answer.

Marshall said, "You going to keep the pizza uniform?"

Cohen thought about it. He said, "Maybe just the cap. For when I'm cooking homemade."

"You kill those two guys in the Tahoe?"

Cohen took a moment, like it wasn't quite reality until you put it into words. He said, "Got the driver over the line, but the other one's only halfway there. Just have to hope."

Marshall wondered if that was a wish for dying or surviving, but he didn't ask. He said, "What are you going to do?"

"I'm going to call Loretta, tell her how much I love her and that sort of thing. Right now that's the sum total of my intentions."

Marshall didn't answer.

Cohen said, "Maybe the one savin' grace of this kind of thing. You see the world with a bit of extra clarity, and you know pretty well what your priorities are."

Wisdom applicable to himself, but in a slightly different way. Marshall sipped his coffee, careful to hide the noise. He said, "I'm glad you're all right."

Marshall drank and watched the light show.

Vance dead by the Chrysler. The other thug dead in the Tahoe. The two men dead in the motel room. To him it was the natural outcome, but it would be nice to know the odds. If somehow there existed a great accounting of the world with a cosmic tally of human traits he could see the number that had brought him to this moment alive.

He'd done this a long time and he'd always been on the side of good fortune. But one thing he knew was that all safe bets run their course and eventually even the slimmest chance will manifest as the thing you're facing. Maybe this was his final win. Maybe come next time whatever good luck he'd ridden would be gone, and Marshall with it.

Who would they tell? Probably his mother, wherever she was. His father, wherever and whoever. His private self so carefully concealed, Sarah could never know. Abby would say: Where's Marshy Marsh?

He'd just be a bygone element of someone else's life. Perhaps he already was.

He drained the mug. The waitress asked if it was to his satisfaction and he smiled and told her it was.

Last night's phone call with Rojas was playing in his head:

I'm planning on killing you. That lady cop, too.

Lady cop.

Lauren Shore.

He had another cup of coffee while he thought about what to do. Without exception he placed the mug in the same position after every sip with the handle perpendicular to the counter edge. He had his sleeves down to hide the blood from the two men he'd killed in the motel room, and he buttoned each cuff in turn. When the coffee was finished he picked up the phone again and dialed information and asked for the New Mexico MVD. The call was redirected to an automated service. He listened to the prerecorded options and pushed the button to speak to an operator. A woman picked up.

"New Mexico Motor Vehicles Division, you're speaking with Diane, how may I help?"

Marshall, talking in a murmur, said, "Yes, hi. My wife's just re-registered her car, you might have actually spoken to her. Her name's Lauren Shore, the car's a Chevrolet. Let me see here." He recited her license plate number from memory. "What I was wanting to check, she's actually overseas right now but we're moving in three days, but I don't know if she's swapped the car over to the new address. Sorry, I'm not being very helpful, I don't actually know if she had it on our house, or if it was registered to the office, I normally just leave this stuff to her."

He waited. He could hear typing.

The woman said, "Shore. Chevrolet. Uh. Loma Del Norte Road, Northeast?"

"Oh great, she must have changed it. And number twelve hundred, I think? That's the new place."

"Uh. No sir, I've got eighty-one fifty-six here."

"Oh, of course, twelve hundred's the new office. That's fine, thank you for your help."

"Have a good day, sir."

Marshall put down the phone and walked out.

2010

One of the taskforce safe houses was on Foster Avenue in Brooklyn, a temporary lease above a grocery/deli on the ground floor, only a short walk from the PD's 70th Precinct. When Marshall arrived at nine A.M. the three of them were waiting:

Lee Ashcroft from the NYPD's Organized Crime Control Bureau, Sean Avery from the FBI, and Avery's supervisor, a guy in his midforties Marshall had named the Ray-Ban Man on account of his eyewear.

They were at the table by the window, blinds partially drawn. A narrow view across the street of brownstone frontages, the steel fire stairs a thin black sawtooth on the brick. On the glass in reverse gold print was written EZRA SILVERSTEIN, DIVORCE ATTORNEY. Marshall didn't know if it was part of the ruse, or if Ezra was a former tenant. He sat down.

Ashcroft said, "We sent a unit down along Eighty-sixth, no Mikhail."

Marshall said, "There must have been witnesses. I saw about a dozen people."

Ashcroft nodded. "He was only there a few minutes, two guys came and got him."

"How'd they find him so soon?"

"I don't know. Maybe Lloyd called and tipped them off. Who knows."

Marshall didn't answer. Ashcroft was fiftyish, a big guy going bigger, stomach the main culprit. Neck approaching the girth where the top button would be a touch-and-go affair. Avery was your standard government man: polite in a kind of cool and detached way, no real spark. Nothing unpleasant, but nothing you'd look forward to seeing again. The Ray-Ban Man seemed to be cut from the same cloth: a trim gray suit to match his trim gray haircut, quiet and concise, an air of oncologist about him. Accustomed to bad news, and good at being polite with it. Right now he sat with arms folded, back against the wall beside the window, head turned so he could look out along the street. On his right Avery held his mirror pose, between them both directions covered.

Marshall said, “I want out.”

Nobody answered.

The Ray-Ban Man’s sunglasses were on the table in front of him, folded in a square by way of hinges at the bridge and temples. He looked at them and then looked back out the window and said, “Is your cover compromised?”

“I don’t think so.”

“So as far as he’s concerned, you’re just a bent cop?” Trying to be gentle with it.

Marshall said, “Uh-huh.”

“So what’s the issue?”

All three of them looked at him, like this would be good.

Marshall said, “The issue is my morals are compromised.”

The Ray-Ban Man looked at Ashcroft, a silent question exchanged: Will you do it, or shall I?

Ashcroft leaned forward, arms on the table, poised to deliver a difficult truth. He said, “It’s the nature of the work. You might have to do things you don’t like.”

“I shot a guy in the stomach. I don’t even know if he’s still alive.”

Nobody answered. Avery traced an eyebrow very carefully with a thumbnail.

Marshall said, “What about that tail job we had last week? That guy in Koreatown who Jimmy Wheels shot?”

Ashcroft said, “Who’s that, the little wheelchair guy?”

“Yeah. Wheelchair guy.”

Ashcroft said, “Midtown South said the transfusion almost saved him.”

“Almost.”

"Yeah. Not quite."

Marshall said, "Wonderful."

Ashcroft said, "This is New York organized crime. Sometimes people get hurt."

Marshall looked at him and smiled. "I appreciate that, Lee. The problem I've got is I'm supposedly doing this for the greater good, except I've got no sense of where the end is and I'm complicit in things I'm going to regret for the rest of my life."

Ashcroft said, "Killing people."

"Well. Killing people who maybe didn't need it. Like maybe that Russian guy from the night before."

The Ray-Ban Man said, "So what do you propose?"

"What do you mean?"

"Well." Delicate, like he knew how this would go. "You want out, how do you think you're going to do it?"

Marshall said, "Like any job. Just don't show up on Monday."

The Ray-Ban Man smiled, doctor with the prognosis. He said, "Are you going to take your uncle with you?"

Marshall didn't answer.

"Or were you just going to disappear and see what happens? Assume Tony won't think to ask Eddie where you've gone. Or that he won't hurt him, either."

Marshall said, "I've been doing this nine months now. I didn't write you a blank check so you could work me forever."

The Ray-Ban Man said, "Yes. But you've got to stay with it long enough for us to make an arrest."

"And when's that going to happen?"

"Eventually."

Marshall said, "What's the Bureau's priority?"

"All kinds of things. We've been through it."

"Yeah, but what's the big-ticket item you want to hang on him?"

The Ray-Ban Man said, "I'm retiring in a month, so goals might get a shakeup. But if you find me the Dallas Man, it would make a nice retirement present."

The Ray-Ban Man chasing the Dallas Man. Marshall liked the namelessness of it. He said, "Lloyd mentioned him the other night."

The Ray-Ban Man nodded slowly, like some private mystery had just gained clarity. "What did Lloyd have to say?"

"Nothing we don't already know: Tony uses him on the tough jobs, makes people just disappear."

"How'd you get onto that subject?"

Marshall said, "He said he was going to have him kill me if I didn't stay in line."

Not a glimmer, nothing. As threats went he'd probably heard worse. "And that was it?"

"I guess it struck him as a pretty good line to close on."

Nobody answered.

Marshall said, "I can't believe after nine months you still don't have enough."

Avery said, "Keep digging."

His one curt contribution, didn't even deign to look at him.

Marshall said, "Did you read my report?"

The Ray-Ban Man said, "All it seems to say is you shot a guy, and Tony Asaro poked someone in the eye with a spoon."

Marshall didn't answer.

Ashcroft made a steeple with his fingers, tips only just touching. He said, "It would be nice to get him on something bigger than assault with cutlery."

Marshall said, "So is this Dallas Man going to be big enough?"

The Ray-Ban Man checked his nails. He said, "If you find him and prove he's been killing people on Tony's dime, then we'll make an arrest."

Marshall said, "Make me a cake, too?"

The Ray-Ban Man smiled. "We'll fly one up from Quantico."

After the Bureau guys had gone they sat in Ashcroft's car, Ashcroft at the wheel with a pastrami sandwich in one hand, coffee in the other. He liked a good deli.

Marshall said, "Do you even know what his real name is?"

"Who?"

Marshall looked at him. "Mr. Sunglasses."

"Uh-huh."

"What is it?"

"He swore me to secrecy."

"Jesus Christ, Lee."

Ashcroft kissed a drip of mayonnaise. "Some of these fed guys get funny about their privacy. I dunno. The guy's very sorta . . . you know. Particular."

Marshall didn't answer.

Ashcroft took a bite, followed it with coffee. Every few seconds he checked his mirrors.

"Shit, you're jittery. We're not having an affair."

"Yeah, well. If there's someone watching I'd prefer to know about it."

"There's nobody watching. I guarantee it."

Ashcroft didn't answer.

Marshall ran a hand through his hair, let that sit between them a while. He said, "Eddie's got a debt with them. They're chasing him for it. Lloyd told me."

"Ah, shit. Eddie your uncle?"

"What other Eddie would I be worried about?"

Ashcroft said, "How much?"

"Sixteen grand."

Ashcroft tilted the sandwich a few different ways, lining up a good mouthful. "Should I ask why he owes it?"

"No. You better not."

Marshall looked out the window, listened to him chewing. He said, "If NYPD gives me the money I can clear the debt."

"Marsh, Jesus."

"It's only sixteen K. Asaro has me on two a week, I've been booking that as evidence for nine months, just take a little back."

"Marshall, I can't."

Marshall turned and looked at him. "So what can you do? Let's try and be positive, if we can."

"Ah, Christ."

Ashcroft tossed his sandwich on the dash, wax paper on vinyl sliding to the corner. He cradled the cup in his lap and looked at his side mirror. "I'm trying to get you out, okay? I'm doing my goddamn best."

Marshall didn't answer. He climbed out slowly and was very gentle with the door.

Round two was at the Hilton on West Twenty-sixth Street. Afterward they lay in bed in the dark, no noise from the street, and across the ceiling the city lights cast long and random through the gap between the curtains.

Marshall, head on one arm and Chloe in the other, said, "Does anyone wonder where you are?"

She arched her back. "I doubt it. I don't have a bedtime anymore."

He said, "What about your credit card?"

She turned and lay against him. Just a darker shape in the dark. Her breath on his neck. "What do you mean?"

"You put the room on Visa. But who gets the bill?"

"I do."

"So it's private."

"Yes, Marshall. It's private."

"I just wondered."

She didn't answer.

He said, "How do you pay for it all?"

"I have money."

"From your father?"

"How else do you think I could afford this?"

"I don't know."

Quiet a little while. He watched the lights and then he said, "Do you ever wonder how he made his money?"

"No. I know how he made his money. Buying property and then selling it for a profit."

Marshall didn't answer.

She said, "Why are you even asking me this?"

Marshall didn't answer.

She said, "Normal cop suspicion? Or cynicism or whatever."

"Something like that."

She said, "You think he's hiding something?"

"Everybody's hiding something."

She propped herself on an elbow and looked at him. She ran the other hand through his hair. "What are you hiding?"

"I don't know."

"That's not an answer."

Marshall said, "Yes it is. I don't know if people hide how much they know about me."

She didn't move, this vague rendering above him in the dark. She said, "That night you called me. How did you get my number?"

Hard to lie in this context. She could feel his warmth, his heartbeat, his breathing. He kept it vague. "I'm a police officer."

"I didn't know the NYPD was that efficient."

He said, "Depends on the situation."

She laughed gently through her nose, and he smelled alcohol from earlier. "Did you tell them there was a girl you wanted real bad?"

"Not quite. I didn't want that on the file."

She didn't answer, and he thought she'd let it go. Her hand was on his chest. Maybe nothing, maybe tracking rhythm, listening for the truth.

At length she said, "Are you hiding how much you know about me?"

"No."

"So you don't know very much."

Marshall gave it a moment and said, "There's only one thing I want to know now."

She lay down again, her head on his shoulder, lips on his skin. "Which is?"

"Would you ever leave here?"

No movement, but he knew she was holding her breath: no

cyclic warmth on his neck. She said, "I don't know. It would depend why. And for whom."

Maybe this was too far, too soon. He said, "What about for me. Because I asked you to."

Still holding her breath. "I thought this was just fun."

"It is."

"So that's a pretty serious invitation."

"You can still think about it. If you want."

She didn't answer. He watched the ceiling, and after a few seconds she started breathing again.

THIRTY-SIX

Wayne Banister

Back at the motel.

Regret was always a delayed effect. Getaways took some concentration. It was often an hour before the don't-be-seen imperative gave way to other thoughts. Not that he wanted to confront it, but the quiet made it weigh on him. You've just killed two people, trapped a kid with a dead body.

He rationalized it based on past experience. Not that he thought it was right, but he'd learned to apply some moral relativism: the world had given him much, much worse. Whatever wrong he'd dealt was negligible in the grand scheme of horror.

They'd been married eight years when she started getting symptoms. Night sweats, back pain, weight loss you could notice week-to-week. She called it early: cancer. He told her don't be stupid. He ascribed it to job stress. He said relax. He came on too glib: most people would kill to get that slim. But then the tests came back: Hodgkin's lymphoma.

Sweetheart, you've got a year.

He had good medical. It covered her exorbitant chemo and pill costs. But she was a fighter. Support groups talked in terms of life lived: you've had thirty-five wonderful years. She saw the flipside: you've got forty-something more ahead of you. She couldn't die and miss out.

She researched and sourced extra drugs. Trial meds lacking FDA approval. The monthly tab ran a solid four figures. He needed more work to meet the costs. The choice was obvious, given his training. He knew how to do it, and he knew how the system operated.

He killed a pimp off Rockaway Boulevard, out by JFK airport. The guy had snitched on one of Tony Asaro's dealers, put the guy in federal for ten to fifteen. Tony wanted the pimp dead. Wayne got wind and put an offer in: thirty thousand, and I can make him disappear.

Tony accepted.

Wayne did the deed and caught the train home afterward. Shakes and nausea at the Broadway Junction transfer. He almost fell on the tracks, but a homeless woman pulled him back.

He remembered getting home early morning, cracking the bedroom door, hallway light across the bed and there she lay curved, thin beneath the covers and weak breath the only motion.

His head a crescendo: chants of What Have You Done drowned all else.

Sitting in his office with the muzzle of the .38 in his mouth and a round waiting. Taste of smoke and iron and the barrel shaking in his clenched teeth. He closed his eyes as he dropped the hammer. No last words and barely a last thought. He screamed down the muzzle and sat gasping when it clicked.

Dud load.

He took it as a sign. If there was a God, God would have killed him. The fact he'd made it through meant there was no higher power keeping watch. He knew unequivocally that the only rule is the rule you make.

She died in August, a month shy of their nine-year anniversary. He remembered the funeral, the hearse pulling away, petals lifting in its wake. Love of his life taken by an unjust world. He felt it set a datum for what was permissible. Whatever you dream of, someone has suffered worse. He called Tony Asaro, tears still in his eyes.

Wayne said, "Let's make this a long-term thing."

THIRTY-SEVEN

Lauren Shore

Shrink day.

There was a room set up at police headquarters on Roma Avenue. She thought of it as the psycho suite. The therapist was one Dr. Cullen, prim and reserved, her office fittingly austere: paperless desk with the laptop computer that always sat closed, the two consultation chairs precisely square, every surface clean and clutter-free. In a sad attempt at warmth, a framed print of a vase with two roses adorned one wall.

Cullen sat down and crossed her legs and smoothed her skirt hem, propped her notes on her thigh. Shore still wasn't used to it, being questioned and observed: a sharp inversion of her normal role. The note-taking was the worst part: this private log of flaws steadily accruing. Every week some new quirk to document. She smiled to herself. It could give someone a complex.

Cullen said, "I understand you had a difficult evening."

Difficult evening. She had a flair for euphemisms.

Shore said, "Yeah. Something like that."

"Are you sure you want to do this now? We can reschedule if you'd like?"

"No. It's okay."

"I'm actually quite surprised you made it in this morning."

"I never left. I stayed the night at the office."

"I certainly would have understood if you wanted to postpone."

"It's fine. I don't sleep much anyway."

The doctor lifted a page, read through prior jottings. "You've mentioned before it's not stress or anxiety that keeps you awake."

"Yeah."

She glanced up, looked back at her notes. "But are you comfortable that's still the case?"

"How do you mean?"

"I just want to make sure you're not losing sleep as a result of something you're dwelling on."

Shore said, "I'm a light sleeper. Always have been."

Cullen noted something, shorthand, appeared to underline it. "Do you want to talk about what happened last night?"

"Well, I don't know. You ask the questions."

Cullen said, "I prefer to think of this as a discussion, and I can just prompt you to address things that could be beneficial."

Shore smiled. "I told the story on repeat for about two hours straight last night, so I'd be happy to talk about something else today if it's okay with you."

"What would you like to talk about?"

"I'm blank. Pick something."

Cullen nodded slowly, read back a couple of pages. The pen waved slowly in her hand. "Okay. Have you been drinking?"

"I didn't really have time."

"I meant in general."

Shore nodded. "Yeah. Every now and then."

"Do you feel you're in control?"

"Control."

"I mean: Do you ever feel that you can't stop yourself?"

Shore said, "No." What she should have asked: Do you ever feel that you *can* stop yourself.

"Do you ever get the impression you're using alcohol as an escape?"

"Okay. I'm not quite sure why we're discussing this."

"Lauren, this is just a routine inquiry. I'm a bit concerned at your defensiveness."

"Well no, it's just you've obviously gone: police detective suffering trauma, must have an issue with alcohol. It's not always the case."

"Yes, you're absolutely right. I'm just trying to establish if it's the case with you."

"I don't have an alcohol problem."

Cullen made a point of noting that. She said, "Okay. Are you still sleeping with a loaded firearm in the bed?"

"Yes."

"Why do you choose to do that?"

"I've explained it."

"Yes, I remember. But I just want to confirm it's a choice that is reasoned and pragmatic and not something irrational."

Shore said, "I'm a drugs detective. People want me dead. I think it's reasonably straightforward."

Cullen appeared to write something to that effect. She stabbed the period with some finality. "You've been a narcotics officer eight years, is that correct?"

"That's right."

"And have you always slept with a loaded gun, or is it just something that's developed recently?"

She didn't answer.

Cullen moved on. She said, "Have you rehung the photographs at home yet?"

"No. Not yet."

"Do you plan to?"

"I'm not sure. I haven't really thought about it."

"Have you spoken to your parents about any of this?"

"They wouldn't understand."

"What about your sister?"

"Same thing."

"Do you discuss work with friends at all?"

"I don't really have friends. I just sort of, well. Over the years I've seen less of them and more of work. But I guess that's often the way it goes, doesn't matter what your job is."

"No relationship?"

"No. I don't think I can risk it."

"Can you explain that?"

"I'd rather be by myself than risk losing someone again. I think that's the safest way. And I can deal with it."

Cullen studied her a while, like she'd admitted she really couldn't cope at all. She made some notes, separate lines, like annotating her last few responses. She looked up.

"Okay. Lauren, what concerns me a little is that you seem to be repeating the same high-functioning behavior from a few weeks ago."

Shore smiled briefly. "High functioning's the aim."

"Not if it's concealing a deeper problem. I want to be sure any issues are being confronted and processed rather than suppressed, so we're not postponing a more severe event."

Shore didn't answer.

Cullen said, "Please bear in mind my comments will be considered when you're reviewed for active duty."

Shore didn't answer.

Cullen said, "I want to be sure you're not just pushing aside what happened last night. Or anything else, for that matter."

Shore stood up. "I'll see you next week."

Back in the car she checked her cell and found a missed call from the main office line. She dialed Martinez.

"Did you just call me?"

He said, "Yeah. Are you still in the building?"

"No, I'm outside. I just had my shrink session."

He said, "We had Bernalillo sheriff's on the phone. They've caught a big shooting at some motel up there, four people dead."

"God. When, just now?"

"About ten A.M. That guy Lucas Cohen from the marshals was there, apparently he's saying Troy Rojas was involved."

"But he's not dead?"

"Rojas? No. They didn't get him."

She turned the key so she could run the air-con. The radio started, and she killed the volume. She always drove with it on. She couldn't sit alone in the quiet.

She said, "So what happened?"

"Well, from what I can gather, Rojas was at the motel and Cohen was lined up to get him, but there was some third-party interference, ended up with a major shots-fired."

She said, "Third-party interference."

"Yeah. I don't have the whole story yet."

"Was it cartel?"

"Sounds like it could be. I'm not sure."

"So what the hell was Cohen doing up there?"

"I don't know."

She said, "Have you spoken to him?"

"No, not yet. Look, you should come back in. I'd feel much better about having someone drive you home."

"There's a unit watching my house."

"Yeah. Well two, actually."

"So I'll be fine."

She clicked off.

THIRTY-EIGHT

Marshall

He'd given the cabdriver vague directions, said he thought the house was on the 8000-block of Loma Del Norte Road. As they approached Shore's address he saw there were two APD patrol cars out front, one at each curb, both directions covered.

"We getting close, boss?"

Marshall was in the middle seat in back, leaning forward to see through the windshield.

"Just keep going. I'll know it when I see it. Maybe speed up a little."

He sat back as they cruised past the first car, speedometer showing twenty-five, the two guys up front ignoring them.

Nothing happening at Shore's place. No sign of her Chevy.

Marshall, counting houses, said, "I think it's actually the next street over. Just take a left when you can. Funny how you think you know a place, but then when you haven't visited for a while it all looks a bit the same."

"I know, boss, I know what you mean, exactly. We just take our time. No rush with anything, eh?"

More than happy to keep the meter running.

"I take a left here, you think?"

"Yeah. Here's good."

As the car made the turn he could see through the side window the two cars just sitting there and no one on the mike.

"Where now? I go left again?"

"Yeah, take another left. We'll do the other side of this block."

Counting down now as they doubled back. No police in sight. A few cars out on the street, but no red Jeep. Marshall's count hit single digits.

"This will do."

"This is the place, boss?"

"This is the place."

The guy coasted slowly to a halt, really eking it out. Marshall took a hundred dollars from his pocket and set it on his knee to fold, make sure the crease was perfect. He handed the bill across the seat.

The guy reached across himself to take it. "Eh. Boss, that's too much, even plus the tip."

Marshall said, "Have a good day."

He stood at the roadside and watched the cab pull away. Its putter the only sound, fading weakly into nothing.

He walked along the street. Beyond the nearside row of houses he could see Shore's roof, just above the fence line. He paused and removed the sunglasses and hooked them in the neck of his shirt and stood smiling in the harsh light. All still. No one watching. The vast cloudscape borne as one on a slow current, like the sky was some fixed socket in which the world turned blindly.

He listened briefly and then he moved off the sidewalk and cut down a right-of-way along a line of town houses to the rear property. Laidback, nonchalant. A small dog yipping, a woman cursing it. Without breaking stride he threaded through the low planting along the boundary and vaulted the fence into Shore's property and stepped out of the shrubs and ran lightly across the yard and stood at the corner of the house with his back to the wall. The gun drawn and raised. His footprints already fading: blade by blade the short grass recovering. He waited. No sound from inside. He eased his head out and risked a look. No one.

He counted to thirty, patient, a little more than half a minute. Then with the gun at his leg he walked down the side of the house toward the road. There was a frosted-glass door just before the garage. He crouched and listened. The little dog still carrying on.

From his pocket he took the canvas lock pick bag and unfolded it on the ground. This bright ladder of utensils, snug in their loops. He put down the gun and noticed the little telephone junction box, twenty feet away at the corner of the garage. The short wire at the base had been clipped. A break-in precaution: cut the phone line so the alarm system can't dial out.

He waited there a moment. The crouch starting to burn.

Do it. You're not going back now.

He looked at the junction box. Close enough to the corner the patrol car up the street could probably see it. He considered that. Then he took a torsion wrench and a small rake pick and on a single held breath opened the lock and returned the tools to the bag and pocketed it. Then he quietly picked up the gun and stood with his back to the wall on the handle side and opened the door cautiously: a gentle underhand motion, thumb and index only, barely a sound.

Gun up as he went in. Left through an empty hallway. The empty garage. The oil-stained slab with cracks wending through. Into the house proper. The curtained living room. Churchlike in its dusty gloom. Police files abounded. Her makeshift home office.

Nothing in the kitchen. She'd removed pictures from the hallway wall. He could tell from where the paint hadn't faded. Her bed made, the quilt rumpled. He pictured her lying across it.

Back down the hallway. He stood a moment at a closed bedroom door. The files in the living room and the photos gone from the wall and he just knew without looking what lay within. Nobody hiding. One of those things you just know and know for sure. It had that long-unopened look.

He went back to the kitchen and sat at the table with his legs crossed and the gun resting on his knee and waited to see who would show first.

2010

Still at the Hilton, still in bed, watching her get tidy. She sat on a corner of the mattress, legs crossed one way and then the other as she slipped on her boots.

"Can you zip my dress up?"

She leaned back so he could reach.

He ran a knuckle up the valley of her spine, her skin soft and sleep-warm. She laughed and arched catlike. He said, "I only know how to take them off."

"Give it a try. It's easy."

He did the zipper up smoothly, kept his hand there when it reached the top. He said, "I want to get out of here."

She moved away and tugged the sheet with her. He made a grab and trapped it waist-high and laughed. She said, "So get dressed."

"Yeah. I mean, away from here. Out of New York. Do something different."

She walked to the window and drew the curtains. On the carpet the narrow band of morning growing wider and her stretched shadow through the middle of it. She said, "How come?"

"Various things."

She sat down again on the edge of the bed. "Work?"

He pulled the sheet back up and ran his hands through his hair. "Yeah. Mainly."

"You don't like it?"

"Basically."

Looking at him quietly, features hidden by the bright window behind. He draped an arm over his eyes against the glare. She said, "Why?"

He said, "I have to do things I don't want to."

"That's a bit vague."

"It'll give you nightmares." He smiled. "I've made you lose enough sleep as it is."

She said, "I'll risk it."

He thought a while, arm still covering his face. He said, "I hurt people."

"Hurt people how?"

He didn't answer. After a moment she said, "So quit."

"It's not quite that easy." He rubbed sleep from an eye. "I think I might have to run away."

"And join the circus."

"It's the circus I'd be running from."

She didn't answer.

He rolled on his side to face her. "Are we always going to do it like this?"

"What do you mean?"

"Well, like . . . Meet at a hotel and then go our separate ways."

She found his hand under the sheet and held it. "I don't know. We've only done it twice. And it's still fun."

He smiled. "Feels like an affair or something."

She said, "Probably help if you weren't trying to hide from my father."

He nodded but didn't answer. He waited a few seconds, building up to it, and then he said, "Would you want to come with me? If I went somewhere?"

His heart thumping with the wait. She squeezed his hand and said, "Where would you go?"

"I don't know. I haven't thought that far. But I will."

She leaned over and kissed him and stayed there beside him. Her shampoo and her perfume. She could probably feel his heart racing.

She said, "I'll think about it."

THIRTY-NINE

Rojas

Shakes made it hard to drive. He held the bottom of the wheel and clamped the wrist with his other hand, trying to keep steady in the lane. He was running on survival instinct, a white-knuckle fear of dying. Not a new experience. He'd been shot at in the Gulf, Khafji in '91, but that was wartime danger. He'd never been a sole target. This morning had been different. A peril for him alone. Sitting with a pistol in his hand in his quiet room, a departure lounge of sorts, he knew that doorway had been given all-new meaning. Those years and years behind him, and in the weighing of good and bad you could reach a judgment about which way he leaned, but the only ruling would be whether he was in the cross hairs and that would be final.

And somehow he'd made it out.

Not a word to his mother but he wasn't a spiritual man, no time for guardian angels or anything like that, but if someone said the devil himself had taken him beneath his wing he wouldn't have argued. If his escape had been a miracle then it was hell's doing, because no moral god would see this as justice. Not with what was planned.

He was southbound on I-25, still very conscious of the tracking unit somewhere on the car, Leon probably watching on his screen, pissed off but not worried.

Getting south toward the airport now. He took the 223 exit and coasted down the ramp. The shoulders just brown-yellow and as he turned west into the suburbs he could see a thin shelf of desert wavering beyond the city, arid out there, like a vision from his new watchman.

He made a right onto Broadway Boulevard and pulled to the curb and sat idling with the turn signal still counting tick-tock. Quiet residential, stunned lifeless in the heat. The bag on the seat beside him with the zip open and the .44 Anaconda waiting beneath the flap.

He patted his pockets for the phone, feeling light when he came up empty. A frenzied dig through the money and he found it at the bottom of the bag. He called Troy Junior, but the kid didn't pick up. Probably spaced out on something, too fried to reach the phone. He tried his mother. It went to voice mail. He almost hung up, but he stayed with it.

"Um, Ma, thought I'd just leave you a message, let you know where things are at."

He tapped the back of his hand on the wheel as he spoke, make it an absolute promise: "I got some things to fix up and then I'll be on the way. I'll be coming. It'll just take some time." He leaned back and pinched the bridge of his nose with his other hand. "I know I keep saying it, but it'll just be a couple of days. No more than that. Anyway, I dunno, I just wanted to say, all the things I've done or been involved with or whatever, it was always because of other people. Like, I kinda get swept along by it. All my life, I dunno, I've been in other guys' slipstreams and it's all just bad luck. But I'm fixing it. I've just gotta do these couple of little things and then I'll come see you, bring you that money."

He paused, thinking of something nice to finish on. He wasn't sure if promises were any good if you made them in a stolen truck with a dead man in pieces in back and three million bucks on the next seat, but he said, "I'm on the good path, Ma. I'll see you soon."

He hung up and tossed the phone aside. Then he bit his lip and sat with his elbow on the sill and the web of his thumb like a visor across his brow. Instinct told him to vanish, never surface again, but he couldn't. Leon would kill his mother, kill his boy.

You have to get rid of him.

He sucked a breath and checked the mirrors, tasting blood. How long had he been sitting here, three or four minutes? He pictured the transmitting unit on the truck, the little dot on the map just hovering there.

Scalding hot in the car. The fan was fucked. He wound the window half-down and reached in the bag and put his hand on the gun. It had a nice clearing effect, made plans come together.

They're tracking the car, so you need new wheels.

Cyrus was still in back, but Rojas had never touched the plastic. Plus Vance and Leon's prints would be all through the car. There was nothing that definitively said:

Troy, you cut the guy up.

Even if they hung it on him, he'd held a police detective at gunpoint last night. Killing an ex–federal convict would just be like a bonus round.

He checked the mirrors again. A car maybe every fifteen seconds. He shut off the turn signal but left the motor running. One knee jiggling anxiously. He could just picture that shot-up Audi creeping nearer in the mirror, swimming out of the haze. Leon with some god-awful weapon on the seat beside him: No rush, just looking for my money.

3.1 million cold.

It had felt good this morning, but his brush with dying made it feel more like a liability.

He kept his hand on the gun. Come on. Shitty little sedans, good to no one. He needed something with guts. A cop car cruised through a junction up ahead and the world went very quiet as he held his breath. But it didn't turn around.

He leaned back in his seat and tried to relax. How long is it now, five or ten minutes?

A little beat-to-shit hatchback coming toward him, and then a white car in his wing mirror. He sank lower. Oh Jesus. Like he'd had a premonition.

Please don't be an Audi.

The vehicle's image sharpening in the heat shimmer as it neared and he saw it was a Mustang, two-door, only a couple years old. Some shaven-headed moron in a flat-peak cap driving. One hand on the top of the wheel, head doing a back-forth rooster thing to the stereo.

He swallowed and felt the adrenaline, and everything mapped itself very quickly. He let the brake off and started rolling, and as the Mustang drew level he swung in behind and accelerated. He reached in the bag and cocked the Anaconda and then he closed in on the guy's fender and started hitting the horn, flicked his lights a few times for good measure.

They reached a red light and both cars came to a stop. Rojas waited a few feet back and put the car in reverse and kept his foot on the brake. Then he leaned on the horn and wound his window down at the same time. He saw the guy check him in the mirror and throw up his hands. Rojas flashed his lights. The guy popped his door. Thud, thud, thud off a subwoofer.

Out you come. Good boy.

Rojas reached across the console and took the cocked .44 from the bag and held it upright just below sill level with the butt resting on his thigh.

The guy got out of the car and left the door open. He had his arms wide. "Man, the fuck. You got a problem?"

Rojas took his foot off the pedal and the Jeep starting rolling backward at walk speed, the guy from the Mustang keeping pace easily.

"Yeah, I thought so. Actually comes down to it, you ain't much. Man, the fuck's your problem?"

Rojas raised the gun six inches to bring the muzzle above the sill and pulled the trigger. The hammer dropped too light: a misfire, just the click. It was like flipping a switch on the guy's attitude: all that posture gone, face suddenly slack. In his hurry to get away he tripped and hit the ground. Rojas opened his door and put a foot on the road and leveled the gun across the sill and waited for the guy to come upright again, and when he did he pulled the trigger a second time and shot him through the back.

The boom took his hearing. World mute beneath ringing, like being deep underwater. He swapped the pistol to his left hand and dragged the bag across the console and stepped out of the truck and didn't bother to close the door.

The guy from the Mustang was spread-eagled, staring at the sky. The left half of his chest in tatters. A pool of blood beneath him, the edge creeping in a very careful pattern through the blacktop. His back arching as he coughed feebly. Pink foam at his mouth. Rojas stood there a moment, as if paying his regards. Like a fleeting overseer embodied some small mercy.

Everything fading out. In what order did the world dissociate? Was there vision till the last, or were there a few seconds' darkness, just before the very end. Alone with yourself long enough to think:

Well, this is it.

The Mustang's engine was still running. Rojas wondered if a broader context could make a thing less wrong. Then he got in the car and drove away.

FORTY

Marshall

Early afternoon by the time Shore arrived. She parked in the garage and came in through the door he'd used earlier, Marshall quietly waiting. When she saw him at the table she stopped with a jolt like she'd walked into something. "Holy shit."

She closed her eyes briefly and glanced in the living room.

Marshall said, "Just me."

She didn't answer. She came around the edge of the counter and leaned against it, not looking at him. She placed her keys in a bowl. "You're lucky I wasn't carrying, might've shot you on reflex."

He said, "I didn't think you'd have a gun."

"What made you think that?"

"I just knew."

"You just knew." Spoken under her breath. "What are you doing here?"

"Protecting you, hopefully."

She seemed more worn out than impressed.

He said, "You escaped a kidnapping. I can guarantee there's at least one person who wants you dead."

"That's why there're cops out front."

"I'm backstop."

She didn't answer.

Marshall said, "Sorry I had to ditch you last night. At the diner."

She folded her arms. "I thought you were going to say sorry for breaking into my house."

"No. The break-in's doing you a favor."

"Right."

"Well. You've had at least two now, so I think you need a better alarm."

She didn't answer.

Marshall said, "Your junction box's been clipped. And it wasn't me."

"Might have happened today. You could have come in and had someone waiting for you."

He shook his head. "Guys out at the road would have seen it. So it wasn't recent."

She didn't answer. Arms still folded she walked around the counter into the kitchen. Very upright and sort of regal, the way her head didn't really move. She lifted the kettle to check how full it was. "Coffee?"

He shook his head. "I've had a few already. But you go ahead."

She leaned against the counter and watched him sitting there while the water boiled. Making an effort to seem composed.

She nodded at him. "How long were you planning on sitting there?"

"I don't know. Until one of you turned up. Which I figured wouldn't be long."

"And I'm first?"

"Evidently."

"How did you get in?"

"Drove past in a taxi and then I went round the other side of the block and jumped over your back fence."

"And then picked the lock or something?"

"Yeah. On that door by the garage."

She nodded slowly but didn't answer. Steam from the kettle

flattened beneath the cupboards above the counter. He watched the door and listened to her find a mug and spoon. A metallic grating as she opened a jar. The jug clicked. She poured, and then she came and sat down, just off to his left so she wouldn't block his view of the door.

He laid the gun on the table and lowered the hammer. Not that he felt any safer than a minute ago, but it seemed like the polite thing to do. Someone else's kitchen.

She said, "How'd you get my address?"

"I called the MVD and asked them. Kind of a long shot. Most cops' info's protected."

She didn't answer.

Marshall said, "Which makes me think it isn't actually your car."

She had a sip of coffee, two hands on a big mug. She said, "Some kind of shootout up in Bernalillo this morning."

"Yeah. I heard about that."

She looked at him. Long dark bags curved beneath her eyes. "You heard about it."

He rocked his head a fraction. "I was actually responsible for some of the shooting."

"What happened?"

The table was circular, no way to place the gun tidily without putting it dead center. He liked a square edge on his furniture so he could line things up parallel.

He said, "Rojas called me and said he was in a motel in Bernalillo and if I came and talked to him he'd tell me what happened to Alyce Ray."

"Your Albuquerque girl."

"Not mine. I'm just looking for her."

"You didn't tell me why, though."

"Yes I did. I told you I wouldn't feel good if I did nothing."

"So this is your standard routine whenever someone's missing?"

Marshall didn't answer.

She said, "So did you talk to Rojas?"

"No. He's ended up on bad terms with whoever's he's working with. There were some other guys there wanted to talk to him, too."

"And that's how the shooting got under way?"

He said, "Mmm."

"I heard Lucas Cohen was involved."

"He was. I'd say he probably still is."

"You're not the easiest person in the world to talk to."

"Yeah, well. Some things're best not discussed too freely."

She didn't answer. Eyes still on the door, he pulled another chair around next to him and laid his arm along the back.

She said, "Why are you doing all this?"

The gun thing was irking him. He put it back on his knee. He said, "Because I want to find out what happened to that girl."

"Yes, but why?"

She didn't mind talking in circles.

Marshall took his time, deciding how to say it, how to pitch it as rational. He said, "Because she reminds me of someone I knew. Few years ago now." The clean and simple basics.

She waited.

He let his breath out, the tough parts imminent, looming in his thoughts. He said, "I thought I could protect her, but I didn't, and I should have. And I'm tired of regretting it." He held the gun up, the muzzle flat at eye level. "So this is my atonement. Finding Alyce Ray."

She didn't answer.

Marshall looked around the room, a smile on his face as a thought came to him. He said, "It's good how luck works. You know. Someone just straight vanishes from their bed, not a trace, it's getting close to the worst kind. But then to have someone like me looking for you just because I'm reminded of somebody else is a hell of a good turn. So I like to think I'm doing my bit to balance things out. Agent of karma, something like that."

She didn't answer.

He said, "Anyway. Least you can say about it is I'm party to a hell of a slim chance."

She said, "Are you in some kind of program?"

He smiled. "Like AA or something?"

"No. Through the marshals."

"You been talking to Lucas Cohen?"

"He said the marshals know you. I guessed you were more likely witness protection than a federal fugitive."

"Federal fugitive." He nodded, like maybe he'd try it sometime. "Reckon I'd give them a pretty good run for their money if I was."

She had some coffee.

He said, "Yeah, witness protection. Keep it to yourself. Apparently it's meant to be kind of a secret."

She smiled. "How'd you end up in WITSEC?"

"I'm not supposed to tell you."

"Maybe given you're sitting in my kitchen with a gun you could make a special exception."

"You first."

"I don't have anything to tell."

"Oh. I think you do."

"Based on what?"

"I don't know. This and that."

She drank and didn't answer.

Marshall said, "My story takes a bit of effort to talk about. But I figure if I hear yours first it might warm me up enough to share."

She didn't answer.

He said, "I won't ask again. But if you want to hear my story I've got to hear yours. And I'm not going first. One of those quid pro quo things I suppose."

Quiet a little while, and then she said, "What do you want to know?"

He said, "Whose car are you driving round?" It came out more accusatory than he'd intended.

She looked at him and then she took a good long look at her coffee. She said, "My son's."

"What happened?"

She pursed her lips, chewed her mouth. She took a breath like she was set to embark on some long telling, but she didn't say anything.

Marshall tipped his head a little behind him. "That his bedroom?"

She looked at him quickly. "Did you go in?"

"No. I didn't open the door."

She didn't answer.

He said, "What's his name?"

"Liam."

"What happened to him?"

She sighed and looked past him, back to whenever it was. She blinked carefully. "We had a break-in, three months back. What's the date, maybe four, now." She had some coffee. "I was out. Liam came home, didn't realize there was anyone in the house. Just a burglary and they ran, but he chased them, and so, yeah."

She made a fist and coughed lightly against it. "They shot him."

She jutted her jaw slightly, moved it gently left and right like it was tender. "Died on the driveway. Stomach, so."

He waited.

She said, "It wouldn't have been quick."

He said, "God."

"Yeah. Exactly."

They sat there a while. He figured she knew he was sorry, and he worried verbal condolence would sound insincere. So he didn't say anything. In light of her story he saw that his uninvited entry had been a fairly sizable faux pas.

At length she said, "I was okay for a while. I could just kind of . . . You know, cling on by the fingertips for a bit, even after he'd died. But then it got to the point where it was too much. I've been off six weeks now."

Marshall said, "How old was he?"

"Seventeen."

"Don't you find it . . . You know." He looked around.

"What, hard?"

"Yeah."

"Of course I do, but . . . What else are you going to do? Could get even worse."

"You could move."

"Yeah, I could. But . . . This is where he was, so . . . Kind of a good and bad thing really. I'm not sure what I'm going to do."

Marshall didn't answer.

She said, "My dad used to say, you never know if your current self is the person you'll envy. I always remembered that, because it's like: any bad luck might be your absolute worst, or it might be a prelude to something harder. So you just carry on, pretend life's on a downhill trend, right now's the very best moment you'll have until you die. Pretty sobering thought, I reckon."

Marshall didn't answer.

She smiled, too bright, suddenly self-conscious. She said, "All right. Your turn."

He said, "Will you ever put the pictures back on the wall?"

"Someone asked me that today."

"What did you tell them?"

"I said I don't know." She shook her head, ridding a thought. "I don't want to talk about it. Your turn."

He left it at that for now. He said, "What do you want to know?"

She said, "You're not local, are you?"

He shook his head. "New York. I've been down here about five years."

"So what's your story? I figured you were some. I don't know. Special Forces guy or something."

He took his time answering, venturing into things he'd never really talked about before. He said, "I was NYPD. I worked undercover with the mob. It was a joint police/FBI thing."

She said, "That's not the full story."

"No."

"So can you tell me?"

He said, "I was with a guy called Tony Asaro. East Coast mob. Ran protection and stuff for him."

"How old are you?"

"Thirty-four. I was twenty-nine at the time."

"So how'd you end up doing that?"

Marshall said, "I lived with my uncle in New York. Asaro was his brother-in-law. My uncle had laundered money for him through his business for years, so Asaro knew him and he knew me before I was a cop."

Getting back to details he didn't want to share, but the way she was calmly watching, like this was any old story, he felt safe to go all in. And he had to. It was reciprocal disclosure. He couldn't back out now.

He said, "He wanted me working for him as well. They get you fast, this was when I was only just out of the academy." He smiled. "They backed off long enough for me to get a transfer to organized crime, and then it was all on."

"So he thought he had a bent cop on his payroll."

"Yeah. And he got an undercover one instead."

"So where is he now?"

"Prison. Federal tax evasion, like they got Al Capone."

"And how did you get out?"

"Not easily."

"Hence the WITSEC thing."

"Yeah."

"Is Marshall your real name?"

He nodded. "Well, kind of. I wanted to keep Marshall, but I could only have it as a middle name. So I'm James Marshall Grade."

She nodded. "I like it. It's got a . . . I don't know. It's got a ring to it."

He mouthed it a few times, testing the claim. He said, "Yeah, I guess. I've always thought of myself as just Marshall rather than Marshall-something. Or whatever, something-Marshall-something. The other bits never really meant anything."

She gave that a few seconds to settle, and then she said, "Who was it you were supposed to protect?"

Marshall said, "Her name was Chloe."

She waited.

Marshall tipped his head back, like it could shift the memory, make it clearer. He said, "She was shot."

"You going to tell me about it?"

He said, "Put that kettle on again."

2010

About five P.M. he sat with Ashcroft in his car on Flatbush Avenue, crime scene tape over Eddie's window where the glass had been shot out. They were parked diagonally opposite. The block was cordoned at the next set of lights, a small crowd behind the police cruisers, cell phone cameras rolling for posterity. A long line of marked and unmarked cars at both curbs.

Ashcroft was slouched down in his seat, ball cap pulled snug like he was worried he'd be seen. He raised his coffee cup. "Look, sorry. This is kind of my little routine, didn't really think about it."

"It's okay."

"I mean, yeah. No disrespect or anything."

Marshall looked at him. "Lee. I don't care about your coffee."

Ashcroft made the most of the ruling and had a mouthful. The radio was on, status codes coming through at a murmur. "You doing okay, Marsh? You're looking way too calm."

Marshall looked in his side mirror. The reflection of the sidewalk receding to a point. Things all converging. He said, "When have you ever seen me not calm?"

Ashcroft sucked a tooth, lowered the visor a little and raised it again. "Yeah, well. If you were going to make an exception now would be the time."

Marshall said, "Still no witnesses?"

Ashcroft shook his head. He leaned forward to see the upper-level windows. "Few people came out after the noise, but they said it just looked like a normal street. Other than over there obviously."

Marshall said, "Probably a drive-by. Guy in the back, pull up alongside, bang. Cabin'd catch all your brass. Late afternoon, no customers to worry about, either."

Ashcroft said, "Even just the one guy in a car. Drive in from this way, zip the window down, boom, and then you're off."

Marshall said, "Exactly."

Ashcroft said, "You want to have a look inside?"

Marshall looked across the street. A few guys in blue jumpsuits picking through the mess, CSU doing their thing. He said, "He's dead, isn't he?"

"Well. Yeah."

"So that's all I'm going to see. Stuff out on the street's what's worth looking at. I don't need to see his blood."

Ashcroft studied him. "How come you're all normal?"

Marshall looked in the mirror again and shifted in his seat so the vanishing point of the sidewalk was sitting dead center. "What did you think I'd be like?"

"I dunno. I just . . . I didn't think you'd be going over it with one arm up on the sill."

Marshall looked at him. "This is how I always sit. I think of good stuff while I'm sitting like this."

Ashcroft said, "Are you upset?"

"A bit."

"A bit."

"I only knew him eight years."

"Who did you know before that?"

"My mother. In Indiana."

"You need to call her?"

"What, to tell her about this?"

"Well. Yeah."

Marshall shook his head. "I don't think she'll mind. Eddie's my dad's brother, not hers."

"Jesus. Is your whole family like you?"

"Like me how?"

"All sort of . . . Ah. Don't worry."

Marshall said, "I'll put a checklist together, hunt my dad down wherever he is, see how we stack up."

Ashcroft looked at him as he sipped his coffee.

Marshall said, "He was in debt sixteen grand to guys normal people would try and avoid talking to, let alone doing business with."

"So?"

"So this here is a pretty natural by-product of the lifestyle he chose."

Ashcroft touched his hat brim and said, "Fuck, I end up getting clipped one day I hope I don't have someone looking at it and going, Well, you know what? This here is a pretty natural by-product of the lifestyle he chose. Yada, yada."

Marshall said, "You know what I mean."

"Yeah, I think you're going too fast. He wasn't necessarily whacked because he owed something."

Marshall said, "I'd say he was. You get threatened one week for owing money and then end up dead the next, there's probably some kind of correlation."

Ashcroft popped the lid on his cup and took a look, sealed it again. He spent a moment looking at the crowd up the street. He said, "Might be right. Way I understand it though is if you're dead you're not much good for paying money if you owe any."

Marshall said, "Yeah. But you reach a point where you realize you're never getting back what you've loaned. So you assess your options a little." He nodded at the scene across the street. "Take some appropriate action."

Ashcroft shook his head, adjusted his mirror. "I don't think you're right."

"I think I am."

"Asaro wouldn't have him clipped like that. I mean, shit. You're working for him."

"This is a serious business. I saw him put a spoon through a guy's eye the other night. Getting someone in a drive-by probably seems civilized. Like, this is probably a courtesy."

"Are you sure you're all right?"

"Stop asking me that. I'm fine."

Ashcroft looked his jacket over. "What're you packing under there? Doesn't look like proper issue."

Marshall didn't answer. It was the Beretta M9 Asaro had given him, the gun he'd used to shoot Vicki B.'s man, no silencer this time.

Ashcroft said, "Had old Tom Whatshisname on the phone, from the range. Said he reckoned you'd been doing draw-fires three hours straight the other day. Said lucky he knew you were PD or he would've worried it was some Timothy McVeigh shit or something."

Marshall said, "If I'm ever in a shooting, I don't want to be putting them wide."

Ashcroft didn't answer.

Marshall said, "You need to give that Ray-Ban Man a call, let him know I've had enough of undercover."

"I think you're making too many assumptions."

"Well. I'd say if they've murdered my uncle it's probably a conflict of interest or something. Probably a bureau guideline somewhere deals with it." He opened his door.

"You going for a look?"

Marshall said, "No. I'm going for a walk."

More like a subway ride. He got a Q train at the Parkside Avenue station. Standing-room only in the peak-hour traffic. These blank and tired faces and nobody talking, everyone swaying in rhythm, well-practiced moves. North and west across Brooklyn to the Manhattan Bridge, west to Seventh, north through Midtown. He got off at Fifty-seventh and shuffled with the crowd. Exhaust and hot trash aroma, the chatter of thousands. Up the stairs and he emerged into the cool evening, gentle by contrast, even with blaring traffic gridlocked on Seventh.

He walked the two blocks up to Central Park and made a left at Fifty-ninth, headed for Columbus Circle. Right onto Central Park West. Walking north in the shadow of the elms and across the street the grand old apartments tall-windowed and ornate, dour-looking in the evening light, an almost grim opulence.

He crossed CPW in front of the Dakota Building and cut north again over West Seventy-third, walked in the front entrance of the Langham.

The guy at the desk recognized him and smiled primly. "Hello, sir. Are you expected?"

Marshall said, "I'd say I probably am."

The guy dialed Asaro's room and said a visitor was waiting. He listened briefly and then said, "Yes, sir, that's right." Then to Marshall as he lowered the phone: "You can go on up, sir."

Marshall rode the elevator to five. Lloyd was waiting at the door. Marshall stepped inside to the foyer. Asaro's office on his left, separate doors to living and dining straight ahead. A hallway to the right. All very quiet.

Marshall said, "Where's your father?"

Lloyd closed the door gently, leaned against it with folded arms. He said, "You can't just show up and start demanding things."

"It was just a question."

Lloyd didn't answer.

Marshall said, "Where is he?"

"On a plane somewhere. He has to go to Miami for this real estate thing."

"Real estate."

"What do you want?"

Marshall in the center of the foyer, his back to the entry. He tugged his lapels gently, get the jacket shoulders sitting right. He said, "My uncle's dead."

Open-ended, see where it led him.

Lloyd said, "He did business with some hard guys. I guess that's what happens."

Quiet a while, in case he took it further.

Marshall said, "I never said it wasn't natural causes."

Nothing. In the living room the TV was paused on some car game.

Marshall said, "You wouldn't know anything about it, would you, Lloyd?"

He didn't get an answer. Lloyd crossed the room to a side table holding an old rotary telephone and opened a drawer and took out a little Smith .38 and let it hang at his leg.

"I don't like the way you're talking."

He pushed the drawer closed. Nothing twitchy to it, nice and easy, like he was fixing a drink.

Marshall said, "I don't think that's how you want to do this."

Lloyd didn't answer, drifted a little closer.

Marshall said, "There's a few different ways we can part but as long as you're holding that you're narrowing the options a bit."

"All right."

Six feet between them.

Marshall said, "Just so you know. I don't want to embark on anything without you and me both knowing where we're heading. But if you're sure."

Lloyd raised the gun and closed one eye to aim. The pistol at arm's length. "Pretty sure I know how this is going. No crystal ball, either."

He cocked the hammer. "I've just got a way of knowing."

Marshall said, "Shooting cops is one of those things, pretty hard to pull off. Need to dress it up good for it to fly."

"I'll keep it in mind. You need to take that piece out of your jacket and put it down for me."

"No thanks."

Lloyd didn't answer, just kept aim.

Marshall said, "I'm not going to take it out, and you're not going to shoot me unless I do something pretty rash. Too much hassle really, isn't it?"

Lloyd didn't move.

Marshall said, "Only way you're getting it is if you come over here and make a play. We could give that a go. Otherwise I think we'll just go sit down, have a talk about things."

He gestured with a thumb, raised his eyebrows invitingly as he walked through into Asaro's office. On the left was his desk in front of a tall bookcase, one shelf serving as dry bar. Straight ahead two high-back chairs sat at mirror angles on either side of the tall window looking out over West Seventy-fourth. He chose the right-hand one and sat down so he was slouched comfortably, and laid an ankle across the other knee. Elbows on the rests with his fingers in a steeple just below his face. The Beretta under his jacket a nice weight on his chest. Lloyd took the other chair and laid the Smith sideways on the armrest.

Marshall said, "So. You going to tell me what happened?"

"I don't know what you're talking about."

"Someone killed Eddie this afternoon. Drive-by."

"Where? The shop?"

Marshall nodded.

"I don't know anything about that."

"Your father might."

Lloyd didn't answer.

Marshall said, "If it was him I'm going to kill him. Same goes for you, too."

"I think one day I'll put you in the ground."

"I don't think you will. But okay."

Lloyd didn't answer.

Marshall said, "Anyone else home?"

Lloyd shook his head slowly, air pocket in one cheek, like it was bad news. He sighed through his teeth. "Just you and me, I'm afraid."

Marshall said, "Where's Jimmy?"

"Not here."

"You know if he's taken any drives up Flatbush Avenue lately?"

"No idea."

"Yeah. That's a long way from saying you had nothing to do with it."

"I can't say what he's done or hasn't done. Because I don't know."

"I know. That's why you're going to put the gun down and we're going to call your dad. See what the situation is."

"I don't think so."

Marshall said, "You remember what I said?"

"About what?"

"How you've set things moving on a certain road." He looked out the window, an oblique angle down along Seventy-fourth. "There's still time to back up."

Lloyd lifted the gun, lowered it again. He said, "Room's soundproofed. Won't need to dress anything up." He smiled. "Quick tidy, no one will know."

Marshall said, "Well. That's good to bear in mind."

Lloyd didn't answer.

Marshall said, "You know something?"

"What?"

Marshall said, "Universe is infinite." He dropped his chin a little, like trying to follow something distant. He said, "Means even the very slimmest luck has either already come to pass or will eventually. Anything you can think of, you give a thing endless chances, one day it'll happen. Somewhere, at some point. Which is good because it means even if you make a wrong turn you've got the comfort of knowing that in another dimension your parallel self made a better choice. Maybe you already have. You could have done something that let you avoid sitting here altogether."

Lloyd didn't answer.

Marshall said, "Anyway."

He looked at Lloyd, the steepled fingertips bouncing in a small amplitude, half an inch. He said, "I guess there's three things we can do. We can call Tony and see what the deal is. Or we can just wait until he gets back. Take a lot longer, but it's nice and peaceful."

Lloyd smiled. "What's the third way?"

Marshall said, "Well. It'll depend on what you do, I guess. Sort of a reactive thing on my part really."

Quiet between them. No traffic noise at all and he wondered if the room really was soundproofed.

Lloyd crossed his legs, Marshall's antipose. He said, "I think I'll give you to thirty to get out, and then I'll start firing."

Marshall waited. He said, "Have you started?"

Lloyd smiled and slouched lower, spread his legs. "Uh-huh. Twenty-five."

"Oh. I thought you might count it out loud or something, doesn't matter."

He slipped his phone from his right pocket, passed it to his left hand, let the right drape easy on his stomach. He said, "I'll try and get hold of Tony, see what he can tell me in twenty seconds. Or however long it is."

Left arm cocked with the screen at eye level, he made a show of punching the numbers. Lloyd watching him. Marshall put the phone to his ear, frowning slightly, let's see what he has to say.

Two seconds' pause. Then the landline on the desk began to ring.

Marshall said, "Oh, wrong number."

He looked toward the noise, surprised. Quite a suggestive action, and Lloyd just couldn't help but glance over too, and without moving his head Marshall drew the gun from his jacket and shot him twice in the chest.

The bullets caught him high up on his right, maybe an inch spread. The Smith hit the ground but didn't fire.

Lloyd gasped and curled into himself, started to scream but kept it to a low croak in the back of his throat. As he fell forward Marshall could see the twin holes in the chair back, delicate threads of white stuffing visible.

Marshall kept the gun on him. "This is option three. The peaceful wait, with you injured a little bit."

"Fuck. You shot me."

"Mmm. Twice."

"Jesus. You're crazy."

"No. I want to know what happened."

"I don't know."

"That's why we're going to wait for Tony."

"Oh, god. I can't. Shit, I'm bleeding. Help. Oh shit."

"You'll be fine. Just think of Mikhail."

"He's probably dead."

"Oh. Well think of someone else then."

Marshall looked out the window and sat listening to him panting. The evening turning pretty as the sun fell away. The traffic fading to paired lights on Central Park West and the park itself a lush green he could not see the limits of. He said, "You saw what I did to Vicki B.'s man. Why did you think I couldn't do the same to you?"

Lloyd didn't answer.

Marshall said, "I might give Tony another call soon. But I need to think about what I'm going to say."

Lloyd had his hands to his chest trying to staunch the flow. "If you . . . There's . . . There's a safe in the bookshelf behind the desk. I know the combination, it's, it's CY160. There's two hundred grand and a gun, clean, never been used. You could just take it and go. Two hundred K."

Marshall said, "I'll think about it."

"It's a Colt .45, never been used."

"I'll think about it."

The foyer door opened.

He swung the Beretta round to cover the entry, Lloyd going slack with relief, almost falling off his chair, calling for help.

Marshall stood and moved behind Lloyd's chair for cover and sighted two-handed, lowered the weapon as Chloe rushed into the room. She screamed when she saw the gun, her brother bleeding. Both hands at her mouth and he thought she'd turn and find cover, run for the foyer, but she came toward him, diving, and with the chair between them he couldn't block her from the Smith .38, and she grabbed it.

Only one thing he could do.

Walking south just past Columbus Circle, the bag from the safe slung on his shoulder: two hundred grand cash and a silver Colt M1911, just as Lloyd had promised.

He turned east on Fifty-sixth to miss the patrol cars from Mid-town North coming up Eighth. He called Ashcroft.

"Where are you?"

Marshall said, "Lee, I think I might have blown the op."

FORTY-ONE

Rojas

The club was down the western end of Central Ave., pink stucco, CALOR in red lettering on the lintel. He slowed as he drove by in the Mustang. Suit-clad doorman lighting a cigarette, just a few guys drinking at the bar. He watched a moment, anonymous in the new car. Traffic built behind him and someone leaned on the horn. He accelerated and made a right into the parking building next door and followed the ramp up to the top floor. The V8 in a low growl as it came slowly round the loop.

He parked at the edge of the building and sat a few seconds with the engine running. The desert stretching westward and in the distance Mount Taylor just a shallow knoll at the right of the yellowed pan. A blurred white band where the sky came down to meet it.

He shut off the engine and left the key in the ignition and dragged the bag across the console and got out. Then he took the vehicle ramp down to the street and turned left and walked back along to the club. The doorman ignored him as he approached, but as Rojas entered the guy stamped out his cigarette and followed. Low light in here. Contrast with the bright street wasn't helping.

The two guys at the table over to the left were just silhouettes as they stood and buttoned their jackets.

He headed for the door to the back room. A guy seated at the end of the bar swiveled smoothly on his stool and stood up to block his way, drink still in hand. He knocked the dregs back and set the tumbler down, ice tinkling a little.

He smiled as Rojas drew near. Tattoo on his neck just visible above his collar. "Didn't think we'd see you in here."

"Why's that?"

He closed his eyes briefly, shook his head. "Oh. We just didn't."

Rojas said, "Is he in?"

The guy touched his cuff links, one and then the other. "Are you carrying?"

Rojas said, "In the bag."

He looked at it. "What else you got in there?"

"Nothing to worry about."

The guy stood aside, gestured with one arm. "Come on through. Take a seat."

Rojas passed through the door and the four others filed through behind him. Like some funeral procession in their dark attire. He went and sat at the red leather booth curved against the left corner and set the bag on the table by the stripper pole. The cigarette man went back to his post and the guy he'd spoken with turned away to make a call on a cell. The two others standing near the door, hands clasped.

He heard the guy on the cell say his name. Something else in a low tone Rojas couldn't catch, and then a long spell of nodding. One foot on its heel, watching the toe as he listened.

The guy said, "Yeah, okay. Good."

He clicked off and came over, passing the phone hand-to-hand as he walked. He said, "Five minutes. I gotta pat you down first."

Rojas stood and let himself be frisked. The two others just watching.

"I got a .44 in the bag."

The guy with the phone didn't answer, just unzipped the

duffel and looked in. Colt's finest, sitting on 3.1 million cold. He said, "Don't lunge for it. You want a beer?"

They brought him a Corona. He sipped as he sat waiting. He wasn't sure of the time. Midafternoon, maybe. The beer half gone by the time Jackie Grace arrived. Tidy as always in a gray suit and tie, white shirt, collar so crisp it looked like you could break a piece off. He was wearing black boots with gold spurs, black cowboy hat tilted forward a little, covering one eye.

He tipped the hat back as he reached the table, gave Rojas some eye contact as they shook hands. Then he spun a chair round from another table so they could sit facing each other. A nice little move, all in the wrist. He took off his hat and placed it on the table, ran a hand through his hair as he sat down.

"Hot out there. Shit." He glanced around. "Hector, get me a napkin or something, would you. Fucking sopping."

The guy with the phone slipped out and returned a moment later with a napkin and laid it in Jackie Grace's outstretched hand. Jackie mopped his brow, folded the napkin, blotted again a little more carefully.

"You want me to take that, Mr. Grace?"

"No, it's okay. I'll hang on to it. Troy, you met Hector?"

Rojas said, "Yeah, I seen you a few times."

Jackie hiked a thumb. "Tyrone and Carlos over there by the door."

Rojas nodded at them. He didn't get anything back.

Jackie Grace clapped his hands once. "Hooray, everyone's met. That's terrific."

He stretched his legs and crossed the boots at the ankle, ignoring the bag but no doubt looking forward to the story. Rojas had met him a few times. Jackie Grace was the club owner, one of Leon's middlemen: he'd married into some good cartel contacts, helped facilitate deals when Rojas and Leon were bringing meth up from Durango. The marriage had come apart a few years back now, but he was still tight with the cartel guys, if not the wife.

He pointed at Rojas's beer as he took a pull, looked back over his shoulder. "Get me one of them as well. Corona. And tell him not to cut the lime too fat."

They waited a minute, not talking, both of them gazing idly at different walls, trying to seem patient. Eventually Hector set a beer on the table, a thin wedge of lime floating in the neck. Jackie took a long pull, throat pulsing. "Oh, that's good." He held the bottle at arm's length, eyed the label like it was a new brand. Then he set the bottle down and pulled the bag toward him. The zip was still open.

"All right. What've we got."

He tilted his head back to see in. "Ha. Shit, that's heavy stuff. Anaconda, haven't seen one of them in a while. What're you packing, Colt .45?"

Three million bucks looking back at him and it was the gun that got him going. Rojas said, ".44 Mag."

"Man. Yeah, I had a Smith 29, used to take .44s. Had to just about hang a weight off the end, stop it flying over your head when you pulled the trigger. Jeez it could kick."

Rojas said, "I've got some trouble with Leon."

Jackie Grace laughed. "Let me guess. This is your severance pay?"

Rojas said, "Yeah. Not quite."

Jackie shook the bag. "What is this, two million?"

"Three point one."

Jackie didn't answer. He looked around. Hector was in the other booth, arms stretched along the top of the chair, shoulder holster showing beneath his jacket. The phone on its flat in one hand, flicking his wrist gently to make it spin. Tyrone and Carlos leaning by the door. Jackie said, "Carlos, pull that door, would you?"

Carlos pulled the door. It felt like business now. Jackie had some beer. He said, "So what's the story, Troy?"

"How much do you want to know?"

"I don't know. I figure you rehearsed something in your head, so why don't we start there."

Rojas said, "Leon's gone funny on me."

Jackie smiled, looked up and down the length of the pole, like checking it was plumb. He said, "I reckon if someone took three point one mil off me I'd be pretty funny, too."

Rojas said, "The funny came first."

"The funny came first. All right."

Rojas didn't answer.

Jackie said, "So what do you want from me? I guess that's why we're sitting here." He looked under the table as he swapped his crossed ankles round. "You're after something."

Rojas said, "There's three point one in the bag. I'll split it with you if you get rid of Leon for me. Call it one point six."

Jackie took his time with that. Rojas's head pounding in the quiet. After a moment Jackie said, "Well, that suddenly got pretty serious, didn't it?"

Rojas didn't answer. He felt his voice drying out. He took a sip to get him over the line: "One point six million to whack him."

Jackie Grace said, "Leon's not easily whacked." He ran a hand through his hair, wet spikes raked back all quill-like. He said, "I heard about what happened to the Frazers."

Shit, he thought at that price even Leon would be an easy sell. Rojas said, "What, you mean Emile?"

"Yeah, and the kid, whatshisname." Jackie gestured vaguely. "Cops found Senior out west by Tohajiilee, real mess, like dead in his car, backup guy shot in the head, and then just this morning they found the kid at this restaurant over by the rental place, just stabbed right in the throat. Actually in his car too, so I don't know. Guess there's a nice . . . You know. Like-father-like-son angle to it. But anyway."

Rojas said, "I don't think that was Leon."

"Yeah, I don't know. Senior was pretty neat and tidy, had Leon written all over it. Used Emile's gun was the thing. Popped Chino and then did Emile. Not the easiest thing in the world."

"So what's the issue?"

Jackie spread his arms and leaned toward him, and when he spoke his voice was softer. He said, "Issue is, you don't want him after you, shit, I completely understand, because I wouldn't want him after me, either. But, you know, frankly, one point six mil isn't enough to offset the risk of blowing a hit and having him coming for me, too."

Rojas finished his beer. "Look. No offense, can we talk by ourselves?"

Jackie shook his head. "No offense. I don't do business unless I got guys with me. Just how I do it, sorry. Especially since this Frazer thing."

Jackie took another long pull. Rojas waited. He said, "Name your price."

Jackie laughed. "What if I said four, what would you do then?"

"I'd say three point one is a pretty good down payment."

Jackie shook his head. He knitted his fingers in his hair, tugged his forehead taut. He said, "You see that? Up along my hairline."

Rojas saw a scar running just below his widow's peak, bone-white, suture marks right across.

Jackie said, "That's about fifteen years old now. Dealing with some guys, a bit of product they'd sent up went missing, and they were under the misconception I had something to do with it vanishing. So they said: Tell us where it is, or we'll cut your face off. And yeah, luckily by the time they got the call to say it'd been found, they hadn't got too far." He lowered his hands. "Coulda been like that movie with Travolta. You know the one? With the faces?"

"Yeah."

Jackie put his hat back on, the brim covering one eye like when he'd walked in. Maybe conscious of the scar now he'd brought it up. He said, "Some people in life I really do not want to cross, and Leon is one of them. And I'd be stupid really: I set up a lot of business for you guys, I take a good cut, I want him as an ongoing client."

He held a hand edgewise on the table, slid it away from him. "It's like a long-term investment thing. I don't want to snip a decent revenue stream. I've got a good setup. And look, you want my advice, you come into that sort of money, you don't fuck about. You say sayonara and take off for, I dunno. Swaziland."

Rojas shook his head. "He'd kill my boy. Or my mother."

Jackie sucked a tooth. "Yeah, well. I guess you gotta look after number one though, don't you?"

Rojas said, "I'll give you the bag. Three point one to make it happen."

Jackie shook his head, palms raised. "No, you're not getting me. I'm not going to do it. I mean, shit, if we're taking sides, I'm with him. In fact, jeez. Who'd you think it was sent those cartel guys out this morning? Up in Bernalillo."

Rojas didn't answer, but Jackie must have seen him pale. He waved a hand like it'd been too easy. "Troy, come on, Leon wants cartel guys to do a hit, who you think he's going to call? I mean, god. Who else does he know with my kind of connections?"

Rojas didn't answer.

Jackie read his mind: he reached across and took the .44 out of the bag, laid it on the table with his hand on the grips. He smiled. "Can't be too cautious."

"Fuck you. You're going to rat me out?"

"Well, I kind of already have. I'd say he'll be here soon." He killed his drink, paired the two empties side by side. He said, "You want another beer?"

FORTY-TWO

Lucas Cohen

On the drive back to Santa Fe his phone wouldn't stop ringing. He kept his eyes on the road, almost worse than answering, made him speculate about the nature of the call. Bad news and that sort of thing. Deputy, we're somewhat puzzled at your actions. Deputy, we're not wholly convinced that shooting was kosher. However it was that they put these things. When he pulled up at the courthouse on South Federal Place he stayed in the car and checked his messages.

A sheriff's CID detective he'd already talked to, wanting more of a statement.

State police, requesting some clarification.

Marshal's office, same again.

He called the sheriff's guy, figuring he'd be the friendliest of the three, on account of being least in the dark.

Cohen opened his door for some air and said, "Detective. Lucas Cohen speaking."

Traffic noise and wind crackle at the other end. Cohen pictured him out on 550, trying to comprehend it all.

"Deputy. Just wondering about your whereabouts."

Cohen said, "Santa Fe. I was hoping to stay put if that's all right."

"Right. Well, our officer-involved shooting people would like a word."

Cohen said, "I ain't an officer, I'm a federal marshal."

"Yeah, I conveyed that. Hang on." Notebook pages turning, letting Cohen know this was someone else's view on the matter. He said, "Something to do with how you were pursuing a state fugitive and therefore you were executing the duties of a sheriff's employee, so they'd like to talk to you. Just for completeness' sake, I'd say."

Cohen said, "I handed in both my firearms with about twelve bullets missin', so I would've reckoned it's all pretty self-explanatory."

"Nonetheless."

Cohen said, "You get anything out of those cars?"

"Not so far. Guy from the Chrysler had a phone on him and some fake ATF ID. So that was something. Haven't got into the phone yet but I'll let you know soon as we do. Sometimes these fancy ones take some cracking, but they'll do it. They've got this whiz girl at the state lab, she's quite something. I've seen her do one of those Rubik's cubes in about ten seconds flat, maybe she can do the same with a phone. Not that I've asked."

Cohen said, "Kids these days."

"Yeah. Kids these days. Anyway, well. I'll call you, but are you gonna come back down?"

Cohen said, "I'll give them a call."

He clicked off and tossed the phone on the seat beside him, sat there a moment with his door open and his head tipped back on the rest, just watching the comings and goings. Everyday courthouse stuff he could have seen from his office, but he liked how one tough morning could give an old scene fresh splendor. He could have sat there all day. That was the payoff, though: you make it through, you get the warm contentedness of knowing you're still a part of the world, and goodness it's a fine place. He wondered how long it'd last. Might be reveling in the sunrise for weeks to come.

He picked up the phone again and called Loretta at home.

When she answered he said, "Thought you might still be at work."

"So whyn't you try the office?" A smile in her voice.

"Thought I might get lucky."

She laughed. "How's the day been?"

"Oh. Not too great. I had some trouble this morning." He thought about how to say it, and then he realized there was only the one way. He said, "Had to shoot a man."

"God, Lucas. What, just now?"

"Yeah. Just this morning."

"Oh, no. He make it, or has he passed?"

"He's passed. Actually two of them. First one moved along fairly promptly, second man's still hanging on. Could go either way."

"Lord. Are you all right?"

"Yeah. I'm all right."

"What happened?"

"Well, I just . . . We had to go down to Albuquerque, pick up a coupla guys. But they didn't want to come quietly."

"And they shot at you?"

"Yeah. I shot back a bit straighter."

"Sweetheart. You've hit some bad luck recently. Only just been the Farmington thing."

"Yeah, I know. Haven't been shot myself, so must be some good in it."

"Oh, Lucas. Are you sure you're all right?"

"Yeah. It just weighs on you when you think about it, you know?"

"Sweetheart, I know. But you shouldn't let it. You have to be strict about what goes into your head. Keep the regrets out."

"Yeah."

"And I'll keep pulling them out long as you keep putting them in."

He laughed but didn't answer, moral issues tugging on him the more he talked.

She said, "Is it this drug violence business or is it a new thing?"

"It's a bit of everything I think." He smoothed his tie, making sure it was good and central. "Shouldn't tell you about it, give you the heebie-jeebies."

"Why don't you come home a bit early? Or are you still doing interviews?"

"Yeah, I still got some interviews to get through. They'll probably want me to write a novel about it, as well." He thumbed his star, watched the metal cloud and then clear. He said, "Funny. Much as I wish I hadn't done it, idea of killing a man doesn't bother me nearly as much as getting killed myself. I don't know. Maybe that's callous. How it's been put to me in my own head, anyway."

"And that's the exact same way I'd put it to you, too. And the girls."

He closed his eyes and pinched the bridge of his nose. On the courthouse lawn the flag was shifting and popping faintly in the breeze. "Yeah, I know. I just . . . Sometimes I worry if I got hurt I wouldn't see you again."

"Sweetheart. Don't be silly."

"I know. It's just . . . Something like this happens, puts all the things you care about in real sharp perspective, so I thought I'd better call you, case I got clipped by a truck or something coming home. Ten o'clock news they'd all be like: and just today he'd survived a major shootout with cartel fellas, but now he's been hit by a drunk driver. Something like that."

"Now you are talking silly."

"Yeah. Just makes you wonder about things though, you know? Like whether people have always agonized over the state of it all, or whether it's a new thing." He studied the mirror, like somehow with his own reflection lay a broader image of the world. He said, "Place's actually getting worse maybe. You know what I mean?"

"It's not getting worse for me. I get to see you every day."

He knew he needed to wrap it up, things at risk of snagging in his throat, but he said, "When I die I want to be in bed with you.

Having just had a nice long evening playing Scrabble. And drinking something good."

"Well, we can get the Scrabble out, and I think there's a bottle of something somewhere. But you're not going to be dying."

He smiled, eyes still closed. "Not tonight?"

"Not tonight. Not for a very long time."

FORTY-THREE

Marshall

"How long are you going to sit there?"

Marshall was still at the table, look in his eye like he maybe enjoyed the wait, gun the only sign he was expecting conflict. He said, "I don't know. Until it's over."

"You think he's actually going to come here?"

He was nodding slightly, not an answer to the question, just working on his own thoughts. He said, "Someone will. Rojas came to my house, no reason he won't come to yours, too."

"Do you want something to eat?"

The way he looked at the ceiling he seemed to consider that in some depth. Eventually he said, "No thanks."

She said, "So what happened to everyone?"

"In New York?"

"Mmm. In New York."

He picked up the sunglasses and angled them so they fell open and slipped them on, somehow easier to talk when he was slightly hidden. He said, "Asaro's in federal lockup like I said. Lloyd's doing seven years at Sullivan on a Class D felony. Menacing me with a firearm. Probably out by now."

"And what about the sister?"

"Chloe."

"Yeah."

Marshall inspected the ceiling again and said, "I think she's probably okay."

"Probably."

Marshall said, "Last I heard she was in ICU. Only meant to shoot her in the arm, make her drop the gun, but I got her in the chest, punctured a lung. She had to have a transfusion. All that training, and I missed anyway."

Shore didn't answer.

He said, "Far as misses go it's probably not bad, better than shooting fresh air. I don't know. She would've just got a misdemeanor, if anything. But I almost don't want to check."

"Case you shot her better than you thought."

"Well, yeah. Or worse, depending how you look at it. Something like that anyway. I call the apartment every so often but it's never gone through, probably disconnected. Dumb habit really, sort of thing you could find out so easily but I keep thinking if I call, one day she might pick up and say . . . I don't know. Don't worry, you only shot me a little bit. Water under the bridge."

She didn't answer.

Marshall said, "Stupid, but . . . That's what I do."

She said, "I sleep with a loaded gun in the bed."

Marshall nodded. "Did that for a while, too." He raised the Colt's muzzle off his knee. "Actually had it under the bed so I could just hang an arm down and there it was. Used to wake up all out of breath and have to check it was still there, put my hand on it. You know that real thumping anxiety? And then it just goes."

She nodded. "You feel like you're in danger?"

He traced a thumb lightly around the edge of the table, one way and back, like testing a blade. He said, "Saw Asaro in court, this was just before I went into the program. His lawyer gave me a letter, opened it up, all it said was 'Dallas Man.' Only thing he'd written. That was the name of the cleaner he used. The Dallas Man. Don't even know if he was from Dallas, but anyway. I just knew it was his way of saying, Sleep with one eye open. He wasn't going to let anything rest. I don't know. Part of me always wanted to stay where I was and face it all down and see an end to it, whatever it was. WITSEC kind of felt like running. Right now feels better though, feels a bit like atonement. Who knows, I do this long enough, it might bring me back to what I should've finished before I left. But we'll see. Right now I feel like I'm waiting. I'm not running from anything."

"You think you'll see them again?"

He nodded. "Probably. Everything in life's got a ripple, every so often something bumps into something else. So. We'll see. People always telling me how it's a small world, I'm putting it to the test. See if it'll rise to the occasion."

She didn't answer.

He said, "Are you going to go back to work?"

"I hope so. I'll always do it, maybe not officially."

Marshall said, "I saw your files in the living room."

She nodded. "Yeah. I've got old robbery cases I'm working through. Slowly compiling stuff. One day I'll find who did it. I've promised myself that."

Marshall said, "I could help you."

She didn't answer. After a while she went into the living room and closed the door behind her.

He was checking the phone for messages every thirty minutes. He had the SIM and battery routine down to a fine art now. Nothing all day. Or, nobody he wanted to speak to.

In the strip of glass beside the living room door he could see Shore hunched at the coffee table making notes. Every so often he'd catch her looking at him, interesting how she'd give it a few seconds before looking away. Safe behind the sunglasses he wasn't bothered. Pink as they were.

At four P.M. he reassembled the phone and switched it on and found a message.

Rojas's number, but a new voice: "Call me back."

He waited thirty seconds, coming down off the little jolt of discovery. Trancelike he was so still, the gun in one hand and the phone in the other, Marshall contemplating how things might come to a close.

An end of some sort approaching and maybe it's yours.

He dialed.

"Yes?" The same voice from the message.

Marshall, watching Shore, said, "Is my friend Troy there?"

"Marshall. I'm glad you rang back. This is Leon. We spoke yesterday morning."

He took himself back there. The hot car and the circling of the birds. He said, "I remember. Life and death and that sort of thing."

"That's right."

"Is Troy there?"

"He is. He can't actually talk, though. A bit indisposed right now."

Marshall said, "I need to come see you. Ask you about Alyce Ray."

"All right. You sure you want to do that?"

"Yeah. I'm pretty sure."

"Remember what I said yesterday. About how looking for disappeared people's a good way to end up disappeared yourself."

Marshall said, "I'll take my chances. I've done all right so far."

"Not going to last forever, nothing does. But okay. You know where Calor is? Central Avenue in Albuquerque?"

Calor. He remembered it from the DEA photographs. That pink building where Alyce Ray had last been seen.

Marshall said, "When?"

"Where are you?"

"Close."

"Well, how about thirty minutes, then?"

Marshall said, "Good," and clicked off.

Shore had noticed him talking and was coming in from the living room. Marshall finally stood up, pushed the chairs in. He took a step back to check everything was correctly spaced and put the gun in his belt.

He said, "I've found him."

He went into the bathroom and locked the door. On the shelf above the basin a long display of pill bottles, prescription and off-the-shelf. He turned them so he could read the labels. Sleeping pills. Anti-anxiety. Codeine. Vicodin.

He placed the gun on the medicine cabinet and rolled up his sleeves. Blood from the Bronco men still on him, hair on his arms crusted with it. He ran a basin of hot water and soaped his fore-arms, and using a small nail brush removed the lather one long stroke at a time, elbow to wrist. A delicate pinstripe of foam remaining. He splashed water from the faucet to get the residue and rinsed his face and hunched dripping over the bowl. A pink tint in the dimpled water and this odd distorted figure looking back. Just the shape of a person.

He leaned close to the mirror and ran a hand along his jaw. His beard just showing. He took a step back and crouched slightly to see his reflection and turned his head left and right and then up and down to check his hair. Scissors from the medicine cabinet to clip a rogue strand. It fell in a gentle curve on the water and frayed slowly to its composite threads.

There was a five-pack of razor blades in the cabinet as well, and he unwrapped two of them and set them on the shelf in front of the pills, short side flush with the edge. Then he removed his belt and held it up to compare widths, blade to leather, and marked the midpoint of the belt with his thumbnail. In a drawer beneath the basin he found a single Band-Aid and cut the adhesive tab from each end, and one after the other peeled off the protective paper and taped the razor blades to the inside of his belt at the position he'd marked. Then he threaded it carefully back through the loops and did the buckle and turned and looked over his shoulder to check his reflection, but all was hidden.

He drained the basin and ran the tap to get the last of the blood and dropped the scrunched remains of the Band-Aid and the razor papers in the trash can beside the toilet. He stood square to the mirror and crouched again to center his face.

Could be the last time you see it.

He turned some pill bottles to restore disorder and then he picked up the gun and walked out.

FORTY-FOUR

Wayne Banister

He hadn't changed motels yet. He was still at the Gibson Boulevard place, guest numbers low enough the safe option was to stay put rather than be seen at the desk.

Sitting at a table in a Starbucks just up the road, working through coffee and a newspaper, the blue phone rang. He checked the time. Four thirty P.M. He looked out the window as he answered. Not even the traffic moving. A clear afternoon, and on the sidewalk the long shadows of the streetlights reaching eastward.

The Patriarch said, "Thanks for the file. It's taken a while to break the encryption, but there's a lot here."

"Anything useful?"

"Yeah. The Frazers seemed to think their main rival is a guy called Jackie Oswald Grace, working with someone called Leon. No surname. I'd like to know who did their intel, it's good stuff. Spreadsheets and everything."

"Junior said they used some ex-Mossad guys."

"Interesting. We might have to look into that."

Wayne said, "Sure."

"Anyway, they've catalogued all their assets, including the vehicles. It says Leon's got a red 1994 Jeep Cherokee, a white 2013 Audi Quattro SQ5, and a black 2013 Chrysler 300C."

"Okay."

"But I saw just now the State Police down there have a BOLO out on an Audi SQ5 involved in a shooting yesterday, and APD've caught a homicide, someone dead next to a red Jeep Cherokee."

"I haven't seen the news."

"No, well I checked the local stations to see if TV had caught anything, and there's been a shooting at a motel in Bernalillo too, looked like they tried to reenact the O.K. Corral. But one of the cars there is a Chrysler 300C."

Wayne said, "So Leon's been busy."

"Seems so. Either he's after someone, or someone's after him."

Wayne closed the paper and folded it. People at adjacent tables hunched over laptops. He was just background, no one even glanced. He said, "You want me to look into it?"

"Yeah, I just don't like the coincidence. First I hear Marshall's in Albuquerque, and then the news is full of shootings involving drug dealers."

"That's pretty standard down here. Cops love it."

"Yeah, I've just got that feeling. And I don't want any missed opportunities. Even if it's a slim chance it's still worth checking."

"You think he's hunting dealers?"

"I don't know. It's the kind of thing he might be up for, though."

"I'll look into it. How many people has this Leon guy got?"

"Four. Assuming they're not all dead."

Five-on-one, potentially. Wayne thought about it a second and said, "Okay. I'll check it out."

"Thank you. I don't have the file in front of me, but it says he's got a place up in Santa Fe. I'll text you the details."

"Sure. I'll head up there now, see what's going on."

"Great. The file said there's no alarm, and the lock's a Schlage Camelot, apparently. I'll send you the code."

"Thank you."

He finished the coffee as he walked back to the motel, the paper under one arm. Camouflage against anyone not focused on the car ahead.

In the room he put the bag on the bed and checked the load in the guns. He clipped the SIG on his hip and tugged his shirt over it. Then he put a foot on the edge of the mattress and strapped the .22 in its holster to his ankle.

A nice added weight. He always liked that comfort of metal.

This is your place in the world.

In the bathroom he took a leak and looked at himself in the mirror as he washed his hands, tipping his head different ways to check his hair. He turned off the tap and leaned on the sink so his reflection was centered.

Could be the last time you see it.

He checked that both phones were in the bag before he left.

Afternoon traffic pushed the trip out to an hour.

When he pulled into the driveway he saw the garage was empty. He slowed and came popping in over the gravel. The broad curve of a house becoming evident as he drew nearer, and he saw the windows were all curtained. He stopped and set the brake and with the engine running opened his door and sat half off the seat with a foot outside and the SIG held low.

Ding, ding, ding.

He thought of Frazer and Chino, probably still out west, getting pretty leathery by now.

He shut off the engine and removed the key. Without looking he reached across and took both phones from the bag and pocketed them. He got out and closed the door. Very quiet without road noise. The car slowly ticking. He felt the heat from the wheel arch. The house dark and lifeless.

And you're going in.

Gun raised, he ran lightly to the entry and punched the lock code. The mechanism clicked. He turned the handle and nudged the door back with his knuckles and waited, staring down the sights. Just the creak of the hinge as it eased back around. He went in. The weapon held close and two-handed, snapping left and right to cover doors as he passed them. No one in the living room. The place a mess. Needles and coke. The crack house standard.

He checked the hallway. Empty bedrooms, an empty bathroom, two locked doors. He kicked them both in. Product and gun storage. Stairs to a basement as well, but he decided to check them later. He headed back toward the entry. There was another door with a combination lock, maybe an office.

He stood straining to hear. Then he took a step back and trained the gun chest-high and kicked the bolt in. The door flung open and bounced off the adjacent wall and swung almost closed, caught by the ruined tongue. He shouldered in.

A computer sat humming on a desk, laser prints spread out next to it, people in various states of dismemberment. Anatomy texts, open at the relevant sections. He turned and trained the SIG on the door and walked backward to the desk, sifted through the papers.

Like a morgue file. Nothing that wasn't severed.

Next to the monitor he found a printout from the Motor Vehicle Division. A standard registry entry, personal and vehicle stats, together with a photograph.

James Marshall Grade. He kept Marshall as a middle name.

He waited there a moment, gun up, seeing how it all fit together. Then he left the smashed office door hanging wide and went and stood at the top of the stairs. A dull hammering from somewhere. He hadn't noticed before, but he had an idea what it might be. He started down, back to the wall, gun swinging left and right for cover. Halfway there and he could hear voices. He stopped and listened, head cocked. Two women calling for help, cries going in and out of sync. At the bottom of the stairs, he stood with his ear to the door and listened. Some kind of cutting suite adjacent. The table still wet, a trace of water along the bottom of the drain. Serrated tools on the pegboard. The door beside him shaking as they hit it.

He said, "Jesus Christ."

He took the red phone from his pocket as he walked back up the stairs, sat in the living room and called his daughter. He was shaking as he held the phone to his ear.

"What are you up to, sweetheart?"

FORTY-FIVE

Marshall

Southbound on I-25. Shore driving, Marshall in the seat beside her, looking out the window, but not really seeing the view. He had the pink glasses on and the Colt held two-handed between his knees.

She said, "How do you think she saw you?"

Marshall took a few seconds to surface. He said, "How do I think who saw me when?"

"The Chloe girl. How did she know to come upstairs after you shot him?"

Marshall ran a hand round his jaw but didn't turn from the window. He said, "Hard to say. She was only one floor below, she could've heard the noise. Or she might have seen me on the street, I don't know. Maybe she just decided to come upstairs. Might've just been bad luck."

She didn't answer.

Marshall slid low in the seat. He took the lock pick bag from his pocket and put it in the glove compartment.

"What's that?"

He said, "Lock picks. For breaking into people's houses."

She looked out her window. The low sun in the glass of the

buildings. The city had a silver clarity against the hard, blue folds of the mountains. She said, "You carrying anything else I should avoid being seen with?"

He said, "I don't know. The usual."

"Which is what?"

"Money, and a gun, and my keys. Got a phone too, but that's kind of an exception."

She glanced at him. "Carrying it round in three pieces is pretty exceptional."

Marshall said, "Stops it being tracked."

"Yeah. Except when you turn it on again."

He shook his head. "No onboard GPS, so they'd have to triangulate the signal. Less cell towers out here than on the coast so I don't think it's that precise."

She looked at him. "You don't think."

"Well. That's the theory. It's working for me so far."

She said, "If you're going for normal, you could try using a wallet."

He shook his head. "No. You have to put things in them."

"Like what?"

"I don't know. Credit cards and ID and stuff."

She said, "What's wrong with credit cards and ID?"

Marshall said, "Nothing. Unless you happen to be in my situation. In which case everything's wrong with them."

"So no plastic?"

He shook his head. "No plastic."

She looked at him. "How do you drive?"

"Easy. You just need a key and a car." He pushed the glasses up the bridge of his nose. "And to avoid being pulled over."

She said, "What about voting?"

"I don't vote."

"Right."

She kept working on that for a minute and said, "Don't you think that's worth an exception? Like, have some ID on you long enough to mark a piece of paper."

"Partake in democracy and all those good things."

"Exactly."

Marshall said, "I'm on the periphery. Whether the country goes blue or red doesn't affect me." He mused a little while, watching traffic overtake, sun flares sliding off the paintwork. He said, "Plus if democracy's worth anything, the right to *not* vote's just as crucial as the right *to* vote."

Looking pleased now, like here comes the punch line. He said, "So in that sense I'm helping exemplify an important principle."

She said, "Right."

Marshall said, "Anyway. I'd say if things ever reach the point where it's essential I'm involved, it's got to be pretty dire."

Turning west off I-25 onto Central Ave., they cruised through low-rise: diners, fast food, motels, and at the very end of the street the sun hovering on final approach.

Marshall said, "Are you doing this because you think you owe me a favor, or is it actually what you want to do?"

She took her time with that. She said, "Normally I'd say I'm just paying back a favor, but getting held at gunpoint makes you take things to heart a bit more."

Marshall said, "So it's both."

"I guess."

Marshall nodded. He liked that just fine.

She said, "Why Stella?"

He looked at her. "Why Stella when?"

"That night in the bar. I dunno, I thought if you have your pancakes one at a time you'd go for Stone, or Great Divide or something."

Marshall shook his head. "Too local. People might guess I'm from around here." He adjusted the air-con vent so he could only see the thin edge of the fins. He said, "Stella's more common, so I could be from anyplace."

"So it's always Stella?"

He nodded. "It's always Stella."

Spoken curt enough it seemed to put an end to beverages. She said, "Did you have some sort of plan?"

"Kind of."

"Kind of."

Marshall said, "Well. I was just going to go in and order a drink and see what happened. React to whatever needs reacting to."

"I thought all that time sitting quietly you were coming up with something."

"I was just deciding whether simple is best."

"And is it?"

Marshall said, "I'm still undecided, but we'll give it a try anyway. See what eventuates."

A brief cool darkness as the road swooped beneath the railway overpass, and then they were broaching the high-rise stretch.

Eyes forward he said, "You're actually kind of pretty."

A bit out of nowhere and maybe not the best timing, but he thought he'd see where it got him.

Nowhere, as it turned out: she pretended she didn't hear, not the slightest reaction.

Marshall responded in kind. He said, "Do a drive-by first. Maybe we'll see them at the bar, having a cold one."

"You know where it is?"

"Next block."

He could see it coming up on the right. The cracked pink stucco and a parking structure on the next lot. He lowered his visor against the glare. A doorman outside smoking a cigarette. Marshall remembered him from the DEA shots. It was hard to see past him. Two or three people at the bar, but no one he recognized. He held the gun between the seat and the door to keep it hidden, and leaned forward to see past the edge of the roof and scan the parking structure. Plenty of cars nosed up against the edge, no people visible.

Marshall said, "I'll get out in a couple of blocks."

"And what am I supposed to do?"

"Park somewhere you can see me, and then follow if I get kidnapped."

"Kidnapping's not in the plan though, is it?"

Marshall turned in his seat and checked the other side of the street. He said, "No, it's not. But you've got to be flexible."

Approaching the light at Fourth Street the traffic slowed, and the instant the car stopped the rear door opened and a man slid in, and behind his seat Marshall heard a gun being cocked.

Shore said, "Shit," the car rolling again as she looked in the rearview, their belts locking with a jolt as she hit the brake. Marshall, still holding the .45 low by the door, used his other hand to jiggle the tension out of his restraint and then reached up and turned the mirror so he could see their passenger. A man in his late thirties, short hair and a lean, sharp face, little ball of sinew in his jaw as he looked out the window.

Marshall said, "That a Middle East tan, or just a local one?"

The guy said, "I'd say it's mainly UV bed by now." He met Marshall's eyes in the mirror. "Take a right and go round the block, and we'll head back along to Third."

Marshall said, "Are you Leon?"

"Yes I am. Are you Marshall and Detective Shore, or have I got the wrong car?"

Marshall said, "No. You're spot on."

"Nice glasses."

"Thanks."

"What are you holding down there by the door?"

Given a lie would be seen for what it was fairly promptly, Marshall said, "Colt .45 semi-auto."

Looking out the other window like he was taking a cab ride, Leon said, "Just leave it there and put both hands on the dash."

Marshall complied. He said, "Did you get your money back?"

Eyes in the mirror again. "What money?"

"Troy said he stole some."

"Oh. Yeah." A sound like the flat of a gun tapping on his leg. "Troy likes to think he's more trouble than he is. But you probably found that out for yourself."

Marshall didn't answer. Leon turned and looked out the rear window. He said, "And how are you, Detective Shore?"

Shore didn't answer.

Leon said, "I think I'll take that as a good sign. Not far to go, anyway. Just take a left on Third."

They went into the garage of a condo building three blocks off Central. Shore took the ramp down to the second basement level. Fluorescent-lit concrete, the squat columns all raw-faced, two black SUVs and three more sedans.

Leon, in the center seat now, said, "Park over there by the elevator."

Shore followed painted arrows, tires squealing faintly in the turns. She came slowly to a stop, set the brake, shut off the engine.

Leon spent a long moment looking round, check they were alone, and then slid behind her and opened his door wide. He said, "Belt and door, Detective."

Shore unclicked her belt and popped her door. Leon leaned forward and reached around the pillar. He grabbed her by the front of the blouse, stitches tearing as he pulled her out of the seat, dragged her backward around the car to the elevator. He hit the button, looked at Marshall across her shoulder.

"You too. Six feet clearance, or the detective loses a kidney."

Marshall slipped off the sunglasses and folded them carefully, placed them on the dash. Taking his time. He was hoping the Colt would fall on the ground when he got out and there'd be a fuss getting it back in the car, but somehow it stayed propped against the seat.

Leon said, "Shut your door."

Marshall knocked it closed with his heel, just enough to catch.

The elevator dinged and opened. Leon backed in, his arm around Shore's throat. He pushed her into a corner and took a key from his pocket and inserted it in a lock below the button panel. Then he pulled Shore close again and held the gun at her spine.

He turned and jerked his head to beckon Marshall. “In you come.”

Marshall followed, stark echo of his footsteps, and stopped just inside the threshold.

Leon said, “Hit the P button.”

Marshall hit P.

The doors closing solemnly. He felt them brush his shirt. The light a fraction dimmer. Silence.

They rode up to the penthouse, the dial above the door counting floors, Marshall watching the reflection in the mirrored rear wall.

That brief lightness in his gut as they stopped. The doors opened.

Leon smiled. “Out you go.”

Marshall turned and stepped out into the apartment. Through a short, narrow entry and into a kitchen floored in gleaming timber, late sun a bright oval in the gloss. At a polished granite counter, two guys in shirtsleeves perched on barstools, between them Troy Rojas lying hogtied and bleeding, one eye half-closed and purple, mouth a pulped mess.

The timber floor continued into the living room. It looked like a catalogue: a leather sofa and two armchairs forming three sides of a rectangle, and a TV and sound system that must have cost five figures. Two guys on the sofa, and a man in a gray suit and black cowboy hat in an armchair, a half-empty Corona waiting on a coaster. He stood up as Marshall came in, brought his drink with him.

“Man, that was fast, thought it might take you a couple hours or something. Ah, god, Troy’s made a puddle.”

One of the guys on the stools said, “It’s okay on wood, Mr. Grace. Long as you got the polyurethane, yeah? Just mop it up. Just gotta not leave it too long.”

The guy in the hat didn’t answer. He put the bottle on the bench and looked at Marshall, standing there in his kitchen, Leon behind him with Shore still hugged close and the gun in her back. He clapped his hands and said, "Right, introductions: I'm Jackie Grace, we've got Tyrone, Carlos, Hector, and Miguel." He pointed them out in turn, smiled as he said, "And I guess you already know Leon."

Jackie Grace. It rang a bell, and Marshall hunted for the name. It was in that DEA stuff. Jackie Grace: Calor club owner.

Marshall said, "How's the bar business doing?"

Jackie Grace laughed and rolled with it, all suave, took a hit off his beer. He walked a little loop behind the counter, hands spread and elbows tucked, a little behold-the-glory gesture. He said, "It's doing okay. Yeah. I think we can say it's doing pretty good." He put a knuckle to his nostril and sniffed.

Leon said, "We'll need some more cuffs for these two."

Jackie had some beer. The four others did a little pocket-pat routine. Jackie said, "There's a bag of those plastic ones in the office."

The guy called Hector went to get it. Jackie stepped over the back of the couch and stretched out. He tipped his hat low on his eyes and said, "Shit, this is going to be one hell of a party."

Leon put Shore on the ground facedown and knelt beside her, pat-searched one-handed, the gun hanging by his knee, aimed at the floor. It was a Ruger SR22, boxy polycarbonate, like a compact version of a Glock. Hector entered the room and dug a mess of cable ties from a fat Ziploc baggie. He shook the bunch until he was holding just one, hangers-on falling to the floor. He threw it over beside Shore. Leon locked her wrists, an expert job, three seconds tops.

Marshall was by himself, no one in grab distance, the guys on the stools watching him hand-to-gun.

Leon patted Shore's backside. "Thanks for being so cooperative, Detective."

He aimed at Marshall. "On the ground."

Marshall didn't move. Hands bound he wouldn't have much of a show. Somewhere back there had been the chance for control, and it was before Leon got in the car. Now he had a gun on him, and two others on the brink of a draw. His exit options were shrinking.

He said, "What happened to Alyce Ray?"

Leon said, "I'll tell you as you're dying. Which might be soon if you don't get on the ground."

"Kidnapping a police officer's not a great idea."

"Only if you're planning to let them go. On the ground, now."

Everyone watching him. Jackie's bottle catching the light as he had a drink. Marshall's pulse hammering as his options shrank.

Do something, now.

Leon's gun right there, almost in grab range. Take it and kill the others. He's close enough. Do it.

"I'll give you a bullet through the knee."

Marshall waited. Make him come closer.

Leon shouting now: "I'll count you in. Three, two—"

Marshall took a knee.

He let his breath out, the moment gone, tension collapsing.

Leon pushed him prone, crouched and ran a hand up and down Marshall's leg, Jackie Grace saying, "You see I pimped out the bathroom, Leon? I've got those new taps, kinda like the kitchen. Bit sorta, I don't know, culinary. But still pretty slick, you should have a look. All polished metal. Should show you through the building, too. It's a bit ghost town at the moment 'cause everything's been ripped back for the do-up, but we're going to decorate like in here, make it real smooth inner-city living, you know? Real sought-after shit."

Leon said, "Yeah. Maybe later."

Marshall put his head up on his chin, and there was Rojas looking back at him blank-eyed. A drool-line feeding the bloody puddle and Marshall saw his lips move in something that looked like:

Help.

His ruminations in the diner that morning about luck, the good grace of the world wearing thin, and maybe this was the end.

Leon finished his pat-down and picked up a cable-tie from the floor, bound Marshall's wrists at the small of his back. Marshall's cash and keys and pieces of phone in a neat little pile.

Leon said, "You got any longer ones?"

"What for?" Hector's voice.

"Put one round his neck. Make a little yank leash if he gets out of order."

Jackie Grace called, "Yeah we got some longer ones. Next drawer down, Hector. Orange ones you want. Jesus, how much cash has that guy got?"

Leon didn't answer.

Quiet while Hector fetched the cable tie. A drawer opening, plastic sounds as he rummaged. Then Marshall felt Leon thread the strap beneath his throat, heard him feed the end into the little buckle and ratchet it firmly against his carotid. The skin above it swelling fractionally, blood trapped in his head.

Nothing in Rojas's face. A this-is-how-it-ends blankness to him. He couldn't see Shore.

Leon said, "Need someone to go down and move the woman's car. Just down outside the elevator there. Keys are still in. There's a gun by the passenger door, better bring that up, too."

Marshall heard him stand and move away. Then he paused.

Marshall counted it, growing cold—

Six, seven, eight.

Jackie Grace said, "What?"

Leon came over and crouched again. Marshall felt his hands at his waist, lifting his shirt. Folding his belt over.

"Huh. That could have been interesting."

He felt Leon pluck free the two razors, the delicate metallic tinkle as he tossed them on the bench. He laughed, heard a larger blade spring open, Leon pulling his head back, holding a switchblade below his nose. Marshall tried not to blink. The thing so close his breath clouded on it.

Leon said, "You bring a blade to a meet, this is what you need. That other shit just won't cut it. See how sharp this is."

He let go of Marshall and stepped over to Rojas, knelt again and scored the blade cleanly across his forehead, Rojas yelping and hissing through his teeth, blood already starting from the wound, a sheet of it hanging off the straight cut, a crimson shelf at his eyebrows.

"Whoa, Leon, easy. I don't want too much mess if we can help it."

Jackie put his beer down and leaned in close. "Don't want any soaking into the wood, be a right hassle."

Leon said, "Move Shore's car, and then bring the SUVs round. We'll take them over to my place."

They dispatched Carlos to deal with Shore's car. Ten minutes later he returned with Marshall's Colt, passed it to Leon.

Leon held it low on flat hands, tipped it back and forth. He dropped the clip and inspected the load.

"Nice piece."

He clicked the magazine home and put the gun in the back of his belt, shirt pulled tight as he reached behind him.

Carlos said, "I brought the cars round too, so we're all good to go."

Leon looked down at Rojas, leaned against the counter. He spread his arms. "Well, the news just keeps getting better."

A pleasant look on his face as he looked out at the view, like he could see more than just the end of the day. "Jackie, why don't you take Troy now, I'll look after Marshall and the detective."

"Yeah, fine. You want to see the new bathroom before you go?"

"Not today, but I will soon. Is that garage okay? I don't want a walk-in or anything while we're loading up."

Jackie waved it off. "Yeah, contractors aren't in for another week, don't worry about it. Look, I'll give you the number for the bathroom guy anyway, might see something you want. You never know. Or even just look at their Web site. Some classy stuff, I tell ya."

Rojas gurgling as they dragged him away, smearing his own blood. Marshall heard the ding as the elevator arrived. A pause, and then a very faint rumble on descent. When he looked back at Leon, the man was watching him, waggling the knife, still red at the tip from where he'd cut Rojas.

Leon said, "Best behavior for the trip, or I'll have to use this."

He folded the blade closed, a gentle snick, dropped it in his left pocket. The Ruger on his right hip beneath his shirt and Marshall's Colt in his belt at the small of his back.

Marshall looked across at Shore but she was turned away from him, Leon laughing as he saw the failed contact. He said, "All right. Who wants the girl?"

A minute later the chime of the elevator, the muted rumble as Carlos and Miguel took her down.

Just Marshall left.

Leon watching him with a funny light in his eye, like good things were imminent. He said, "Don't forget what I said. Never had to gut a man in a car, don't want to make today a first. Imagine the mess." He nodded at Rojas's puddle. "Make this stuff look like nothing."

Marshall didn't answer.

Tyrone collected his suit jacket from the back of an armchair and donned it with a flourish, swung it high to slip his arms in.

Leon gripped Marshall's bicep and pulled him upright.

"Three feet ahead and left of me at all times. Understand?"

Marshall nodded.

Three feet ahead because that was his comfortable clearance, and keep left because the Ruger was on his right hip.

They walked to the elevator. Tyrone pushed the button to call it.

They waited.

Leon tugged his throat leash gently. "Be a good doggie now."

He laughed. Then he reached behind him and drew Marshall's Colt and pushed it against his kidney.

The elevator pinged. The doors withdrew.

They turned one-eighty and backed in: Leon on his right,

Tyrone left, both of them maybe three feet behind. The doors closing. The penthouse view narrowing to a slot and then nothing.

The pause and the silence. Leon watching Marshall watching the counter waiting on P.

Tyrone leaned carefully and pressed B2. The gun hard in Marshall's side. A revolutionary firearm that Colt: incredibly reliable, the basics of it barely modified since 1911, but one of its few disadvantages was that by pushing back the slide just a fraction of an inch, the interrupter could engage and lock the trigger.

Leon nodding to himself. He said, "Need some music."

The weightlessness as they began the drop.

The counter descending—

Eight.

Seven.

Six.

Leon's hand on Marshall's right elbow, Colt muzzle in his kidney. Tyrone with a pistol on his right hip. The knife in Leon's left pocket—

Four.

Three—

Marshall leaned right and felt the Colt's mechanism shift that golden fraction, just enough to seize the trigger, and took a fast backward step and twisted left, lunged from the waist and headbutted Tyrone clean on the temple. A huge impact, and the guy was out cold and falling, but Leon was fast enough he'd already dropped the Colt and had the Ruger clear, so Marshall leapt backward and smashed into him, pinning the arm against the wall. He heard the pistol fall, head pounding and his face almost bursting as Leon yanked the leash around his neck, and Marshall slammed into him with all his weight, trapping him against the elevator corner, snapping his head back to hit Leon in the face. With his bound hands, he felt for the guy's left pocket, tore the seam when he got a hand on the switchblade. Leon thrashed and kicked, and Marshall almost dropped it, his vision blurred and red as he sprung the blade and thrust it deep in Leon's thigh. The guy twitched and jerked as Marshall dragged upward, a savage wound, bone-deep and femoral, all the way to the hip.

He felt the man go slack, Leon biting back screams as his breath hissed warm and spit-laden on Marshall's neck, pure animal now as he flailed. Marshall kept his weight on him, gasping. His face was puffed and throbbing from the pressure of the noose. He turned slightly and kept Leon pinned with a shoulder, almost slipping in the blood on the floor, pushed the knife blade up between his own bound wrists.

Felt like he sawed a long time before the plastic finally gave. A desperate pounding in his head. His face felt like it could split. The noose so tight it had cut a little furrow in his skin, almost have to dig it out. He tilted his head back and wedged the point of the knife up inside the plastic, through the shallow valley between his throat and carotid. He rotated the blade slightly and pushed outward, and he felt the edge catch, and a second later the cable broke and he felt the pressure release from his head, the red throb subsiding.

He leaned there gasping and exhausted and finally saw the details of it:

Leon trapped pale and weak against the corner and the blood from his leg halfway across the floor, making steady progress. This wide, gaunt grin, almost reptilian, and the morbid sibilance of his panting.

Tyrone in a heap, dead, just beneath the button panel. Maybe a better head butt than he thought. The elevator doors open, and the basement beyond. White exhaust smoke drifting from the right and a heavy stereo beat faintly audible. Their SUV, patiently waiting.

The elevator light flickering gently.

Last thoughts, eyes closing, deathbed moments.

He kicked Leon's gun into the corner out of reach. Then he picked up the .45 and sat the dying man down in the pool of his own blood. He held the switchblade in front of him on his palm.

He was going to say something glib like: I promise I'll bring it back. But what was the point, other than spite. So he didn't say anything.

Leon on the brink of slipping away.

Marshall didn't stay to watch.

FORTY-SIX

Lucas Cohen

At his desk in the courthouse on South Federal Place, typing up a day best forgotten, his phone started ringing. He was tempted to leave it, wouldn't be anything cheerful, but then Miriam put her head through and said it was that guy from Bernalillo Sheriff's. If she came and told you the caller, you'd better answer, meant she was sick of having them in her ear.

Cohen picked up and said, "You're the closest thing I ever had to a stalker. Actually kinda flattered."

"One meeting and a few phone calls isn't much of a stalk."

Which was a fair point, but Cohen held on a little longer: "Maybe you're just getting started, building yourself up. Mighta caught you early."

The guy said, "Mmm. Anyway. They cracked that phone I was telling you about. That they found in the Chrysler."

Cohen said, "Okay."

He hovered a pen over his blotter.

The guy said, "It had like a GPS tracking thing in it. Funny thing was, getting into it wasn't even that hard. The password was just one of those things where you have to draw a line that's a certain shape on the screen, you know those ones? But if you just angle it in the light a bit, you could see the grease marks where he'd done it, and the whiz girl at the lab reasoned, well, it's gotta be one continuous movement, and there's only two combinations because you start at either one end or the other. So knowing that, she got in."

Cohen said, "Great."

"Yeah, so, like I said, it had this tracking program on it, big mess of lines on a map, like he'd been following something round."

"Okay."

"And we looked at the current position of whatever it is he's tracking, and it's showing this point just off the 25, down South Albuquerque. Called APD to see what's down there, whaddyaknow: it's that red Jeep you were telling me about, feller lying dead beside it, 'nother feller in back all chopped up and wrapped in plastic."

Cohen said, "Can you just bear with me a moment."

He turned the phone against his shoulder to mute it and leaned back in his chair and said, "Miriam. Could you be a darling and get a message to my Mrs. Cohen I won't be home for dinner tonight? Maybe just put it in the lower oven if that's appropriate. The meal I mean."

Back to his call. He said, "Was it Rojas?"

"Well, sounds like his car, but neither of the bodies are him. Homicide guys down there reckoned it was a car swap or something. Pulled a guy over, shot him, took his ride. Actually saying the feller in back could be Cyrus Bolt, but nothing's been confirmed. Too grisly to call it."

Cohen, still leaning back, the phone cord stretched across his chest, swung side to side a little and said, "Where else has that Jeep been?"

"You mean according to the GPS thing?"

"Yeah."

"Well, a bunch of different places really."

Cohen said, "I've got a pen."

FORTY-SEVEN

Marshall

The SUV was an Escalade, seven seats: Shore in back, Miguel in the middle row behind the driver, Carlos at the wheel. They didn't know what was happening until he was in the car. Like some vision of the undead this bloodied figure with a gun outstretched.

Miguel not much now he had a pistol in his face. He shrank back against his door and raised his hands, and Marshall said, "Where's the other car? With Rojas?" To Carlos: "Keep your hands on the wheel." Shouting over the stereo.

"It's already gone, bro. Just chill, man."

Marshall put the gun on Miguel. "Get out."

Eyes on the gun, Miguel opened his door, and Marshall swung a leg up along the seat, kicked him in the shoulder, and the guy fell sideways out of the car, rolling as he hit the ground.

Gun on the driver. "Go."

Carlos hit the gas, the back end dropping with the boost, Miguel in a heap with his jacket up around his shoulders. Marshall waited for the left-hand turn onto the ramp, and as they reached it he leaned across and helped the door closed as it swung toward him.

"Shut that stereo off."

"Yes, sir." Done.

"Yes, sir. We're all polite now, aren't we? Keep your hands on the wheel and catch that other car, you might not get a bullet."

He looked in back. Shore lying across the seats, not quite as composed as last time, but still with it.

She said, "You're covered in blood."

He showed her the switchblade. "Turn around."

She rolled over awkwardly, and he reached down and cut the cable tie securing her wrists. She lay back and covered her face with her hands. He could hear her panting.

He said, "Are you all right?"

"Uh. Yeah. I think so."

She sat up shakily, her balance off, bracing herself against a window. Marshall slid to the center seat and leaned over the console. Eastbound in light traffic on Central.

"You know what that other car looks like?"

"Yeah. Like this one."

"Black SUV."

"Yeah, just like this."

"All right. Your one purpose in life is to catch it, okay? If you can do that you might have a story for later."

He looked in back. "Are you all right?"

"You asked me that."

"You're a bit pale."

"Well, yeah. What do you expect?"

"You're shaking."

"Yeah. Don't sound so surprised."

Marshall said, "You know where they're going?"

Carlos's eyes in the mirror. "Me, boss?"

"Yeah, you."

"They going to Leon's. Up 25 some ways. Maybe Santa Fe, I think?"

"You don't know the way?"

"No, boss. That's why we had Leon."

Marshall cocked the Colt. He said, "All right, well. I just killed him so you're going to need to catch that other car. Okay?"

They picked up speed and reached the interstate. The car listing as they came round the ramp, faint squeal of the tires only just clinging. Pedal flat to the floor as they merged with northbound traffic.

"You don't stop for anything, you understand?"

"Yes boss, okay. Look, I can see it up ahead. They not as fast as us."

Marshall ducked and watched through the windshield, the other SUV maybe ten cars ahead. "Okay. This speed is good. You keep this lane, and then get in behind them, okay?"

"You want right behind, boss?"

"Uh-huh. Right behind."

The needle showing seventy-five. To the east Albuquerque and the Sandias beyond, and westward the sun collapsing orange at the edge of the world. Its heated lip spanning the barren width.

Gaining ground now on the lead vehicle, six cars ahead.

Marshall said, "Get in behind it."

The guy didn't answer. Marshall lowered a window, leaned across and did the same on the other side. Noise dissipation: he didn't want to lose his hearing if he had to fire in the car.

He said, "You honk your horn or flash your lights or anything, I'll put a bullet through your knee."

Two cars behind now. An exit sign: turnoff approaching.

Marshall said, "Come up alongside."

"Stay in this lane, boss?"

"Yeah, stay in this lane. Get up alongside. Faster, come on."

Eighty now. A rotorlike buffeting from the wind in the open windows. The exit approaching.

One car-length back.

"Come on, faster."

Closing now. Fifteen feet. Ten. The exit up ahead.

"Marshall, the hell are you doing?"

He didn't answer.

Jackie Grace in the passenger seat, reaching across the driver to point them out as they drew alongside, something like *holy shit* on his lips when he saw Marshall with a gun to Carlos's head. Too late when his driver glanced, Marshall yanking the wheel, and the two cars clashed with a screech of metal. Shore screamed as both vehicles bucked horribly, rubber squealing and smoking as each driver stomped the brakes. The SUVs skidded as one across the mouth of the exit, a colossal smash as Jackie's car struck the concrete apex of the lane dividers. The truck reared up on its front axle, teetering almost vertical before the drop, back suspension crushed flat as the wheels thumped down.

Their own car still doing thirty when Marshall ripped the brake. The sudden halt sent him sprawling, and he hauled himself off the console into his seat. He threw open his door and ran back along the shoulder, northbound traffic pulling over to assist.

Burnt-rubber smell and four matching black swathes stretched across the exit lane.

The crashed SUV was windowless from the impact, and the edge of the barrier had gouged it from grille to firewall, the engine bay halved lengthwise. The chassis was warped and crumpled like a halfhearted concertina, and Jackie Grace and the driver were sprawled inert beneath a wilted mess of airbags. Steam and radiator fluid spreading, a pungent smell of gasoline.

He opened the rear door of the truck, and there was Rojas laid across the seat. Marshall cut the cable tie at his ankles and pulled him out onto the road, Rojas stumbling, dropping to a crawl.

"Up, get up. Come on."

Crunch of glass under his feet. Stopped drivers watching aghast, the gun keeping them well back. Rojas's face covered in blood. Marshall hauled him limping along the shoulder and shoved him in the backseat of the Escalade. Keys still in the ignition, Carlos in a sprint down the exit ramp. Shore at some guy's window, screaming she was a police detective, call 911.

Marshall slammed Rojas's door and jumped in the front seat and tore away.

Rojas was still dripping blood, and Marshall didn't know if that was from earlier or a by-product of the crash. He pushed the Escalade up to a hundred, a gradual slalom through the other cars traveling at seventy-five.

Marshall said, "Tell me what happened to the girl."

Rojas shook his head. It made things worse, blood in his eyes. He said, "Did you kill everyone?"

"I hope so. What happened to the girl?"

"Oh, god."

"That was the deal, Troy. I get you out of that motel, you'd tell me what I needed to know. You said you'd talk till you bled, and right now we're all blood and no talk."

He lay down across the seat. "Okay, okay."

"So what happened?"

"Oh man."

"What happened, Troy? I saved your life twice. Pretty easy to take it, too."

Rojas spat some blood. "We saw her at Calor. At Jackie's club. This was like . . . Jeez. This was like two weeks ago or something."

"Who's we?"

"Me and Cyrus and Vance. And Leon."

"Why were you in there?"

"Business. Jackie sets stuff up for us. He's got cartel contacts. We were meeting some guys, Jackie put it all together."

"So who took her?"

"The girl?"

"Yes. Alyce Ray. Who took Alyce Ray?" Almost screaming at him.

"Shit." He shook his head, trying to flick the blood from his eyes. "Man, slow down, come on."

Marshall said, "Troy, if you don't answer the questions, I'm going to shoot you in the head."

"Okay, I . . . Shit. We saw her in there and . . . She just happened to be in there. Had some friends with her I think. Three or four maybe. Vance and Leon noticed. They just . . . They've got an eye for that sort of thing, you know?"

Marshall didn't answer.

Rojas said, "Cyrus was in a separate car, but I was with Leon and Vance. They know all this black-ops stuff. Leon did renditions or whatever, got sent to kidnap people after nine-eleven. Like, the government trained him how to do it. So they just . . . They followed her. We followed her, I mean. Just tracked her back to her house, went in at the dead of night. No one would have heard anything. Like, it's their job."

Like when he'd got in the car. Appearing out of nowhere.

Marshall said, "Why'd they take her?"

"I don't know. Why does anyone do anything? They just wanted to. They felt like it, and they knew how."

"They felt like it."

Rojas didn't answer.

Marshall said, "Is she still alive?"

"Yeah. Yeah, she's still alive."

"Where?"

"Leon's basement. They got a room. Oh, shit. They got a room where they keep them."

"Them. Who's them? How many are there?"

"I dunno, three, four, I don't go down there. They have witnesses and shit, from like indictments."

"What indictments?"

"Like, any. I mean, if one of Jackie's guys doesn't want someone testifying, you know? They keep them down there and like, do stuff to them. It's not my thing, man, I promise. That's why I got out, I don't do any weird shit. I just wanted the money."

Marshall drove faster. He said, "You show me where it is, or I'll kill you like I killed the rest of them. Okay?"

"Okay."

One hundred on the interstate made it a short ride: thirty minutes up to Santa Fe.

Rojas in the middle seat, hands cuffed behind him, leaning forward to give directions. They headed into a new subdivision out east of the city. Spanish pueblo–type architecture on big sections. Quiet, well-kept streets.

"Take a right up here. This is it."

Marshall slowed. "Right here?"

"Yeah. Right here."

Marshall swung in. Around the curve of the driveway, over a slight rise, and there was the dark curve of the house waiting for him, windows curtained.

Marshall said, "Anyone home?"

"Can't be. They're all dead."

"So whose car is that?"

The sedan parked by the garage.

Rojas said, "Uh. I don't know. Could be a buyer."

The gravel popping and crunching softly. Marshall stopped and set the brake, left the ignition on. He said, "Not anymore." He opened his door. "Don't get out of the car."

He waited a moment just watching the house, and then he ran crouched to the other car and leveled the gun across the trunk, aiming at the front door. Bone-white grip, and it was still shaking. He ran to the entry and turned the handle.

Unlocked.

He pushed the door back and went in, following the swing.

Through the entry, left through the first door he reached. The living room. Place was a mess: coke and foil on the coffee table, an IV stand lying next to it. On the right by the television, a young woman in a soiled white nightgown, face swollen and abraded, duct tape across her mouth.

Alyce Ray.

And standing behind her a man Marshall hadn't seen in a long time.

He had a gun to the girl's head. He said, "Drop it, Marshall. And let's all sit down."

FORTY-EIGHT

Marshall

There was a sofa facing the television, and an office chair on casters: probably a last-minute effort to accommodate him.

Marshall, gun still raised, said, "Did you know I'd show up?"

"I knew someone would. Maybe you, maybe Leon. Whoever it was, I could guess the rest of the story." He nodded at the chair. "I thought I'd better have something on standby."

Marshall didn't answer.

"You going to put that down, or do I have to hurt the girl?"

Marshall placed the .45 on the ground and took a step back.

"That's better." He led the girl over to the sofa, and they sat down side by side. He said, "You remember me?"

Marshall wheeled the chair so it was opposite him and sat down unbidden. He said, "I always thought of you as the Ray-Ban Man. Ashcroft never told me your real name."

The guy smiled. The gun in his hand was a SIG P226, something else on his ankle, too.

Marshall said, "You still working organized crime for the Bureau, or is this the main gig now?"

The guy laughed. Beside him Alyce Ray sat hugging her knees, leaning away from him, eyes elsewhere and her mind even further. He said, "This is the main gig."

Marshall said, "Now we're on more personal terms, do I get to know your name?"

The guy looked at the girl, back to Marshall. He said, "Wayne Banister."

Marshall said, "You still wear Ray-Bans?"

Banister smiled thinly. "Not so much." He swapped the gun to his left hand so he could prop it on the armrest. He said, "I've got another name, too. You might've heard it."

Marshall said, "Try me."

Banister said, "I'm the Dallas Man."

Feeling the chill now. He'd guessed the name, but it wasn't quite real until he heard it.

New York coming for him. He'd known this would happen, one way or another. The realist or the pessimist in him. He'd given Shore that line about small worlds, ripples hitting other ripples, but he'd still hoped it would be a case of later rather than sooner.

The universe set a task to bring things full circle, and here it was, as they say, rising to the challenge.

He began to hope Rojas hadn't followed instructions. Bloodied man running handcuffed in the street might bring some law along.

Marshall said, "You had a pretty sweet setup."

"How's that?"

"You had me undercover in New York, trying to find the Dallas Man. All you wanted to know was whether Tony Asaro knew more than just your nickname."

"Yeah. It was a good arrangement."

Marshall said, "So what took you so long?"

"What do you mean?"

"Asaro wanted me dead. But it took you five years to find me."

Banister said, "I retired, I've been out of the loop. Just had to hope one day good or bad luck would bring us together. And it has."

"So how'd you find me?"

"It wasn't hard. We knew you were here somewhere. You made that call from the motel. And then my employer noticed Leon was having some trouble. And obviously you're the trouble."

Marshall nodded at Alyce Ray. "I was looking for her."

"I see."

"Who's your employer?"

Banister shook his head. "Sorry."

"Tony Asaro?"

Banister smiled. "Sorry. Client-killer privilege."

Marshall didn't answer. The chair keeping him oddly upright. Banister's expression somewhere between pleasant and bemused.

Marshall said, "Did you ever tell Asaro I was undercover?"

Banister shook his head. "All I needed to know was who to whack. It's just money. It's just business." He shrugged. "You don't owe anyone any favors."

Marshall didn't answer. At length he said, "So what now?"

Quiet in the room. Alyce Ray's eyes were closed and he could see the tape moving, almost imperceptible, like a prayer. Banister looked at her awhile, and Marshall could almost read that same thought, and maybe there was sympathy, too.

Banister said, "We're not all walking out of here. I don't know if you'd gathered that or not."

Marshall shook his head. "I just want the girl. We can go our separate ways. And then if it's meant to be, maybe we'll see each other a little farther up the road."

Banister smiled. He said, "This is farther up the road. Here we are in the moment that was meant to be."

Watching the gun. All these things he could have said to deter him, and all he could manage was, "There's no point."

"There's no point to anything."

Marshall didn't answer.

Banister said, "Seems like a pointless waste to you, but life is pointless. People always clutching for a higher meaning, but there isn't any. You live and then you die, and no matter what you did you're irrelevant. This planet is four and a half billion years old. To call you a blink is an overstatement by an order of magnitude." He smiled. "So don't worry about it."

Marshall didn't answer.

The Dallas Man kept the gun on him. He said, "There are no absolute morals. There's no universal right and wrong. The only rule is the rule you make."

Marshall said, "Okay."

The Dallas Man said, "So if this room was the very end of the earth, and we were the last men living and I killed you, who's to say I'm wrong?"

"We're not the last men living."

"Even so."

"Who's to say it's right?"

The Dallas Man said, "I don't say one way or the other. It's just the way it is. One day everything will be gone, and your life and every choice you made will be meaningless. And that will be reality from then on. Millions and millions of years."

Marshall said, "Okay."

"Any last words?"

Marshall said, "I'll settle for last thoughts."

Banister didn't answer.

Marshall said, "Are you going to count me in?"

"You can do it if you like. Have some control. It's a privilege, really."

Marshall looked down at the Colt. He said, "You going to shoot me on one or zero?"

"I'll drill you on zero. But you won't have time to say it." He raised the SIG.

Marshall said, "Five."

The Dallas Man's eyes on him.

"Four."

The world collapsing down to just the two of them. He thought about how he'd do it. Grab the Colt and dive and fire. Banister leaning forward in his seat.

Marshall said, "Three."

Both of them poised.

"Two."

Alyce Ray made a grab for the gun, eyes closed, screaming mutely as she lunged. Marshall launched off his seat, the girl blocking his shot, her hands at Banister's wrists, the gun raised high like the liberty flame. Marshall crashed into them and the sofa toppled backward, limbs in all directions as they went to the floor. Marshall's hands on the gun now, the three of them in a tangle as they rolled, the girl crawling free as they went over a second time. Banister kneed Marshall in the groin, punched him in the side of the head, breath wet and rasping, his panic writ large: locked jaw, carotid rupture-taut, tendons in the clawed hand. Marshall tried to worm a finger behind the trigger, lock the action, shouting for Ray to get the Colt. Then Banister kneed him again, shoved him clear, and the gun was coming round. He couldn't stand, nauseous from the groin impact, but he spun on his back and kicked out, caught the SIG and sent it tumbling, spinning. Banister found his feet, tried to back away, and Marshall dived, caught his ankle and brought him down again. Banister thrashed, Marshall hugging his leg, a desperate clinch around the wild limb, trying to reach the backup gun. Banister in a fury, kicking, eyes bulging as he clawed, like trying to shed his own skin. He pulled them both across the floor, over to the couch, and when Marshall glanced up he'd reached the SIG and was swinging it—

Crack.

Marshall looked.

Lucas Cohen stood in the door, Glock raised. Alyce Ray screamed behind the tape, ran, tripped, crawled for him.

Banister had dropped the gun. He fell across the toppled sofa, a red stain blooming on his chest. Marshall lay on the floor a moment, hugging his knees, gasping, waiting for the pain to back off. He rose unsteadily and picked up the Colt and stood looking down at Banister. The man coughing blood, chin pulled to his neck as he tried to check his pockets. "My daughter. Just let me. My daughter."

He pulled a red cell phone from his pocket, fumbled it, dropped it on the ground. Marshall bent and passed it to him, the thing dead, not even a battery. Banister draped an arm across his eyes, choking as he put the phone to his ear.

"Sweetheart, it's Daddy. It's Daddy. I'll see you soon, don't worry."

Marshall limped outside to escape the misery. Shadows had come down with the gloaming, and finally it was cool. Alyce Ray lay shivering on the driveway, Cohen crouched with his jacket draped over her. He watched the house as he made a call, stroking her shoulder, the girl screaming there was someone else down there.

Coming round the side of the Escalade, he saw the rear door was open. No Rojas. He swore under his breath and ran out to the road, awkward and shuffling, temples throbbing on each step. He saw him only sixty feet away, this hunched and lurching figure trailing blood.

Marshall watched him a second. Rojas swaying like a drunkard, bound hands oddly cocked, his every fiber desperate. Marshall raised the Colt and breathed out, sighted and squeezed the trigger.

Click.

A dud load. Marshall thought about that. Then he walked back up the drive to the house, Rojas still running.

The sofa was Banister's deathbed.

Marshall went through his pockets. The Dallas Man watching wide-eyed. He had a blue cell phone as well, battery intact. Marshall clicked through the call history:

A New York number, showing up the last three days. Twice today. He wondered how many people in New York used the Dallas Man as their cleaner. Maybe he was just Tony Asaro's man. He looked at the call times. The most recent was only thirty minutes ago, outgoing.

He imagined Banister reporting in while he waited:

I've found him.

Five years, and they'd done it. He remembered the photograph from Lloyd. Vicki B. shot dead. Greetings from Dallas. A threat and a promise that would never expire.

We'll always be looking.

He brought the phone outside. Cohen was just coming in, gun up. Alyce Ray sat against the wheel of the Escalade, huddled in his jacket, rocking back and forth. Marshall hit Redial. Who's it going to be: probably Tony, possibly Lloyd.

Three rings, and then the pickup.

Chloe said, "I figure this is either Wayne or Marshall."

The last voice he thought he'd hear. He did a double-take: looked at the phone, and then put it back to his ear.

She said, "I'm guessing Marshall."

He stumbled through a false start, cleared his throat to get past it. He said, "Wayne won't be coming home."

"Well, that's a shame."

Waiting for his reply.

He said, "I was expecting your father."

"He had to delegate. It's hard to run things from prison."

"So you've found a career?"

She laughed. "No, I actually did this when I knew you, but I've upscaled slightly. They call me the Patriarch now. I thought about Matriarch, but I like the misdirection."

He remembered talking with her that night at the Standard: *I'm with Brooklyn South Narcotics. I go around looking for drugs.*

And her smile and the whisper:

I do that sometimes, too. Though I'm not with Brooklyn South Narcotics.

He swallowed. "So you're in charge of killing me?" His voice was going. Shock more than exhaustion.

She said, "Good guess."

He didn't answer.

She said, "I was worried you'd moved on, but then Wayne called and said he'd found you. So that was a nice end to the day."

That last line almost playful, inviting something back.

He said, "I'll send you a photo. Make a nice start to tomorrow."

"Yeah. I'd been hoping Wayne might send one."

Marshall said, "I didn't think I'd speak to you again."

"Likewise, I guess. But I can't say it's a shame."

All these questions he had, and all he could manage was: "I'm sorry I shot you."

She didn't answer. Blue and red lights out at the road.

Marshall said, "You going to stay in the business?"

She laughed. "We'll see how it goes. This is a bit of a setback. But I think I'll persevere."

Cars coming round the bend. Lights and sirens.

She said, "They for you?"

Marshall said, "Maybe."

The big question irking him: Were we the real thing, or were you just testing how much I knew? But he didn't say it. To ask was to reveal a fear, and he didn't want to give her that.

She said, "Are you going to come looking for me?"

Marshall didn't answer. The dark landscape shaking in the blue-red strobes. Sirens keening as if chased by some greater horror. He ended the call and raised his arms.

ACKNOWLEDGMENTS

I would like to thank the terrific team at St. Martin's Press who enabled the publication of this novel. Thomas Dunne and my editor, Brendan Deneen, deserve a special mention for letting Marshall and me have a shot.

My agent, Dan Myers, was not only instrumental in getting me in the door in New York but has also proven himself a great editor and New Mexico tour guide.

Finally, I would like to thank the North Harbour Club (Auckland, New Zealand) for their AIMES and Emerging Talent awards, which provided invaluable support toward the writing of this novel.